THE OTHER SIDE OF FEAR

EOGHAN EGAN

RED DOG
UK

Published by RED DOG PRESS 2022

First Edition

Hardback ISBN 978-1-914480-96-6

Paperback ISBN 978-1-914480-94-2

Ebook ISBN 978-1-914480-95-9

www.reddogpress.co.uk

To every blogger, podcaster, influencer, book reviewer, bookshop owner and librarian for the time you spend reading, critiquing and helping authors get their book into potential readers' hands. Your selfless service is admirable, and without your support most of us would flounder.

1

SATURDAY 19 JANUARY. 8.30 P.M.

TOMMY MELLON fought futilely.

He screamed and twisted his body, but the stony-faced bouncers on either side straightened him in the chair. A fourth man tossed a piece of wood from hand to hand and swung it again. The shoulder of a hickory pickaxe handle thudded into Mellon's ribs.

The scream gurgled to a groan, and died.

Dessie Dolan tapped the axe handle barrel into his left palm and circled the bound man with slow, measured footsteps. Long shadows added menace and bulk to his small physique.

'I'll ask you once more. What'd you tell him?'

'Nuthin'. I swear I told him nuthin'.' Air whistled in Mellon's throat as he craned his neck and tried to keep his nemesis in sight. He coughed and spat a clot of blood. 'You gotta believe me.'

The pungent scent of desperation and sweat seeped from him; a mixture of ammonia and sour milk. His blond hair, caked with blood, shone black. Overhead, a low-wattage filament bulb dangled like the Sword of Damocles.

'I do. You know I do. It's just that...' Dolan waved the wood in front of the tethered man's face. 'I sent four of youse to pick up some money. Two of ye end up pumping blood like sieves. Jackdaw's nose is putty an' he's pissin' through a tube. An' you come out without a scratch? Dafuk, man?'

'I'm hurt too, Dessie. I—'

'What? You tripped 'n' fell running away?'

'I didn't run. He pinned me. Busted—'

'Think you can play me, huh?' Dolan gauged the distance. Wood caught Mellon's ribs again and shattered them. His shriek echoed through the warehouse, then thinned into silence as a second swipe caught him flush on the mouth and crushed his remaining front teeth.

A tug boat horn moaned three short blasts.

Dolan walked towards a full-length windowless frame, avoided dangling electric wires and twisted copper water pipes. He kicked Mellon's hat out of his way and watched it skid towards a pile of debris. He lit a cigarette, blew a funnel of smoke into the night air, and looked down four floors at layers of neglect and sepulchral bleakness. Light from the full winter moon gave a ghostly glare to dozens of rusted warehouses, honeycombed together. Rejuvenation of Dublin docks hadn't hit this area. Yet. Hunched against the cold, he turned sideways and broadened his gaze, past stacks of forty-foot shipping containers that glittered in the moonbeam, back to the boat as it chugged out to sea. An air horn sounded, and a train clanked out of Connolly Station.

It had stopped snowing.

Dolan shivered in the glacial air, flicked the cigarette butt out the window, and circled the bound man again. A predator's dance.

'This one-man army, fella. Didja get his name?' Dolan rubbed the hickory along Mellon's face, almost caressing him, smearing blood.

'No.'

'Seen him around before?'

'No.' Mellon tried to move and ease the pain from his crushed ribs.

'What'd he look like?'

Mellon struggled to talk through his mangled mouth. 'Big. Six-five, six.'

Dolan looked at the bouncers. 'Sounds like the fella that's sniffin' round the nightclub. So, what'd he say?'

'Nuthin'.'

'Nuthin'? Ye chatted for fifteen minutes and said nuthin'?'

'He was lookin' for a bird. I said I didn't know nuthin' 'bout any bird. Then he asked about you.'

'What about me?'

'Jus'... who you were an' dat. What you did.'

'And?'

'And nuthin'. I told 'im nuthin'. I swear. What could I tell 'im?'

'What else was he askin'?' Dolan nodded at the muscle men. They half-dragged, half-carried Mellon and the chair to the broken window.

Mellon struggled harder, frantic now. Blood bubbled from his nose and mouth, breath rattled in short, wheezy pants. 'He wanted to know where you hung out. That's all. I told 'im I'd met you once. In Whispers.'

'That's it?'

'Yeah.'

'Nuthin' else?'

'Nuthin. I never even said your name, Dessie. I swear—'

'Alrigh' alrigh'. Relax, man,' Dolan said. 'No need to get into a dyin' swan fit.' He removed a splintered piece of wood from the handle's tapered wedge and used it to scratch his neck.

'You gotta believe me, Dessie. I told him nuthin'. I'll find him for ya. Gimme ten minutes with him. Know wharra mean? That's all I'm askin'.'

'Howaya gonna find him?'

'I'll get him. Ten minutes. That's all I'm—'

'An' you'll do... wha?'

'I'll... I'll take his soul. The end.'

'Fergeddit. You've done enough damage. Thanks to you, he's already—'

'Gimme a chance. I'll... listen, I've got money comin'. You keep—'

'You've got nuthin' comin'. What else he say?'

'Nuthin'. Except—'

'Except wha'?'

'He said to tell you to keep away from McGuire's.'

'McGuire's? What about 'em?'

'He said for you to keep away an' call off your dogs. Or else.'

'Or else, wha?'

'Or else he'd shut your game down.'

Dolan stared. 'An' you tell me this now, huh? Didja not think that might be important?'

'I didn't... I'm *sick*, man. I don't...' Mellon was hyperventilating. 'All he said was to tell you to keep away from 'em. Gimme ten minutes, Dessie. I'll make him pay. Please.' Mellon caught his tormentor's eye and tried a reassuring grin. Shadows and blood turned the man's bruised, mottled features into a grotesque grimace, like a Shroud of Turin image.

'I believe you, man, honest, I do,' Dolan said. 'But this isn't a church where you can buy indulgences for a cutback in sins. I'll have the info I need in a few hours. Maybe when I'm finished with 'im, I'll give you a chance.'

A glimmer of hope shone in Mellon's dull eyes. 'Dessie, gimme ten minutes—'

'You've convinced me,' Dolan said. 'Cut 'em loose, lads.'

'No way I'd split on ya, Dessie.' Mellon rubbed his chaffed, rope-burned wrists. He stood and hobbled a step away from the window. 'You won't regr—'

Dolan spun, stretched out both hands, caught Mellon in the sternum and blasted him backwards. Mellon bent his upper body forward to stop himself falling out the window. He tried to break away, but the silent bodyguards grabbed him. 'I'll get you for this, Dolan. Someday I'll—'

'You'll have a long walk back from hell, bud.' Dessie Dolan pushed Mellon into space. The man plunged, legs dancing. His arms flayed and flapped in a frantic effort to halt the flight. Even after the *thunk*, the primal cry resonated around the warehouse.

'Goodbye, cruel world.' Dolan leaned out the window. The fall had split Mellon's head. Blood glistened dark against the slush background. He made a sign of the cross in the air, picked up the pickaxe handle and flung it out. 'Wrap 'im, pack 'im, an' bury 'im,' he said to one of the bouncers. 'Get Decaf to help ya. Tiny?' He nodded to the second man. 'You and me gotta get back to Whispers. We've work to do.'

The men walked down the metal staircase, heavy boots clanging. The smell of fear still stained the freezing night air.

'What about that big guy, boss?'

Dolan kicked out at a rat that scuttled into a crevice between two girders. 'You'll pay him a visit in a day or two. Make 'im sorry he ever heard of "danger" Dolan.'

MIDNIGHT

THE HEAT IN Whispers nightclub was oppressive.

Someone had come up with the idea that the place was classy enough to have a coat check-in area, and Sharona Waters pulled Ronan Lambe past the queue of chattering girls and entered the nightclub. Eyes narrowed against the blinding strobes and dazzling laser lights, her body bounced to the hard-core beat of pulsating, deafening, techno music. 'C'mon,' Sharona shouted to Ronan.

'What?'

'Tiesto vs Diplo. C'mon is the song title.'

'Oh.' Techno electronic wasn't Ronan's music.

Sharona scanned the nightclub and felt old. A churn of teen bodies surged around her. They smelled of wet clothes, cheap perfume, and scrummed for position at the bar. The dancefloor was crammed with clubbers. Some sucked on baby pacifiers to lessen the ecstasy side effect of jaw clenching and teeth grinding. Others waved glow sticks, deciphering the music with their own facial contortions and gestures, spraying sweat with every head shake. A DJ, high up in a Perspex booth, surrounded by machinery, turned and twiddled knobs, using technology and technique to fuse and blend the sound. Waves of relentless bass beats snapped like whips, pumping energy into the crowd. White strobes and flashing lasers beamed and bounded, inducing some dancers into hypnotic-like trances.

Ronan grimaced.

Sharona grinned and stretched out her arms. 'Feel it.'

'What?'

'Feel the music. Let yourself go.'

A fug of heat haze and dry ice radiated from the dancefloor. The music scaled up, building, building... Eyes closed, heads tilted towards the heavens, dancers twirled and spilled into one other, each in their own frenzied world, until the music reached a crescendo.

The house lights came on. Dancers hugged. The DJ spoke a disjointed, garbled sentence, then left his perch.

Ronan checked his mobile. 'Midnight. Is that it?'

Sharona shrugged.

The crowd left the dancefloor, focus shifting. Caught in the wake, the pair went with the flow of bodies. Sharona spoke to a young girl next to her. The teen replied and gesticulated.

'Music break while they pick models for a fashion competition,' Sharona told Ronan. 'Five grand plus guaranteed work at some international fashion show. She thinks Milan.'

'Cool.'

The horde halted by a thick red decorative rope at the edge of the dance floor, held in place by metre high tarnished bronze supports with ornamental heads. The rope seemed to run all the way to the bar. More rope and props were placed parallel, leaving a three-metre wide space between. The babbling teens tussled and elbowed their way to get space at the rope. Two, three or four rows back would lessen their chances of being spotted. Some girls ducked under or jumped over the rope barrier and ran to the other side and jostled for the best position. Two hawk-faced bouncers halted the stampede, got the aisle free again, and stood guard. The babble turned raucous when a small man, surrounded by two huge minders, walked up between the red ropes.

'There's Dessie Dolan,' Sharona pointed and shouted over the din. 'He's a bloody loan shark, not a fashion promoter. Why's he—?'

A twenty-something woman, with flame-red hair and thin as a junkie, trailed behind Dolan. She flitted over and back, selected a few hopefuls. When a girl was chosen, a bouncer unlatched the rope from the support, let her through, and then reattached the rope. In the minute it took the group to reach the spot where Sharona and Ronan stood, four giggling teenagers followed the female Pied Piper. The red-haired woman's eyes caught, held, and brushed past Sharona.

'Hey. Me. Pick… what's wrong with me, Ron?'

'Nothing. 'Cept you're five years too old.'

Sharona tried to move through the crowd. 'I'm gonna ask Dolan some questions.'

'Jesus, that's… You said you wouldn't—'

'That was then. This is a golden opportunity.'

Sharona side-stepped bodies, got hemmed in, jumped across the red rope, ducked under a bouncer's outstretched arm, and ran to catch up with the tight cluster that now had six or seven teenagers in tow. The group skirted the bar and started to file through an interior exit door. Sharona grabbed one of the girls, but got shrugged off. She clutched another girl's arm and yelled into her ear. The teenager shouted back and kept walking. Sharona yelled again. The girl nodded, mimed dialling a phone. Sharona passed over her mobile and the girl tapped buttons and handed it back. Sharona put out her hand for the girls' phone, but the teenager turned away and pushed forward. Sharona dug into a jacket pocket, found a crumpled receipt and a biro. She scribbled down her mobile number, folded the sliver of paper and handed it to the girl. The girl, still on the move, rolled the paper between a finger and thumb and shoved it into the back pocket of her denims.

The redhead stood beside the bouncer in the doorway and ushered six girls through. She frowned and shook her head at Sharona, beckoned the girl behind her to come forward. Then she followed her chosen troop, closed the door and left the glowering doorman to stand guard.

Sharona turned away, frustrated, and waited for Ronan.

'What's the story?' he asked. 'Did you get Dolan?'

'No. I talked to one of the girls, though. Rebecca Greenfield. She's been picked as one of the finalists in the modelling competition. It happens here every month, she said. Fashion industry's always on the lookout for fresh faces.'

'*Young* fresh faces,' Ronan said.

'She gave me her number.' Sharona added the name to her contacts. 'If I can't get to Dolan directly, I'll find another way. She said she'd let me interview her later. It'll make good insight.'

'Why would she—?'

'I may or may not have said that I'm a fashion reporter, and I'd get her story in our magazine. Hint: I did.'

'Jeez, Sharona—'

The house lights dimmed and the music swelled. Sharona leaned into Ronan. 'We'll hang around for a bit, see if Rebecca comes back. You don't mind, do you?'

'No probs.'

'Aww, you're sweet. If you're bored, take a tour around the place.'

'Ah, no. I'll stay here with you.'

'That's the right answer.' Sharona planted a kiss on Ronan's lips, then went back to watching the exit door for Rebecca.

REBECCA GREENFIELD AND six other girls milled around the corridor and surreptitiously checked each other out.

They were all tall and wore clothes that covered everything and concealed nothing. One blonde-haired girl's bare midriff displayed a crystal tattoo that glittered and shimmered. Another leggy teenager, hair the colour of burnt butterscotch that fell down her back in thick waves, checked her reflection on a mobile. A third, with brown eyes and a faint dusting of freckles sprinkled over her fair skin, combed her hair. A multi-spike bracelet slid down her wrist and she kept pushing it back up her arm. A fourth chewed gum, wore purple-tinged tights, and a low-cut jumper with nothing underneath.

Rebecca rummaged in her clutch bag, found a compact mirror and examined her heart-shaped face critically. Her wide almond eyes and creamy skin needed... something. She dug into the bag again and used a black eyeliner pencil along the top and inner rims to make her eyes more defined. Then she finger-combed her long, dark hair over her forehead and fluffed it at the back until it rested on her shoulders. Satisfied, she folded her arms and waited, shivering.

A door opened and a broad-shouldered man came into the hallway. A spider web tattoo spread out from his neck and disappeared under a black tank top. He seemed oblivious to the freezing temperature. He handed out A4 sheets and Bic biros and beckoned the girls to follow him. This room was warmer and partitioned into stalls. The red-haired scout was waiting. Clipboard under her arm, she held an iPad and directed the teenagers into separate cubicles. 'Fill out the form,' she instructed. 'I'll be back in a minute.'

Apart from a chair and a pile of green-cabled Christmas tree lights piled in a corner, Rebecca's cubicle was empty. She sat and glanced through the form. "Talent Agency" was typed across the top. Below it, a list of boxes to fill: Height. Weight. Full name. Date of birth. Address. Phone Numbers. Employment details. Email address. Family members. Marital status. Medical history. She filled out the information and listened to muffled murmurs coming from the other contestants. Rebecca turned the sheet over, but the flip side was blank. A high-pitched giggle from the girl in the next cubicle followed by footsteps. She signed the sheet, knees jiggling with nerves and anticipation. This was worse than a job interview. She'd read about how models got scammed, signed with an agency who had no work for them, but still fleeced the girls by getting them to pay for professional photos to fill a portfolio. She thought about questions to ask. If I'm too forward, maybe they'd dismiss me as a troublemaker, she thought, and I'll never get a chance to—

'Rebecca? Hi. I'm Janice.'

'Hi.'

'Thanks for waiting,' Janice said. 'Won't keep you a minute. Have you filled out the form?' She scanned the information. 'Good. Okay, next step is I take a few photos.'

'Should I, like, brush my hair, or—?'

Janice laughed. 'Just as you are. You look great. One of the big myths in modelling is that professional photos,' Janice used air quotes 'are needed to get discovered by an agency. That's rubbish.'

'Oh?'

'Studio photos can hide the real person. Agents only want a few snaps to show your natural look. I don't wanna see you all glammed up; I want your natural look. That'll give me an accurate representation of you. Does that make sense?'

'Oh, totally.'

Janice lifted her iPad. 'Don't move. Perfect. Smile. Perfect. Can you stand, please? I just need a full length… great. Sideways… and turn around. Excellent. We're done.'

'What now?' Rebecca said.

'Now, I put the information together and send it to our clients. If they like you and have a role, they'll get back to me.' Janice smiled. 'With your looks, well, it's not fair to get your hopes up, but I'm sure they'll be in touch.'

'Ohmygod. Really?' Rebecca's mind romped ahead to what her friends would say.

'Don't quote me, but yes.'

'Will I have to pay fees? I'm a student, and—'

'No registration fees,' Janice said. 'No C.V. or photography services. No expensive workshops or acting schools.' She leaned closer. 'In fact, here's a tip: *never* buy anything from or through modelling or talent agencies.'

'Oh, okay.'

'Reputable agencies won't require you to attend classes or buy anything from them.' Janice ticked off items on her fingers. 'No books, no runway training. No web exposure or videos. No portfolios. No comp cards. No address labels. Ultimately, clients pay everything. If you need something extra to become more professional, that cost gets taken from your modelling wages. Never pay anything up front.'

Rebecca's eyes widened in an I-can't-believe-I've-just-won-the-award expression. 'Wow… that's… wow. Umm. I've never been on a catwalk, or—'

'Neither have ninety-five per cent of models. I'm not saying you'll be on a catwalk in New York next week, but that doesn't mean you can't work as a model. Weekends or evenings, modelling at fashion shows, catalogue work, magazine covers, conferences… Loads of work. Good money. Plus expenses.' Janice took Rebecca by the arm and moved her towards the door. 'You're a natural.'

'Sounds great.' A thought struck Rebecca. 'I don't have a car. What happens if I'm sent to work in, say, Cork? How do I—?'

'One of our drivers will take you,' Janice said. 'Or we'll pay your train fare. But there's never any pressure. If something doesn't suit,' Janice shrugged, 'don't do it.' She stepped aside and eased Rebecca into the corridor. 'Have you got a jacket?'

'Yes, it's in the cloakroom.'

'Let's get it.' Janice steered Rebecca down the corridor. 'Who'd you come with tonight? Boyfriend?'

'No. We split up last week. I'm with Louise, a girlfriend from college.' Rebecca grinned. 'She's gonna be mad jealous she missed out, 'cos just before ye came out, she told me she was leaving with a guy.'

'Her loss, your gain,' Janice smiled. 'So, what happened to your boyfriend? What'd you say his name was? When'd you break up?'

'Michael? Nothing, really. We were together for a month. It didn't feel right.' Rebecca shrugged.

'Ah, okay. Did ye live together, or—?'

'Ah, no. Dad's afraid if I'm with other students I won't study, so he rented me a small place on my own.' Rebecca grinned.

'That's cool.' Janice grinned back. 'Do you have your coat ticket?'

Rebecca dug through her clutch bag, found the ticket, and passed it to the cloakroom attendant. She opened her purse and Janice stopped her. 'That's taken care of.'

'Really? Thanks.'

'Pleasure. Now, you should go home and think about this. Make sure it's what you want.'

'It is. It really is.'

'Well, get ready for some life changes,' Janice said. 'Good money, but the work's hard.'

'It's what I've always wanted to do. I can't believe—'

'Oh, and it's best you keep this to yourself for a few days, Rebecca, just in case things don't... it'll be embarrassing if you'd told everyone about a modelling career, and then it didn't pan out.' Janice shrugged. 'For your own sake, better say nothing 'til you hear from me.'

'Of course. I understand.'

Janice ushered her to an exit door and stepped into the street. 'Gosh, will this snow ever end? Here.' She thrust a fifty euro note into Rebecca's hand. 'Don't hang around, you'll get soaked. Grab a taxi.'

'God, I couldn't—'

'Nonsense. If your friend has hooked up with someone, I'm not gonna have you walking around on your own. Besides, I don't want you sick in bed next week.'

'Oh, okay.'

'Nice meeting you, Rebecca. We'll chat soon.'

'Thank *you*. Thanks for the opportunity—'

Janice shooed the gratitude away. 'Safe home.'

'I can't tell you how much—'

Janice smiled. 'Night.'

'Night, Janice.'

Janice watched Rebecca turn into Ely Place and disappear around a corner. She lit a cigarette and shuffled sheets of paper. A door creaked open and a figure stepped out.

'Five out of seven, Tiny,' Janice said. 'A decent night.' She placed three A4 sheets in his outstretched hand. 'These two,' she tapped the fourth and fifth sheets, 'have just split up with boyfriends.'

Tiny grunted.

'Forty-eight hours,' Janice said, 'then pick them up and get them working.'

2

SUNDAY 20 JANUARY. 8.15 A.M.

THE MOBILE HUMMED on the bedside locker.

Hugh Fallon untangled himself from Ruth Lamero, fingers brushing her warm thigh as he twisted and groped for the phone. He squinted at the caller's name, whispered, 'Sharona,' squashed the mobile between his shoulder and jaw, and snuggled back under the duvet. 'Hi, Sharona.'

'Your mug's all over the Sunday papers,' Sharona said. 'Hogging the limelight as usual.'

'Yep, that's me. Always first in line to get my face on the front page. What are you on about?'

'Ganestown hero saves girl from certain death,' Sharona narrated. 'After she'd been kidnapped by a crazed maniac, blah, blah, blah.'

'Argh, Jesus. That's the last thing—'

'The Sun thinks you and the kidnapper were rivals for my affections.' Hugh heard Ronan Lambe snicker in the background. 'Seriously, haven't you seen the newspaper headlines?'

'Erm, no. I'm—'

'Oh. Still recovering from your date night?'

Ruth turned on her side, tapped Hugh's shoulder, put up a warning finger, then keyed a password into her own phone and started to scroll.

'Date finished early,' Hugh lied. 'I'm, uh, tidying up... stuff. Haven't checked my phone.'

'Well, you've put Ganestown on the map again.'

'Shit. I thought this had blown over.'

Ruth nudged him with her knee and showed him her phone screen. Passport-sized photos of Ruth and himself stared back at him.

'Where'd they get my picture from?'

'Facebook, probably,' Sharona said.

Hugh read aloud from Ruth's phone screen:

Couple risk their lives to save friend.
Kidnapper masquerades as furniture manufacturer.
"In a death-defying car chase, Ganestown resident Hugh Fallon and his partner Ruth Lamero raced to Sharona Waters' rescue, after she was abducted last weekend."

'When did ye become partners, Hugh?' Sharona asked. 'After one date? Aren't you a dark horse.'

"According to sources, unemployed Fallon had no hesitation in putting his life at risk when Sharona Waters (23) was abducted from her home in Ganestown last weekend by Adam Styne, general manager of Hattinger's Furniture, Fine Art and Antiques, and taken to an isolated farmhouse near Birr, Co. Offaly.
This followed Miss Waters' uncovering of an art scam, relating to the switching of genuine paintings for fakes that staff members were running from Hattinger's showrooms. The fraud came to light when eagle-eyed Waters noticed a McKelvey painting, owned by wealthy Belfast art collector, Dorothy Ridgeway, was a fake that had been substituted by one of Hattinger's employees during a routine appraisal.
"Without Hugh and Ruth's timely intervention, I'd be dead," Sharona said.
"Of course I was afraid," Fallon confessed, "but my friend was in trouble. There wasn't time to think of the consequences."

'Where the hell do they...? I haven't spoken to the press,' Hugh said. 'I didn't want my name over this.'

Ruth Lamero, RGN, BSc (hons), NMBI, is currently working at Ganestown hospital, and told sources: "When someone's in danger, your initial instinct is to help."

13

Ruth bit her lip.

Hattinger's offices have remained closed and directors have declined to comment. Staff on both sides of the border have spoken of their concerns that the premises will never reopen. "We're owed wages, but no one has told us what's happening," a concerned employee remarked.

In a follow-up search, police discovered bodies buried on Adam Styne's farm. Whilst he sustained substantial injuries during Sharona Waters' rescue, a spokesman said Adam Styne will be transferred to another hospital for further assessment.

'Bloody hell,' Hugh said.

Sharona laughed. 'Everybody gets five minutes of fame, Hugh. This is your time. 'Look on the bright side. How many people will read this? The attention will help you find a quality management position. Much better than being stuck in McGuire's. You're way better than that.'

'You think?'

'Sure. Look what happened me.'

After Sharona's role in unravelling the art swindle, Virgin Media One approached her to audition as narrator and investigative reporter on a new true-crime series they were planning.

'Virgin Media made the right choice,' Hugh said.

'We'll see what happens when the screen test results come back. But I'm quietly optimistic. Actually, I started some research last night.'

'Oh? How?'

'I told you about the loan shark, Dessie Dolan? Well, I want to expose him and make him accountable for his actions. It would make great viewing… *and* help people see the real—'

'Sharona, I don't think you should—'

'I didn't do anything stupid. I saw Dolan at a nightclub he owns, Whispers, but couldn't get near him. Apart from loan sharking, he's also involved in the modelling industry. Imagine? Anyway, Ronan and me mooched around for a while, took some photos… tried to set up an interview with one of the models for some background. We'll see what happens. Any word from Ferdia? How's he coping?'

'We spoke after Ciara's funeral. Seems okay. But you know Ferdia. Keeps everything bottled up. I think he's up to something.'

'Like what?'

'He's paid off Malcolm's gambling debts, but he's trying to warn Dolan away. He's already had a scrap with a few of his flunkies. That could mean trouble.'

'Malcolm McGuire should stew in his own juices.' Sharona's voice rose a notch. 'If everyone keeps bailing him out, he'll never learn. Hope Ferdia knows what he's doing. Dessie Dolan's dangerous.'

'Most times Ferdia does,' Hugh said, 'but when he's too close to a situation, he lets his head rule his heart. That's also why you should keep your distance—'

'Yeah, yeah. Anyway, how'd your date with Ruth go?'

'Nice conversation switch, Sharona. And keep your intrusive questions for when you become an investigative reporter. You'll get nothing outta me. We had a nice meal and a chat. That's it.'

'Really? Hmm. You'd better check on her so, 'cos she didn't reply to my text messages since Friday night. Gosh, I hope the meal you cooked didn't sicken her.'

'Errr—'

Sharona giggled. 'I'm the investigative reporter, remember?'

'You've been caught, dude,' Ronan Lambe said in the background.

'Don't worry,' Sharona said. 'Ruth'll give me all the details later. Sorry for disturbing you. Go and finish the tidying up…'

'LIAR.' RUTH PUNCHED Hugh playfully.

'Just saving your blushes, ma'am.'

'Oooh, and they say chivalry is dead.'

'Not here, it's not. How can newspapers print a story without speaking to me? Not that I'd tell them anything.'

'I never said that either,' Ruth said. 'Jesus. Keith Abbot will have a stroke when he reads this. Hospital chiefs hate to see staff included in front-page headlines. It's usually a rant about pay, working conditions or letting the public know there's a strike looming. It's never good news and therefore bad for the image.' She scrolled through another feed and read:

'In a death-defying car chase—'

'Well, they got that right,' Hugh said. 'With the way you drove…'

Ruth grinned. 'I'd better go into the hospital and work on damage limitation before these reports and mad rumours grow legs.' She snuggled deeper into the bed.

'If I'm at a loose end for an hour, I'll catch up with Ferdia in the gym,' Hugh said. 'He's always there on Sunday's and he promised to get me fit.'

Ruth turned to Hugh and wrapped an arm and leg around him. 'Will we get a chance to meet up later, partner?' she whispered in his ear. Her breath tickled, and the remnants of her vanilla and strawberries perfume scent assailed his senses.

'After the gym, I'll be with Mum. Maybe you could come over to her place later? We could order a takeaway and watch a DVD.'

'Sounds cosy. What time?'

'Whenever suits.'

'Okay. Let's see what happens at the hospital.'

'Will these newspaper articles cause you an issue?'

'Don't know. I didn't ask or want this publicity, Hugh. I need to explain the circumstances before they get blown out of all proportions. Also, I'll need to reassure my family that despite your best efforts, I pulled myself out of harm's way.'

'Won't happen again.'

'Good. Wouldn't wish that episode on my worst enemy.' Ruth yawned. 'Sorry, I'm tired. Didn't sleep well last night.'

'Really? Were you not comfortable? I thought…'

Ruth winked.

'Uh-oh, you got me there,' Hugh said.

'Tsk, tsk.' Ruth patted Hugh's cheek. 'How quickly he forgets.'

'You can remind me again later.' Hugh dived under the duvet, hands caressing. Ruth wriggled.

'Ditto. I'll help you get Kathleen settled. Ow. Ow.'

'What?'

'Your beard. You need to shave.'

'Sorry.' Hugh pushed away.

Ruth pulled him back. 'I said, you need to shave. I didn't say stop.'

11.40 A.M.

ADAM STYNE'S INITIATION to crutches hadn't gone well.

The plaster cast grazed the ground and made every rod, screw and pin that held his knee and leg together feel like flesh and bone were being torn apart. Pulsing pain danced around the nerve endings in his jaw, keeping time with his increased heart rate. Salty sweat blinded him, and he couldn't release the crutches to wipe his eyes.

The nurse looked on, arms folded, robotically telling him to "hop," but didn't assist. Another agonising step got him to the doorway. The Garda on babysitting duty sat in the corridor, looked over the top of a newspaper, and refolded a page. Styne saw Hugh Fallon's photograph.

'Let's go.' The nurse clapped her hands. 'And hop. Hop. And again. And again.'

Styne gritted his teeth and blanked her out.

Hugh Fallon. Someday, I'll repay you.

The thoughts of revenge powered him to the end of the corridor, panting and sweating. He turned awkwardly and made it halfway back before he stalled and sagged against the wall. Still no assistance from the nurse.

Bitch.

Styne struggled on. Wanted to get back into bed. He hopped into his room and stopped. In the time he'd been out, the bed had been removed and replaced by a wheelchair. For a moment, he thought he was in the wrong room. He twisted.

'What's going on?'

'You're moving.'

'Moving where?'

The Garda came in, pointed at the wheelchair. 'Sit. You've been detained under section 3 of the Mental Health Act.'

'Why?'

'Your barrister already told you. To be assessed.'

The nurse plopped a black plastic bin liner on Styne's knees and he got wheeled back down the corridor, through double doors and into a cobblestoned alleyway. An ambulance waited, engine running. Hands gripped his elbows, and he got lifted onto a stretcher. Two paramedics strapped him down. A Garda helped slide the gurney into the ambulance and snapped a handcuff bracelet onto a steel pole, the other end onto Styne's wrist, and sat on the bench beside him. The black bin bag was thrown in, almost as an afterthought.

The paramedics jumped off the tailboard and slammed the doors shut. Styne closed his eyes.

This is too fast. Everything's happening too fast.

Drugs and pain clouded his brain. He needed time to think.

1 P.M.

'JAB,' FERDIA SAID.

'C'mon, Hugh, jab and circle to your right. *Your* right, man, for feck's sake, not my right. I'm right-handed, so you gotta circle away from it.'

'Oh.'

'Stop talking. Concentrate. Hit me. C'mon. Hit me. Move. Move.'

Hugh hunched, bobbed, weaved and threw a punch that hit Ferdia's shoulder. Tried again. Missed. Regrouped, steadied himself. Let go with a thunderous uppercut. Missed again.

'Move.'

Hugh pulled back. Ferdia tapped his jaw, enough to hurt.

'Ow.'

'You pulled back with your chin up in the air. Could've knocked you cold with a sweeping right. That's a schoolboy error, Hugh. Told ya to move.'

Hugh rubbed his jaw. 'I wanted to, in theory, but in practice, it's different.'

'Aye. Sit on your stool, lad. Have some water. You've tired me out looking at you waving your arms around like a feckin' windmill. Hitting someone isn't easy. Lots of great boxers get physically sick before a fight. Fight or flight; it's a biological reaction. Nothing to be ashamed of.' Ferdia stood in the middle of the ring and shadowboxed. 'You gotta dominate the setup. Jab. Boxing begins with a jab. That's how you control range. Makes your opponent react and dictates the direction of the fight. Your rest minute's up. Let's go again.'

Hugh came forward.

'Yeah, good. Like that. Jesus, don't run at your opponent in a straight line: he's gonna shove a fist in your face. You're swinging wild, like an amateur. Oh, and sticking out your arm and moving *back* in a straight line won't help your cause either, Hugh.'

Hugh's heart pounded. 'Enough.' He gasped for breath. 'I'll work on the punchbag.'

'Hitting punchbags is easy; they don't punch back. Try again. Keep moving. Take risks. Adapt to any change your opponent makes. Left, right, step to the side. Change direction. Pop, pop to the ribs. Uppercut. Duck. Dodge. Faster, man! Speed of directional change is critical. Good, that's good. Hit me. Go on. Sit on the punch. Put your weight behind that right hook. And again. Come on. There's no *menace* in your punches. Put some mustard on them. Let your hands go, for feck's sake.'

Ferdia's giant frame loomed. Hugh swung at his jaw.

'Jesus, lad. Why aim for my chin, and ignore ninety per cent of my body? Huh? You're like a man thrashing water, trying to get to dry land. And now I'm behind you. Never let anyone get behind you in a fight. You can't attack someone who's... Hit me, can't you?'

Hugh tried, wary now, afraid to commit. Ferdia defended himself with a high guard and bobbed his head at the same time. 'Use your fists and arms to protect yourself,' he said. 'If you keep leading with your face, you're gonna get planted. That's better. When you're striking, push off with your back foot. That's where the power comes from. I said back foot. Argh, for feck... okay, that's not bad. Now, double-tap with your right hand, bap-bap, and follow up with a big left.'

Hugh's arms felt like lead weights. He sagged against the ropes, panting.

'Don't stop now, Hugh. Less punches, but get maximum return on the one you throw. Steady. I told ya, if you charge in head first, you're gonna get face planted.'

'Ah, shut up, Ferdia.'

'You're acting emotional now. You gotta act rational, not emotional.'

Hugh dropped his hands. 'I'm done.'

'No, you're not. This is a controlled environment. I've put you in legitimate danger so you'll be comfortable meeting a real threat.'

'I'll never get in a real fight,' Hugh wheezed. 'I only want to get fit.'

'And you will. Now, kick. Remember, there are no rules in street fighting. Kick me.'

'I'll hurt you.' Hugh gasped for air. 'Remember, I broke Adam Styne's jaw with a kick last week.'

'He must've had calcium deficiency.' Ferdia moved out of range. 'Again. You can't be just *close* with your shots. You've gotta be precise. Dancing around, throwing leather that isn't connecting, will land you flat on your back. Hit me, for feck's sake.'

Hugh's punches became laboured. He circled, fists cocked. Waited for an opening... and pounced. His right hand skimmed Ferdia's jaw. For his trouble, he got a box to the ear that staggered him. Crashing waves roared in his head.

Blinded, he swung again and his fist whistled through air.

'Open your eyes, Hugh. I'm over here. I've turned southpaw.'

'What?'

'Southpaw. A Lefty. To knock you off balance. Right hand to jab. Left hand to power punch. Traditional or orthodox stance is the opposite. Left hand to jab, right hand to punch.'

'Oh. That's not fair.'

'You're getting thick now, Hugh. You gotta keep cool. Talent isn't enough in boxing. You need discipline.'

Hugh swung at Ferdia's body mass and got popped on the nose.

'See? There ya go again, Hugh. You can't get mad or angry in a fight. It knots your muscles and burns adrenaline. Time out. Here, catch.' Ferdia threw a towel at Hugh. He dabbed it against his nose and sopped up a trickle of blood.

'That was bloody sore, Ferdia.'

''Twas only a tap, lad. You hafta feel some pain. World's full of armchair boxers who never see the inside of a gym. It's only after getting hit an' hurt, you find out whether you're made for this. Only way to learn is to engage.' Ferdia hadn't broken a sweat. 'You'll be grand,' he said. 'Once you get started, you'll improve. Go have a shower.'

HUGH FELT MARGINALLY better after the shower. He towelled his jet-black hair, poured coffee into two mugs, and watched Ferdia Hardiman stride across the gym. He had a badly set nose, hairline scars under both eyes, and his overgrown russet hair was tinged with grey. He'd worked in Pharma-Continental for thirty years, rising through the ranks. Now aged forty-eight, he held the title of National Sales Manager. He'd appointed Hugh as a regional manager four years earlier, and even with a twenty-year gap between them, the two men formed a friendship. Three weeks earlier, Hugh had been made redundant, along with a third of the workforce. Ferdia had helped him get part-time work at a hardware store owned by his brother-in-law Charlie McGuire. Twenty years earlier, he'd married Charlie's youngest sister, but within six months, she'd died from an aneurysm. Ferdia never remarried. Gruff, tough, with a heart of gold, he'd spent years as a lock in Ganestown's rugby team. Now, for exercise, he sparred with the local boxing team.

Ferdia blew into his coffee and sipped. 'Everything alright?'

'I think so.'

'Huh. I see your mug's all over the front pages today.'

'Yeah. Lucky me.'

'Any publicity is good,' Ferdia said. 'Still on for Dublin tomorrow?'

'Sure. But I thought you'd stay in with Niamh tonight.'

'Yeah, I was going to, but I'll take Master David tonight. Give Charlie a break. Niamh's gonna drive down to Ganestown tomorrow and have some grub ready when we get back. So, if you're still—'

'Sure. I'll drop you off at the hospital before I head into McGuire's. Charlie and I are gonna have a chat. See what exactly he wants me to do. Have you spoken to him?'

'Talked to him and Master David earlier. He'll never get over the last few weeks. After being beaten up, getting a heart attack and losing his only daughter, he's got a long road ahead. No one should have to bury their child. He needs support, and I'm not sure how much help Malcolm's gonna be. Anyway, I reckon ye'll figure it out. Assume nothing until you get settled in. Then challenge everyone.'

'What about David?'

'He's with Charlie today. We'll drop him off at the childminder in the morning.'

'Sure.' Hugh rolled his shoulders to relieve some pain. 'What's the latest at Pharma?'

'Like swimming through molasses.'

'And Denis Wiseman?'

Ferdia rolled his eyes. 'It's like peeling a feckin' onion. Layers and layers and then nothing when you get to the core.'

'He's doing his job.'

'Too many meetings,' Ferdia said. 'Too much red tape.'

'Do what you normally do.'

'What's that?'

'Dodge it, duck it, jump over it, cut through it... or just ignore it.'

'Yeah. I always think common sense works better than lists of rules and regulations. The latest now is: he wants me to identify the ten per cent of the remaining workforce that adds the least value to the organisation. Sticking his oar into—'

'Down, boy,' Hugh said. 'See? You're letting emotion take over, Ferdia. It'll knot your muscles and burn up adrenaline.'

'Huh.' Ferdia left down his mug. 'I'm gonna do a bit more sparring, seeing as you couldn't give me a workout.'

'That'll get rid of your aggression, but you should rest before the operation.' Hugh drained his coffee.

'I'll be grand. It's only a biopsy. No big deal.'

'Stop, Ferdia. It *is* a big—'

Ferdia slapped Hugh's shoulder and studied his friend's six-foot frame. 'You're getting fat. Couple weeks in the ring will improve your upper body strength and give you more muscle and power. You're what now, thirty-five?'

'Twenty-eight.'

'That's worse. By the time you're thirty-five, you'll have the body of a sixty-year-old. Still, a few lessons and—'

'No, thanks. I'll stick to running.'

Ferdia walked Hugh to the gym door. 'You're right. Twenty-eight's too old to learn. Boxing isn't complicated; it's all about exploiting chinks in your opponents' defences, but there's a lifetime of learning how to use your fists, an' figuring a route to knock him out. Heard anything from Malcolm?'

'God, no. He has enough on his plate. It's only twenty-four hours since he buried his sister.'

'He's not answering his feckin' phone.'

'Give him space and time to mourn, Ferdia.'

'Huh. See ya in the morning.'

4 P.M.

'ALL IN.'

Malcolm McGuire pushed piles of poker chips into the centre of the green baize. The towers fell and cascaded over the mountain of coloured tiles already there. He took a swig of energy drink and glanced at the other players. God, he was tired. Five hours without even a toilet break. He eyed the chips, fifteen thousand euros worth. But it wasn't real money; they were measuring counters used to gauge his ability against other players.

Two punters threw in their cards. A third, immediately to his right, fiddled with a chip stack, hesitated, then matched Malcolm's bet. Malcolm hadn't expected that. He checked the five communal cards again: Two red aces, ten of spades, seven of clubs and six of hearts. The quiet murmur stopped. Silence spread. The fourth player chewed an unlit cigar.

Malcolm rolled the cold energy drink can across his forehead, left it down, and watched the condensation trickle down the sides. Surely, they could see his heart thud. What, he wondered, were they waiting for? The player to his left had a possible run from six to ten. The bettor across the table had a pair of tens, Malcolm thought, giving him a house. He had no idea what the guy to his right was doing. He'd played fast and loose all day, betted and folded erratically. Maybe he thinks I'm bluffing and he's keeping me straight, Malcolm supposed.

'See you.' The man on Malcolm's left added his tokens to the pile, and the player across the table folded. Everyone looked at Malcolm. It felt like the world was waiting as he turned over his hole cards. Two black aces. A release of breath from the bunched spectators. The remaining gamblers dumped their cards, and the low murmur of talk resumed. Malcolm pulled the chips towards his chest, like a lover's embrace and stacked them into trays. Then he stood and stretched, relieving the kinks and tension. After a dry spell, it felt good to be back winning.

DESSIE DOLAN PUSHED through people lined up at a mobile ATM and wandered through the Park Hotel foyer in Clonmel like he owned it.

With flyaway blonde hair and small build, he wore designer gear and resembled a mellowed bass player of an ageing rock band. His scowling companion, square-jawed with a crew and a chin cleft, was twice Dolan's size. He gripped a black leather briefcase and had a scar running from the side of his mouth to the corner of his eye. A neck tattoo disappeared under a Slipknot T-shirt.

An army of slot machines dotted the foyer's perimeter; their flashing bright lights, celebratory jingles and lure of clinking coins, attracted hordes of gamblers. Poker tournaments tend to generate a carnival atmosphere. Dolan ignored the pleading eyes of early tournament losers, desperate to find a sponsor. He stood on tiptoe and glanced around, eyes bouncing like a stone skimming on the surface of a lake. Nothing caught his interest.

He moved into the large ballroom. A roulette table had a throng of punters, ten deep, throwing money onto the table as if it was going out of fashion. Scattered around the floor, dozens of blackjack tables had been set up, to maximise the overall gaming experience and keep players interested. Dozens of patrons waited for an opportunity to sit around the half-moon tables. The tables were staffed by attractive blackjack dealers, who quickly exchanged money for chips and flicked cards with a magician's speed and precision. Ball-shaped security cameras had been installed over each table, and suited secret service types roved discreetly, ready to intervene or eject. Each player had their own winning blackjack strategy. Some stuck at fourteen or over, hoping the dealer would bust. Others pushed their luck and called for another card, even when they were at sixteen or seventeen. Regardless, the end results remained the same: the dealer always won. Dolan nodded in approval and prowled, looking for opportunities.

Dotted around nooks and alcoves, poker players who'd been eliminated from the tournament, continued to play in groups of five or seven. There was no clink of chips here; only paper money allowed. Dolan watched a middle-aged man cry, drop a car fob on the table and push his chair away. He'd just lost a Mercedes.

Dolan nudged his companion. 'Gamblers' greed, wha? Never know when to stop. Why bet twenty euro when they can bet fifty? A hundred? Why stop at a hundred? Go for a thousand? The car. Why stop at the car? Fuck it. Bet the house. Wife's gonna get it in the divorce deal, anyway.'

The minder grunted.

The sound of silence from a room off the ballroom drew Dolan's attention. The men ambled through a curtained doorway and into a small room where serious business got played out.

The forty thousand euro prize fund had drawn a full house. Circular poker tables were placed around the room, and heavy cabled rope strung between upright stanchion posts, separated the spectators from the players. Dolan's gaze swept across the players. He elbowed his companion again. 'Lookit tha'? McGuire's here, an' he won.' They watched Malcolm separate and stack his chip pile. When the murmur arose again, the minder macheted a path through the onlookers, and Dolan approached Malcolm from behind. He hopped over the cabled rope and sidled up like a street dealer.

'Wasn't sure you'd make it, seeing as you buried your sister a few days ago. Sorry for your troubles.'

Malcolm jumped and pulled the chip trays protectively to his chest. 'Thanks. It helps me forget.'

'Well, she's lookin' down on ya. Four aces, wha? Must've netted you twenty, twenty-five grand?'

'Something like that.'

'Hear tha'?' Dolan elbowed his companion again. 'Somethin' like tha', he says. See? That's wha' I was sayin'. Professionals like Mal here doesn't give a fiddlers 'bout the money. It's winning that counts. Beat the bookie, beat the other fellas at the table. I'm right, aren't I, Mal? Aren't I?'

'You're right, Dessie.'

Dolan caught Malcolm's elbow and lifted him from the chair. Malcolm tried to grab his trays, causing them to spill across the table. 'My chips. They're mine.'

'Let's discuss it, Mal. We'll go to the bar an' have a drink. In fact, seein' as you're minted, you can buy. Don't worry 'bout the chips. We'll rack 'em an' pack 'em for ya.' The minder opened the briefcase and shovelled chips into it. Dolan gripped Malcolm's sleeve and steered him away from the poker table. 'An' while we're havin' a nice social chat, you can tell me your plans 'bout how you're gonna pay me back. I'd have given ya a week's leeway, on account of your family troubles, an' shit, but as you're here...' Dolan shrugged. 'I've got bills too.'

'I was going to pay you—'

'I know you were.'

'I'll settle up now. How much do I owe?'

'Lemme see.' Dolan pushed Malcolm into a chair and sat beside him. He took a mobile from his pocket, hit some buttons, frowned, shook his head, tried again. 'Twenty-seven. Even.'

'Twenty-seven?' Malcolm's voice rose. 'How——?'

The minder sat across from Malcolm, boxing him in.

Malcolm lowered his tone. 'I only borrowed six. And Ferdia told me he was going to pay you back the other loan.'

'An' he did. He did. An' soon, I'll get a chance to thank 'im, personally. But there was collateral damage along the way, an' that hasta be sorted. Know wharra mean?'

'No. What do you mean?'

'Don't worry your head 'bout it, Mal.' Dolan patted Malcolm's cheek. 'Something I need to discuss with the man himself. In private. Who is he? Where can I find him?'

'Ferdia? Ferdia Hardiman. He's my uncle. In law. Through marriage.'

'And where does Ferdia live?'

The bodyguard leaned forward, eyed Malcolm.

'He has a house in The Demesne, just outside Ganestown,' Malcolm said. 'Let me talk to him. I'll set up a meet—'

'You've enough on your plate, Mal. We'll sort it out. You alrigh'? You look a bit pale.'

'I'm fine. Just tired. I need coffee.'

Dolan clicked his fingers at the minder. 'Coffee here for the champ, pronto. Black with loads of sugar. You need to keep fresh. There's a long night ahead. And then you've got the Deepstack Poker Championship tournament in early February. Jaysus, Mal, you'll be a millionaire in a month.'

'Yeah.'

Dolan put a small clear plastic bag into Malcolm's hand. 'Here. Hang onto these.'

'What's that?'

'A little something to help keep ya fresh. Make you go on for longer. Keep you sharper. Give you an edge.' He winked. 'Know what I'm sayin'?'

'I don't do drugs, Dessie.'

'Everybody does drugs, Mal. Prescribed, recreational, street… whatever. Consider it a gift. From a friend. Look, I'd love to chat, but time's money. How much was in that stack?' Dolan asked the minder.

'Thirty-two grand.'

Dolan nodded. 'Well, go on then. Give Mal his five grand back. We're not fookin' thieves.'

The minder reached into the briefcase, delved around to find the correct combination of poker chips.

'There ya go.' Dolan stood and made a show of searching his pockets. 'Sorry, Mal, I've no change to buy your coffee. But sure, you're loaded. My treat next time. Sorry again for your troubles. Oh, what number is Ferdia's house…?'

4.40 P.M.

ADAM STYNE TRIED to ignore the jarring pain.

Shackled to a mattress that was hard enough to allow for compressions during CPR was uncomfortable. But with the stretcher sitting over the rear axle, whose suspension was tuned to accommodate a heavy vehicle going fast, the effect multiplied the severity of the bumps. He'd lost his sense of direction within minutes.

Stick to the story. The tale that's heard most often is the one that's remembered.

A walkie-talkie squawked. 'Three minutes,' one of the paramedics said. The ambulance slowed and turned. It bounced and jolted like a bucking bronco as it sped over a speed ramp. Styne's spine slammed back onto the hard trolley and caused the pain in his leg to vibrate.

Did I leave any traces? No.

Is there evidence that can be linked back to me? No.

Did anyone see me? No.

The ambulance sprung over another hump and stopped.

They can't pin anything on me. Deny. Deny. Deny.

The back doors opened, the Garda unlocked the handcuffs, and the paramedics manhandled the gurney onto the tarmac.

'Where am I?' Styne looked around while the Garda unlocked the handcuffs. 'Where've you taken me? I know my rights.'

Impossible for some bodies to be found. The ones to worry about are buried on the farm, especially Roberta Lord and Ciara McGuire.

Styne got lifted into a wheelchair and strapped in. His plastered ankle hit against the footrest. He yelped as rivets of pain shot through nerve endings and caused momentarily blindness. When his vision cleared, he examined the building he was being wheeled towards. A wide, three-story grey, cold Victorian building with a red Lancet door in the middle, brooded over a large expanse of snow-covered ground. To his right, Styne could hear a faint hum of traffic.

I didn't use my real name. Let them go through my laptop. I never used it. Always used internet cafes... 'Where is this? Where am I? Where are you taking me?'

'A special place,' the Garda walking alongside said. 'A holiday home. Peace and tranquillity for troubled minds.'

'I want to make a complaint with regard the way I've been treated like non-human cargo. And I want my barrister.'

'He knows where you are. Once you're declared insane—'

'What are you talking about?' Styne said. 'May I remind you who I am? I'm not insane.'

'We know who you are, Mr Styne. *And* what you've done.'

Maybe they'll get saliva samples from Ciara McGuire. That could be a problem. Could forensics tie me to the disappearances? Would the acid have had time to work? Madeline had taken the garage car, so they don't know I used it. And I cleaned all the physical evidence at the farmhouse...

A paramedic held an A4 size file and walked towards the red door. Clumps of tall Scotch pine and Norwegian spruce trees overshadowed the grounds. There were no cars, no sign of life.

Two issues: One, the stun gun was a problem. That's where most questions would arise. Should have got rid of it after Ciara McGuire.

The red door opened. A porter in a white coat stood in the entrance. A string of keys dangled from his fingers and a lanyard with a swipe card hung around his neck. He used a shoulder to open the door wider and stood aside as the wheelchair was pushed into a hallway and wheeled left. The porter riffled through the black bin bag, slung it over his shoulder and walked ahead. He used the swipe card to open a door, and Styne got wheeled into a corridor. Boots thumped on the concrete floor as they passed locked metal doors that had two sets of hinges. Another locked door. The cortège waited while white coat man fumbled with keys. After a few tries, he opened the ancient metal Chubb lock. This door looked heavier. Made of reinforced steel. The porter grunted with effort and pulled the door open. The door clanged shut behind them.

The second issue: I used my mobile to trace Sharona Waters. Premeditated. Stupid. So stupid.

Styne blinked in the white fluorescent lighting. A rank smell assaulted his senses; industrial-strength bleach coupled with sweat and stale urine. Doors along both sides of the corridor opened, and heads peeped out, like rabbits from burrows, but the shush of lethargy was palpable. It was like going from a busy street into a church. Styne glimpsed through the doorways as they passed. Small rooms. Cells. A bed and chair were all he could see. They were all painted the same colour as the corridor; a pastel pink, and devoid of any pictures, murals or tapestries. Some cells were vacant. Others were occupied by people dressed in blue tracksuits. A few people wandered around the corridor. At an intersection, they veered right around a cube of thick glass. A security man sat inside. A middle-aged man was on his haunches in the corridor, crying to a nurse. She shook her head. He went down on his knees and joined his hands, imploring. Another head shake.

I'll practice until I convince myself. There's no evidence I killed anyone. I'll cite stress and the emotional trauma of losing everything I'd worked for. That's what caused me to go over the edge with the Waters woman. I'll say my father used to lock me in the boot of his car whenever I made him angry. Childhood trauma. Plus the stress of Jana Trofimiack and my company. My fears. Anxiety about my wife. Her behaviour. Going to Paris and leaving me on my own…

'Are you the doctor?' A wild-eyed young man with tangled black hair and a rumpled orange tracksuit trotted alongside the wheelchair. 'Are you? Are you?'

'Derek, go to your room.' The porter glanced over his shoulder.

'If you're not a doctor, you're doomed,' Derek said. 'Why don't you end the pain? Go on. I bet you wanna do it. I know you're in pain. You *know* you want to do it. Do it. Do it.'

'Thank you, Derek. Everything's fine. Go to your room.'

The man laughed.

They swerved around an overweight middle-aged man talking to himself. He didn't seem to notice the file of people bearing down on him. At another corridor intersection, they stopped. To the left, a TV blared cartoons from a dayroom. A man stood on a stationery treadmill, lifting one leg, then the other, marching in time, going nowhere. Three hunched figures sat at a table. On the right, a windowless canteen was filled with chrome tables. Each one had four metal chairs welded to it, and unit was secured to the floor. A few plastic pot plants hung from nails hammered into the wall. Straight ahead, it looked like more rooms. Whatever this place was, it wasn't fit for purpose.

Styne got wheeled past the day room. The corridor went on forever. The air got chillier, and the smell got worse. More fetid and acidic. Hums of conversation floated from doorways as they passed. Then, an ear-splitting siren blared, and red strobes flashed. White coats rushed into the hallway, looking for the cause of the alarm.

'Number eleven,' someone yelled, and like a murmuration of starlings, they turned in unison and moved in a single entity to head off trouble somewhere in the cavernous building. The porter pointed at a door, dropped the plastic bag and disappeared among a confusion of white coats.

The paramedic knocked and entered. There was no nameplate, no indication who was inside. The Garda and technician guarded the wheelchair until the door re-opened and Styne got pushed inside.

A short stout woman with white permed hair stood, arms folded. She smelled of hot chocolate. Half a dozen Styrofoam cups were stacked on one side of her desk. A laptop, a pile of folders, and a half-eaten quiche on a paper plate with a plastic knife and fork took up the remainder of the space. Styne noticed a panic alarm button screwed onto the wall and had a sudden urge to plunge the fork into her eye.

Another white coat crowded into the small office. The paramedics and Garda left. The woman sat in her chair, kept the desk between them, while the newcomer sat beside Styne.

'Mr Styne, I'm Josephine,' the woman said. 'Have you been in a psychiatric hospital before?'

'No. And I want to make a formal complaint about the way I've been treated. I've got rights. I haven't been told where I am, or why I've been sent here. Where am I?'

'You're in the Central Mental Hospital, just outside Dundrum village, south county Dublin.'

'Why was I brought here?'

'You've been referred here because the state has asked for an evaluation to determine whether or not you've a diagnosis that needs treatment,' the doctor said. 'Similar to those used in community mental health or private practice, but more detailed. If necessary, a treatment plan will be created, and referrals provided. Understand?'

'Yes. When will I be seen?'

'It's Sunday. Psychiatrists aren't available twenty-four seven. Next week. Sometime.'

'I'm being held against my will. I'm a prisoner.'

'You've been legally detained. You're here to be evaluated and I'd appreciate your co-operation.'

'Evaluated for what?'

'Your mental health.'

'My mental health is fine.'

The doctor sat back and scrutinised Styne. 'First, we don't have prisoners here, Mr Styne, we have patients, and we evaluate each one. Second, our position as psychiatrists is that we work with the law in an advisory manner. We advise. The court decides.'

'I want my barrister, Alistair O'Brien.'

'Mr O'Brien knows where you are. Once you're checked in, we'll need your basic medical history, and then find out about any conditions you have, or treatment you need. What medications you're taking or have taken, what diagnoses you've gotten, what therapists you've seen—'

'I've been in hospital for the past week. I don't know what medication they've given me. Don't you people talk to—?'

'At the same time, each patient entering the system receives a quick mental health screening,' the doctor interrupted. 'This is designed to identify urgent medical and mental health concerns and stabilise anybody in need of immediate treatment. Understand?'

'Yes. Doctor.'

The white coat picked at a dirty fingernail.

'Okay. Let's start.' Doctor Josephine took some papers from a folder. 'Do you want to see a priest?'

'No. I want my solicitor.'

'Have you any…'

THE DOCTOR TICKED boxes and Styne answered. Moved to page two. Education and employment record. From page three onwards, Styne paid more attention and thought more about the answers he gave regarding childhood developmental and family history, education, employment records, marital history, next of kin and social life.

And then it was over. 'In a few days,' the doctor said, 'you'll be assessed by two psychiatrists—'

'Two? Why—?'

'It's the law, Mr Styne. One for prosecution, one for the defence. If a case goes to trial, they can inform the jury if they believe the accused was insane, or not, at the time of the offence.'

'Who are the psychiatrists?'

The doctor stared. 'Why would that matter? When they're assigned, they'll conduct a detailed mental health screening.'

'Why?'

The doctor sighed. 'Because patients with limited cognitive function are at increased risk from victimisation.' She leaned forward, elbows on the desk, and spoke slowly. 'They may also need a staff member to assist them with court hearings, follow directions and or writing. Understand?'

The white coat gnawed a fingernail.

'I don't have limited… yes,' Styne said. What a bitch, he thought. *Someday, someway, somehow, I'll kill her.* 'Can I get something to eat?'

'Of course.' Doctor Josephine stapled the sheets and pushed them into a folder. 'Normally we'd do a physical, but in your condition, I think blood tests will suffice.'

Styne's blood pressure was checked, and two vials of blood drawn. She shone a flashlight into his mouth and tut-tutted.

'How long am I going to be here?' Styne asked.

'Once you're here, there's no out date, Mr Styne. Let's take each day as it comes, shall we? John will get you something to eat. Dining room's closed. You can have it in your room.' Josephine peered at her laptop. 'Room nine, John.' She spoke to Styne. 'John will organise something to eat. Make sure it's soft, John. Oh, and crutches. You need to start exercising a little bit, Mr Styne. Some painkillers too, John.'

John turned the wheelchair around and trundled down the corridor. Halfway down the hallway, he opened a door and pushed Styne inside.

'Don't stir.'

Styne looked around. There wasn't much to see in the windowless prison cell-sized room. A single bed. A wafer-thin mattress. A pillow that looked like a small cushion, and a dirty light-brown blanket no bigger than a beach towel. A grey hard-plastic chair sat in a corner.

John returned with crutches, an orange tracksuit, a pair of slippers and the black plastic bag with his clothes. He removed the clothes, placed them on the bed, folded the bin liner and tucked it into his waistband. Then he pulled the tracksuit trousers over Styne's legs. 'Let's see if you can manage the crutches. Just a few steps.' With Styne standing, John got his arms into the tracksuit top and zipped it up. He stepped back and observed Styne wobble. 'You'll do. Here, let's get these on.' He placed the slippers on Styne's feet.

'They're too big.'

'Yes. Sorry. Everyone gets oversized slippers. Now, what do you fancy to eat?' John grinned. 'I'm sure you'd like a nice medium-to-well steak, but I'll get chef to rustle up a nice omelette, and I'll see if they've got jelly and ice cream.' He stepped towards the door.

'Thanks,' Adam Styne said. His eyes narrowed, thinking. 'Hey.'

John turned. 'Yes?'

Styne took a wallet from the black bag, peeled off a fifty euro note and handed it over. 'Thanks, John,' he said.

John hesitated, took the money, nodded and walked out.

8 P.M.

'WHAT THE HELL happened your face? And nose?'

Hugh recoiled from Ruth's touch. 'Light sparring with Ferdia. I'll never be a boxer.'

Ruth stared. 'For God's sake—'

'Hugh?' Kathleen's voice floated from the sitting room. 'Who's there?'

'It's Ruth, Mum.' Hugh limped down the hallway.

'Why are you limping?' Ruth asked.

'Strained leg muscles. Need more exercise,' Hugh said.

'Brilliant, Hugh,' Ruth followed him. 'Starting a new job tomorrow and you're going in with a black eye and a swollen nose? How'll that look?'

'It's nothing. Honest. Charlie won't mind. He knows what Ferdia's like.'

'So stupid,' Ruth shook her head. 'Ferdia's a bad influence on you.'

'Aww, that's not fair. He's—'

'Hi, Kathleen,' Ruth smiled.

'Oh, hello, dear. 'Are you the new housekeeper? I'm glad. I didn't like the last one.'

'No, Kathleen. I'm Ruth. Hugh's... friend.'

'Who's Hugh?' Kathleen asked.

'Hugh, your son.'

'I don't have—'

'Mum, please.' Hugh swallowed his irritation and stretched his shoulder blades to relieve neck pain. Seeing his mother act like a child was becoming a strain.

'I need to take my tablets.'

'You've had them, Mum.'

'No, I didn't. You're trying to kill me.'

'I forgot, Mum. Thanks for reminding me.' Hugh gave Kathleen a few Smarties and the sugar treats satisfied her. She looked at Ruth again. 'I remember you. Were you at the dance last night?'

'No. But I spoke to Emily and she said you had a great night.'

'Where do I know you from?'

'I looked after you when you were in hospital.'

'Hospital? When was I in hospital?'

'Last week.'

'Was I? Did we dance?'

'She's got dancing on the brain,' Hugh murmured.

'This is my son,' Kathleen pointed to Hugh. 'Do you know him?'

'Yes.' Ruth knelt in front of Kathleen. 'We were in school together.'

'I'm going back to the hotel,' Kathleen tried to stand. 'I want to dance. My son will collect me later.'

'It's okay, Mum. I'm your son.'

'Indeed, you're not. My son is…' Kathleen paused. 'But you seem nice. Do you dance?'

'Badly,' Hugh said.

'He's not able to walk, never mind dance.' Ruth smiled at Kathleen.

'I'll teach you both,' Kathleen said. 'What do you do for a living? I used to be a nurse. I have a son, you know.'

'I know.'

Kathleen frowned. 'How? Do you know him?'

'Yes.'

'Oh. That's nice.'

Hugh gripped his mother's arm. 'Are you tired? Do you feel like—?'

'I feel like dancing.'

'Okay, let's dance then.' Hugh waltzed his mother around the small space. She lilted The Blue Danube and giggled like a schoolgirl.

'What happened at the hospital?' Hugh asked Ruth.

'Potential panic diverted, I think. Keith brought me to his office. I'd to write out a report stating who, what, where, when, why and how. He didn't like it but had to accept I wasn't after headlines. Bad for the image, he said and warned if there's a repeat performance where I'm implicated in any way, I'm out. I'm still on probation. I can't afford—'

Kathleen stopped dancing and wandered into the hallway, towards the kitchen.

'There won't be a repeat performance.' Hugh sat on the settee and rubbed his leg. 'Styne's locked up. The paper's got their headline. They'll move onto something else tomorrow.'

'I hope so.' Ruth sat beside Hugh, put her arms around his neck and pulled him towards her. He flinched. 'Ow. That's sore.'

Ruth pushed away. Hugh pulled her forward again and kissed her. 'I said I was sore. I didn't say stop.' They grinned and held each other tight. Ruth massaged Hugh's neck.

'Hmm,' Hugh said. 'That's nice.'

Ruth worked on the neck muscle. 'Shh,' she said. 'Silence is golden.'

Hugh closed his eyes, relaxed under Ruth's touch, listened to the timber logs crackle in the fireplace, and tuned out... almost.

'Silence,' he said, 'is also suspicious. It's too quiet.'

They looked at each other and sprang to their feet. 'Mum?' Hugh called. 'Mum?' They ran to the kitchen. The toxic smell of smouldering plastic made Hugh cough. Kathleen was standing in a cloud of noxious smoke and steam. 'Mum?' Hugh bounded over, took her hand and led her away to safety. Ruth switched off the cooker and used a dishcloth to yank away the electric kettle Kathleen had placed on the cooker ring. She opened the back door, threw the half-melted kettle out, and left the door open to disperse the smell.

'I want to make tea for the lady,' Kathleen smiled.

'That's great, Mum,' Hugh said. 'I know we've another kettle somewhere.'

'I think the electric ring is banjaxed,' Ruth said. 'The plastic has melted into it.'

'No problem.' Hugh hugged Kathleen. 'We'll get a new one tomorrow.' He spoke to Ruth out of the corner of his mouth. 'Alzheimer's is turning me into a victim too.'

Ruth patted Hugh's arm as she passed. 'You're doing great,' she whispered. 'Agree with everything. The easiest way to survive is to adopt the course of least resistance.'

'I'm switching between feeling important and being useless every five minutes. It's frustrating, but...' Hugh smelled the ammonia before the puddle of urine seeped into the carpet.

Kathleen started to cry.

'It's okay Mum. Let's go to the bathroom. I'll help change you.'

'I'll do it,' Ruth said. 'You...' she gestured at the cooker. 'Do something with this.' She took Kathleen's arm.

'Is nobody going to ask me to dance?' Kathleen asked.

'Let me help you change, Kathleen,' Ruth said. 'Then we'll dance.'

3

MONDAY 21 JANUARY. 6 A.M.

THE LACK OF natural light meant Adam Styne had no idea what time it was.

He must have dozed off at some stage and been woken by a nurse shining a flashlight in his face. Now, voices floated into the room. Styne strained to hear.

'Danny Carrey is a brilliant drummer. The reincarnation of John Bonham.' He swung his legs over the side of the bed.

'Who's Danny Carrey?'

'Danny Carrey. Tool.'

'Don't call me a tool.'

'Not you. Tool. TOOL. The band. Ba-dum-bum-CHING.'

'Never heard of them. Jason Bonham is the reincarnation of John Bonham.'

'He's good, alright. Who do you think is the best drummer?'

'Meg White.'

'Meg…? Jesus. A chef in a bad mood, rattling pans would make a better—'

'Okay, okay. Karen Carpenter.'

'Who?'

'Doesn't matter. Anyways, drummers aren't needed in bands.'

'Bullshit, George. Bull. Shit. The drummer is the most important—'

'*You're* the bullshitter. Just 'cos you're a so-called drummer, Ronnie. It's sound engineers that make the magic happen an' they *never* get credit.'

'Bullsh—'

'Okay, answer me this, then: When a band's playing in the middle of a field, who gives the crowd the sound they hear on a studio album? Huh? Who? The sound engineer, that's who. It's not rocket surgery. Without a sound man, the band'll sound like a duck's fart.'

'Bullsh—'

'An' singers never sing. It's all mimed. How could anyone sound like they do on a CD, when they're jumping around a stage, like a donkey with a wasp up its—?'

'Bullsh—'

'Only thing drummers want is a big finish. Makes 'em look good.'

The voices and shuffling feet stopped outside.

'Ow. Piss off, George.'

'Stop cursing, Ronnie. Bill Berry's an underrated drummer.'

'Super underrated.'

Styne could hear one of the men use the wall as a drum, accompanied by a hissing sound to replicate the snare drum. He eased onto his good foot and hopped to the wheelchair.

'Ow. Ow. Leave my drums alone. Get your own drum kit, George. Ow.'

A small man, bald on top with thin wisps of frizzy black hair over his ears, staggered into Styne's room. He was wearing a blue tracksuit. The bottoms had been bought when he was fifteen kilos lighter.

'Oh, hello. You're new.'

The second, taller man stuck his head in to see who his friend was talking to. He had a short, tidy businessman haircut and dressed in an orange jumpsuit.

'There's been a mistake,' Styne said. 'I'm here for an assessment.'

The small man cackled. 'We all are. What's your name?'

'Adam.'

'I'm Ronnie. This is George.'

'Are you patients here?'

'There are no patients here,' George said. 'We're clients. I'm here 'cos I'm mad. Mad as a hatter.'

'He is,' Ronnie nodded. 'He's super mad. An' I'm mad too. But only 'cos the Government did scientific projects on me. Chemicals, mind control stuff. Shit like that. Now I'm schizophrenic, bipolar, depressive and psychotic. My solicitor's working on it. We're gonna take these bastards to the cleaners. And I'm writin' a book. Sure-fire bestseller. Doc says I'm gifted.'

'Yesterday you thought you were a chicken,' George said.

'You're a chicken. Baawk, baawk, baawk.' Ronnie scratched his left wrist. It had a dirty bandage wrapped loosely around it. 'Why're you talking funny, Adam?'

George pushed Ronnie. 'You thick or wha'? Can't you see his jaw? Someone broke it.'

Ronnie rubbed his own jaw and stared at Styne.

'Who'd you get?' George asked.

'Pardon?' Styne said.

'Who did you get when you came in?'

'Shhh,' Ronnie stepped into the room and sniffed. 'You got Josephine. Didn't ya? Ya did. I can smell her.' He leaned closer. The smell of cabbage almost made Styne vomit. 'She's a walking—'

'Stop cursing, Ronnie.'

'What's wrong with her?' Styne asked.

'You'll find out. She's a nosy bitch. The more you want to forget, the more she'll force you to remember. She likes to see us cry. Shows you're... what's the word I'm looking for?' Ronnie looked at Styne for help.

Styne stared back.

'You know, when you're...' Ronnie clicked his fingers. 'Open to her suggestions. Can I tell you the secret of this place, mister?' Ronnie's wild eyes danced in their sockets. Both men came closer and knelt beside the wheelchair. 'The only goal here,' Ronnie said, 'is to get out. So, never complain, never tell them anything's wrong. Don't *ever* mention that the tablets they make you take, is givin' you migraine headaches, and make you sad. If you do, you'll be given extra days. That bitch controls your fate.'

'He's right.' George stood, scooted to the door, looked along the corridor, then ran back to Styne. 'The only way outta here is by lyin' through your teeth. What *we* do is, we think of a number we need, in order to get out. Say fifty. Every time you agree with the bitch, that's one point. Attend group therapy? That's a point. Smile and say hello to a nurse? That's a point. See what I'm gettin' at? Get thick with a white coat about something, an' that's a minus point. Be negative or angry in front of them, that's more points taken away. Geddit? If you want another blanket or pillow, don't ask. If you do, they'll put you down as a troublemaker. You gotta get to fifty points, an' keep it there for about two weeks, see? Tell her an' show her what she wants to hear, an' you'll be outta here in no time.'

Ronnie nodded. 'Yeah, we're not people to them. We're *conditions*. She'll deffo try to make you cry, she will. She's the real psycho in here, not us. See, she *wants* you to lose points. She's the worst of the white coats. Got a spare ciggie?'

'Don't smoke,' Styne said.

'George, Ronnie. What are ye doing here?' John stood in the doorway.

Ronnie held up an imaginary rifle and aimed it at John's head. 'P-kuk.' His arms jerked. 'Missed. P-kuk. Shit. Missed again.'

'I've got clearance to go,' George said.

'Go where?'

'Home.'

'I've clearance too,' Ronnie said. 'I've drum practice in an hour.'

'Who gave you clearance?'

Ronnie tilted his head and frowned, like someone listening to a voice on a mobile phone with a bad connection. 'The universe,' he said and slapped the wall in a fast two-hand double beat.

'Canteen, now,' John said. 'Both of ye.'

'Sorry, chief.' George ignored John and spoke to Styne. He jerked his head at Ronnie. 'See, with Ronnie there's always high drama, but he's harmless. He's not usually this bad. They changed his meds yesterday and…' George pointed a finger at his temple and made a circle. 'They've made him a bit loo-lah.'

Ronnie joined his hands in prayer and knelt in front of John like a pious penitent. 'Give us this day our daily meds.' He opened his mouth and stuck out his tongue.

'He'll be a raving lunatic 'til he settles,' George added. 'It'll take a few days. Won't it, Ronnie?'

Ronnie stood up and dusted off his tracksuit trousers.

'He useta drum, years ago,' George added. 'In his own head he's John Bonham, 'cept no-one's ever heard of 'em.'

'I—'

'Now, John, here, always was, and always will be a complete assho—'

'Breakfast's ready in the canteen, boys,' John said.

George pushed Ronnie. 'Walk and breathe, Ronnie. Walk and breathe.' The men moved into the corridor.

Ronnie popped his head back in. 'Vul-ner-able. She likes to see you vul-ner-able.'

John pointed a finger and Ronnie disappeared.

'Where's the toilet?' Styne asked.

'Across the hall.'

Ronnie came back into the room. 'I'll teach—'

'Ronnie? Canteen,' John said.

Ronnie ducked. 'You can practice on my drum kit,' he said to Styne. 'I'll teach you how to—'

'Ronnie? That's enough. Go to the canteen, now.'

Ronnie vanished.

'I've a headache, John,' Styne said. 'Can I have tablets? And something for the pain in my leg?'

'Of course. I'll get for you at the canteen.'

'I need to phone my barrister.'

'Phone's at the nurse station. I'm sure he'll drop in as soon as he can.'

Styne straightened his plastered leg. His good leg was numb. He tried to push himself from the wheelchair. Failed. 'I can't do this,' he said.

'I'll help,' John said. He wheeled him to the doorway. A dozen zombie-like figures scratched, stretched and stumbled in a drug-induced fog towards the nurse station and dining room. John waited for a break, then push the wheelchair across the hallway into the toilet. 'Wash,' he said. 'I'll be back in a jiffy.'

The door wouldn't lock. There wasn't any knob, hook, handle or bar to help hoist himself up. Styne gripped the sink, eased himself from the chair and used the toilet. There was no mirror either. He ran a hand over his face. He hadn't shaved in a week. Styne pressed a button on the sink and water trickled from the single tap. Exhausted, he sat back in the wheelchair. 'Hey,' he called. 'Hey.' No one answered. Styne back-combed his hair, managed to turn the wheelchair around and reverse out the toilet door.

'Finished already?' John was back. 'That T-shirt got wet. Let's get you a dry one before we go to the canteen.'

Seething and helpless, Styne allowed himself to be changed and wheeled along the corridor, his thoughts beating in time to the sound of voices and rattling crockery.

Someday, somehow, they'll all pay a hundredfold.

9 A.M.

PHILIP WALDRON, MCGUIRE'S accountant, ignored Hugh's proffered hand.

He steepled his fingers and hooked both thumbs under his chin. A semi-smile, inscrutable as the Mona Lisa, didn't reach his eyes.

Hugh pulled back his hand and sat at the round conference table. Philip opened a notepad and wrote Hugh's name in precise block capitals. Hugh wondered what way the conversation would go. And where was Charlie?

'Charlie informed me you're to be kept on.' The accountant looked out the conference room window and Hugh followed his gaze across Mullingar's snow clad Business Park. Philip motioned with his hand. 'The company can't afford... we've no *requirement* for another employee, but... Charlie has a history of hiring, ah, unnecessary staff.'

'I appreciate the work.'

Waldron added the date under Hugh's name. 'Friend of Charlie's or not, let me give you a head's up. Keep searching for another job. This one has a limited lifespan. We've completed the cost cuts, streamlined the business, brought in the glossy new and improved products, upped customer services, and here's what we're left with.' He ticked off options on his fingers. 'Bankruptcy. Yes, it would buy time, give us access to additional finance, *maybe* help us reorganise... but, negotiations drag on while the company's value declines further. In fact, we're too *broke* to go bankrupt. Lawyers' fees, advisers... but *if* we file, it must be executed now, or there won't even be dregs left to scrape up. Actually, we've *passed* that stage; there *are* no dregs. Two, NAMA's a possibility. Three, sell the business as a going concern. There are no more miracles we can perform to change the inevitable. The barbarians are at the gate.'

'Malcolm said—'

'Malcolm.' Waldron blew air through his nose. 'Another lame duck with daft delusions who thinks a college degree can... And speaking of which, where is the elusive Malcolm?' Waldron made a show of looking around the room. 'If we're dependent on Junior as the saviour of team McGuire, God help us.' He banished the notion with a flick of his hands and placed his fingers back in the steeple position. 'I won't permit any unauthorised spend. Bottom line: I'm the company watchdog.' He glanced at his watch, drummed his fingertips on the table, before putting them back in the steeple position.

Who watches the watchdog? Hugh wondered and looked at the A3 sized framed photograph of Ciara hanging on the wall. She was gazing out to sea, pointing into the distance, unaware of the camera;

a smiling, carefree image, frozen in time. And why didn't Philip make some comment about Charlie's assault or Ciara's death?

'Sorry about that.' Charlie McGuire came in. 'I'd a strange conversation with Milo Brady.' He closed the office door and sat beside Hugh. 'This isn't an interview, Philip. Hugh's already got the job. He's the new manager in Ganestown.' Charlie looked wretched. Years of pumping his lifeblood into the company had taken its toll. High rent, the collapse of the building trade during the recession, and the arrival of big-box hardware outlets, had sounded the death knell on his family hardware business. The murder of his only daughter, Ciara, a week earlier, and the minor stroke he'd suffered in the aftermath, had left him an echo of his former self.

'We're losing Milo,' Charlie said.

Good, Hugh thought. 'That's disappointing,' he said.

Milo Brady was a leech. He was also Charlie's nephew. The previous week Hugh and computer whizz, Ronan Lambe, had discovered Milo was stalking Sharona Waters. He'd damaged her property and had gained access to her private emails. Sharona had given a statement to the Gardaí, and a court summons was being prepared. He'd been handed a role in the Ganestown hardware shop, but did nothing to justify his job. The decision was made to let him go.

'Malcolm had words with him about leaving,' Charlie said, 'and when I questioned him, he didn't seem to know what I was talking about. He hasn't any job lined up, but he'd decided to move on. Spread his wings a bit. Strange that. Leaving, without—'

'One less to worry about when the place closes,' Philip said.

'Now, Philip. We've a corporate responsibility—'

'Jesus, Charlie. A few hardware shops isn't Tesco. My advice is the same as it was last week and the week before. Shutter up the shops.'

'And *you* know how I feel about letting employees down,' Charlie said. 'That's what drives me. I want Hugh on board to help Malcolm implement a change management policy.'

'Change management?'

'Yes.' Charlie nodded at his accountant. 'Hugh starts in Ganestown. Malcolm in Mullingar. From there, we'll roll out changes to the other branches. Hugh's excellent.'

'So, you're the idea man.' Waldron snapped his fingers at Hugh. 'Let's hear them. What experience of crisis management do you bring to the table? Huh? How are you going to save us from rising debt and declining customers? How are you going to adapt and deal with—?'

'Maybe give Hugh a brief outline first,' Charlie said. 'Give the man time to settle—'

'Time is a commodity we don't have, Charlie. I want to hear what he has to say. I'm interested to hear what these... *management policies* are. Well? Hmm?'

'I'll start by benchmarking us against multinationals—'

'Why? Past results are irrelevant, Mr Fallon. This is a new landscape. We've been under the business bonnet. We need a new approach, fresh thinking, but your tactic is not it. The deadly sins of business are...' Waldron started the finger count again. 'Poor cash flow, undercooked ideas, bad employee choices, tunnel vision, over-promising, ignoring the numbers... With all due respect, I don't see us becoming better with your input.' Waldron looked at his watch. 'Our time is up.'

'Maybe,' Hugh said, 'but I haven't had my say.'

'Have you forgotten what I just told you? We've tried and tested every possible—'

'The internet.'

'What?'

'You haven't used and aren't maximising the internet.'

'We can't afford upgrades. The bottom line is—'

'It's not about affordability or bottom-line costs. It's about return on investment.'

Waldron clenched his jaw and glanced at Charlie for support. 'I've told you, there's nothing left. What part of that sentence do you not understand? We've got zip. You're naïve in your aspiration, Mr Fallon.'

'Malcolm says there are stock issues,' Hugh said. 'Most of the shops are out of stock. Hard to sell products when you don't have them.'

The two men measured each other with their eyes. Hugh waited out the silence.

'Now, there's a point.' Charlie looked at his accountant. 'What's happened with our JIT system of having the right stock in the right place at the right time?'

'Must've got shelved,' Hugh said.

'Who shelved it?'

Hugh looked at Waldron.

Waldron added additional notes to his pad. 'It's under control.'

'So, is there an order due?' Hugh wasn't letting Philip off the hook.

'If there's an invoice query, deliveries can get delayed.' Philip skirted the question. 'Anything else?'

'Can you explain the order process?'

'The company's run for eighty years without your input, Mr Fallon. With all due respect, what business is it of yours *how* our order system works?'

'It would help him, going forward,' Charlie said.

Waldron scratched an eyebrow. 'Store manager makes a list. I order it. I've no idea what comprehension level you have of accountancy practices, but if a company is in dire straits, it is *vital* the finance department administers and manages all aspects of the business. I've the final say on all orders sent to suppliers. Now, I'm overdue at a conference call, so—'

'Malcolm says sales increased weekend before last.'

'For a man who isn't a wet week in the business, Malcolm says a lot,' Waldron said. 'It'll take a divine intervention to change the inevitable outcome. Regrettably, spreadsheets don't have columns for miracles. I deal in figures. Now, if you'll excuse me—'

'Sit for a minute, Philip,' Charlie said. 'We're all on the same side here. Hugh's right. Like it or not, the internet passed us by, and our current policy measures aren't working—'

'And *his* ideas will work? That's straining the bounds of plausibility.'

'We're dinosaurs, Philip. The next generation are the new leaders, the vanguard of change in technology, innovation and entrepreneurship.'

Philip snorted. 'Cop on, Charlie.'

'We both need reverse mentoring. It's time we tapped into the knowledge of our younger colleagues—'

'If you're asking me—'

'I'm not. This business was built to help people, and by God, that's what we'll continue to do.'

Philip tore the page from his notepad, wadded it into a ball, and flung it in the direction of a trash can. 'Open your eyes, Charlie, as to why you've lost the competitive edge. You're crippled by debt, battered by falling prices and discounts. Competitors with buying power… even if by some marvel we repair the balance sheet, your credibility within the trade is shot. Pah! Benchmarking against multinationals? More costs, less profits, equals job losses sooner or later.'

'Still, Philip, the man's willing to try, and there can be compromises—'

'Aspirational at best.' Waldron waved Charlie's words away. 'Compromise brings more headaches. More problems. More…' Waldron ran out of arguments.

'The explosion of credit killed us,' Charlie said. 'The banks…'

'You can't blame banks for everything, Charlie. *You* lost the run of yourself. *You* forgot the basis on which the business foundation was started.'

Hugh noticed how Philip interchanged "we" and "you" when it suited.

'Banks look at balance sheets and forget to take a commercial view of your trading history, management and customer base,' Charlie parried.

'And there ends today's lesson,' Waldron put the pen into his shirt pocket. 'Extended good times breeds complacency. The borrower pays the price. And now you expect staff to work for Fallon? A newcomer? With no—'

'I don't expect anyone to work for me. I expect them to work *with* me. How's Malcolm getting on with trade customers?' Hugh stayed in attack mode. 'Has he met suppliers yet?'

'Haven't had a chance. Waste of time teaching people who're untrainable.'

Charlie pinched his nose. 'I asked you to bring him along, Philip. He can't learn if—'

'What's the point, Charlie? Managing accounts wouldn't be conducive to… Impulsive habits like gambling can lead to rash decision making.'

'Philip, Mal's gambling days are over. I asked you to take him under your wing and show him the ropes. Now, do it.'

'I—'

'Adapt and deal with it.'

Philip puffed out his cheeks and glowered. 'Simplistic solutions to complex proble—'

'Force yourself to change your linear thinking process,' Charlie said. 'And I want no more talk about downsizing.'

'It's not downsizing, it's rightsizing.'

'I disagree—'

'Then you're wrong. I'm sick of saying this, Charlie: You've spent all your good will equity. Get out before…' Philip took a breath and changed tact. 'So, Mr Fallon, what's your first objective in turning McGuire's fortunes around?'

'I propose—'

'You propose. I dispose—'

'Let him speak, Philip.'

'Check competitor pricing and steer away from their discounted items. Compete in other areas—'

Waldron pushed back his chair. 'As I said, undercooked ideas and ignoring the numbers never works. Charlie, this is… your hopes are unrealistically high. Mr Fallon has no concept, no idea how to—'

'What's the worst that can happen, Philip? We need a balanced perspective. Hugh qualifies.'

'Qualifies, maybe. Suitable? No. God, that's been the theme of your management style for years, Charlie, and now we're seeing the consequence of your incompetence. And there'll be more predictable non-results once this… salesman comes on board.' Philip spoke as if Hugh was invisible. 'He'll struggle to master the most basic… Investing in the internet? Rubbish. You can't. Companies reinvest from profit, not from cash flow. And there *is* no profit.'

'We'll give these boys a chance, Philip. It's our only option.'

'A nonsense option. Your view is too simplistic, Charlie. I'm grounded in reality. You'll spend more money, and there'll be no significant sales improvement. What we need are decisions. This will be another build-up before a let-down.'

Charlie said: 'You're a cog, Philip, as I am. We all make up the wheel. I've made my decision.'

'Noted,' Waldron said. He stood. 'I can't listen to any more of this. At least, you've now found a definitive way to fail, once and for all.' He walked out.

Hugh knew he'd made an enemy.

11.30 A.M.

HAIRY SPIDER'S LEGS crept over Malcolm McGuire's face.

They stroked his skin and tickled him with their light touch. He tried to brush them away, but the legs dug into his skin, sharp as rat's teeth. Then something bit his toe. Malcolm jerked his leg and tried to dislodge whatever was attacking him. The claws burrowed deep into his face, ripping flesh from bone. He shook his head violently, fingernails tearing at the tormentors. Other creatures joined their comrade at his foot and began to nip and bite his legs, across his stomach. He scratched one away. Two more took its place. He couldn't grab the vicious attackers as his fingers and hands were numb.

Malcolm jumped out of bed and scrabbled for the light switch. Couldn't find it. Where was the...? He coughed, gagged and swallowed, throat parched and tasting of soap. Then the biting bugs reached his back. His fingers scrabbled to dislodge the bloodsuckers, but there were thousands of them. They attacked with increasing ferocity. His eyes, his scalp... his whole body was being eaten alive. He rolled on the floor, desperate now in his attempts to shake them off and opened his eyes wide. He couldn't see. He was blind.

Panic.

'I'm dying. I'm gonna die. I. Am. Going. To. Die.'

Malcolm banged against some obstacle, and that seemed to appease the parasites. A chink of light flowed through the edge of a curtain. He sunk knuckles into his eyes. Now he could see, but wished he'd stayed blind.

In the semi-dark, he could make out the invading leeches' shape: strange creatures that hopped about on stick-like legs. Thousands of them. Silent. Waiting. Their heads the size of gobstoppers, with eyeballs dangling on wires. In unison, they attacked again. Their jaws opened and became shark mouths' of jagged teeth, gouging and gnawing...

Malcolm woke. His eyes burned and his head throbbed from where he'd hit it thrashing around. Someone was using a jackhammer. He blinked, clamped his mouth shut in an attempt to stop his teeth chattering. His whole body was shaking, spun out from withdrawal symptoms. The creatures disappeared, carried away on a chemical cloud.

He stood, weak as a newborn foal, fell back onto the bed. Tried again. Found the light switch and looked around. This was his apartment, his bedroom. He stumbled to the window and opened the curtains. Daylight.

What time is it? What day is it?

He felt his wrist. No watch.

Malcolm turned and saw the bed. The duvet and pillowcase was covered in blood.

'What…?'

He rushed to the bathroom, looked in a mirror. Nose bleeding, his face and neck were covered in dried, crusted blood. His forehead and chest were scratched and torn where he'd ripped skin, and his pupils bulged three times their normal size.

'What happened?'

Malcolm switched on the shower and turned his face to the spray. Shivery waves flowed up and down his body. The hot water made his nerves tingle and he could feel his fingertips again.

He tried to remember where he'd been. Who took him home? Did he drive? How…? Car. Dripping wet, he stumbled through the apartment bedroom, looked out, and sagged against the windowsill in relief. The Audi was parked in its space. Malcolm opened and closed his mouth, trying to release pressure in his jaws. His gums and tongue were covered with lesions and cuts from teeth grinding.

What happened?

He'd no memory.

What the hell happened?

2 P.M.

'WHERE WERE YOU yesterday?'

'It was Sunday, Adam. Spending time with my family. Plus, working on your behalf.'

'And? Am I being released from these trumped-up—?'

'Not yet.'

'Then you're not working hard enough.'

Alistair O'Brien frowned. 'How are you coping?'

'Ending up in a mental hospital isn't something I'd planned for.'

'I can imagine.'

'Why'd you put me here? This is *your* fault. I'm *not* a basket case.'

'Consider the alternative, Adam. A prison? With no privacy? Where the cops tell other prisoners what you're in for before you arrive? Guilty until you're found innocent. Prisoners would give their right arm to get transferred to a place like this. Guess why? Less crowded. And,' O'Brien leaned closer, 'it's a far easier for me to convince and manipulate psychologists, than try to persuade streetwise cops that you're innocent. Remember, I'm a barrister *and* a psychiatrist. I've worked in mental institutions, plus I'm experienced in forensic evaluations. Our job here, is to complicate the circumstances that's been considered by the law, to a considerable extent.' O'Brien sat back. 'Have you been fed? I believe the food here is nutritious, healing and life-enhancing.'

'If you call under-cooked, over-starched food nutritious, then I suppose so,' Styne said. 'There's nothing healing or life-enhancing about it. This place is a pigsty.'

'Twenty-five per cent compliant. Twenty-five per cent non-compliant, and fifty per cent non-applicable, are the latest figures. The powers that be expect an improvement in the next inspection. There's nothing healing or life-enhancing about mental hospitals, full stop, Adam. Let's call a spade a spade. This place is designed to hold people in and keep society safe. It's not intended to *heal*. Speaking of healing, how's the leg?'

'Sore.'

'Hmm.' O'Brien surveyed the plaster cast. 'Have you had physio?'

'No.'

'Oh dear.' O'Brien pursed his lips. 'I'll see if I can get a nurse to help you with that. Prolonged lower limb immobilization in plaster carries the risk of deep vein thrombosis. Did nobody—'

'No,' Styne said again.

'Yes, well,' O'Brien said, 'physical wellbeing isn't the main priority here. Have you been told the name of the psychiatrist assigned to you?' O'Brien asked.

'No. A woman, Josephine, told me there'd be two. Whose side are you on? How long will it take?'

'Your side, Adam, and the timeline depend on lots of factors. The law trundles along at its own pace. Annual budgets dictate duration and evaluation. Have you been told why you were brought here?'

'Only that I'm being assessed.'

The barrister scribbled a note.

'Why'd you send me here?' Styne asked. 'The guard said I was detained under section 3 of the mental health act. What's that?'

O'Brien held up his hand. 'Dundrum is part of the National Forensic Mental Health Service. And you're correct, the place isn't fit for purpose. Should have closed years ago. A new facility will be opened in North County Dublin next year. We'll see. Section 2 lasts for twenty-eight days, and its main purpose is to assess a patient. It does not permit treatment. Section 3, on the other hand, lasts for a maximum of six months, and is for the purpose of treatment.'

'Six months? Are you insane?'

O'Brien smiled. 'Perhaps we're all insane. But in this case, there's a method to my madness. You're going to be assessed whether you like it or not. If you need medication, best you're here where dosage can be monitored. It also gives us time to prepare for a mental health tribunal, and it'll let some of the heat die away from, err, what you were arrested for. Believe me, this place is Disneyworld compared to our open prison system.'

'What mental health tribunal?'

O'Brien held up a finger. 'Let's not jump too far ahead of ourselves, Adam. One step at a time. An assessment will be carried out by two senior doctors, who are independent of each other, as well as—'

'I'm innocent.'

'—when you're admitted to any approved psychiatric centre, you *must* be examined by a consultant psychiatrist on the staff. You may be detained for a maximum of twenty-four hours in the centre for the purpose of this examination. If psychiatrists are satisfied that you are suffering from a mental disorder, he or she will make an involuntary admission order. If they are *not* satisfied that you are suffering from a mental disorder, you must be released immediately. In your case, back to the Gardaí. That's the law.'

'Why did you allow me to be sent here?'

Allister crossed his legs and cleared his throat. 'Let's look at the evidence from Gardaí perspective. On Monday night, January fourteenth last, you drove to Ganestown, entered the property of Sharona Waters without permission, knocked her unconscious, tied her up, used a *stun gun* to knock her out, and then you dumped her in the boot of your car and drove to your farmhouse. You were followed the whole way by a man and woman, who managed to... impede you doing whatever you'd planned to do next. They phoned the Gardaí, and the rest, as they say, is history. Gardaí and the forensic teams arrive. At this stage, they are investigating an abduction. You were brought to hospital. A few hours later, in the cold light of dawn, the team started a general sweep of your outbuildings and land. They found what looked like a fresh grave in one of your fields, and when they opened it, they found a body. A woman. Ciara McGuire. She'd been reported missing on...' O'Brien consulted his notes, 'Tuesday, January fifteenth. The body had been doused in Paraquat and wrapped in tarpaulin. The empty drum was beside the body. Incidentally, they've traced where you purchased the weed killer back in May last year—'

'Yes. I bought it for—'

'—and that discovery led to a more extensive search. Another body was found. Roberta Lord. Missing since January seventh last. Again, the body was wrapped in tarpaulin, but her head had been cracked open with a blunt instrument. A hammer, maybe. Something like that.' O'Brien raised his eyebrows. 'You don't seem surprised, Adam.'

Adam Styne mentally roused himself. 'I'm... I'm beyond surprised. I'm shocked. This is...' he shivered, 'bizarre.'

'Indeed. Forensics think your Hitachi digger was used to bury the bodies. They've removed it for further examination. Your house is being dusted for DNA, as are the bodies. Even as I speak, forensics teams are scouring your farm, looking for more graves.'

'It wasn't me.' Adam stared, unblinking, at his barrister.

'Kidnapping brings a mandatory prison sentence of eight to ten years. First offence, you might get five to seven. But, if they find a *single shred* of your DNA on the bodies or a *hint* that Ciara McGuire or Roberta Lord were in your farmhouse, they'll throw the book at you.'

'They can't. I'm innocent.'

'Of course, there's lots of Sharona's DNA in the house. You nearly tasered her to death. Plus Hugh Fallon's—that's the guy who followed you. You—'

'He was an intruder. I didn't know... I defended myself. He could've been—'

'You always go around with a Taser, Adam? On the off chance someone will attack you?'

The men stared at each other.

'Perhaps you'd bought it for your wife,' O'Brien said. 'I'm sure you're not comfortable with her walking around Paris alone without personal protection. Perhaps you were... charging it for Mrs Styne when Mr Fallon confronted you? Hmm?'

Styne looked away.

'So far, no evidence has turned up,' O'Brien continued, 'but I repeat, if they find a *grain, a scintilla* of DNA—'

'Why are you telling me all this?' Styne cut in. 'I need you to get me out of this mess, which is none of my makings. I need to be released and find out who set me up and tried to ruin my life. I had nothing to do with...' he waved his hands, 'burying bodies.'

'I have to tell you the facts, Adam. I don't want you to have unrealistic notions that this is a walk in the park.'

'I understand the seriousness of—'

'Well then, start showing a little empathy towards the deceased and their families. Roberta Lord and Ciara McGuire both left young boys behind.'

'Yes, I read about Roberta Lord someplace... Shocking. Tragic.'

'Good. Now, if you could show a *teeny* bit more *genuine* emotion, Adam, and remorse for what happened to those people? That would be excellent.'

Styne glared at O'Brien.

O'Brien laughed. 'I'm not the bad guy here, Adam. The questions I ask you are the tip of the iceberg. The prosecution will drill into every detail, like, what were your intentions when you kidnapped Miss Waters—'

'I was on painkillers and—'

'You used a *stun gun*, man. You could've killed—'

'I'd been drinking. Had a bad reaction—'

'How did you know where she lived?'

'I must have heard it somewhere—'

'How can you explain that you Googled her address on the electoral website? The evidence is on your phone.'

'I... this...'

O'Brien stood. 'I'm meeting the management here in ten minutes. I'll rattle a few cages and get things moving.' He turned away; then spoke over his shoulder. 'Think about questions you could be asked, and how you'll respond.'

'Fine, fine. What's happened my business? The art galleries?'

'O'Brien frowned and opened the door. 'Art galleries aren't my area of expertise, Adam. My role here is to safeguard your rights while the State considers its case against you, and to keep you out of prison if they decide to prosecute. However, if you want us to get involved in business dealings, I can have one of my colleagues look into them on your behalf.'

'Do it.'

'Fine, Adam. It's your call. Incidentally, was there any good news in the letter Madeline wrote?'

'No.'

'Pity. Well, may I suggest you forget about business and concentrate on pre-empting my learned friends' legal manoeuvrings, so to speak? I'll be back later to discuss further.'

HUGH'S MOBILE RANG. Emily, his mother's carer.

He's stabbed at the connect button, fearing the worst. 'Emily?'

'Hugh? Kathleen's a bit agitated. Wants a word with you. She hit me with a hairbrush earlier when I was changing her.'

'Oh, God, Emily. I'm—'

Emily laughed. 'It's nothing. One of those days. She smacks my hand away when I try to hold hers. Here she is now.'

'Hugh? Where are you?'

'I'm at work, Mum.'

'It's very late. Where've you been? I thought you'd crashed and you were killed.'

'I'm fine, Mum. I'll be home later.'

'Okay. Listen, there's something I've meant to ask you. Hugh? Are you there?'

'Yes, Mum. I'm listening.'

'I wonder if you need a teaspoon.'

'I don't think so, Mum. I've—'

'I've got lots of them,' Kathleen said. 'I don't need them all. I'd like to give you some.'

'No thanks, Mum. I don't need any teaspoons.'

'Teaspoons are very… lovely,' Kathleen said. 'I think you'll find them useful. Can you call now? I've got… those things ready for you.'

'Okay, Mum. I'll drop in—'

'I've got lots of… tea things, Hugh. I'd like to give you some.'

Hugh swallowed his irritation. Alzheimer's was slowly shutting down Kathleen's brain, blowing some words away and leaving others almost within her grasp. His helplessness frustrated him. It amazed him how the deep love he had for his mother, could turn out to be shallow as a puddle in a split second. Kathleen wasn't being deliberately aggressive or attention-seeking. It wasn't her fault she couldn't remember that she'd asked the question three times; her brain was becoming a sieve, and her memories were pouring through the holes. Thought looped before they disappeared forever. Hugh was learning to divert, occupy, soothe over. Diversion and distraction. But it was a continuous cycle and difficult to ignore that his mother was being replaced by a monster.

'I'd love teaspoons, Mum. But I'm at work now. I'll be home later.'

'I'll mind them for you.'

'Thanks, Mum. I'll see you soon.'

EVENING

REBECCA GREENFIELD COULDN'T hold in her news any longer.

She dialled her friend, Louise. 'You okay?'

'Oh, God. I haven't been able to move all day,' Louise groaned. 'What time is it? This hangover is like dismantling a nuclear bomb. I need someone to talk me through it.' She coughed, throat raw from alcohol and cigarettes.

'I'll phone you back—'

'No, you're fine. I'm not in a mood; just too tired and lazy to pretend I like people today.'

'How was the guy from Whispers last night?'

'Devastating... ly bad. My knight in shining armour turned out to be an asshole in tinfoil. At one stage, he asked me if I was ready for round two. I told him I'd like the rest of round one first.'

Rebecca giggled. 'Oops. Better luck next time. Anyway, I've got—'

'Yeah. I kicked him out before breakfast and went back to bed. He wasn't making any effort and there was too much dead air between us. I lost my dignity, but on a positive note, I found a scarf I thought I'd lost. Now, for my next trick, watch me develop feelings for the next random stranger, while I give my soul away again. That reminds me, I've gotta go to the chemist before they close.' Louise groaned again and yawned. 'How'd you get on?'

'Good. In fact—'

'You okay? You sound stressed.'

'I'm great,' Rebecca said. 'Couldn't be better.'

'You're up to something.' Louise's tone sharpened. 'I can hear it in your voice.'

'Okay, I've got some news.'

'What news.'

'You're tired,' Rebecca teased. 'I'll tell you tomorrow.' She waited for a reaction.

'You bloody won't. I want to know now. You're pregnant.'

'Give over, Louise.'

'You won the lottery.'

'I wish.'

'What then?'

'I may have landed a new job,' Rebecca said.

'Good for you, girl. Where? Penny's? McDonalds? Can you get me free coffee refills?'

'If this works out, we won't be drinking coffee, Louise. It'll be caviar and champagne-on-ice lifestyle all the way.'

'Oooh,' Louise squealed. 'You found a sugar daddy.'

'Hah. Funny, but no. Keep guessing.'

Silence. Then: 'What in hell did you do, 'Becca?'

'Nothing.' Rebecca couldn't wait any longer. ''Cept I got picked as a model last night. God, Louise, you should've seen me. I was a ball of nerves. But they were dead nice. Paid for a taxi home an' everything.' Rebecca embellished a little. 'The woman I talked to? She said chances are with my looks I'll probably end up working for Gucci or Versace.' Rebecca scaled back. 'Nothing definite yet. Hafta wait and see what's in the contract, but, yeah, it's all good. What diya think?'

'You lucky cow, 'Becca. Wish I'd stayed with you.'

'I know,' Rebecca said. 'You'd definitely have been picked too.' She opened the wardrobe. 'God, these clothes. Looks like they're taking part in a crime scene. Can I, maybe borrow some of yours? When I earn my first paycheque, I'll buy you a whole new rigout, I promise.'

'Anytime, babe,' Louise said.

'Great. Soon as I hear anything, I'll let you know.'

NIGHT

'HOW'D YOU GET on with Charlie? Have you implemented the plan?'

Ferdia's raspy voice sounded as if he'd spent the day gargling with pebbles and boiled tar.

'What plan?'

'The plan where you get the team to deliver.'

'Deliver what?'

'Deliver on the feckin' plan that you've come up with.'

'You're talking in riddles, Ferdia. We agreed terms. The plan is a work in progress.'

'That worked out well, five minutes up the road from your mother. So, what's the plan?'

'Give me a chance, Ferdia. It takes time for the dream and reality to meet.'

'No point carrying the ball from one end of the field to the other, Hugh, and doing nothing. You need to score. There must be some areas to focus on. Aim for them.'

'Yeah, bigly,' Hugh said.

Ferdia laughed.

'If I can engineer a shared enthusiasm between all the staff,' Hugh said, 'I'll—'

'You've always been good at bringing people together,' Ferdia said. 'Talent and teamwork always get things done, but McGuire's also needs an injection of enthusiasm. You're the best man for the job.'

'Needs an injection of capital,' Hugh said, 'plus enthusiasm. Companies that spend on growing brands in the downturn, capture market share on the upswing.'

'Yeah, but money's tight, Hugh, and Charlie's not in the best place to inject passion. Or capital. You've gotta find another way.'

'Yeah. Well, there'll be no collaboration with Philip Waldron. He's… I don't know, there's something… and he says: "With all due respect, Mr Fallon.".'

'Aww, man. That's the kiss of death. Don't know much about him, but I've heard he treats Charlie like a skivvy. I'd say he'd be feckin' great craic at a party.'

Hugh told him about Milo Barnes.

Ferdia shook his head. 'Dear Jaysus. What's wrong with that feckin' lad?'

'Don't know. How'd it go at the hospital? What did the doctors say?'

Ferdia coughed. 'Argh, they stuck tubes, cameras an' yokes down my throat. Took swabs and tissue samples. Wasn't as bad as I thought or as good as I hoped. Wants me to cut out… doc gave me a list the length of your arm. Coffee, alcohol, chocolate. Nothing fatty, acidic or spicy. Oh, and lose weight. A lifestyle change, he called it. Have to take tablets; some sorta blockers before eating. And from now on, I've to sleep with my head flat. Hate that. I like two pillows. If all that doesn't help, then in a few months, they'll put me under the blade. Can you phone Charlie for me? I want to say goodnight to Master David before he goes to bed. My phone battery's dead since dinner time. Blasted car chargers burn out phone batteries like—'

'Sure. It's connected to the car speakers, though, so it won't be private.'

'It's grand. You can say hello too.'

Hugh dialled. Charlie answered and passed the phone to David.

'Uncle Ferdie?'

'Howaya Master David? I'm coming home now with Hugh. Didya have a good day?'

'I asked the babysitter why did Mummy die, and she said she didn't know. She gave me a teddy bear to play with. I *hate* teddy bears.'

Ferdia looked across at Hugh. Hugh concentrated on driving.

'We talked about this last night, Master David,' Ferdia said. 'A bad man took her away. She's in Heaven now, looking down on you. Keeping you safe.'

'But if Mummy's in Heaven, why was she put into the ground? Why didn't they get a plane for Mummy and bring her *up* to Heaven?'

'When we die, God gives us wings, and we become angels in Heaven.'

'How do you know she's in Heaven? Maybe she got lost, and… and went the wrong way.'

'Nah. Your Mum always knew the right way.'

'When I die, will I become an angel, uncle Ferdie?'

'You sure will, Master David. But that won't be for a long, long time. Not until you're very old.'

'Mummy wasn't old.'

'No.'

'I hope I die tonight. I want to see Mummy.'

Ferdia looked at Hugh again, running out of answers. He waited for the next question.

'Why can't God let her come back? Even for a holiday.'

'Because she works in Heaven now.'

'Has she got her own office?'

'I'd say she runs the place, Master David.'

'I don't like God,' David said. 'He's *horrible. Everyone* gets holidays. Teachers get holidays. *You* get holidays. Why can't Mummy?'

'I don't know what God's plan is, Master David.'

David thought about that. 'Maybe he didn't like her here with us 'cos we were happy. Maybe God isn't happy, and he didn't want me to be happy either.'

'Everyone wants you to be happy, Master David.'

'Is the bad man happy that he's sent Mummy to Heaven?'

'If I ever see him, I'll be sure to ask him, Master David.'

'Where's the bad man now, uncle Ferdia?'

'The police locked him up.'

'Will he be coming back?'

'Never. He'll never come back.'

'Like Mummy. She'll never come back either, sure she's not?'

'No, Master David. But she's looking down on you, keeping you safe.'

'Is the bad man going to die soon?'

'I hope… don't know, but he won't be back. Now, tell Charlie to read you a story before you go to bed, and I'll see you tomorrow. Okay?' Ferdia's voice cracked. 'Okay, Master McGuire?'

'Okay, uncle Ferdie. Bye, Hugh.'

'Night, David.'

Hugh disconnected and Ferdia released a long breath. 'Non-stop since the funeral. It's like been feckin' interrogated. I've to try and remember what I've told him, or he'll pull me up if I change a single word. He's a thinker. Everything's black and white.'

'It's hard for a five-year-old to understand,' Hugh said.

'It's hard for a feckin' forty-eight-year old to understand. Part of me dies when I see him like this.'

'You're doing better than I could.'

'Hafta do our best for him. It's a tough road, though.' Ferdia blew on his hands. 'Christ, I'm as cold as a corpse and my throat is burning. Niamh texted me just before my phone went dead. Said she's got a litre of fresh orange juice in the fridge. Can't wait.'

'You're going to introduce me, right?'

'Sure. You'll have a bite to eat with us. We're going away next weekend. For my birthday. You can organise a party when I get back.'

'Thanks.' Hugh turned up the car heater and they listened to the radio.

'Ganestown, eh?' Ferdia got back on the work conversation when the song was over. 'I've heard Charlie say he has good people there. The key is to get the staff on side. Identify opportunities, delegate and then roll it out to the other stores. Cover yourself in glory. Sure you're on the pig's back.'

'Yeah, yeah.'

'Bish-bash-bosh. All done. Easy.'

'We'll see.'

'Someone's gotta lead the charge, Hugh. There'll always be resistance to change and new ideas, but you're the right man for the job. Charlie hasn't had time to get stuck in. Lately, he's only scratched around the surface like a dog with fleas. And now with Ciara gone, it's—'

'Hmm.'

'Did Malcolm show up today?'

'No.'

'Goddammit. He should be—'

'Relax, Ferdia. You'll hurt your throat. He needs time.'

'What he *needs,* is a boot up the arse.' A waning moon filtered its diminishing light into the car. Ferdia looked out the passenger window at the starry, frosty night sky. 'He hasn't the sense God gave geese.'

'Responsibility will make him man up,' Hugh said. 'Once he gets the business bug, he'll forget gambling.'

'He'd better. He promised me. I told Charlie to cut off the money supply. Zero dinero. He needs to stand up on his own. Time to take off the training wheels, plus get rid of the temptation. Know what I'm sayin'?'

Hugh sensed Ferdia was building up to something. He wasn't sure he wanted to hear it.

Ferdia shifted in the seat. 'Heard from Eilish?'

'Not since Ciara's funeral.'

'Me neither.'

Two years ago, Ferdia had introduced Eilish, his baby sister, to Hugh. They'd started a relationship, moved in together, and everything seemed fine until Eilish phoned Hugh to tell him she'd met someone else and was leaving. Hugh was with his mother in hospital when he got the call, and by the time he'd got home, Eilish had cleared out her belongings.

'You disappeared fierce quick when you spotted her coming over,' Hugh said.

'Argh, I knew ye'd have things to talk about.'

'We've nothing to talk about, Ferdia. She made her choice. It's over between us.'

'Well, ye're still talking. That's a start.'

'Hmm.'

Ferdia coughed. 'This Dolan fella, the loan shark.'

'What about him?'

'I need to see him. Wanna let him know I'm serious about leaving Malcolm alone.'

'No, Ferdia.'

'What?'

'No. I'm not getting involved.'

'I'm not asking you to, no way. It's just,' Ferdia scratched his head, 'I thought maybe you'd give me a hand to pin down his whereabouts—'

'Not a chance, Ferdia.'

'It's nothing serious. The thing is, Dolan isn't around his usual haunt, an' I need to take him out of Malcolm's reach. I know he hangs around a nightclub off Grafton Street. Whispers. Ever hear of it?'

'I'm not listening,' Hugh didn't answer the question.

'Huh. Trying to pin Dolan down is like trying to nail soup to a wall. Still, he'll turn up at some stage. Creatures of habit always revert to type. I know where a contact of his hangs out. I thought, maybe you'd follow him, an' see where he goes.'

'No.'

'It's not complicated—'

'Answer's still no.'

'All you'd have to do is—'

'Ferdia. I nearly got killed a week ago. Not gonna happen again. But, go on, give me a laugh. What have you in mind?'

'Follow one of his men. See where he goes. Maybe take a few photos on your phone—'

'And that's the plan?'

'Yeah. As I said, it's not complicated. Might need a few minor adjustments, but yeah, that's it.'

'And what would following some guy achieve?' Hugh asked.

'All part of a planned strategy,' Ferdia lied.

'Then definitely not.'

'So, you'll think about it.'

'Jesus, Ferdia. Give up.'

Ferdia laughed.

Hugh didn't. 'You don't listen. I said no. You've already given the message loud and clear to his goons, remember? The ones you beat up?'

'Argh, it's grand. No big deal. I need someone to follow this guy. I'm too big and awkward. You'd fit in better, that's all I'm...'

'Third and final time, no. I won't put myself in danger again.' Hugh tuned the radio to a news station. A squabble of politicians argued across each other, creating a barrage of noise that allowed no one to get their point across. Each tried to shout over their opponent, offering populist sound bites with no real solution to the myriad of issues facing the country.

Ferdia pointed through the windscreen. 'Bit early for a bonfire.' From this distance out, Ganestown was a dotted carpet of white and yellow high mast street lighting, with a flickering orange glow at one edge of the town.

Hugh exited the motorway, and the glimmer disappeared. 'What's Niamh like?'

'Niamh? Argh, she's great. Pull in here.' Ferdia pointed at a convenience shop. He got out, stretched, and Hugh watched him hunt for something on the shelves. Back in the car, he opened a bottle of water and drank half it. Then he opened a second bottle and mixed some of the contents into the water bottle. Hugh smelled vinegar.

'What are you doing, Ferdia?'

Ferdia drank again, swallowed, shuddered, and screwed the cap back on the bottle. 'Old boxer's trick. Vinegar's the best thing for internal healing after a fight. Clears up bruises. Stops bleeds. Reduces swelling.'

'Jesus. Ugh.'

'Aye. Not the nicest taste, but it works wonders. You'll need it when we get serious in the gym.'

Hugh shook his head. 'No more gym for me. Yesterday was a one and done.'

'Nonsense, lad. You gotta practice. Everyone needs to be able to defend themselves if they're attacked.'

Hugh held a hand up, palm out. 'Yesterday you told me I was too old. I don't want to know how to avoid or confront danger. I'm happy with my boring life. I'll go to the hotel gym and use a treadmill to get fit.'

'Grand. What were we talking about?'

'Niamh.'

'Oh yeah. You'll like her.'

'More important, do you like her?'

'Sure, you know yourself.'

'No, I don't.'

'Early days, but we seem to be in tune,' Ferdia said. 'Similar likes and tastes. We get on well. She seems to understand me and knows what I want. What more do I need?'

'Wish I knew what women want,' Hugh said.

'Huh. Same things as men, 'cept they go about getting it in different ways,' Ferdia said. 'Same circuit board, different wiring. Anyway, Niamh's good fun. Isn't shy. You'll like her.' Ferdia coughed. 'I still want to meet Dolan. Get him away from Malcolm.'

'Jesus, Ferdia, you never give up. Don't ask me again. Loan sharks are ruthless.'

'I owe it to Charlie. It'll pay off.'

'What if it doesn't?'

'It will.'

An ambulance blew past, siren screaming. The fiery dirty orange glow, straight ahead, was brighter now.

'I'm sure you'll figure out a plan—'

'Guaranteed. Don't have the details worked out yet, but there's no danger.'

'That's what Judas said to Jesus when he led him into the Garden of Gethsemane.' Hugh turned towards The Demesne, the small secluded estate of two-storey houses where Ferdia lived. Flames and sparks shot into the air. Black smoke billowed, turning the clear sky into a murky smog.

'That looks like one of the houses in your estate,' Hugh said. 'It's more than a chimney fire. God, that's—'

'Speed up, willya.'

Hugh pressed the accelerator. Smoke permeated through the air filters.

Half a kilometre.

Ferdia stared at the flames leaping over the rooftops.

Hugh swung into The Demesne and powered down the estate. He careened round a corner, jammed the brakes and skidded to a stop beside two squad cars that were nose-to-nose across the road. A hundred meters ahead, he saw the wrath and fury that a fire can unleash, as torrents of red-orange flames rose into the night sky. When he opened the car door, he heard the noise.

'HELLO, GORGEOUS.' REBECCA smiled at her reflection in the wardrobe.

She unhooked clothes from hangers and put them into the wash basket. T-shirts got thrown in on top. She spotted a food stain on the track suit she was wearing, peeled it off, peeled another garment from the rail, held it up, shook her head, tossed it on the pile, and picked out the jeans she'd worn in Whispers. She pulled then on added a top, pushed her mobile into the back pocket, checked her reflection again and picked up the laundry basket.

A knock sounded on the apartment door.

'Hold on,' Rebecca called. She jammed the basket between her body and the wall and opened the door.

Two men, wearing National Ambulance Service green uniforms and gloves pushed their way into the tiny hallway. 'Rebecca?'

Rebecca looked from one to the other. 'Yes? What's wrong? Has there been in an accident?'

'No accident.' The taller of the men looked at her.

His companion nodded. 'No accident.'

'What's going on? Why are you—?'

'Boss wants to meet you. Thought it best to collect you personally. Your own private transport, see?'

Rebecca frowned, 'No, I don't see. You've got the wrong apartment.'

'Don't think so,' the tall man said.

Rebecca's eyes darted at the doorway. She dropped the laundry basket and took the phone from her pocket. 'If you're not outta here in five sec—'

The smaller man edged sideways. His leg lashed out and the toe of his boot caught Rebecca's wrist. Her eyes widened in shock and pain. The mobile flew from her grasp.

'No mess, Rusty. Keep it clean,' the tall man said.

Rebecca screamed and lashed out.

'Easy, Rusty,' the big man said.

Rebecca's kick connected. Rusty sniggered, grabbed her shoulders, spun her around, pulled back her hair and tightened his grip in a rear neck chokehold.

Rebecca moaned. Her jugular vein compressed, reducing the return of blood from her brain to her heart. She felt her face flush. The arm tightened. Her eyeballs bulged as blood engorged her face and forehead, the extra pressure narrowed the carotids and reduced the blood flow further. Her vision flared, blurred and then the pressure eased up.

'Easy, Rusty. Tone it down a notch, willya? Don't damage the goods.'

Rusty loosened his grip and Rebecca gulped air. 'Let me go. I promise I won't tell anyone—'

'Shut up. Rusty? Clean up here.'

'Please, please, I swear I won't mention this to anyone. Take whatever you want.'

The tall man sighed. 'Don't make this hard on yourself. Once you pay off the debt—'

'What debt?' Rebecca's eyes widened in terror and confusion.

The man shrugged. 'Your ex-boyfriend owes us money. He can't pay. I only collect the merchandise. Now, be nice. I've got your home address. Don't make me hafta pay Mammy and Daddy a visit. Or, I can get your little sister,' he clicked his fingers, 'just like that. Rusty? Hold an arm for a second.' He took a syringe from a coat pocket, found a vein in Rebecca's arm, and pressed the plunger. 'Cha-ching!' he said. 'Inject and collect.'

Rebecca sagged in Rusty's grip.

The man pressed a number on his own phone and spoke into it. 'Stretcher, Tiny.' He moved around the sofa, found the remote control and turned off the television.

A mobile hummed. The men looked at each other. Their eyes followed the sound. Rebecca's mobile screen flashed from where it had fallen. The big man picked it up, and stared at the screen, waiting for the ring to stop. It cut into voice mail, and after a few seconds it beeped, signalling a message. The man dialled into the mailbox and held the phone between them to listen to the message: 'Rebecca? This is Sharona again. Sharona Waters. I left a message earlier. We

met last night, remember? Whispers nightclub? Erm, I'm just… well, I can't wait to catch up with you and get all your news. Let me know how you got on. Sorry again for bothering you. Hope all went well.'
The tall man grunted. 'Might hafta do somethin' 'bout that.' He pocketed the mobile. 'We'll ask the boss if he wants us to check it out. Where's Tiny?' He opened the apartment door and peeped into the corridor. 'Come on, Tiny. Chop, chop. Haven't got all night. Here, gimme.' The man tore the stretcher from Tiny's grasp. 'Find her passport, Rusty, an' follow us downstairs. Tiny, grab hold of that other end. Move it. Move it. We've more kitties to catch.'

FIRE. THE CHEMICAL process makes a terrifying noise. Ferdia leapt from the car and cut between lines of onlookers like a scythe through corn, using his arms to push bodies aside as if they were suits on a rack. He leapt over a yellow crime scene tape. A Garda tried to stop him and was driven sideways by a shoulder charge. A fireman tackled him, but he broke free, leapt over a car bonnet and ran towards his house, now engulfed in flames. Plumes of smoke seeped from roof tiles, windows and wall crevices. Flames licked and devoured the fascia band under the roof edge, crackling, spitting and hissing like a live serpent, shooting sparks into the night sky.

Hugh tried to pass the cordon and got pulled up by a Garda. He watched Ferdia in the distance as he skirted the ambulance and move towards the fire brigades. Two firemen strained to keep the high-pressure water hoses pointed at the flames. A third stood on the fire engine's tower ladder with another hose and directed a water jet through a broken window into the inferno. A Garda videoed gawkers craning for a better view of the whirlwind of violence and carnage. A large pane of glass in the sitting room bulged and splintered. A man in a Hi-Vis jacket ran towards the onlookers, waving his arms to get back, seconds before there was a loud "whump" and the window blew out, raining shards of glass across the roadway. The gawkers scattered, then drew back together like iron filings to a magnet, fascinated by the fire's fury. More glass, from an upstairs window, showered the street, and this new oxygen source increased the fire's ferocity. The cold night air boiled with toxic fumes.

There was no sight of Ferdia.

A dull roar, like a train barrelling through a tunnel, and half the house roof caved in. In control now, the reckless inferno cackled with glee and growled with anger. It ripped through plasterboard and wood, flames shooting from the roof like an active volcano.

Whomp.

A gas cylinder shot into the air like a launch rocket. It rose above the dancing flames, reached its peak, arched, and whooshed as gravity took over. It hit a neighbour's car and set off an ear-splitting alarm. A streetlight popped, fizzed and extinguished. A pall of thick, heavy smoke and soot churned and danced and shifted in the night air. It attacked the throats and lungs of those present, making inhalation seem like breathing in hot flour. But still, they stayed.

Hugh burrowed his mouth and nose in his jacket sleeve and blinked away the stinging, piercing pain as smoke attacked his eyes. The firemen fought hard, pushed forward, breaking up the fire, trying to cool it enough to get a chance to go in and quench its heart. But the battle was lost. Water sizzled and turned to vapour before it could dampen the flames. A command from the ground made the firefighters divert attention to the house next door. They turned water hoses on the gable end, using the space as a fire break to control the flames and stop them spreading. Damage limitation time.

The rest of Ferdia's house roof caved in.

'Ferdia?' Hugh shouted. 'Ferd—'

Ferdia's Mercedes, parked in his driveway, exploded, and a fireball ballooned into the sky. Its sudden searing blast of heat made the bystanders scramble for cover, adding to the mayhem. The car's bonnet blew out, pranged off the footpath, and crashed into the side of a squad car.

'Jesus, that was close,' someone said.

'Move back, move back' a Garda waved frantically. Overhead electric wires hummed and pinged. One snapped, trailing a shower of sparks as it swung through the air. A wheezing, middle-aged man collapsed and got lifted to the side. More Gardaí arrived, forcing a path through the onlookers. Hugh recognised Marcus Mulryan, the detective that had questioned him about his role in the capture of Adam Styne.

'Detective? Detective Mulryan?'

Mulryan stopped. 'Hugh?'

'Ferdia's gone to the house. There's a person in there. His girlfriend, Niamh. You've got to—'

'We've got this. Stay back. Stay back.'

A squad car carted the wheezing man to hospital. Nobody else left, hypnotised by the raw power of nature. Fingers of flames still appeared randomly. The putrid smell of smoke and water, mixed with wood, grease, plastic and creosote permeated the estate. Ash and soot continued to rain down on the bystanders and turned the area into a lunar landscape. Amid the odours of wet timber, soot, and rubber, came the distinctive smell of barbecued pork.

The firemen looked at each other.

Two of them, equipped with air tanks and masks, charged through what used to be the front door, and disappeared into the swirl of smoke. A comrade fed them more hose. Hugh watched a Garda direct an ambulance crew towards the smouldering ruins.

'How'd it start?'

'Who'd—?'

'Why would—?'

The mutterings grew in volume.

'I saw the smoke and tried to phone Ferdia. His mobile was off.'

'Yeah. He told me he'd be in hospital today.'

'Must be an electrical fault.'

'These houses are only seven, eight years old. No way was it an electrical fault.'

The firemen emerged, carrying a body bag.

A slight breeze made the black smoke swirl, and like a spectre, Ferdia materialised, grief etched on his soot-streaked face. He stopped on the roadway and spoke to a fireman.

The murmurings stopped.

The body bag got placed on a stretcher and pushed into the back of the ambulance. A fireman caught Ferdia's arm, urging him to get in as well, but he brushed the man aside. The ambulance eased away from the carnage.

'Listen up, everyone.' Detective Mulryan spoke into a bullhorn, in the calm monotone of emergency workers everywhere. 'We'd appreciate if you'd give contact details to one of the Gardaí, and we'll be in touch over the next few days. As a precaution, we're moving the other twelve families from the estate to Ganestown Hotel. *Don't* go back into your houses. For anything. Make yourselves known to us, and you'll be taken directly to the hotel. You too, Ferdia. Anyone not from the estate, please leave once you've given us your details.'

Rivulets of sweat, or tears, swam down Ferdia's face. He swayed, fragile and brittle as an old oak tree getting battered in a storm. Flesh bubbled from a mass of burns and abrasions on his face and hands. His jacket was missing, shirt hanging off him in tatters, russet hair covered in soot, eyebrows burned off. Either he didn't notice, or he'd blanked out the pain and cold. People swarmed around him, asking questions. He edged past the throng, shoes squelching as the burnt rubber soles stuck to hot tarmac.

Hugh caught up. 'How'd it happen, Ferdia? Are you—?'

'Move on everyone.' Mulryan said through the bullhorn. 'Show's over.'

Ferdia climbed into Hugh's car and looked out at his smouldering home. Perspiration and caked blood mingled and streaked his face. 'Can I stay in your place for a few days?'

Hugh watched thick grey smoke roll around the car. 'Of course. I'm with Mum, so it's yours as long as you want. Eilish's keys are… there's a spare set of keys in the house. And you can have this car. I'll use Mum's. It's not like she'll want it.'

'Thanks. Let's get outta here. I need a phone charger.'

'There's one in the house.'

'Grand. An' what we talked about earlier, Hugh? Dessie Dolan? Forget it. I'll take it from here.'

Hugh drove away and opened his window to let fresh air circulate. He still had trouble breathing. 'Don't jump to conclusions, Ferdia. Could've been an accident.'

'No accident,' Ferdia said. 'Definite arson. The floor burned first. It's usually electric sockets or roofs where house fires start. But they know for sure, not this time.'

'Jesus, Ferdia.'

'Gimme your phone,' Ferdia said.

Hugh passed over his mobile and Ferdia weighed it in his big hand. 'How the feck am I gonna tell Niamh's mother that her daughter's dead, huh?'

'The Gardaí will do it. They've specially trained staff that deal with—'

'It's my responsibility.'

'Leave it to the cops, Ferdia. They'll—'

They're only interested in the *how* and the *what*. I know *who* and *why*.'

'That's rubbish, Ferdia. Arson is a major crime. They'll… listen, don't do anything stupid. You're gonna start a—'

'Circumstances just changed, Hugh. I'm moving from a defensive to an offensive position. Action, not reaction.'

'That's... listen to yourself, Ferdia? You're no better than...'

Ferdia's hand cut through the air. 'Even the bible says "an eye for an eye." Anyway, this isn't your battle anymore. I'll take it from here.'

4

TUESDAY 22 JANUARY. MORNING.

A NOISE WOKE Rebecca Greenfield.

She tried to move, but it felt like she was swimming through sludge. Every bone and muscle cried out in agony. What had she drunk? This never happened before. She struggled to remember and gave up. She rolled over and banged her head on something that shouldn't be there.

It seemed to take forever to reach up her hand and feel whatever she'd hit. She groped something unfamiliar. It felt like a bedpost. But she didn't have a bedpost. She opened her eyes, blinked. There was something gluey in her eye, and she tried to force her brain to take in the blurry image she was seeing. She must be still in her nightmare. It wasn't a bedpost. It looked like the back of a shaved head. It *was* a shaved head. Attached to a body. And it snored.

She closed her eyes. Opened them again. The snorer was still there.

Rebecca shook her head to clear her vision. *'Help.'* Her voice sounded croaky, unnatural. She cleared her throat. Her eyes moved around the bright room. 'Where am I?'

That snore again. It sounded like the low growl an angry bull makes, and the mountainous body beside her shifted.

Rebecca froze.

His neck was pockmarked with blackheads, and his back, covered with black hair, was slathered in glistening sweat.

The image of the two men in her apartment flooded back.

The man-mountain turned towards her, slow, like a fat slug; a sweaty, gelatinous, bloated whale of a man, with fat rippling under his skin. Unsightly as a bullfrog, he grunted in his sleep and threw a massive arm across her body. His breath reeked of cigarettes and alcohol. The man was a monster.

'What? Who…?' Rebecca clamped her mouth shut.

She rolled from the bed, tripped over a sheet, and fell. Then she realised she was naked, and tried to pull the sheet around her, frantically looking for her clothes. She rummaged around the side of the bed, keeping one eye on the snoring figure. Nothing. She crouched in a corner, stared at the bed, too scared to check the other side for her clothes. But she had to. She *had* to get dressed and get out of here. How did she even get here? Where was here? Heart hammering, she strained to patch events together. Her mind was blank, but blurred bits and pieces jig-sawed in her brain. Someone whimpered. It took her a moment to realise the cry was coming from her. Rebecca bit down on her knuckles to stop herself screaming. She shivered, noticed the scratch marks on her arms, legs and body.

What have I done? What. Have. I. Done? Fuck clothes. Get out of here. No, I need clothes.

Heart slamming against her ribs, she low-crawled around the bottom of the bed, peeping around the other side. Everything was in slow motion. What had she done with her clothes? Her hand encountered something hard; an empty vodka bottle. The man's other hairy arm dangled inches over it, fingers brown with nicotine stains.

No clothes.

Forget the clothes. Escape. Get out, her brain screamed.

Door, where's the door?

There has to be an exit. Rebecca turned on her hands and knees, still half-thinking this was a nightmare and she'd wake up.

But she couldn't stop the flashbacks. She remembered two men in her apartment. What did they want? She tried to recall the rest. How did she end up here? What happened? What day was it? Is it day or night? And where was she?

Rebecca looked around, desperate now, trying to orient herself. The room was bathed bright in fluorescent lighting. There was no furniture, apart from the bed. Her eyes travelled across the bloodied, yellow-stained sheets. She panted, short, harsh gasps, and crept to a corner, and sat on her haunches, shivering.

Whose blood is that?

Then the pain came. In waves. Every move was agony. It felt like her insides had been ripped apart. She looked again at the bed, at the grotesque person lying on it, his whole body a hedge of glistening black hair.

Rebecca gagged, placed a hand across her mouth, swallowed the bile, and breathed hard through her nose. This wasn't a bad dream.

Break out. Somehow.

Bathroom. There *must* be a window or an exit door, she thought. Anything. I'm in here, so there has to be a way out.

Have to get out.

Rebecca looked around again. Slower this time. Her gaze avoided the bed. Four bare walls. No window. Okay, there has to be a door. She twisted her head, eyes travelled the three walls she could see.

Nothing. Panic and anxiety made her weak.

Where's the fucking door? It must be behind me. Has to be. There's no place else. Just find it, Rebecca.

She spun around, searched for a doorknob, a door handle. *Something.*

There. A gap between...

'Here, puss-puss.' The bed creaked.

Rebecca lunged for the door. Then she felt her head being jerked back as the man bunched her hair, spun her around and yanked her face towards his groin. The smell of body sweat, stale garlic and rancid butter washed over her and made her retch. She jerked away. The man threw back his head and brayed like a donkey. His fat, sumo wrestler belly moved and jiggled in waves as he rammed it closer to her face. Rebecca tore at his flesh, scratching and ripping.

'Good,' the man said. 'Fight me.' He gripped her hair tighter and slapped her face with his other hand. 'Fight harder. From now on, I call you baby bear. Later, I share you with my friends. You like that? I think you like that verrie much.' He stooped, lifted Rebecca like a small parcel, and flung her onto the bed, snorting and grunting like a wild animal. 'Fight me harder.'

Helpless, vulnerable, struggling uselessly, Rebecca felt the tearing pain start again.

I'm going to die.

She thought of her parents and sister. She would never see them again. How would they ever find her? You're alive, she thought. Stay that way. Do whatever it takes to stay alive. In the corner, she saw a fly entangled in a spider's web. She focused on that.

You're still alive. You're still alive. You're still...

The pain made her scream and Rebecca felt an arm press across on her throat. Her body was on fire. She couldn't breathe. Couldn't hear. There was no air. Her screams faded to a gurgle.

MID-MORNING

HUGH PHONED RUTH, Sharona and Charlie and told them about Ferdia.

He spent a few hours on the shop floor and observed McGuire's staff at work. At lunchtime, he bought a kettle, dropped it off at his mother's house, cancelled his dole allowance at the Post Office, and swung by the Demesne on his way back to work.

An unmarked Garda car, lights flashing, blocked the entrance.

Hugh wandered around the corner and looked at the still smouldering, charred main walls which were all that remained of Ferdia's home, and thought of the times he'd been inside. Wisps of white, gassy smoke wafted in a vaporous heat shimmer that surrounded the site. Black, wet sludge and mud covered the front garden and roadway. Even in the freezing temperature, the housing estate road was still warm.

A knot of men stood around the remains of the blackened structure. One used a shovel to sift through rubble. Hugh wondered if he'd find evidence buried in the wreckage.

'Is Ferdia with you?'

Hugh turned. Detective Mulryan came from a house across the road.

'He stayed at my place last night. He was gone when I called around earlier. I've rung him a few times, but no answer.'

'Huh. He's not answering me either.'

They stood in silence, staring at the ruins. A wind whipped up and embers glowed amid the black and white ash.

'Fire's nasty,' the detective said. 'I've seen cases where people poured petrol in houses, hoping to claim insurance money, and the flame goes out because the windows are shut, or something. Other times, a tossed cigarette butt can bring down a building.' He shrugged. 'Fire does whatever it wants.'

'Ferdia said the firemen suspect arson,' Hugh said. 'Any clue how or who started it?'

'Early days. That guy,' detective Mulryan pointed to the man with the shovel, 'is looking for pour patterns.'

'Pour patterns?'

'Yeah. Not many fires start at floor level, so pour patterns show if an accelerant was used. Wherever it burns longest and hardest, that's where the diesel or petrol was poured.'

'Oh. How do you find—?'

The detective tapped his nose. 'Trade secrets.'

'So, are you definitely saying—?'

'All I'm saying is that patterns show the evidence of the crime. You don't get certain burn patterns or pour patterns on accidental fires.' Mulryan jerked his thumb towards the smouldering site. 'These guys will gather as much evidence and information as possible. But,' he shrugged, 'there'll always be loose ends. I've never worked a case yet that was absolutely tied up with a bow and string, complete with everything explained and accounted for. Anyway, you should go. There's nothing here for—'

'How long will it take for them to—?'

'Not long. Every contact leaves a trace. Somebody will have left evidence. Or one of the neighbours will have spotted something... If it's arson, we'll get the culprits. People with that particular skill always leave a signature. When you see Ferdia, tell him to phone me.'

'Sure. Is this your area now?' Hugh asked.

The detective looked at him.

'What I mean is,' Hugh hurried to explain. 'The first time I met you, was near Birr. Now you're in Ganestown. Two crime scenes, so far apart...'

Mulryan shrugged. 'Cutbacks.' Then he stepped closer and smiled. 'We've specialised units that cover three or four counties. We can pop up anywhere. Depends how busy we are. Now, don't go telling the bad guys we're shorthanded.'

'What's the latest on Adam Styne?' Hugh asked.

'He's in a secure unit, being assessed—'

'I hope he's kept there, freaking psychopath,' Hugh said. 'Do you know yet how many he's killed or how many families he's ruined?'

'We're still gathering evidence,' Mulryan said. 'It'll take a while to pull it all together.' He slapped Hugh's shoulder. 'Get outta here. And tell Ferdia to ring me...'

HUGH SAT IN his car, thinking. Even now, fifteen hours later, the air was filled with noxious smoky menace. Each breath he took burned his lungs like a knife slash. He'd never been in a smoke-filled building but tried to imagine Niamh's last moments. The panic. Perhaps she'd tried to get downstairs, and the flames drove her back. Or maybe the smoke disorientated her. It would've been impossible to see anything through the fumes.

He said a prayer and hoped she'd died peacefully, losing consciousness through lack of oxygen, before the flames got to her.

'ANY IDEA WHAT "Hungry like the Wolf" means, Adam?'

Adam Styne glared at his barrister. 'I'm sure you don't mean some silly song by a stupid pop band.'

'Oh, come, come,' O'Brien said. 'It wasn't that bad. Duran Duran. '82, or thereabouts, if memory serves. No, I'm thinking more within the realm of a legal and criminological stroke psychological area. Briefly, 'hungry like the wolf' is a computerised text analysis that studies the language and speech patterns of psychopaths and homicide offenders. Experts believe various words or expressions match psychopathic personalities.'

Styne stared at O'Brien. 'And your point is?'

'My point, Adam,' O'Brien re-crossed his legs, 'is this. In fact...' O'Brien tapped on his mobile phone, 'let me quote directly from a learned colleague's research paper: "Results show that psychopaths' speech contained a higher frequency of disfluencies, 'err', 'uh', 'um', which indicates that describing powerful, emotional events to another person is difficult for them. They also tend to use past instead of present tense verbs, which specifies a greater psychological detachment from said emotional incident.".'

'So?' Styne said.

'Past tense, Adam, is less emotionally intense, which has the effect of disassociating the narrator from—'

'You're talking in riddles.'

O'Brien smiled. 'But I know from your expression you're with me, Adam. These identifiable language differences which are presumably beyond conscious control, support the notion that psychopaths operate on a primitive, yet rational level. A point of distinction between them and the rest of us.'

'Will this be used at my interview?'

'Your use of language? Yes. But the use of automated tools to detect distinct speech patterns? No. Not applicable in court.'

'When is the interview?'

'Tomorrow afternoon. I'll call in the morning to prep you.'

'Have you found out anything about Hattinger's?' Styne asked. 'What's happening to the business?'

'Adam,' O'Brien shook his head as if he were reproaching a young child, 'I told you. Concentrate on the job in hand, not on issues beyond your control. I made a few calls on your behalf. Nothing has happened… yet. Madeline, Ambrose and the rest of the family are meeting later this week to decide what to do.' He held up his hand. 'No, I don't know when this conclave is, and furthermore—'

'It's my business,' Styne cut in. 'I need to know—'

'I've said it before, Adam: Let's discuss ways to get you out of here. I'd suggest avoiding any talk of business.'

'I'm innocent. I'll prove it. And I want my business back.'

'Forget this innocent until proven guilty lark, Adam. In the eyes of tax inspectors and Gardaí, you're guilty until you can prove innocence. Now, let's discuss your upcoming meeting with the board.'

'What is the difference between orange and blue tracksuits?' Styne asked.

'What?'

'What's the difference between—?'

'I heard you, Adam. I can't believe you're asking such a nonsensical question that has no relevance…' O'Brien sighed. 'Mentally insane wear blue. Criminally insane wear orange.'

'Do you know anything about George and Ronnie?' Styne asked. 'They're clients.'

'Clients? Who have you been talking to, Adam? There are no clients here, only staff and patients. Yes, I know them both. They were patients back when I worked here. Ronnie Carr is… was a plumber by trade, and a musician by night. A drummer. If a good session musician was ever needed, Ronnie was called on. He was working on a gas installation in his home and didn't close off some pipes properly. Left to play at some gig. When he got back in the early hours, his wife and child had died from carbon monoxide poisoning. Total accident, but Ronnie went off the rails. He's completely harmless, but mentally insane. George Higgins, on the other hand, is a pure psychopath. He was and still remains totally unmoved by the plight he's caused. George was a teacher. London born, but moved to Ireland when he was young. Very bright. Worked his way up to Vice Principle, and used his position to molest teenage girls. Told them he'd ensure they'd get higher grades if… Anyway, one girl told her parents and George got a phone call from the father saying he was going to the Gardaí. George asked him to hear his side of the story. The man agreed, and night before the meeting, George went to the house, calm as you please, and knifed the father to death. Then he went upstairs and butchered the wife and daughter. That was back in '91, '92, I think. After that he picked another family; a random elderly man and wife. They lived on the outskirts of Palmerstown. He broke into the house Sunday morning while they were at Mass and set the stage to kill them when they returned. His motivation? Pure blood lust. But what he didn't know was that the couple's children, two cops, would be visiting. The old folk arrived home. George was in the middle of slashing the woman's throat when the sons walked in. He was caught, as they say, red-handed. In custody, he also admitted killing a Polish grocer and his wife, in Fairview,' O'Brien clicked his fingers. 'Just like that.'

'Why's he walking around without a care in the world?' Styne asked. 'Mixing with… why isn't he separated?'

'No staff. No resources. No other facility to put him into. This place isn't big enough. It looks big from the outside, but only two stories are used. There's a basement that used to be the living quarters for… anyway, George is being drenched with drugs to keep him docile. My advice is, keep away from him.'

'He doesn't look like a psychopath.'

O'Brien snorted. 'Do *you* know what a psychopath looks like? I don't. I can be ruthless, charming, manipulative, and dominant. It goes with the territory. I've excelled academically and professionally. I think at times, my heart is colder than most people because of the nature of my business. Does that make me a psychopath? Or the businessperson who fires staff without a thought for their families? Is he or she a psychopath? As a successful businessman, I'm sure you've made hard choices; tough, cold decisions. Does that make you a psychopath? Hmm? The hungry-like-a-wolf test fits George perfectly. He never admits being wrong, doing wrong, or having wronged anyone. When it suits him, he says "voices" told him to do it. Other times he blamed the stress of his job, drinking too much, the weather, the season… Whatever he cheats, lies, manipulates, hurts people emotionally and physically, he manages to blame those around them. He always looks for an angle and continually reframes reality to fit his own narcissistic delusions. The only time George will be released is in a box.

'I shouldn't be in here, mixing with the likes of him.'

'We have to work within the rules, Adam. George isn't a threat, but be careful. Keep him at a distance. Now, can we discuss the assessments, please? We need to tease out some facts and get them clear in your head.'

'Fine.'

'Good. Perhaps we can start with your whereabouts in the days leading up to Roberta Lord's disappearance.'

AFTERNOON

'HELLO? HELLO?'

'Huh. That's odd.' Sharona Waters looked at her phone.

Ronan Lambe stopped scrolling his own phone screen. 'What's odd?'

'That's the third hang-up today. Caller unknown. I think Rebecca Greenfield's trying to get through.'

'Why would she turn off caller ID?' Ronan Lambe yawned and stretched out on Sharona's couch.

'Don't know. When I ring her number back, the phone's switched off.'

'Then it's probably someone else. Text me her number. I'll see if I can trace her.'

'Ta. It's great having a techie boyfriend.'

'No probs.'

Sharona watched while Ronan scrolled, swiped, and checked settings. 'So?' she asked.

'The number belongs to a smartphone,' Ronan said.

'That's it? I thought you were a computer genius. No brownie points for that bit of useless information.'

'Greenfield. Any idea where she's from?'

'I'm guessing Dublin.'

Ronan scrolled through Facebook images. 'Recognise anyone?'

Sharona leaned closer. 'Nope. No, no, no… there.' She stabbed her finger at the screen.

'Cool. Let's see. Hmm.' Ronan sounded dubious.

'Hmm what?'

'Hmm. That's odd.'

'Is there an echo in here?'

'Huh? What? No. It's just…'

'Odd?'

'Yeah. Here's the thing,' Ronan said. 'She's active on Facebook, several posts a day, but nothing since Sunday. See her last message? Big news coming later. Three exclamation marks. And then… zilch.'

'I'm not big into social media,' Sharona said. 'Anything else?'

'Yeah. She posted pictures from Whispers on Instagram. She took a selfie getting into a taxi. And… more photos of… where's that?' Ronan enlarged the image. 'A pub. Greenfield's. Now we're getting somewhere. If I copy that and paste into Google Images… Voilà. Greenfield's pub. Westport, Co. Mayo. That's where she's from.' Ronan clicked back to social media, scrolled and pointed. 'That's UCD. Must be a student.'

'Dear God. How did you—?'

'Geotags.'

'What?'

'Geotags. They're like… Hansel and Gretel's breadcrumbs. Digital tracks that you leave every time you click or post stuff on social media—'

'Forget this new phone,' Sharona said. 'Bad enough having Milo Barnes stalk me. Last thing I want is to have him—'

'No, no, it's good. Seriously. Well, it *can* be good. Say you got lost or went missing? If your history location is on, the GPS coordinates can be tracked and—'

'Okay, I get it. Wait, you said *can* be good?'

'Yeah, I always turn off location services on sharing apps. See what that sixty-second scroll showed us about Rebecca Greenfield? Bet you in another two minutes I could find out about her family, favourite food, where she drinks, friends, holidays, concerts she's been to.'

Sharona shivered. 'Kinda feels like an invasion of privacy.'

'Yeah,' Ronan said. 'Social media companies have several hundred pieces of information on all of us, and they use them for marketing specific products they think we want or need or have searched for. But all this stuff I picked up from her own posts, the photos, they're there for anyone to see. But, if we were… um, stalkers or private investigators or thieves, geotagging reveals a lot of information about you, which could be used negatively. And the more you use them… like, where you go, daily routine, what you buy, all that information builds up.'

'Jesus. That's it. I definitely don't want a smartphone.'

'You gotta get with the times, Sharona. Use the technology to your advantage. Learn the pitfalls. If you don't want to be located, turn off the location features. End of story.'

'I sort of get the geotag thingy,' Sharona said, 'but I don't get the photo. How did that work? Google Images? Is it new?'

'It's ancient. Must be twenty years old. See, the way it works is, when you take a photo, its metadata—'

'You lost me at metadata—'

'—EXIF format.'

'What?'

'Exchangeable Image File Format… okay.' Ronan held up his hand in apology. 'I'll step off my soapbox now.'

'I accept apologies in the form of kisses,' Sharona said. 'Shhh. Stop talking and come here. We're still no closer to locating Rebecca.'

'Technology only works when it's switched on. If the battery dies or the phone's turned off…' Ronan shrugged.

'Thanks for trying. You've earned a tonne of brownie points.'

'Yes! Ronan rocks. I'm the greatest ever.'

'That's a bit strong. Maybe the greatest so far today.' Sharona cuddled closer. 'I might give Greenfield's a ring in a bit. See if Rebecca's been in touch.'

'I doubt if your old Nokia could even bounce a signal that far.' Ronan ducked the cushion thrown at him. 'Careful, you need me to get you connected with your new phone. It'll change your outlook. Make you—'

'What are you implying? That I need to change?'

'No. God, no. It'll… all I'm saying is—'

'Am I not perfect the way I am?'

'Yeah, you are. But—'

Sharona pinched Ronan's cheek and kissed his ear. 'I'm teasing. Now, where were we?'

EVENING

'WHAT'S THAT?' Kathleen peered out the kitchen window.

'The moon, Mum.'

'Never saw it before. What does it do?'

'It gives light and has something to do with sea tides,' Hugh said. Ten minutes in from work, and already he could feel tension tighten the back of his neck. Once the consultant said "Alzheimer's," the word had the concussive force of a bomb. Everything changed in a heartbeat. It was impossible to predict anything. It could be hours of silence, where his mother swam in memories. Other times, the same question over and over, sprinkled with episodes of sustained rage that tested his patience, love and endurance. He didn't know which is worse; being inundated with the same query over and over, or silence. It was difficult to hide his grief at the loss of a person he loved but who was still alive.

Kathleen started a conversation with the weatherman on television. Hugh prepared dinner.

'That was very rude,' Kathleen said.

'What was, Mum?'

'That man I was talking to. He just… left.'

'He'll be back later.'

'Where does this go?'

'Hmm?' Hugh's thoughts were on McGuire's. And Ferdia hadn't answered his phone all day.

'This. Where does it go?'

Hugh glanced across at Kathleen. She was holding a piece of paper. 'In the bin, Mum.'

'What bin?'

'The rubbish bin. Under the sink.'

'What sink?'

'The sink here.' Hugh pointed.

'We don't have a sink.'

'It's okay. Give it to me.'

'No. I want to help. I don't want to be a burden.'

'You're not a burden, Mum. I'll take it.'

'What's this?' Kathleen held up an elastic band.

'What do you think it is, Mum?'

'I've no idea. Never saw one before.'

'Really?'

'Never. What's it for?'

'It holds things together.'

'Where does it go?'

'In the drawer. It must have fallen out. I'll take it.'

'Okay. What's for dinner? I'd like fish.'

'It is fish, Mum.' Hugh stopped preparing the chicken casserole and hunted in the freezer.

'How long will it be?'

'Not long, Mum.' Hugh's phone rang. Ruth, looking for an update.

'What time are you coming over?' Hugh asked. 'I've enough food cooked—'

'I can't, Hugh. We're short-staffed, and I know I'm being watched like a hawk. A few journalists turned up again today at reception, asking questions and looking for background information on me. This hasn't gone away and I don't want to give any excuse—'

'Aww, damn. I don't like it, but I understand the position you're in, Ruth.'

'Any word on Ferdia?' Ruth asked.

'Hasn't answered his phone today,' Hugh said. 'And he wasn't in my house half-an-hour ago. He's up to something. I know he is.'

'Hugh? Whatever it is, don't get involved. Please? Seriously, I can't afford any—'

'I hear you. Don't worry, I've enough on my plate. And I've a group meeting with McGuire's staff in the morning to try and convince them to change their work patterns. Last week's episode with Styne was a once in a lifetime deal. Trust me.'

'I do, Hugh. I just don't want any grief, and I know how close you and Ferdia—'

'We are, but I'm not getting involved in his fights.'

'MALCOLM? WHERE ARE you? Are you alright?'

'I'm fine, Dad. It's, you know…'

'I haven't heard from you since the funeral.'

Malcolm coughed. 'Yeah. I'm in the apartment. Can't sleep.'

'You can't stay cooped up forever, Mal. You should've been in the office today. The business… Philip's ready to take you to meet some clients. It's time you—'

'I need a day or two,' Malcolm fingered the scratches on his forehead, 'you know, to process—'

'It's not healthy to be alone all the time, Mal. Too much time to think. I know it's difficult, but you'd be better off concentrating on… other things.'

'I… I keep thinking about Ciara,' Malcolm said. 'How maybe I could've done something to—'

'Me too,' Charlie said. 'Have you seen the news reports about Ferdia?'

'Ferdia? No. Why?'

'His house was burned down last night. An arson attack.'

'What?' Malcolm's legs buckled.

'Yes. Ferdia had a hospital appointment yesterday, so he wasn't there. But a friend of his, a lady he met recently, was in the house, and she didn't survive. Apart from investigating arson, Gardaí have started a murder inquiry.'

'Jesus.' Malcolm gnawed a fingernail, struggling to make sense of what his father was saying. He needed to get off the phone. 'Dad, I'll phone Ferdia—'

'He's not answering his mobile, Mal. Also—'

'I'll go search for him. He must be—'

'The police are dealing with it. Also, the manager in Ganestown handed in his resignation, and I've offered Hugh Fallon that position. Thankfully, he accepted. Cousin Milo also resigned yesterday. Funny, he didn't seem to remember that you and he had a conversation about—'

'What? Really?' Malcolm's head reeled with this onslaught of information. He wondered if Milo had dropped him in the shit. He mustn't have, or he and Charlie would be having a different conversation now.'

'Did you know about him stalking Sharona?' Charlie asked.

'Milo? No. Why?' Malcolm needed to phone Milo and find out what the hell was happening.

'Hmm. Cops are involved in that as well.'

'Look, I'll be in the office tomorrow, Dad. I've… I'll see you then.' Malcolm pressed the disconnect button and stared at the phone. 'Dessie,' he whispered. 'What'd you do? What the hell did you do?'

FERDIA KNOCKED ON the open church door.

He walked inside to the first pew. The body of the church was dark, but the altar was bathed in bright lights. 'Father?' His voice echoed in the emptiness. 'Are you here? Your housekeeper told me to shout.'

'Who's that?' A voice called from behind the altar.

'Ferdia Hardiman,' Ferdia said.

'Ah, Ferdia, come on up. You can give me a hand.'

Ferdia walked up the aisle and around the back of the altar. 'God bless the work, Father,' he said. 'Still spreading love the Ganestown way?'

'Still trying.' Father Kelly was perched on the top rung of an aluminium double extension ladder, attempting to seal a leaking roof. He looked down. 'I didn't get a chance to say hello at Ciara's funeral Mass last Saturday. Hold the ladder, like a good man.'

'You shouldn't be doing that, Father,' Ferdia said. 'Surely there's a local handyman that can do a repair job?' He watched the priest descend.

'Handymen cost money, Ferdia. Cheapest quote I've got almost gave me heart failure.'

'Then, why don't you get Our Lady to appear in Ganestown?' Ferdia said. 'She always seems to surface in remote areas that need a tourist boost. Surely the Irish Midlands qualifies for some sort of vision, or a moving statue at the very least.'

The priest laughed. 'Doesn't work like that. Whole roof has to be stripped and retiled. Then there's paint and wooden floor damage.' He appraised Ferdia and shook his hand. 'Money's tight. Church attendance is worrying. Next generation will probably turn this place into a pub or a nightclub. Apart from funerals and the odd wedding, I haven't seen you at here lately, have I?'

'No, Father.'

'Why?'

'Argh, you know yourself, between one thing and another...'

'People tell me there's an App you can download to watch Mass on your phone, Ferdia. Is that what you do?'

'Nah, Father.'

'So what stopped you going?'

'Huh. Maybe my sins keep me away.'

'Remember the third commandment?' the priest said.

Ferdia shuffled his feet. 'What was that one again?'

'Keep holy the Sabbath Day.'

'Oh, yeah. See, last time I was at Sunday Mass I came away...' Ferdia scratched his head.

'Encouraged?'

'Nah.'

'Engaged?'

'Yeah, maybe, but—'

'Enthused?'

'Not really.'

'Enriched?'

'Hmm, a bit, I suppose.'

'So, what changed?'

'I get kinda itchy in church.'

'And yet, here you are.'

'This is different. More a personal thing.'

'Okay.'

Ferdia tried again. 'Maybe my absence is a... I don't know, a form of protest against the lukewarm response the church hierarchy had to all the abuse that went on. The lack of closure, or something concrete for the victims, kinda gets on my wick.'

'Placing blame is easy,' the priest said. 'Finding a solution is hard.'

'You need a war, Father. Nothing like a world war to get people back into the church.'

'God forbid,' Father Kelly said. 'But, we're going through strange times. The quantity of communication increases daily, yet the quality decreases. We live in social media bubbles, where we only interact with people who like, follow or share our content. With the press of a button, we can block, unfollow or unfriend those who disagree with us. We've become resistant to change, and that resistance is closing in on us. Easier that way, than accept another person's point of view.' Father Kelly sighed. 'Maybe we feel we don't *need* to hear other points of view. That's easier than being open to new ideas. A new world. A new change.'

'Maybe we've changed enough already, Father.'

'Hmm. Maybe. But sometimes we need to shift, even if we don't want to. We've evolved from steam engines to search engines, yet in other ways, we've regressed. Anyway, you didn't come here for a sermon. I heard your tragic news. Shocking. If I had your number, I'd have phoned you.' The priest glanced at Ferdia. 'Looks like you slept under a bridge last night and had a bottle of whiskey for lunch.'

'Just a wobble, Father.'

'I'm sorry this came to your door, Ferdia. One death a week is enough in anyone's family.'

'Thanks, Father.' Ferdia pulled money from a pocket and handed it to the priest. 'Can you remember Niamh in your masses? Thanks.

Oh, and lovely sermon for Ciara last Friday, by the way.' Ferdia watched a steady drip form a puddle next to the ladder.

The priest moved a plastic bucket to capture the water. 'You didn't come here at this hour to give money for masses, Ferdia. What's bothering you?'

'I know who's responsible for her death, Father, and I'd like—'

'You want me to hear your confession, Ferdia?'

'Ah, no, Father. You're grand. It's been a while since I was in confession, but I've no sins.'

'So…?'

'I'm gonna bring those responsible to justice, Father.'

The priest stared. 'Come again? You're going to do what?'

'It's a guy from Dublin. Name's Dessie Dolan. He's a loan shark. Himself and Malcolm… well, I sorted a gambling debt out, but now there are repercussions.'

Father Kelly held up a palm. 'Whoa, why are you telling me this? And where's your proof? Perhaps the fire started accidentally.'

'No accident, Father. I spoke to one of the arson specialists earlier. It started in two places. Someone filled a bottle with petrol, added a wick and flung it through the kitchen window. Then they sprayed a mixture of petrol and oil through the letterbox and set the hall on fire. Meant anyone inside had no way out. Basically, the specialist told me, the fire had two beating hearts, and they couldn't put out both. Niamh was upstairs. They think she was in the shower. Hadn't a chance. The fumes…' Ferdia looked at the water drip.

'Leave it to the experts,' the priest said. 'You getting involved won't achieve anything. You'll exchange one set of problems for another.'

'I can take care of myself, Father.'

'I know *you* can.' The priest placed his hand on Ferdia's arm. 'Listen to me. What happens if it's not *you* they go after? It could be your parents. Or Charlie and Malcolm. Or David. Look what happened in Limerick and several other towns over the years. The simplest of slights can start carnage.'

'I'll make sure that doesn't happen, Father.'

'Then you're no better than a fanatic, a terrorist, Ferdia.'

'Me? Nah. More a rebel. A freedom fighter.'

The priest shook his head. 'Go home to your family, Ferdia. Rest. You'll have a different outlook tomorrow.'

'You're right. A man needs rest before a fight.'

'For God's sake, Ferdia. Stop acting like a petulant child. 'Come,' the priest gestured towards a pew. 'Kneel. I'll pray to God with you.'

'Why would I want to pray to a God I don't believe in and ask for something I don't want? Huh?'

'Ferdia. I know you're hurting. But Ciara and Niamh are gone— '

'Niamh died because of me, Father.'

'No, she didn't. She was in the wrong place at the wrong time. Let the Gardaí do their job. The McGuire and Hardiman clans need your help now.'

'They'll manage.'

'Then have you stopped to think the life you could save is your own? A feud with this guy Dolan will make a monster out of you, because to defeat him, you must become him. Is that what you want, Ferdia?'

'If that's what it takes, Father.'

'You'll lose.'

'You can't lose 'til you quit, Father. And I've no intention of quitting.'

'Now you're ridiculous, Ferdia.'

'You need to see the world as it really is, Father, not how you'd like it to be. I admire your loyalty, but sympathise with your naivety. Everyone isn't holier than thou and sometimes life turns into a boxing match. You either inflict damage or get hurt. Can you say a prayer for me? Or something?'

'What? You want absolution? In advance? Trying to balance how much you can get away with and still get to Heaven?' The priest's shoulders shook with laughter. 'Doesn't work like that, Ferdia, and you're smart enough to know it. Tell me, where's God in your life? What part does He play in your world?'

'Same part as I play in his, Father.'

'And yet, Ferdia, here you are,' the priest spread his arms wide, 'inside a church—'

'Yeah. The irony isn't lost on me, Father. But this isn't a catholic visit. As I said, it's more a personal thing.'

Father Kelly puffed out his cheeks in exasperation. 'Only the weak believe in revenge, Ferdia. The strong have belief in forgiveness. Intelligent people ignore—'

'Sometimes, smart people do stupid things, Father.'

The priest shook his head, at a loss. 'You don't know who you're playing with, Ferdia. Why would you even *consider*...? These people... violence is meaningless to them because human life has lost all value.'

'I'm not playing, Father. If I don't do something, the change you spoke about won't happen. We all have different ways of travelling to where we want to go.' Ferdia looked around the church. 'You take your path. I'll take mine. Maybe we'll meet up at the same destination. Anyway, if something happens to me, I'd like you to break the news to my parents. I want you to be the one to tell them.'

'Tell them what, exactly?'

'That I had to do it. That I... argh, you're good at soft language, Father, you'll come up with the right words. Put whatever spin you like on it. Think of something that'll give them... acceptance.'

'Acceptance, Ferdia? For the last time. This is a big mistake.'

'Sometimes you gotta get into the sewer if you want to kill some rats, Father.'

Father Kelly's shoulders slumped. 'I can't do any more to talk you out of this madness, Ferdia. Do you believe in God?'

'I believe Gods and demons are of our own making. No certainty. Just possibilities of something. At times I believe in a greater presence, Father. I don't always trust it.'

'Do you trust enough to turn this problem over to it?'

'No. Manmade problems can only be sorted by man. Cancer spreads until it's cut out, Father.'

The priest nodded. 'Yes. And it spreads faster when you cut into it.' He made a sign of the cross in the air in front of Ferdia's face, put an arm on his shoulder, bowed his head and murmured a Latin prayer. 'I'll pray for Divine intervention and intercession on your behalf, Ferdia. And of course, I'll honour your request... if needs be.'

'Thanks, Father.' Ferdia turned to go. 'Appreciate that.'

'Let's swap mobile numbers, Ferdia.'

When they'd done that, Father Kelly said: 'Promise you'll ring me every night and let me know—'

'Sure, Father.'

'Ferdia? Do you promise?'

'It's a sin to tell a lie, Father.'

7 P.M.

WHEN REBECCA WOKE again, two men were staring down at her.

The pain was a serrated, relentless agony that invaded every part of her body. Her rapist drank from a fresh bottle of Vodka. 'Stolichnaya is the best vodka,' he smacked his lips. She noticed he'd an Eastern European accent. He tipped some of the liquid onto Rebecca's body, splashed her face then held the bottle up. 'At home, in Odessa, Ukraine,' he nudged the second man, 'we call this the wife beater.'

Both men laughed.

Rebecca pulled the flimsy sheet around her. 'Why'd you kidnap me? I don't have anything to give you. I'm a student. Why are you doing this? I didn't do—'

'It's not personal, baby bear. Jus' bizzness.'

'How can you do this to another human being? Why are you treating me like an animal?'

'Hush now.' He looked at his comrade. 'Fifteen thousand.'

The second man tapped an unfiltered cigarette against the back of his hand and lit it, never taking his eyes off Rebecca. 'Five.' He chewed gum in a lazy, indolent movement. His hair was cropped to the length of his stubble and he wore an emerald in his left ear.

The Ukrainian stooped and prodded Rebecca's stomach. 'Five? She's trained now. Fourteen thousand. You'll have no problem—'

The man exhaled a cloud of smoke and picked a flake of tobacco from the tip of his tongue. 'Seven. Final offer.'

'Isus Khrystos. You're breaking my heart, man. Look at her—'

Rebecca moved away. 'Why are you—?'

The Ukrainian whirled. 'Shut up. SHUT UP. One more word,' he gestured, slashing his throat with his thumb, 'and I'll turn this place into an abattoir.' He slugged vodka, pointed the bottle at Rebecca and spoke to the man. 'See? She has spirit, yes? No bolt-on, no tattoo, perfect teeth.' He nodded. 'By next week, the shyness will have worn off. You'll be paid back in two months. Twelve thousand.'

Rebecca shivered in disbelief that this was happening.

The second man took a small calculator from his pocket, prodded some buttons. Held it sideways, studied the numbers and shook his head.

The Ukrainian scratched his shaven head. 'You'd never be wife material, baby bear.' His eyes roved her body underneath the sheet. 'A nice distraction, maybe. Or perhaps clients will think you're too fat. If so, I'll sell your organs. A kidney, four thousand. Two kidneys? A bargain at six. An eye? Three thousand. Then,' he leaned over the bed and whispered, 'then I get your sister and do the same with her.'

Rebecca slapped the Ukrainian's face. 'Don't you *dare* mention my sister, you piece of filth.'

The Ukrainian straightened. 'I'll pay you back for that later, baby bear.'

The second man smiled. 'Eight.'

'Let me go, or I'll—'

'You'll what, baby bear. You'll do what?' The Ukrainian raised his arm. Rebecca cowered into a ball. The other man muttered, and the Ukrainian lowered his hand. 'Okay, baby bear. We'll talk about it later. Ten thousand,' he spoke over his shoulder to the second man, 'but we keep her until after Valentines night.'

The man ground the cigarette butt into the floor, shrugged and nodded. 'Deal.' The men shook hands.

'Nooo—'

The Ukrainian grabbed Rebecca, and his arm, stiff as a steel band, circled her neck choking off her air supply, and she slid into unconsciousness again.

8 P.M.

'DESSIE?'

'Yeah. S'up?'

'I've been trying to get you all day,' Malcolm said. 'What the hell did you give me?'

'Whatcha on 'bout?'

'Those tablets. You screwed my head up. What the—'

'Kid, you screwed yourself. No one *forced* you to take them. 'Twas left to me to clean you up, get your car sorted out an' shit, which you owe me for. One of our drivers brung you home, even brought you up to your bleedin' apartment and put you into bed. Then, outta pure consideration for you, I leave you alone, let you recover before looking for my money, an' now, two days later, you phone me an' act like it's all *my* fault. Know wha' I'm sayin'? Well, I've had it. Rusty'll be around tonight to collect my money, and then you can piss off, kid. Bye—'

'Dessie? Dessie, wait.'

Dolan waited.

'Listen, I don't know where… my wallet, my credit cards, chips I won—'

'What chips? You bet everything against four kings, ya dope. Who dafuk bets against four kings, wha? That's not a gamble. That's suicide.'

'I'll get it back. I swear. But I don't have any money now. You gotta give me a few days. Get me a stake into the tournament tomorrow at the Jurys Inn, and I'll pay you by the weekend.'

'You've some neck, kid,' Dolan said. 'Call me up an' accuse me of all kinda things, when I've always had the best of intentions for ya, and then, and *then* you ask me for money?'

'I swear, Dessie.'

Dolan let the silence build.

'Dessie?'

'Yeah, yeah. I hear ya. Not a chance, Mal. You owe me too much. I'd be a mug to give you—'

'I've got information for you.'

'What information?' Dolan's tone sharpened.

'Something important you need to know.' Malcolm let the silence build.

'Okay.' Dolan chuckled. 'I'm always on the lookout for dirt. Dish it up.'

'Promise you'll payroll me tomorrow.'

'Are you for real, kid?'

'You'll want to know this, Dessie. Life and death, I swear.'

'Mal, Mal, I admire your spunk, kid. Lemme think.' Dolan stared out the car window for a moment. Then, 'ya know the old sayin' never give up when you lose, or you stay a loser, wha? Nobody likes a quitter, eh?'

'I'm on a downswing, Dessie. I *know* it's gonna change. One more crack, and—'

'Okay, kid. I'll buy whatever you're sellin'. What's this life an' death thing I need to know 'bout?'

'Ganestown,' Malcolm said.

'What about Ganestown?'

'Ferdia's house. You burned it down, didn't you?'

Dolan sat back in the car. 'No idea what you're talkin' 'bout kid. Haven't been to Ganestown in—'

'There was a body in the house.'

'Wha?' Dolan smiled. 'Well, if a man died in a house fire, I'm sorry again for your troubles. Jeez, Mal, your family's havin' a rough week. Between your sister, an'—'

'Ferdia wasn't there,' Malcolm said. 'His girlfriend was. And now Ferdia will come after you. If he doesn't kill you, you're gonna be charged with murder.'

Dolan straightened and forced a laugh. 'Whoopie do. Nuthin' to do wit' me, kid. Shit happens. Man must've a tonne of enemies. Still, I 'preciate you lookin' out for me, so tell you what: I'll stake you for tomorrow's game. Collect the money at the walk-in on Thomas Street on your way over. An' Mal? You'd better not lose, ya hear?'

'Thanks, Dessie. You won't regret—'

'I regret it already, kid.' Dolan disconnected. 'Loser,' he muttered. He reached into the glove compartment for another mobile and punched in a number. 'What's clicking?' he asked, and listened to the reply before blasting the person on the other end. 'What dafuk? I hafta hear from Malcolm McGuire about Ganestown. Where've you been for the past twenty-four hours? Why weren't you in touch? Why wasn't I told? When were you gonna—?' He held his temper for thirty seconds. 'I don't give a flyin'—'

Dolan listened again as the voice on the other end explained. He slapped the steering wheel. 'Yeah, well, tryin' to tidy the loose ends up before lettin' me know, didn't work out too well, did it? An' whaddya mean, you can't find him? He's six foot bleedin' six, wit' red hair. He should stand out like a sore thumb. How many places can he hide?'

The voice continued to mollify, and Dolan calmed down as the broad outline of a battle plan took shape. 'Yeah. Sooner or later he's gonna show up at Whispers. Prob'ly sooner. And you're right, I should disappear for a few days, 'til the heat dies down. Geddit? Heat?' Dolan laughed at his pun. 'Wha? Mal? He's fine. Another day older an' deeper in debt. Still layin' golden eggs, though. Wha? This connection…'

The voice repeated a question.

'Yeah, all good at that end. The boys are back working. Bit sore, but… Yeah, the meat racks are being delivered tonight. Tomorrow, Cork, Limerick and Galway will have fresh supplies. Are you gonna float around for the next few days? That's good. How long should I stay away? Shipment still due on Saturday? Deadly. 'Bout bleedin' time 'n' all. I'll be home for that. And make sure the boys don't kill yer man 'til I get back. I want that pleasure myself. I'll phone ya in a couple days.'

Dolan disconnected and tapped the steering wheel, thinking. He prised the SIM card from the mobile, inserted a new one, and dialled a number from memory. When it answered, he said: 'I'll be there in fifteen minutes,' and eased into Dublin traffic. He swung by Christchurch, down Dame Street. Stopped at traffic lights he broke the old SIM card in two and flicked the pieces out the window. Then, he turned right onto Trinity Street and straight through to St. Stephen's Green car park. He grabbed a briefcase from the car boot, took the escalator to the ground floor and turned left onto King Street. A Gaiety Theatre assistant was removing The Snow Queen pantomime posters and replacing them with advertisements for a new show, The Cripple of Inishmaan. Dolan glanced behind him, suspicious, before turning right onto Clarendon Row and right again onto Chatham Street. Halfway down, he knocked on the window of a tiny shop. There was no sign over the door and the only window was covered with posters for a concert long past. He heard the shuffling footsteps before a light came on. The door opened. A small, fat, white-haired, man, with a full beard and glasses, bowed. 'Apologies for keeping you, sir.'

Dolan grunted.

He watched the man close and lock the door. 'It's a pleasure to see you again, sir.' The shop owner was the relic of a bygone era: old style deferential manners and charm. Dolan followed him to the back of the shop, while the man kept up a line of banter. 'I must say, I can't believe how quickly the month of January has flown, even with the terrible weather.'

'Huh. Whatcha got?'

The shop owner fiddled with the gold chain of a pocket watch. 'Something I think you'll...' he bent and disappeared under the counter, '...be interested in.' He appeared again, out of breath, and placed a folder on the countertop and tapped its cover. His jacket sleeves had ridden up his arms, exposing liver spots on both wrists. 'This came into my possession last weekend. An auction. It belonged to a retired army general who served overseas. He accumulated quite a collection over his lifetime, most pretty ordinary, but a few particularly fascinating items.' The old man opened the folder and took out a plastic cover. His fat, stumpy fingers shook with Parkinson's as he held the plastic surface delicately. The veins in his wrinkled wrists throbbed as he removed four stamps. He clasped a loupe to his right eye and studied them before pushing them across the counter. Then he looked at his customer, smiled and offered him the loupe. 'It takes diligence, patience and a keen eye, but the astute stamp collector can sometimes find hidden gems, sir. This,' he pointed, 'is a 1964 China Peonies Flowers Stamp. This one, a U.S. 30 Cent Postage Stamp, dated 1869. Quite valuable. Now, this 1841 1d Grey black Pl.11? Very fine. Used four margin—'

'Lovely,' Dolan said.

The philatelist clapped his hands. 'But wait, sir.' He placed the plastic cover on the counter and reverently pointed at the fourth stamp. 'This is an 1840 1d Black Pl.11. A superb unused o.g. four margin horizontal pair lettered CD-CE. A magnificent exhibition piece of the highest quality. A rare find.'

'How much?'

'The Chinese flower stamp? Three thousand. The 1869 United States stamp? Seven thousand. The 1d grey black P1.11 is currently eleven thousand. The 1840 1d Black, I value at eighty thousand.'

'Eighty grand? Huh.'

'Conservatively.'

'Them your prices or catalogue prices?'

'My prices.' The old man pointed at the 1d stamp again. 'Anyone with this stamp in their collection would have a baseline market value of ninety thousand on it.'

'How much for the four?'

'Let me see. Hmmm, eighty, plus seven, plus… one hundred and one… For you, a hundred thousand. Even.'

Dolan didn't haggle.

He unlocked the briefcase, removed stacks of fifty and hundred euro notes, and placed the piles on the counter. 'Anything else?' There were still four thick wads of currency in the briefcase.

'Not today. But I'm expecting a very big consignment on Friday or Saturday.'

'Me too,' Dolan said.

'Meantime, sir, I'll keep searching.'

'Search harder,' Dolan said. He pointed at the money in the briefcase. 'There's lots more where that came from.'

The old man handed over the plastic sheet. Dolan placed it in the briefcase, twisted the combination lock and turned away.

'Enjoy,' the old man called after him. 'If you hold them for eighteen months, you'll double your money. The Chinese market has opened up, lots of new buyers interested in European stamps—'

'Huh.'

Dolan heard the door click and lock behind him. He retraced his steps through Stephen's Green centre. He'd no interest in keeping stamps; had no emotional attachment to them. All he wanted was buy, sell and recoup what he paid for them. A washer would run the money through a legitimate business and charge thirty per cent. This was cleaner. Traceless. Easy to take through customs. Easier still to resell. None of this suitcases-full-of-cash-through-customs bullshit. Stamps worked a treat because they traded for the same price in Madrid, Milan or Moscow. On a few occasions, he'd turned a small profit on the resale—enough to pay for return flights and a few nights' fun.

Dolan exited the car park and followed signs for M50 north and the airport. I'll chill in Europe for a few days, he thought. Any European city will do.

MIDNIGHT

DESSIE DOLAN DOMINATED Ferdia's thoughts.

Propelled by a desire for revenge, he moved towards Whispers nightclub. Even if the loan shark didn't show, he'd made up his mind to do something that would pull the man who'd killed Niamh into his orbit.

He'd seen the looks Father Kelly had given his face and clothes, so he'd bought new garb in Ganestown and had a shower in Hugh's house before heading to Dublin. He parked in Trinity Street car park and strode towards Grafton Street, ignoring the pelting sleety rain. At Stephens Green, he passed the shopping centre and cut right, through a narrow, cobbled-stoned, rat-run alleyway, thick with the smell of stale alcohol, vomit, cheap perfume and urine.

Whispers nightclub had no signage to announce its presence, except for a thin, flashing LED sign that showed two faces pressed close together. Ferdia joined a jagged human chain that slouched and pushed each other, guzzled cans of cheap beer and head-banged in time to the heavy metal tracks that blared from loudspeakers attached to the outside wall, as if their collective fingers were stuck in an electric socket. Heavy metal attracts all ages. Tonight's metalheads ranged in age from fifteen to sixty.

Stick-thin girls showing off barbwire tattoos, fake tans and enhanced white smiles. They wore short vinyl skirts and dresses, shivered in the freezing cold and tried to look hot. Boys, in denim and leather, acted macho and tried to look cool. Sodden cardboard boxes had been ripped apart to use as umbrellas. Two drug dealers sidled in and out through the crowd, selling their wares like fruit vendors on Moore Street.

In a doorway, a young man and woman attempted clumsy sex. The man concentrated more on not spilling whatever drink was in the plastic cup he was holding. Half-a-dozen onlookers videoed the scene with mobiles amid a smattering of cheers and applause. The man raised his plastic cup and grinned for the cameras. It would be all over social media in a few hours. There wasn't a cop in sight. A scuffle broke out among four raucous males. Bursting with aggression and soaked in alcohol, they looked for attention. The girls observed covertly, unimpressed. The weed-scented air was filled with possibilities and potential.

Ferdia felt old. He hunched his shoulders, tried to make his large frame smaller. The metalheads at the top of the queue were funnelled, single file towards the nightclub entrance and three gatekeepers barricaded the doorway, watchful and alert like Cerberus, the three-headed dog, reputed to protect the entrance to Hell. The men were similar in appearance, not huge, but stocky. They all had tight crew cut hairstyles, no necks, and tight-fitted black suits. Various sized pieces of metal hung from ears, eyebrows, noses and lips. Two had moustaches and the third was trying to grow a Fu Manchu. The ends trailing off like a mouse's tail and he wore more sovereign rings than an ageing dart player.

From what Ferdia could gather, the bouncers admitted or denied access on a whim. Some were allowed entrance with backpacks, others weren't. From a group of five, two girls were given the nod, the other three a quick shake of the head. No explanation. Ferdia got a nod because money talks. His face was known now, and he was a good tipper. He'd visited twice since he'd paid off Malcolm's debt to Dolan's goons. The loan shark himself was never around, but tonight was different. Tonight, he'd stir the pot and make his presence known.

He palmed the bouncer twenty euro and stepped through. Strains of a Bon Jovi power ballad pounded into the passageway, the thick insulated walls vibrating with the bass beat. He pushed through a chattering throng that milled around a cloakroom, and shouldered his way into the club, like he was meant to be there, eyes canvassing the crowded floor. A ceiling of 1970s mirror-balls twinkled and glittered, creating a kaleidoscope of colour. Two gangly dancers wearing tasselled bikinis gyrated on a platform suspended over the DJ's booth. Ferdia edged towards the bar, jockeying for position. A stout, sweaty, middle-aged man sat sideways on a red plastic sofa, right hand tunnelling under his companion's skirt; a girl less than a third his age. His bald head glistened, as his other hand roamed her curves, grabbing and pinching flesh. She fiddled with a mobile phone and looked bored. He licked his lips like a lascivious lizard and gnawed her ear lobe. Over in a corner, a group of students huddled together, easy prey for the two older guys pouring drinks. Within an hour the men's conquests would be separated from the bunch.

A thick fog of dry ice and marijuana hung over the dancefloor, where people pressed against each other, dry-humping to the screech of shredding electric guitars. A couple of big-bellied musclemen waded through the metallers, shepherding and hustling troublemakers towards the exit. One got rough with a teenager who was using the floor as a mosh pit, hit him harder than was necessary, then himself and a companion dragged the unconscious figure through the crowd towards an exit. This was his opportunity. Ferdia followed and watched them manhandle the crumpled bundle out the door and toss him into a back alley. The bouncer pulled the door shut, turned, and got dropped by Ferdia's left hook.

Someone screamed.

The second bouncer slugged Ferdia from behind. Ferdia turned and countered with a right that busted the bouncer's eye. He ripped him again with a body shot. The bouncer staggered back and crashed into a table. People scattered. From the corner of his eye, Ferdia saw two of the doormen pushing through the crowd. No trace of Dessie Dolan. Yet. He tried to get his back to a wall and manoeuvre some space for the coming attack. It was impossible with tables, chairs and screaming metal fans in the way. He watched Fu Manchu charge his way through the dancefloor, oblivious to the bodies bouncing off his shoulders like tennis balls from a racket. Ferdia hoped the doormen would arrive separately, to give him some chance.

That didn't happen.

Fu Manchu stopped outside Ferdia's range, caught his breath and waited for his comrade to catch up. The headbangers pushed and shoved, stampeding over tables. Some males formed a moving half-circle around Ferdia, looking for a ringside view. Girls screamed and clawed their way out of danger, losing shoes and bags in the process. Others stood on chairs and brayed for blood. The second doorman arrived, panting. His momentum carried him past his comrade, closer to Ferdia.

The music stopped.

'You murdered her.' Ferdia's voice roared through the sudden silence.

The house lights came on. Ferdia grabbed the bouncer by the throat and shook him. The man's tongue protruded, and he gargled like an actor in a poorly performed B movie death scene. Ferdia swung his arm, a vicious backhand swipe that knocked the man sideways into the bouncer who'd just disentangled himself from a table. Fu Manchu didn't get involved. The onlookers parted as a tight sea of black suits descended, moving fast, crushing plastic pint cups under their boots. Someone pushed opened the exit door, and the damage to the nightclub became more apparent. Fresh air lifted the dense roll of sweaty heat and dispersed the marijuana and liquid carbon dioxide haze.

A general melee started at the bar. Another scrum broke out on the dance area. Remaining chairs were overturned and smashed and bodies got draped across tables. The red plastic lounge seats were in tatters, gouged by stiletto heels. The bouncers ignored everything; all eyes on Ferdia. Three surged forward, en masse, crowded him along with half-a-dozen onlookers and pushed them all out the exit door. This cobbled-stoned back alley, Bell Lane, was similar to the one they'd walked through to enter the club, except it was narrower, and used as a rubbish dump. On the left, a high wall prevented escape. To the right was freedom, but that path was blocked by the three bouncers who watched and waited for instructions. Ferdia watched and waited back, hands by his sides. A few hundred metres behind the bouncers, the alleyway opened onto Ely Place. Buses passed by the entrance, the hiss of tyres loud as they sloshed through a build-up of water and slush. Five more security men came from the nightclub and formed a half-circle around Ferdia. His gaze scanned the area. No CCTV. Bell Lane was a blind spot. A steady downpour helped quench the fight in the young troublemakers. They pulled jackets over their heads and ran. The ones that remained were spoiling for a fight.

One of the bouncers hawked and spat, the spittle landing at Ferdia's foot. Ferdia reversed a few steps, not to avoid the saliva; he wanted to get his back against the high wall. Fu Manchu appeared in the doorway, pointed at Ferdia. 'Kill him.'

There was a rush of violent physical contact. Three bouncers pushed forward. Using the wall as a brace and his right foot as a pivot, Ferdia shot his left leg out in front of him. His size fourteen boot rammed into a stomach; a foot higher than he'd intended. The man folded. The second took a thumb in his eye. He covered his face and howled in agony. The trio guarding the alleyway shouted encouragement. Fu Manchu joined his comrades. Ferdia twisted away as both men tried to find an angle of attack. He sidestepped the first rush and ripped his right fist into a man's unprotected belly. The bouncer looked like he was trying to go opposite ways simultaneously; from waist up, his body continued its forward momentum, and from the waist down, he went into reverse. His feet left the ground from the force of the blow, and he doubled over, vomiting. Ferdia spun and drove his elbow backwards. It smashed into Fu Manchu's breast bone, making his forward momentum halt like he'd hit a brick wall. Ferdia followed up with a short uppercut and laid the man out. Another bouncer, smaller than his companions, looked around and decided this wasn't his night. He made a run to get back inside the club, got the door half-open, before Ferdia slammed it shut, catching the man's arm.

The onlookers applauded.

The man howled. 'Me arm. You've broke me fuckin' arm.' A bottle was thrown by a bystander. It caught the bouncer on the back of his head. He moaned in agony.

'I'll break your feckin' neck,' Ferdia said.

'Get Tiny,' the man screamed through the doorway. 'Get Tiny. Get Tiny.'

Ferdia dragged the small bouncer back and gripped his neck. The remaining bouncers pushed forward, half a tonne of bad intentions.

The bouncer struggled in Ferdia's grasp. With his other hand, Ferdia gripped the man's belt, and like a weightlifter, he swung him off the ground, knee-high, chest high, and then over his head, before he flung him like a sack of potatoes into the advancing charge. Two were knocked over like skittles. The third, more agile, dodged the human bowling ball and kept coming forward. His momentum carrying him straight into Ferdia's fist and his face disintegrated. The other pair scrambled to their feet, faces set, intent now on causing carnage. Ferdia clamped hold of the first one to reach him and spun around like a hammer thrower building up speed to release the ball and chain, focusing on speed to send the man the maximum distance. The other bouncer ducked as Ferdia released the goon. But Ferdia miscalculated. Instead of the man colliding with his comrades, he missed them completely, and disorientated by the swinging motion, he'd no control over his movements. He tripped over his legs and smashed headlong into the wall.

The spectators groaned in sympathy.

Fu Manchu had recovered and jumped onto Ferdia's back. He swept his arm around Ferdia's neck in a rear chokehold. If he tightened on the carotid artery, it would mean unconsciousness in seconds. Ferdia drove back his right elbow into the bouncers' ribs, with the power of a battering ram. He felt the rib cage give way. The man groaned and released his hold. Ferdia spun and landed a quick body to head combination that put Fu Manchu down. The remaining bouncer ran.

The onlookers bayed and booed.

A spectator in a sodden white t-shirt and jeans, blocking the exit to Ely Place, stuck out a Doc Martin and tripped the bouncer. He slid face-first along the cobbled pathway. The small security man scrambled to get back on his feet and screamed again, 'Tiny.'

The exit door swung open, slammed against the outside wall, and a shape stood in the frame.

Tiny was huge.

Built like a potato, Tiny had no neck and a thick powerful body. The small bouncer and a comrade got to their feet and made shapes. Ferdia discarded them from his fighting equation and concentrated on this newcomer. Tiny had little pig eyes, buried under flesh, but they flashed around, taking everything in an instant. This was the danger man. A crusher, Ferdia reckoned, who liked to pin you to the ground and use his body weight to sap your energy and then ground and pound with hammer fists until you were unconscious. His triceps protruded like handles. He had a trapezius muscle that bulged from his shoulders like a linebacker's neck roll, and he wore Robocop biker boots with oversized buckles, straps and thick rubber soles.

Belying his bulk, Tiny moved fast. Ferdia didn't want those arms to get anywhere near him. He tucked his chin into his chest and charged, relying on height, strength and muscle. He threw a roundhouse that would knock out a bull. All his weight was behind the blow, but it never landed. Tiny ducked under the swing, and his right fist went through Ferdia's guard, gun-barrel straight. Knuckles drilled into flesh and thudded gelatinously on Ferdia's nose. His head snapped back and blood gushed.

Ferdia blinked and shook off the pain. He ripped a brutal shot into Tiny's body that folded him, and followed up with a powerful backhand to his jaw. Tiny staggered back. Ferdia, overconfident, stepped in and got drilled with a punch to the side of his head, causing his brain to slam against the skull walls with such force he almost lost consciousness. He shook his head as stars danced in front of his eyes. Tiny pushed forward again. His foot shot out and caught Ferdia in the solar plexus. His leg went from under him. He folded at the knees and never saw the kick coming. Boot leather exploded on the side of Ferdia's jaw, and he toppled like a tree, as siren's sounded and a squad car turned into the laneway, blocking the only exit. The onlookers barged back into the club. Tiny grunted. Four bouncers lifted Ferdia. Groggy and helpless, Ferdia had no choice but allow himself be dragged through Whispers, which looked like it had been bombed. He was yanked through the front entrance, out to a taxi with its engine running. Tiny grunted again. Two bouncers pulled Ferdia upright, and Tiny smashed a fist into the soft skin behind Ferdia's ear, knocking him out. The men lugged Ferdia, now dead weight over to the taxi and rammed him into the back seat. 'Docks?' a bouncer asked Tiny. Tiny nodded. More car engines started, and the vehicles dispersed like mice at a crossroads.

2 A.M.

UNDER COVER OF darkness, Rebecca Greenfield and three other women were herded outside.

Rebecca stumbled, dazed and disorientated from the drugs that had kept her compliant all day. The Ukrainian gripped her arm and bundled her into a people carrier taxi. Her head lolled against her companion as the driver drove through the city suburbs. Every sinew was sore. Every joint ached. Her whole body cried in a symphony of pain. She tried to open her eyes and see where they were going, but heavy sleet blurred her vision. The effort was too much. Her head was a tonne weight. Was this all a nightmare? All she wanted to do was sleep. She heard the girl on her shoulder whisper something, and strained to hear the words: 'don't wanna die, don't wanna die, don't wanna—'

'Shut up bitchin'.' The growl came from the Ukrainian seated in the front passenger seat.

The driver laughed, turned into an estate and the Ukrainian made a call on his mobile. Rebecca peered out. An apartment block. A person dragged two small figures towards the people carrier. The Ukrainian got out, spoke to a man as he helped push the two teenagers into the taxi, slammed the door shut and mashed the women together like peas. One of the newcomers curled into a ball and sobbed quietly. The Ukrainian got back in, and the taxi moved off.

Signs for Kimmage and Crumlin flashed by. Then they were on a dual carriageway. The Maldron hotel at Newlands Cross loomed on Rebecca's right. The waft of strong Turkish tobacco came from the front seat. An exit sign for Naas… Zzzzzz.

SHE WOKE, STARVING, disorientated, and with a pounding headache.

Still in the taxi. Still dark. No idea what time it was. The buildings gave no indication where they were. Rebecca looked out the side window. Black. Through the windscreen, there were lights on the skyline. Could be any town, in any country, anywhere in the world. Then they were on a motorway. The Ukrainian and the driver talked low. She looked at her companions, counted them, and then counted again. Four. She thought there'd been five. Had they dropped one off somewhere? She couldn't remember. The girl curled in a ball was still there, now nestled into Rebecca's side. Rebecca put an arm around her shoulders. The driver slowed, coming into another town. Rebecca looked for signs.

Adare.

They passed through the deserted town. More motorway. A speed ramp jerked her awake. They swung left onto a bridge. Charlotte Quay and Rebecca realised the side windows were blacked out. A set of traffic lights. Red. The taxi stopped. Another car pulled up beside them. This could be my only chance, Rebecca thought. She leaned across her sleeping companion and groped for a door handle.

'Only opens from outside,' the Ukrainian said. 'Scream. Go on.' He nudged the driver. 'We like to hear girls scream, don't we? Or try breaking the glass. It's reinforced, but, please, try. See if you're able.' He laughed. 'Relax, baby bear. We'll be there soon.'

'Where are you taking us?'

'You're going on tour. Like rock stars.'

The driver turned down a side street, away from the river. Rebecca squinted, tried to see street signs. Castle Street. That was no help. There was a Castle Street in every town. Another right turn. She spotted Chapel Lane and straightened up, alert now. Cecil Street. Barrack Street. Bishop Street.

Cecil Street. Castle Street. Barrack Street. Bishop Street. C, C, B, B. Adare. The river. We're either in Limerick or Galway.

Another right turn. Convent Street.

Three C's. Two B's. Cecil Street, Castle Street. Convent Street, Barrack…

The taxi stopped. The Ukrainian dialled a number and opened the car window. Somewhere in the distance, a tower bell rang five times. An electric gate opened. They drove into an apartment complex and parked around the back beside an emergency exit door. Two men waited, arms folded. They came forward, opened the taxi doors and hauled two of the women towards the building. The Ukrainian pulled Rebecca out, and the taxi driver shoved the fourth girl through the emergency door. They were led down a long corridor with doors on either side. The Ukrainian stopped beside one. The handle, Rebecca noticed, had been removed and replaced with a heavy-duty barrel bolt. He shoved back the pin, opened the door, pushed Rebecca into the room, and switched on a light.

The smell of unwashed bodies and bleach hit Rebecca like a punch. She looked around the sparse windowless five metre square room, with a small open wardrobe and a single bed. Mould grew from a corner of the ceiling and had encroached two walls. A jagged crack ran halfway down one wall, and the yellow paint, rippled with damp, peeled in patches. The orange-coloured linoleum was so worn in spots that the threaded backing showed through. Two nails hammered into the wall served as clothes hooks. There was no linen on the bed, and the flat, lumpy mattress was covered with a plastic sheet. It didn't hide the dark stains or the cigarette burns that dotted the mattress. A broken spring peeped out from one end.

'See? I give you room with en suite,' the Ukrainian said. He switched on another light, and jerked his head at a doorway, inviting Rebecca to take a look. 'Only the best for baby bear.'

Rebecca looked where he was pointing. There was a toilet with no seat. The sink had rusted taps and a grey-coloured facecloth hung on the sink rim. A small, tarnished mirror hung above it. Condensation and damp had turned the tile grout into dark green gunk. The joining between the floor and the walls were black with mould. Added, almost as an afterthought, was a shower stall with the door missing. The shower fixtures were yellowed and crackled, the shower tray rimmed with grime. Beside it, a discarded condom clung to the side of a metal wastepaper basket.

The Ukrainian stepped aside to let a small old Asian woman enter. Wizened as a dried apple, with her hair done up in a silver beehive, she edged past and left bed sheets, a bath towel and a sports bag on the bed. She smelled of chip pan grease and assessed Rebecca, dark eyes narrowed with suspicion. 'For you.' The old woman pointed at the sports bag. 'Get dressed.'

'I'm sick.'

'Your job is to work.' The Ukrainian clapped his hands. 'Work. Work. Work. On your knees. On your back. On your belly. You display. They pay.'

'I'm sick. And I'm sore. You hurt me. I need sleep.'

'No sleep. Work. Work. Work. Take tablets.' He said something to the old woman. She nodded and left. 'Wear this.' The Ukrainian pulled a see-through blouse from the sports bag. 'Is good for bizzness. No more jeans.'

'I'm not wearing that.' Rebecca's heart thumped. 'You can't force me to—'

The Ukrainian stepped towards her. Blood vessels bulged in his temples. 'Don't make me hurt you, baby bear. I hurt you without leaving a mark. Nobody will know. And then I get three more to take your place,' the Ukrainian clicked his fingers, 'like that. Lots of housewives looking for extra income while husband at work. Or... I take your sister, remember? I can be in Westport in two hours.' He wagged his forefinger in front of her face. 'There are many ways I can hurt you, baby bear. Is like, how you say, putting down family pet. I don't want to do it, but,' he shrugged, 'is no big deal either. You mean nothing to me. You're my money-maker until debt is paid.'

'What debt? I—'

'No talk. Work. Work. Work, baby bear.'

The old woman returned, threw four tablets on the bed and left without saying a word.

'I'll be back in ten minutes.' The Ukrainian pointed at the sports bag. 'Those clothes only. Nothing else. I want you to look like a duck on water. All smooth on the outside, all party underneath.'

'I'm... I need to wash. I need a shower. My hair—'

'Dry shampoo. Whore's wash only. Use towel. No time to shower. Work. Work. Work.'

'I can't do this. Why—?'

'Your debt will be paid soon. Then you leave, no problem. Until then—'

'What debt?'

The Ukrainian looked at her. 'Why you keep asking me questions? You don't know? Your ex-boyfrin' didn't tell you?'

'Tell me what?'

'Tsk. Tsk.' The Ukrainian shook his head. 'He owes me money.'

Rebecca stared. 'Who?'

'Michael,' the Ukrainian said.

'Michael would never have anything to do with you. He—'

'He was one of our street dealers, baby bear. I gave him valuable merchandise and he didn't pay me. Now I must get, how you say, refunded.'

'That's a lie. You're a lying piece of sh—'

'Is true, baby bear.' The Ukrainian plucked a cigarette pack from a pocket, lit and inhaled. 'Until debt is cleared, you're just flesh, a sack of skin. Nothing else.'

'How... how much is owed? I can get my parents to—'

The Ukrainian peered at Rebecca through a cloud of exhaled smoke. 'Be ready in ten minutes.'

'What's your name?' Desperate now, Rebecca tried to stall.

'No names. No more talk. Work. Wor—'

'I swear, I can't—'

'Enough,' the Ukrainian shouted. 'I put you unconscious again and let my men do what they want—'

'Okay. I'll... get dressed.'

'Ten minutes. And keep room tidy.' The door banged shut. Not the soft thud of wood, but the cold clang of metal. Rebecca heard the bolt slide home with an oily clunk. She doubled over and gagged.

'Help me, God, help me, God. Dear God, please…' her stomach rumbled. How long would it take to starve to death, she wondered. She'd refuse to eat. That way, as least… What day was it? She'd no idea how much time had passed since Sunday. She heard a sound. What was that? Rebecca straightened, staggered to the wall and put an ear to it. There it was again. Someone crying. Her eyes searched the door, then looked around the room, looking for something to jam against it and… Nothing. Like the last room, the door frame was almost invisible. If there's a fire, I'll die, she thought, and wished she smoked. Then she could set fire to the bed and die in the flames.

Rebecca rubbed her hand over her eyes and looked at the sports bag her captor left. She rummaged through it. A black dress, neon halter tops… she shivered. Another Lurex dress. Lipstick. Cheap perfume. Condoms. Makeup…

Condoms?

Reality hit home, and she sank onto the bed. Plastic sheeting scrunched beneath her. Death would be a relief because God wasn't coming. She was all alone.

Someone banged on the door. 'Five minutes.'

Rebecca grabbed the sports bag, ran to the en suite and tried to push the door closed. Swollen with damp, the door wouldn't shut.

She undressed, pulled the low, short black slip dress over her head, afraid now that the Ukrainian would come back and see her naked. She picked up the makeup and lipstick, trowelled on cosmetics to hide the bruise on her jaw and the dark lines under her eyes. She wouldn't wash. Maybe nobody would want her if… She looked in the sports bag for a comb or hairbrush. Neither.

Footsteps in the hallway.

'Oh Jesus. What the fuck am I gonna do?' Rebecca spotted the tablets on the bed. Painkillers. Four. Not enough to overdose. But if I can get more… She dry swallowed one to help ease pain and put the other three under the bed. She picked up her jeans, automatically searched the pockets for a comb. Nothing, except… it felt like a piece of chewing gum. Rebecca looked at the rolled-up piece of paper, so small it had escaped the searches, and unwrapped Sharona's mobile number. Another thump on the door.

Panicking now, Rebecca looked around for some place to hide the paper. No place in the room.

Bathroom.

She ran back into the bathroom and glanced around. No place to hide it there either. The door bolt snapped open. Rebecca rolled up the piece of paper again and pushed it into the lipstick lid. She applied another daub of mascara while the Ukrainian stood, arms folded, and glowered in the doorway.

Rebecca didn't care.

She flushed the toilet. The plumbing system gurgled and cranked like an old tractor starting on a cold morning. She turned on the sink tap, and a jet of brown water shot into the basin. No soap. She took her time drying her hands.

'Enough, baby bear. Come.' The Ukrainian pointed at the hallway.

Rebecca mixed water and toothpaste in her mouth, swirled it around, spat, and picked up the lipstick. Anything to delay the inevitable.

The Ukrainian clapped his hands. 'I said, enough. Don't worry about makeup. The drunker they are, the prettier you'll get. Time to meet your new family.' He turned, and Rebecca glimpsed the gun, tucked into his waistband. He walked ahead. Rebecca was ready to run in the other direction, then saw another bodyguard lounging against the wall in the corridor. He had a blond crew cut, wore black jeans and a black tank top that showed off a hammer and sickle tattoo from shoulder to elbow. He gestured at her to follow the Ukrainian and then took up the rear. In convoy, they walked down the long hallway, around a curve and into a sitting room. Hammer and sickle man placed an elbow on a mantelpiece and began to pare a thumbnail with a knife. Rebecca looked around. A few mismatched chairs and a dark red carpet. There was a three-piece suite, upholstered in a faded floral-patterned fabric, with a blanket thrown across the back. The cushions on the sofa and armchairs sagged from use. The portable sized television in a corner was switched off. An aroma of dirty washing and stale smoke hung in the air. Standing in a circle were six women. Three Scandinavian-looking blondes had gold bracelets on their ankles and wore stilettos and short dresses. The fourth, a dark-haired, swarthy twenty-something who looked Italian, wore knee-high black boots, a short skirt and a low-cut tank top. Numbers five and six were two of the women who'd arrived with her in the taxi. Overall, there was an array of flesh on display that ran the gamut from insignificant to extreme. Rebecca's eyes searched for the girl who'd curled into her during the drive. She wasn't there.

A studded partition wall with an open arched doorway separated the sitting room from a kitchenette. The old Asian woman took a load of washing from an industrial-sized machine, transferred it to a tumble dryer and refilled the washing machine with towels and sheets. She pressed buttons and the machines rumbled to life. The woman's expression never altered; stoic, weary, seen-it-all-before. Above the sink, street lights poured through a small single window that looked out onto rows of apartment blocks. The tower bell rang six times.

No one spoke.

The Ukrainian clapped his hands. 'Line up.'

The girls formed a line, motionless as skittles.

The Ukrainian pointed at Rebecca and the new girls. 'In here, you wait for clients. If you're not with client, you stay in this room. When client calls, he can pick quickly. Is good for bizzness.'

The girl who'd cuddled into Rebecca in the taxi arrived with a bodyguard. Dishevelled, she stumbled as the bodyguard pushed her towards the other women. She wore a short-sleeved flimsy blouse and denim skirt. Her bare legs were the colour of bleached bones and goose bumps covered her arms. Her hair was lank. She had the grey pallor of a ghost and the dead eyes of a hostage. The bodyguard grinned and gave a thumbs up to the Ukrainian. The girl swayed and fell. She looks about sixteen, Rebecca thought. Nobody assisted, so Rebecca reached to help the shivering girl to stand.

'Stand straight,' the Ukrainian said.

The girl moaned. 'I can't do this anymore.'

The Ukrainian came closer. 'Why? Are you a lemon? Have your juices all dried up?'

'Please, let me go. I'm hungry and sore. He...' She pointed at the grinning bodyguard. 'Please?'

The Scandinavian women looked away. Indifferent. Or afraid to get involved.

'Shut up or I kill you,' the Ukrainian said.

The silence hung like a thick fog.

Then, 'you won't kill me,' the girl said. 'I'm too valuable.'

The Ukrainian's eyes twitched, jaw muscles clamped. The girl cowered into Rebecca, and the man laughed. 'You're only valuable when you work. No work, no value.' He held up a finger. 'One hour.

I can have you replaced in one hour. Now, move away and stand straight.' The Ukrainian pushed the girl back.

'Oh, sweet Jesus. What've I done wrong to deserve—?'

'You work to pay off your debt.' He pointed his finger like a gun barrel. 'Work. Work. Work. When debt is paid, you free as a bird.'

'It'll never be—'

'Save breath for clients. They'll be here soon.'

Please don't say anymore, Rebecca thought. She watched the Ukrainian's expression. No hate, no regret, no pleasure. This was something that had to be done. Please, please don't say another word, she prayed.

'I'm not doing anything until I get food.' Scared and frightened, but hunger made the young girl defiant.

The Ukrainian drew the gun from his waistband, stepped over to her and pushed her to the ground. She covered up, arms folded to protect her ribs and kidneys, expecting a physical attack. The man squatted and pressed the rim of the handgun to her lips. 'If you're hungry, eat this.'

Rebecca's heart thumped.

'I said, eat it.'

'I don't—'

The Ukrainian snatched a Tesco plastic shopping bag pushed it down over the girl's head and wrapped it around her neck, holding it in place with his giant paw. The girls' breath deepened. Her fingernails clawed at the Ukrainian's arm, and he laughed. 'Good. Fight me. Fight me harder.' He pushed the gun barrel into her forehead and pulled the trigger. A soft "pufft," barely audible over the rumble of the machines in the kitchen. The shopping bag expanded like a balloon as the back of the girls head blew off, then it deflated around her. Trickles of blood swam down her neck.

Six women screamed.

The man with the hammer and sickle tattoo continued to pare a thumbnail. The old Asian woman looked on, unmoved.

'She's… dead,' Rebecca said.

'Have I got your attention now?' the Ukrainian clicked his fingers at the old Asian woman. 'Clean up.' He pointed to the two bodyguards. 'Dump her in a ditch on your way back. Use gloves.' He turned to the six women. 'I do the same to you if I hear another word. You eat *after* you work. Not before.'

Stunned, Rebecca tried to take in what had happened. She struggled to listen to the Ukrainian, unable to tear her eyes away from the small bundle now wrapped in bin liners. Blood and brain matter stains remained on the carpet.

'This,' the Ukrainian shrugged, 'is of no importance. Is the cost of doing bizzness.' He clapped his hands. 'Pay attention. Here, we work on quantity, not quality. Is your job to make man feel verrie special…' he wagged his finger, 'but no longer than fifteen minutes per client, okay? Is very important you understand me.'

The women nodded.

The bodyguards carried the body out. The old Asian woman scrubbed the blots with bleach and sopped up the mess with a mop.

The Ukrainian's phone rang. He answered, disconnected and said, 'good.'

A doorbell rang.

'Stand straight,' the Ukrainian said. 'Remember, when you finish, you wipe down bed. You wash. You come back here. You wait.'

Rebecca forced herself to stand straight. A trio of testosterone-fuelled young men, topped up with beer and bravado came into the room. They pushed, jostled and talked loud, a macho display of virility, filled with the expectation of a guaranteed good time. Inside, they displayed a forced casualness, nudged each other, slyly eyed the six women, and muttered among themselves.

'All good girls,' the Ukrainian said. 'Take your pick.'

The men pointed at the blondes. The women, subdued into submission by the Ukrainian's sudden, severe show of strength, were culled and shepherded to their rooms.

One of the men cupped his hands around his mouth and shouted after his friend. 'Hey, Tony.'

Tony turned. 'Yeah?'

'Double bag, man. Ya don't know where she's been.'

'Yeah. You too.'

The doorbell rang again.

Rebecca prayed she wouldn't be picked.

A murmur in the hallway and another man appeared. A cocky muscle-bound gym rat, who had either been to or was coming from the gym. Knew what he wanted and didn't have time to waste. He ogled the three women, pinched, probed and prodded their flesh before deciding. He pulled the Italian from the line and pushed her down the corridor. 'Ow, don't hurt me,' she said. 'Don't hurt—'

The bedroom door slammed, and the Ukrainian bolted it from the outside. Fifteen minutes started to tick down.

The hammer and sickle bodyguard returned. Two of the original three clients came out, smiling, less than ten minutes into their allotted time, and compared notes.

Rebecca prayed so hard she didn't hear the doorbell ring or see the two Scandinavians come back into the sitting room. Two new johns, one overweight, both dressed in leather jackets, checked shirts and denim, came in. About five foot seven. Not attractive. Not ugly. Normal looking. Their eyes roved up and down the girls. One pointed to Rebecca.

Hammer and sickle grunted and jerked his head.

The second john sat down. 'I want that one too. I'll wait.'

Rebecca edged by the punter. He stank of cigarettes and beer and followed her down the hallway. 'You're one lucky woman,' he said. 'You've no idea what a good time you're gonna have. Believe me, no one you've ever been with will come even *close* to what I'll give you.'

They stepped into her room. Rebecca heard the bolt slam shut. She turned to face her client and whispered, 'listen, I don't want to do this. I'm not here of my own free will. I've been kidnapped—'

'Hey, shut up,' he said. 'You're bought and paid for. Don't look at me.' He pawed at the dress.

Rebecca slapped his hand away.

'Bitch,' the man said and clouted her across the face. 'I said, don't fuckin' look at me. Turn around. Strip. Bend over. I wanna see what I've paid for.'

'I don't want—'

'Hey, I don't care what you want. You're mine for fifteen minutes an' I can do whatever *I* want with you. You do what I say, and I say, shut up.' The man beat the back of Rebecca's head with an open palm until she thought her skull would fracture. She inhaled the salty smell of stale sweat and aftershave and wondered if this was the person who'd kill her. She tried to remember phone numbers while he grunted and pounded her flesh. She couldn't remember her sister's number. It began with a three. Three something... God, how long more... She tried to calculate how many seconds there were in fifteen minutes. Sixty seconds by ten equals six hundred. Sixty seconds by five equals three hundred. Nine hundred seconds? Jesus. I'll die, she thought. How many seconds were gone? Seventy? Eighty?

The stale sweat smell was beating the aftershave scent. 'I've heard that some of ye don't enjoy it,' the man panted, 'that ye only pretend. But I've never had that problem. I can see you're havin' fun. Tell me you're havin' fun.'

'I'm. Having. Fun,' Rebecca said. *One hundred and one. One hundred and two. One hundred and three... Barrack Street. Castle Street... No, Rebecca, put them in order. B.B.C.C.C. Barrack Street, Bishop Street, Castle Street, Cecil Street, Convent Street. One hundred and seventeen. One hundred and eighteen. One hundred and...*

5

WEDNESDAY 23 JANUARY. 7 A.M.

THE PLASTER CAST made Adam Styne's skin itch.

He listened. Where was the white noise? The muffled cartoon soundtracks pumped through speakers, the clatter of cups and saucers and the peal of phones. He'd no idea of the time. He wished he had a needle to burrow under the plaster and tear at the itch.

He eased his legs out of bed, sat on the edge, and began doing exercises. Once he got circulation going, he wrapped the thin bed sheet around the plaster of Paris, stood on his good leg, and grabbed one crutch. Slowly, he hobbled around the small room, using the crutch to minimise contact between the floor and his sore foot. Sweat bubbled on his forehead, but he gritted his teeth and limped through the pain. Six laps of the room yesterday. He was going to double that. At least. Had to prepare in case George came after him. Right now, he was a sitting duck. After seven laps, Styne left the crutch on the bed and managed three more, unassisted, before he sank into the wheelchair. It felt like he'd run a marathon. He hadn't achieved his goal but was satisfied with the improvement.

Styne reached behind his knee, loosened a plaster layer and removed two of the painkillers he'd saved. This was the only hiding place he had. He dry swallowed the pills, patted the covering back into place, put the sheet on the bed, and sat back. He wondered why he didn't fear George. He should do, after what O'Brien had told him, but… The drugs worked, and he dozed.

THE SLAP OF shuffling slippers heading towards the dining room woke Styne again. John appeared to help him get ready for breakfast. After a quick wash, John wheeled Styne back to the room and helped him get dressed.

'Thanks for everything,' Styne said, and palmed John another fifty euro note.

'Oh, thank *you*.' John pocketed the money.

'Could you get me some more tablets?' Styne asked. 'This pain…'

'Sure.' John winked. 'No problem.'

'And,' Styne looked at John, 'I wonder if I could use your mobile for a minute?'

John took a step back.

'Nothing serious,' Styne said. 'It's my business. I need to look up something. Find out what's happening to my business. Two minutes.'

John hesitated. Then: 'Okay.' He took a phone from his coat pocket, drew the pattern password on the screen and handed it over.

Styne tapped on Google and typed in 'Hattingers.' In an instant, the screen was filled with articles. He tapped on the first one:

> **"Throughout all this, Director, Ambrose Hattinger was content to provide a veneer of establishment credibility to the group while happily disengaging from the key decisions he had a responsibility to scrutinise. For this deplorable performance, he received a considerable salary. Sources have criticised him for having a docile attitude, and that he represented the apogee of weak corporate governance…"**

He tapped on another article. An interview Madeline did for a woman's coffee table magazine.

> **Question: "What do you enjoy most about Paris?"**
>
> **Answer: "Paris served its purpose, but it's got nothing I need right now."**

Styne's lips tightened. Bitch wants to take over my company, he thought and scrolled again. Dorothy Ridgeway's name popped up, and he clicked on the article. She was an art collector, and it was her painting that one of Styne's employees had decided to forge. Instead of keeping the issue in house where the fallout could be curtailed, she had hired Sharona Waters to check into the forgery, and then went to the police and the press, effectively destroying his business and reputation. Dorothy Ridgeway was his nemesis.

'Err, we need to go,' John said.

'One second.' Styne tapped on an article titled "Redefining Success" and dated January twenty-second. He scrolled, speed reading Dorothy's thoughts on the selective deafness towards women in boardrooms. That female directors were seen as tokenism rather than real talent at work. In the middle of the piece, he slowed and reread her thoughts about "shaking up the establishment and that the time has come to smash the art world glass ceiling." Styne's eyes narrowed. "Going forward, I believe it's up to women to help women," Dorothy told the interviewer.

'Err, Mr Styne?'

Styne handed the phone back along with another fifty euro note. 'Appreciate it,' he said, lips tight.

Bitches want to take over my company. Women helping women? She wants to buy my business. Those new articles are a mushroom cloud starting a quiet, slow build-up on a media rollout concerning my company's future. I won't let that happen.

John wheeled Styne to a table where Ronnie and another man were already seated. Still fuming, he hoped someone else would take the fourth chair before George arrived. John brought Styne his breakfast.

'Look at the shite they're giving us?' George sat and eyed Styne's breakfast. 'Who do they think we are? Kitchen crew are beholden to the psychiatrists an' psychiatrists are the most deluded people in mental health. Not us. *Them.* If you don't see things their way, you're sick. People in Stalin's gulags got better treatment than us. Least they got fed. And if we're lucky enough to survive mad doctors and hunger, we've to be always on guard. It's nonsense to have non-violent people like us thrown in with maniacs like them.' George's wave included the whole canteen. 'And all the time we're being watched. Informers. Staff, doctors… Even when we take a piss. No such thing as privacy. Aren't I right, lads?' George nudged Ronnie for support, but Ronnie was engrossed in his food. George looked from Styne to the fourth man.

'You're new,' George said. 'When did you come in?'

'Yesterday. I'm Paul.'

'I'm George. This is Adam and Ronnie. What're you in for?'

Paul swallowed. 'It says in the rules we're not to ask anyone what they're here for.'

'Rules?' George spat. 'The rules and policies here are ridiculous. They took my belt, shoelaces and toothbrush, then gave me back the laces and belt, but wouldn't gimme the toothbrush. Mad. But that's rules for ya. Lemme tell you 'bout rules, an' this is no word of a lie. Yesterday, I asked a question: "What drug are you giving me?" Simple, right? Well, four white coats grabbed me, tied me to a bed and injected me with all kindsa stuff.' George shifted in the chair. 'My arse is still killing me. But them's the rules. Why can they do that against my will? Why can't they answer a simple question? Huh?' George looked at Paul. 'So why are you here?'

Paul chewed and thought. 'I need rest. Doctor says I'm mentally interesting. I'm not crazy.'

'Course not. Have you seen a white coat yet?'

'No.'

'Diya know which one you've been given?'

'Someone said Doctor Jessop.'

'Sarah Jessop? Oh, Jesus, man. You're—'

'You are,' Ronnie nodded. 'Fucked.'

'What? Why?' Wild-eyed, Paul looked at the men. 'How?'

'Listen,' George glanced around to see who was nearby. Satisfied, he leaned over the table. 'There are two groups in the power structure here: Clients versus doctors. The first thing I do is I size them up. Don't I Ronnie?'

'You do.'

'See, I figure out what they're looking for, an' how much you need to give away to keep them happy. Then, you gotta look for something in return. An angle, an edge. Anything that'll give you a future advantage. Give and take. Simples.'

'What's wrong with Doctor Jessop?' Paul asked.

'Quick fix Jessop, we call her,' George said. 'Let me tell you sumptin, Paul. She can run for Ireland. Has patients in several hospitals, an' she runs in an' runs out. An' don't get me started 'bout writin'. Even before you talk, she's got a big notepad out, and she's writin' like hell. Doesn't listen to you, doesn't look at you. She's read over your file an' made up her mind long before she sees you. One fella, he's sittin' over there,' George pointed across the room, 'he left in the middle of the session, and guess what? He wasn't even missed. She kept writin'. Doesn't ask any follow-up questions, just writes an' nods her head. Twenty minutes, max. In and out. You'll get a dose of tablets that'll give you the scutters an' you won't sleep for a week, my friend, 'cos you're running to the jacks every five minutes. Then, when she meets you again, you'll complain about the tablets, and she'll change them. Then the week after, she'll put you back on the first ones again. Vicious circle, Paul.' George turned his attention to Styne. 'Have you been assigned one yet?'

Styne shrugged.

George winked at Paul. 'Some people get special treatment.' His eyes flicked to Styne. 'Some people have *barristers* who get them *preferential* treatment. I bet he's got Ann lined up for ya.'

'Don't know,' Styne said, his mind on Hattingers. 'And I don't see anything preferential about this.' He looked at the half-eaten scrambled eggs.

'Anxious Ann, we call her,' George talked around a mouthful of food. 'She's new. Easy to get around 'cos she's not the prettiest picture on the wall, an' that makes her insecure. See? We notice these things. It's live ammunition. In fairness, she shouldn't be here; she'd be better with... less *excitable* clients than Ronnie here.' George slapped Ronnie's back. 'But, we're short-staffed, so they've pulled in bodies from wherever. She pretends to find what you say confusin', an' that gives her a chance to dig up follow-up questions and makes you explain and repeat what you've said, over and bloody over. She likes talking 'cos she's got no one at home to talk to.' George sniffed the air. 'You can smell loneliness from needy people. Don't be afraid to tighten the screws, I say. It's the law of the jungle in here: fittest and strongest survive. Simples. At least she doesn't try to ram tablets down your neck.' George looked around the table to check if his audience was taking in the information. 'Yesterday, she put Ronnie on new therapy. Have you met Ronnie before now?'

'No.' Paul shook his head.

'Well, see, if you *had* met Ronnie, say, last week, he was full of beans. Chattin' 'bout drums and rock bands and famous people he's met, that kinda shit. Look at 'im now? Bolloxed. New tablets an' some funky groovy stuff, like acupuncture, but different. Whenever he feels stressed out, he's gotta tap his head, don't you, Ronnie?' George demonstrated by hitting his own forehead with his finger. 'Supposed to relieve tension, for Jaysus sake. Anyways, what was I sayin'? Oh yeah. Anxious Ann. I had her once or twice, but I asked for a change 'cos I got fed up of her saying "I'm still not sure what you're trying to say," or "let's stay on one subject at a time, shall we?" and "I can't help you when you get this agitated." I went in calm as a summer breeze an' *she* made *me* agitated. Freaked me out, she did.'

'Who have you got?' Paul pushed his plastic plate away.

'Dan…? something. Doctor Dan. He's an intimidatin' wanker. I'd a run-in with him already. We all have. Knew as soon as he walked in we weren't going to get on. Sometimes it's just a bad fit, know wharra mean? He sits across from you and says "tell me about yourself".' George looked at the three men. 'That's it. Then, he leans back in his chair and ticks boxes off sheets. Least he doesn't write notes like yer wan. An' he never looks at you while you're talkin'. When your time's up, he'll give you a prescription. Amazin', innit? They spend half their lives in college and still don't know how to treat us like humans. Specimens on a whatjacallit dish, that's all we are to them.' George nodded at his assessment.

Patients began to form a line, queuing for their morning pills. George, Ronnie and Paul joined them. Styne waited in his wheelchair.

'Tap, tap, tap,' George whispered to Ronnie and hit him on the back of the head. Ronnie yelped, turned and swung. George ducked and Ronnie's fist connected with the next in line. The man snarled and hit Ronnie back. George laughed and danced away. In an instant, a dozen men, whose natural habitat was violence, began a full-on, free-for-all aggression-filled fistfight. Calm inducing drugs failed to alleviate the spike in hostility. Nobody had the wherewithal to realise that involvement in violent outbreaks would inevitably restrict privileges, add extra time to their internment, and mess up their sacred routine. This was a release for patients to vent their resentment at being locked up; an opportunity to put their finger up to authority.

An alarm clanged.

Styne watched George go wild with excitement. 'Come on. Time to get one back for our side. This's our chance.' George stayed on the fringes, shouted encouragement as security merged with the brawlers. Someone found a plastic tray and let it fly like a boomerang. Its edge caught another patient over the eye. Blood flowed. Styne wheeled himself towards the kitchen area, out of harm's way. Amid crushed paper cup and plates, he noticed a white plastic knife on the floor. He leaned out, scooped it up, and slowly pushed it into the plaster cast behind his knee.

A chair got torn from its mooring and used as a battering ram to push security aside. Styne watched George dart around, throw vicious leg kicks at people, then dodge away, laughing. Paul cowered in a corner, head down, arms folded across his forehead. Ronnie was missing.

Staff and security personnel converged in the middle of the canteen, broke up fights, pushed bodies away, and quick as it started, the melee fizzled out. George slunk over to Styne, sniggered, then changed his expression to one of deep concern. He caught the handles of the wheelchair and pretended to pull Styne out of harm's way.

Doctor Josephine walked through the throng. 'Who started this?' She scanned the room, looking for the culprit.

Lots of mutterings, but no one looked her in the eye.

'George? George?'

'Here, doctor.' George waved and pushed the wheelchair forward.

'This has all your hallmarks,' the doctor said.

'Me? No way. I was talking to my friends, an' I've no idea what started it. I thought it best if I pulled this man away, seein' as he's not able to walk, and tha'. For his own sake, like.'

'Hmm.' Doctor Josephine wasn't convinced.

A high-pitched plaintive voice asked her when was lunch.

'You're only after your breakfast. We'll organise lunch at the usual—'

'Fire. Fire.' Ronnie stood and ran around the room. He slapped his shoulder and looked behind him in an attempt to escape the imaginary flames.

'There's no fire, Ronnie,' Doctor Josephine said.

'But it's coming. Look.' He twisted, pointed and coughed. 'See?'

'Stop, Ronnie. You can go to your room.'

Ronnie's eyes bulged. 'We're all gonna die.'

'Remember what you were told to do yesterday?' the doctor said. 'Tap, Ronnie, Tap.' Doctor Josephine demonstrated by tapping her temple with her index finger.

'I am.' Ronnie punched his ear until it was red.

'That's not tapping, Ronnie. And you're supposed to think about your problems as well.'

Ronnie squeezed one eye closed, the other watched doctor Josephine, as he banged his head. 'I am. I am.' Voice raised in frustration, his tone becoming more urgent. 'Aww… fuckit,' Ronnie said.

The doctor clapped her hands. 'Everybody. Go to your rooms, please. There'll be no therapy, visits or assessments today.'

John wheeled Styne into the corridor and George leaned close and whispered, 'looks like you won't get to see the bigshot barrister today. Welcome to the jungle.'

9 A.M.
'ANY QUESTIONS SO far?' Hugh looked around McGuire's canteen.

'You've told us how bad things are,' a voice called from the bunch, 'but you haven't given any solutions—'

'It's not our fault that the company's—'

Hugh held up his hand. 'McGuire's have enjoyed eighty years in business. Most of those were uninterrupted growth. Charlie and Charlie's father before him had a clear vision of their company's positioning and strategy. They knew their key customers. Knew their competitors and added new product lines when market opportunities opened up. The company had a clear formula for success, which served it well. Its culture and operations reflected Charlie's vision of treating customers and employees as part of the "McGuire family".'

The canteen door opened and Philip Waldron leaned against the back wall, arms folded. 'Somewhere,' Hugh continued, 'between the recession in 2008 and the arrival of big-box competition, including Ikea in 2009, that formula broke down. The problem wasn't a failure to take action, but an inability to take *appropriate* action.'

'We've always done what Charlie asked,' a voice shouted, followed by rumbles of agreement.

'Companies tend to follow established patterns of behaviour,' Hugh said, 'and approach all new problems with the same tried and trusted processes that got them out of trouble in the past. In a lot of cases, attempts to dig themselves out of a hole will actually deepen it. Some recover after painful rounds of downsizing and restructuring. Many don't. Which is why action isn't always the best defence. *Appropriate* action is.'

'Doesn't matter,' a female voice argued. 'We'll be closed in a week, anyway. And why do you expect us to work for you? You come in here, know nothing about this business, and want to change everything.'

Stony faces waited for Hugh's answer.

'McGuire's won't close in a week,' Hugh said. 'And I don't expect any of you to work *for* me. I expect us to work *together* to help secure the future for everyone here.' Hugh looked directly at the woman. 'Most new managers would want to change every aspect of McGuire's, on the assumption that the old ways weren't working. I'd argue strongly against that approach, because in the clean-up, crucial skills and experiences that takes a lifetime to learn, get thrown out.'

Hugh noticed a lot of the staff look to the woman for her reaction. She was a leader. Now, she said nothing.

'So, what's next?' a new voice asked.

'Forget the "what-can-we-do shrug," and ask, what's stopping us?' Hugh said. 'To succeed, we must build strong relationships with customers and suppliers—'

'We don't have customers,' the woman spoke again. 'Charlie told me we've barely enough money to pay wages. Way I see it, McGuire's only way to survive is to close some stores and restructure.'

Hugh said: 'Does restructuring really improve a business? Sure, it'll buy time and cut costs. It'll make all employees more crisis aware, but what does it transform?'

For the first time, Hugh got nods of agreement.

'What's your suggestion?' The woman again.

'I suggest everyone takes a hard look at every part of the business they've got knowledge of and ask yourself, what else is possible? Can customers be offered better terms for bigger orders, without damaging the business? Have we exhausted the market for our products or services? Definitely not. In the case of consumer products sold through other retail outlets, have you considered selling a different range, direct, or through mail order and the internet? Spend more time talking to customers. Ask questions. What can we do to make their lives better and easier? The great things about a family-run company,' Hugh added, 'is that it's flexible, adaptable and has a faster decision-making process than its bigger, rigid cousins, who have committees and boards of directors.' He looked at Philip Waldron. 'In our case, we only have to make Charlie happy.'

'We do all those things already—'

'Really?' Hugh raised an eyebrow. 'Has anyone mentioned McGuire's on your personal Facebook page?'

No answer.

'How many of you tell your followers on Facebook or Twitter about that special weekend deal that's available? Or post a short video of the new stock that has arrived?'

No answer.

'In the past six months, how many of you made suggestions directly to Charlie?'

No answer.

The woman raised her arm. 'It's impossible to promote when margins are tight.'

'Sorry, I don't agree,' Hugh said. 'Best businesses are run on uncomfortable margins. 'Once you start making big profits, someone will undercut you. Impossible problems get solved when we see that the issue is only a tough decision waiting to be made. Also—'

'Everyone's great at seeing snags.' Charlie walked through the gathering. Hugh hadn't noticed him arrive. 'Can we concentrate on finding ways to solve them? Hugh's right. Instead of waiting for business to come in, go out and hunt for it. Introduce yourself to foremen on development sites. If you see a new housing estate being built, drive in and ask to see the gaffer. Ring our top customers and remind them McGuire's are open. What do they need? What would make their experience in our stores better?' Charlie looked around and spied what he was looking for. He went over to the coffee dock, picked up a cardboard box, and placed it on a table.

'Suggestion box,' he said. 'Hugh'll go through everything you recommend and, between us, we'll figure out ways to act on your proposals. Great start. Anything else, Hugh?'

'I'm going to form team leaders,' Hugh smiled at the woman who'd given him a hard time. She was first on his list. 'You see,' he said, 'I don't *have* to know how to run this business. I only need to know *how* to manage the people who understand it. So, start with the basics. As ideas develop, new ones will form. Once mind-sets change, that will cause a transformation. That's our way forward. I don't believe you can do today's job with yesterday's methods and still be in business tomorrow. I'll speak to you all individually over the coming days.'

The canteen emptied. Staff murmured among themselves. Neither hostile nor hopeful. A slow dawning of a new chapter.

Hugh texted Ronan Lambe and lifted his head when he heard the slow clap. 'Ten out of ten for the motivational speech on...

operation transformation, Mr Fallon,' Philip Waldron said. 'Zero out of ten for credibility and workability. I don't agree—'

'If two people in business always agree, one of them is unnecessary,' Hugh said, and brushed past.

RONAN, SHARONA AND Hugh met in Starbucks. Sharona unwrapped a smartphone, inserted a new SIM card and snapped the cover back in place.

'New phone?' Hugh asked.

'Good deduction, Sherlock,' Sharona said. She wadded up the wrapping and tossed it into a bin. 'Waste of money, but Ron insists. I prefer my Nokia. All I need it for is to call a taxi or phone for a takeaway.'

'Reporters need one with a camera, GPS, email, basic stuff like that,' Ronan said. 'I'll add a device recovery app in case it gets stolen or lost.'

'You're the best.' Sharona pinched Ronan's jaw. 'Write down my new number, Hugh.'

'Why don't you just change the SIM card?' Hugh asked.

'I will, I will, once I've transferred all my contacts.'

'But you can do that automa—'

'I know. But I'll do it myself. Later.'

Ronan rolled his eyes and sipped latte. 'How's the new job, dude?' he asked Hugh.

'Had a meeting with staff an hour ago. Went okay. Picked four assistant managers who'll be my eyes and ears. Spoke about ways to add value to customer service and asked them for ideas. Employees will believe and implement ideas quicker if they come from within their own ranks. If everyone makes an effort and pulls together, it'll buy us some time.'

'Cool,' Ronan said.

'Crises are great because you get to make decisions without being hobbled by bureaucracy,' Hugh said. 'Internal arguments are non-existent because everyone clings to any thread of hope.'

'Any choice is better than no choice,' Sharona said.

'Exactly. We'll see what happens. I want to turn up the volume on social media and get the power of the internet to grow sales, Ronan,' Hugh added. 'How'll I do that? Cost effectively?'

'Great idea, dude. One, I'd pick up all McGuire's antiquated desktops. Two, I'd walk to the nearest bin. Three—'

'Yeah, yeah.'

'Do you have a customer email list?' Ronan asked.

'Um... not sure.'

'Get it updated. Email is still the cheapest and best way to keep in contact with customers. Newsletters, deals, special offers... quickest way to grow business is through email. Hold on a sec.' Ronan took out his phone and started scrolling. 'Lemme go into their website and see what's what. Oh, dude.'

'What?'

'This website ain't gonna win any awards. First, it isn't secure. It doesn't have an SSL cert. Nobody's gonna... And there's no click to buy buttons. Very few products listed, no links to social media sites, and the contacts link is broken. Who the hell—?'

'Attack the problem, not the people, Ronan.'

'How'll you manage to juggle work with your mum?' Sharona asked, watching Ronan scroll and mutter to himself.

'I've no choice. I need a wage.'

'Still,' Sharona said, 'it's tough.'

'Yeah. Hard to come home and find a stranger in the kitchen every day.'

'The events calendar has no events listed,' Ronan said, 'and the news page hasn't been updated since... 2017.'

'That's bad?'

'Terrible is a better word, dude. This website is crap. Looks like someone started the process and forgot about it. Needs to become a shopping basket order site. Customers can then click and you deliver, or have their orders ready when they come in.'

'Can you do that? How long would it take? How much?'

'Easy peasy. Timeline? Twelve, fourteen hours. Building the site is easy 'cos you're starting from scratch. The biggest time issue is photo uploads and adding descriptions. Would suppliers help with that?'

'I'll ask.' Hugh chewed a biro top. 'And cost?'

'Fourteen hours. Sixty euro an hour. You do the math, dude.'

'I'll see if I can swing that.'

'Cool. Once you get clicks and sales, we can include scroll boxes and exit intent pop-ups—'

'You've gone geek again, Ron,' Sharona said. 'Seriously, I've no idea what you said.' She left the smartphone aside, picked up her Nokia and dialled a number. 'Hello? Would Rebecca Greenfield be there, please?' She listened to the reply. 'Oh, nothing important. No worries. I'm just a friend. Wanted to touch base. Haven't seen her for a while. I've lost her mobile number. I wonder if you could...? Oh, thanks a million. Hold on 'til I get find a pen. Okay, zero eight... huh-uh. Great. I'll give her a ring. Oh, really? Well, I'm sure she's... When Rebecca phones, could you ask her to contact Sharona? Yes, Sharona. Yeah, she'll know who it is. Thanks again, Mrs Greenfield.'

Sharona dialled the mobile number she'd written down, listened, made a face, looked at the screen, and disconnected.

'Still nothing?' Ronan said.

Sharona shook her head. 'It's the same number Rebecca gave me at Whispers. Same message: The customer you are calling is not reachable at present. Please try again later. So weird.'

'What's weird?' Hugh asked.

'That girl, I told you I met last Saturday in Whispers? The one that took part in a modelling contest? I gave her my number, but she didn't phone back, and hasn't been active on social media for a few days. Her mother says they spoke last Saturday, to say she'd be home next weekend.'

Hugh's mobile rang. 'It's Ruth,' he said.

Sharona made kissing motions.

Hugh turned away. 'Hey.'

'Hey yourself. Listen, I've to cancel tonight. We're—'

'Aww—'

'I'm swamped. People are Googling every ache and pain. The internet has made it too easy for everyone to think they have a rare, incurable disease that's invisible to the naked eye, so they cram into their local doctor's surgery. Then they get pushed into emergency and clog that up.'

'System has been creaking for years,' Hugh said. 'Sounds like you're having a bad—'

'Staff off sick with flu or stress. Either way, we don't have the manpower to fill the rota. So I'm working dusk to dawn for the next few nights. We've just lost one of our patients. I thought she'd be home by the weekend, and now she's going to her grave. Being short-staffed has made us spend less time with patients, which results in... missed signs.'

Hugh wandered towards the window. 'I remember Mum…
That's always a bad day.'

'Yeah. Sorry for being a whinge. After a while the nursing
profession makes you a bit thick-skinned. If you grieve for every
patient or share the pain of a family who has lost a child, you'd
become a mental case. Death and misery and suffering becomes
routine.'

'I suppose that's self-preservation, Ruth.'

'Hmm. I know I shouldn't, and I don't want to, but when I'm
overtired and stressed, it's easy to get annoyed with everyone for
making me stay late on shift, or keep me up when I should be in bed.
That sounds horrible, but that's the way it is. Anyway, I've to work a
double shift tonight. I daren't refuse. I'm still in the bad books.'

'Reporters should be gone by now.'

'God, I wish. We've treated some of the firemen for burns and
smoke inhalation. Bloody reporters are conning their way into the
emergency department with notepads and tape recorders, trying to
get the inside track without having to go out in the cold. One guy
even got a white coat and a stethoscope… Jesus.'

'That's not your fault, Ruth. You can't be blamed. Was Ferdia one
of the people you treated?'

'No. Why?'

'He's not answering his phone. I don't know where he is.'

'Hugh, Ferdia can take care of himself. He doesn't need you to—
'

'I know, I know.'

'Don't get involved in—'

'I won't. As far as rescuing people is concerned, I'm one and
done. That's it for me.'

'Good. Ferdia will try to drag you—'

'Ferdia isn't like that. He's not the type to—'

'Ferdia doesn't have a type.'

'Will I drop you in a pizza before I head home?'

'Nice deflection, mister. And yes, that'd be nice.'

'See you later.' Hugh sat down.

'What's that about Ferdia?' Sharona asked.

'Haven't heard from him since Monday,' Hugh said.

Sharona frowned. 'That's a wonder. You two are thick as thieves.'

'Not always.' Hugh dialled Ferdia's mobile and listened to it ring
out. 'Still no answer.

'Let Ron try his geek thing with Ferdia's phone,' Sharona said. 'Maybe he'll have better luck this time.'

'Sure, dude. No sweat if he's got the location settings switched on.'

'Whatever way the settings were when he opened the box,' Hugh said, 'Ferdia won't have changed them.'

'Cool. What's the number?'

Hugh read it out, and Ronan copied, pasted and tapped the screen. 'Yeah, it's connected all right. He used his fingers to enlarge a map.

'Well?' Sharona asked.

'It's in Dublin,' Ronan said. 'Dublin port.'

Hugh leaned over to look at Ronan's phone. The small rectangle filled with indecipherable writing meant nothing to him. Can you pinpoint exactly where he is?'

Ronan pointed at a red dot. 'I can pinpoint within a metre *exactly* where his *phone* is, dude. No idea where the man is, though.'

'Huh. I wonder what Ferdia's doing at Dublin Port,' Hugh said. 'Can you send that to my phone?'

'I'll take a screenshot and send it to your WhatsApp account, dude.'

'Thanks.'

MID-MORNING

THE BEST PEOPLE to loan money to are those deep in debt with a poor credit rating.

Malcolm McGuire queued outside Dessie Dolan's walk-in shop on Thomas Street. He'd been here before, sandwiched between desperate customers willing to pay any interest rate so long as they got cash. Now. A drug habit to feed? A communion dress or school uniform to buy? New shoes? Football jersey? Birthday present? No problem. A thousand per cent interest.

The anonymous grey building looked like a dwelling house on the outside. A security man opened the door and let a set number of people in. The internal walls had been knocked out, turning the downstairs into a large office setting, identical to a bank; plush carpets, bright lights, security cameras, a mahogany counter, cubicles and a team available to discuss private matters away from prying ears. The shop worked regular banking hours. Staff collected cash, redistributed it and negotiated loans. They were adept at the business of laundering funds generated by massive interest rates.

Malcolm was handed an envelope. He checked the money and signed a sheet of paper that made the transaction legal. After all, Dessie Dolan was a professional.

JURYS INN HAD been transformed into a casino. The long reception area was festooned with banners, bookies and bettors. Slot machines sang to the tone of C. Air conditioning pumped out a mixture of oxygen and a pleasant sweet scent. Windows were blacked out, giving punters a timeless space. The jingle of coins got enhanced by the creative use of hidden loudspeakers, and lights flashed over poker machines whenever they paid out.

Underneath a giant chandelier, a roulette wheel spun. Three smiling croupiers took money from punters. A woman pushed through the throng and placed a bundle of fifty euro notes on number seventeen. A fourth croupier sent the ball spinning. It stopped, jumped, rolled again and plopped into slot seventeen. The woman collected a wad of winnings and wandered away. Malcolm picked up an energy drink, took some money from his envelope and approached the roulette table. Six spins and one Red Bull later, he'd lost four thousand euro. He tossed the can into a trash bucket and pushed into a lounge area that had been converted into a poker room. He was seated directly across from the dealer, with two players on either side. Not the best spot. Quick scan of the chip stacks beside each player. Four tidy little heaps; the fifth guy had his spread out in front of him, all denominations mixed up. Lazy player, Malcolm thought. That's the first target. He flicked his gaze across their faces as the dealer pitched cards across the table, then lifted the corner of his two hole cards; pair of red tens. Malcolm caressed the pile of chips and settled in.

AFTERNOON
'YOU'RE FOOKED, BUD.'

The pain told Ferdia he was still alive. He floated along the edge of consciousness in waves of agony. His eyes burned from sweat and he tried to blink the discomfort away. Strained to open his eyes but they seemed to be gummed shut. He tried again. A pinpoint of light peeked through. Blinked again. Too sticky for sweat. Must be blood. His side felt as if something was stabbing him. Rib damage. He coughed, tried to swallow, but his throat was swollen with thirst. He licked parched lips. Needed liquid. Cold, warm... any liquid so long as it was wet.

'Willya shut up?'

Ferdia hadn't realised he'd made a noise. Still couldn't open his eyes. He took a breath and was sorry he did; his stomach and chest were molten balls of agony. Pain pulsed in time with his thudding heartbeat. And definitely a broken rib. He tried to open his eyes again. Was he blind? Or was this place so dark he couldn't see? Ferdia wasn't sure. The only thing real was the pain. Where were his hands? Why couldn't he wrap an arm around his ribs to protect them? Why couldn't he feel his hands?

'Keep your whinin' for when the lads get back, bud.'

That voice again. Ferdia tried to focus on where it was coming from. He shook his head, and a chink of light appeared through a blurry haze. A full-length window frame in front of him, its glass long smashed, leaving no block from the cold wind blowing in. Even though the place was freezing, Ferdia was sweating. His vision improved. He looked around and discovered why he couldn't feel his hands: they were tied to a cantilevered girder that jutted out from a side wall. His feet were also bound; the toes barely reached the ground.

'Wakey, wakey.'

Ferdia turned his head, and that sudden movement felt like a lorry had smashed into him. A world of ache flashed a kaleidoscope of colours and stars in front of him, and he lost vision again. His throat was blocked. He couldn't breathe. For a second he panicked, opened his mouth, inhaled, and tasted blood. He tried to swallow. Mucus and blood clots, thick as treacle coated his mouth and throat.

'See that girder you're tied to, bud?' the high-pitched voice said. 'Dessie hanged a lad from it last week. Other times he throws them out the window while they're still alive. Depends on the mood he's in. So, if it's any consolation, you'll be next in a long line of people dropped from the departure lounge. That's what I call this place, 'cos dead or alive, all visitors fly outta here. The lucky ones die quick. One fella, he's a vegetable now, ended up as a chugger for Concern, sittin' in a wheelchair on Grafton Street, rattling a collection box, an' droolin' at the shoppers. Coupla weeks ago, Christmas Eve, I think it was, Dessie tipped him over for a laugh. That's life, innit? One day you're top of the heap, next day you're lyin' in the gutter.'

Images slowly took shape. It was bright outside, but the building was semi-dark. Its only light came from the broken window and the filament bulb that dangled over his head swayed in the breeze.

'Wassup, bud?' The man came closer, sniffed, ran a fingerless glove across his runny nose, and blew breath onto his fingers. He was small, emaciated, with thin lips and a snub nose that had a septic boil on the side of it. Red, watery eyes, pupils too large for his pale face, showed the blank desperate stare of an addict. He wore a black beanie and a grey tracksuit three sizes too big. Ferdia recognised him. Decaf. They'd met the previous week in a laneway off Parnell Square, when he'd paid off Malcolm's latest gambling debt. Then, Decaf was driving a taxi. Now, in constant motion, he twisted, gestured, scratched an arm, rolled his shoulders, pulled at an earlobe and hopped from foot to foot.

'Hah!' Decaf said and fell into a martial arts crouch, arms extended. He shuffled sideways towards Ferdia.

'Hah, yourself,' Ferdia managed.

'You're some spanner, wha?' Decaf said. 'Dafuk you think you were gonna do in Whispers, huh? Didja want a gold sticker for turning up? Just 'cos you eat your porridge in the morning doesn't mean you can burst into a man's gaff an' tear the place apart. That's some shady shit… and lemme tell you somethin': once you came inside the Pale we'd got you in our sights.' His gesture encompassed the whole city. 'You were like a goldfish in a glass bowl, bud. In our town, there's no hidin' place.'

Decaf sat, pulled a plastic bag from his pocket and removed the contents with religious reverence. A syringe, a dessert spoon, another small plastic bag with a block of something inside, a thick elastic band and a bottle of water. He looked at Ferdia and gave a black-toothed grin. 'I'd share it, but it's too good to waste on ya, seein' as you're gonna die in a few hours. I'm not psychic, but I see pain in your future. When the lads get finished with ya, we'll need a brush to sweep you up. You'll fit in a matchbox. Anyways, while I'm waitin', I might as well bake. You'll get cooked when the lads get here.'

Decaf bent the spoon handle until the bowl rested level on the floor, then poured in a sprinkle of water and added the dark block. He picked up the syringe, patted his pockets, found a Bic lighter, and rolled the metal wheel. The lighter sparked but didn't ignite. 'Shite.'

Decaf shook it and tried again, knees jerking with agitation. This time it worked, and he brought the syringe needle to the orange flare for a few seconds before running the flame around the spoon bowl to boil the heroin. Ferdia watched the chunk melt into the water, and now in a liquid state, the mixture bubbled. Decaf's body shook with anticipation. He grabbed the elastic band and rolled up a sleeve to reveal a mass of festered blisters and scabs running the length of his arm. He strapped the elastic band around his bicep and pumped his fist, peering intently for a vein. Then he syringed up the liquid from the spoon and pressed the plunger until a drop appeared on the tip of the needle. 'Showtime, bud,' he said, pushed the needed into the vein, and released half the contents. Then he syringed blood back into the barrel, where it swirled and mixed with the cloudy heroin mixture, before he pressed the plunger again, pushing the cocktail into his bloodstream. 'Ahhh.' Decaf lay back. The arm, with the needle still attached, dropped to his side. His face relaxed into a smile and his pale skin flushed from the high.

Ferdia moved his fingers, tried to clench his fists and move his feet a fraction. Piercing pain lacerated his chest. His heart slammed against his ribs like a head-on collision. He controlled his breathing and waited for the agony to pass.

'Waste a time, bud.' Decaf grinned. 'This isn't Lourdes; there'll be no miracles here. Back in the day, if we'd to get rid of someone, it was purely business. But these European lads? They kill for sport. It's a thing of beauty to watch.' Decaf sniffed mucus back up his nose and swallowed. 'There's a shit storm comin' down, an' you're in the middle of it. Shoulda stayed in Smalltown, or whatever defuk you call that place out in the sticks.' He giggled, the heroin doing its work. 'The lads are gonna churn you into bleedin' butter. You'll be screaming like a banshee.' Decaf shrugged. 'It's your own fault. You bought the ticket, now you gotta take the ride.' He squinted at Ferdia. 'Do you ever say anythin'?'

'Tick-tock,' was all Ferdia could manage.

'Hah, funny man. We'll see how funny you'll be when Dessie an' the lads get here. They'll go through you like crap through a goose. Now, give me head peace.'

Ferdia tried to ease the discomfort. If only he could let his feet take the weight, it would help the ribs. He explored the space around him, looking for a purchase or any foothold to relieve the strain on his arms. His visual search got nothing. He looked out. In the distance, a boat that looked no bigger that a cork, bobbed on foamy waves. A seagull shrieked, wheeled in the wind, and dipped below his eye line.

Ferdia used the pain to try and piece together what happened, his brain shuffling through thoughts like a deck of cards. He remembered the nightclub, but nothing after that. Maybe it had been a mistake taking on Dolan in his own backyard. But he owed it to Niamh. He wondered how this could help her. There was no way out from here. He'd have to tweak the plan as the game unfolded, if he got an opportunity. Trying to conjure up solutions helped him forget the physical and mental pain. What day was it? How long had he been here? Had Niamh been buried yet? Had he missed the funeral? Punish the living for the sins of the dead. Was he hallucinating? He didn't know. He relaxed his arms, embraced the physical pain, and accepted it as punishment for still being alive, while Niamh was dead. It should have been the other way around. The image of her remains being removed from the burning house was branded into his memory. I'll be dead soon, Ferdia thought. Maybe we'll meet up again.

His shoulder blades knotted. The muscles in his arms screamed for release. He closed his eyes, willed himself to stop panting. He slowed his breathing to conserve energy for later, and concentrated on listening to the squabbling gulls and wave's boom against the shoreline.

In the silence, his mobile rang.

Decaf jumped to his feet, eyes wide. 'Defuk?'

The phone kept ringing.

Decaf pulled the needle from his arm, scratched at a scab, stood, edged around Ferdia, patted his pockets, and lifted out the phone. The ringing stopped. Decaf looked at the phone, looked at Ferdia, looked at the phone again, dropped it, smashed it underfoot and turned away.

Ferdia braced himself. He knew what was coming and there was nothing he could do about it.

Decaf wheeled and clubbed Ferdia's liver with an elbow, causing pain to jump through his body like an electric current. 'Now, *dat's* funny, bud. What else ya got in there?' Decaf searched again and found Ferdia's wallet. 'Well, well.' Decaf walked over to the window and pulled out some notes. 'Fifty, seventy, hundred 'n' twenty, hundred 'n' forty, hundred 'n' fifty. He held the money up to Ferdia.

'You killed me buzz, bud, but more cheddar makes it better. I'm gonna get some gear to keep me going 'til Dessie gets here. Dessie's dead sound. He always looks after me.' Decaf stuffed the money into his tracksuit jacket and looked at the wallet.

Ferdia held his breath.

Decaf tossed it on the ground and kicked it towards a pile of rubble. 'Now, don't go anywhere.' He laughed with a bronchial wheeze. 'I won't be long. Don't wanna miss a thing when the lads get here.' He passed Ferdia and lashed out, kicking him in the thigh. 'That's for nearly chokin' me to death the other night.'

When he couldn't hear the footsteps any more, Ferdia breathed a sigh of relief. The wallet was essential. His eyes searched and honed in on the spot where Decaf had kicked it. His gaze narrowed when he saw the crumpled hat beside it. He knew that hat. He'd fought with its owner a few nights ago. Looked like Tommy Mellon didn't make it. They weren't friends, never could be, but the man was doing his job, and Ferdia didn't wish him any ill will. Behind the rubble came a frenzied squeal as rats fought over some morsel. Ferdia looked up. The free end of the girder had a large piece of steel welded to it, preventing anyone from slipping their bonds. He was trussed tighter than Houdini, with no way out. He hoped an opportunity would appear from someplace, later.

HUGH FROWNED AT his mobile screen. Ferdia's phone had rang out, and when he tried again, it had been switched off. Or the battery has died, he though. He looked at the screenshot Ronan had sent. On the large computer screen, it made more sense. Roads and markings were clearer. The red dot looked like a beacon. He tried Ferdia's number again. Nothing. It was none of his business, but… He checked the time. 4:20 p.m., made a calculation and dialled Emily. When she answered, he said, 'I'm running a bit late. Is it possible for you to stay with Mum until I get there? I should be home around… eight. Half-eight at the latest.'

Emily agreed, and that made Hugh's mind up. 'Is Mum awake? How is she today?'

'We went through a few hours of Kathleen taking all the clothes out of drawers, me refolding them and putting them back, and she pulling them out again. She's having a little snooze now.'

'God,' Hugh said.

'You know, Hugh…' Emily hesitated, 'many well-meaning people continue to care for their relatives long past the point where… a residential care home would be a better option. For everyone.'

Hugh listened. Emily ploughed on. 'Family caregivers engage in crisis management but believe, understandably, that they are doing the best thing, and the thoughts of sending their parent to a care home feels as if they've failed in their care of duty. It shouldn't. I'll be leaving in a few weeks. Um, have you considered other options?'

'I'm doing everything I can to not think about it, Emily,' Hugh said. 'I'm still coming to grips with seeing my feisty, strong-willed, opinionated, loving, infuriating, funny Mum being transformed into someone who isn't able to hold a conversation and can't make simple decisions, like deciding what to have for dinner. Or, at the other extreme, she develops a fixation on bloody teaspoons.'

'Kathleen still has the power of speech, Hugh, but she's lost the art of conversation.'

'Hmm, it's a hopeless situation,' Hugh said. 'All that keeps me from giving up is that I know sooner or later I'll have no one to argue with. That day will be worse than anything Alzheimer's throws at me now.'

'Many caregivers are raising families and working full time,' Emily said. 'They're exhausted, and that, in turn, causes feelings of hopelessness, because they've no control. Caregivers experience symptoms similar to the patient; denial, confusion, fear, depression and resentment. Most of them have very little support or help from others. Even with a strong foundation of family and friends, they can feel isolated and alone because people don't know how to help. The caregiver is often too overwhelmed to even *ask* for help.'

'I know the feeling,' Hugh said. 'It's at times like this I miss not having siblings to shoulder some duties. I promise I'll think about what you said, Emily. And thanks. For everything. Don't know what I'd have done without you over the past few weeks.'

Hugh printed the Dublin port map, and nosed his mother's car onto the motorway.

EVENING

'I GOT COMPLAINTS,' the Ukrainian said.

The women shivered and rubbed their shoulders in silent anxiety. In this quiet time between afternoon and evening rush, the sitting room was meat locker cold. Their darting eyes flickered from one to the other and then back to the floor. Since early morning Rebecca had only seen the other girls sporadically, as they passed each other on the corridor coming from or going to their rooms, but their high-pitched screams and muffled sobs mingled with gruff curses told her she wasn't alone. Maybe they listened to her cries too. The Italian girl wasn't there, Rebecca noticed, but she'd been replaced by another. Late twenties, anorexic thin, long curly black hair framing her face, she had deep-set brown eyes and wore blue jeans and a kimono. No makeup, no lipstick. She held her head high, looked straight ahead, shoulders back. One hand clutched the neck of the kimono, squeezing it closed around her. Rebecca hadn't seen her during the day, didn't know when she arrived, but with the relentless doorbell announcing a constant stream of johns, and the Ukrainian barking orders, it was impossible to keep track on anything except the immediate job in hand: Living room. Bedroom. Count to nine hundred. Tidy up. Memorise Sharona's mobile number. Repeat.

Rebecca had lost track of the times the Ukrainian had clapped his hands, shouted at her to hurry up, and the number of men who'd picked her. Six? Seven? Being constantly herded and watched and anaesthetised by the murder of the young girl earlier, had numbed her reaction at which the speed her life had been upended. She couldn't think straight. Couldn't believe how fast being pimped out became the norm.

The tumble dryer rumbled in the background. The old Asian woman pottered around, gathered up empty pizza boxes and Styrofoam cups and stacked them in towers on the sink. She hummed an indiscernible Taizé chant and dragged a hoover into the corridor.

Two new bodyguards.

One, a narrow-eyed, jut-jawed, bearded, beer-bellied bouncer type with cauliflower jug ears, and a craggy, pockmarked face, shifted a toothpick from one corner of his mouth to the other as he scrolled through a mobile phone. The second, a scar trailing from an eyebrow to the side of his lip, had a crew cut and stubble both the same length. Gym muscles bulged underneath a Hard Rock café tank top, while a detailed diary of symbol tattoos ran down both arms from bicep to wrist. He lounged in the doorway, flicked through a tabloid.

The Ukrainian peeled a stick of gum from its wrapper and folded it into his mouth. There was a nick on his chin where he'd cut himself shaving. He chewed, looked at the women standing in the sitting room, like sheep waiting to be slaughtered, and rammed his right clenched fist into his left palm.

'Complaints,' he said again. 'Verrie bad for bizzness.' He pointed at Rebecca. 'They say you cold as Eskimo, baby bear.'

The hoover hummed, and Rebecca stared at the spot where the girl was murdered. The Ukrainian wandered around the room, his boots clumping a slow, measured pace. The footsteps stopped behind Rebecca, and she could feel blasts of fetid breath stain her neck. She wasn't expecting the kick to the back of her knee. Her leg caved, and she fell. 'Ow.'

'Shut up.' The Ukrainian shouted over the hoover whine. 'Stand straight, baby bear. You stand like a drunk donkey.'

Rebecca stood, wobbled, and tried to keep weight off the sore leg. The other women stiffened, ramrod straight, and stared at the ground. One of the Scandinavian girls chewed lipstick from her lips and her trembling fingers pulled down her short skirt hem a fraction; dignity trumping respect, even in a brothel.

'Complaints means fines.' The Ukrainian roved again, a petulant prowling presence. 'You and you,' he turned and pointed at Rebecca and one of the blondes, 'you owe me extra money. Clients not made feel special. You don't show passion. No smile. Clients don't want to see grumpy wife face. No emotion. Perhaps you start to hate men and think of them as, how you say, objects, huh? You give minimum... *happiness*, like you've been married fifty years.' The blonde woman shifted, and Rebecca saw yellow bruises on her neck and leg. The six-inch stilettos she was wearing were calf-killers. 'You must make them feel like they're giving you the best time ever,' the Ukrainian said. 'All the girlfrien' benefits but no fuss. If they want wife experience, they go home. Let yourself loose. If you can't do that, I hit you. I won't break skin, but I break your spirit. Then, I kill you.' He clapped his hands. 'Are you listening?'

Rebecca looked at the Ukrainian and saw the violence blaze in his eyes. A vein bulged in his forehead. She nodded.

The Ukrainian stared back. 'I will add to your debt.'

Another blonde with a bruised lip spoke. 'I've a kidney infection. I need something.' Eyes low, she talked slow. It was the first time

Rebecca heard any of the others speak. Although she looked Swedish, her voice sounded British.

'What, you want time off? And leave me short-staffed?' The Ukrainian lifted his shoulders and opens his palms in a what-do-you-expect-me-to-do gesture. 'Is not possible.' He wagged his finger. 'You should have told me sooner. Now is too late. I need you to work, work, work. I got complaint about you too. You scratched a client. He say you've nails like cats claws. Why you do that? Hmm?'

'Because he—'

'I don't care,' the Ukrainian cut in. 'Is verrie bad for bizzness. How will he explain scratches to wife, huh? Maybe he won't come back. For that, you will be fined. And cut your nails.'

The tumble dryer beeped. The old Asian woman shuffled past the girls, pulled bedsheets from the machine and bundled them into a wicker basket. The Ukrainian said something, and she nodded. He turned back to the girls. 'When doorbell rings, you smile. This is your boyfrien' coming to spend time with you. You are his special girl. But,' the Ukrainian wagged his finger, 'only for fifteen minutes. Work, work, work. Get them in and get them out. If you were home, you'd be doing it for free. Here, you earn money. Lots of money.' He pulled a fat wad of euros from his pocket and waved it at the women. 'You get cash at end of week, after expenses. Tax free. The happier you send man home, the more you make. And you're doing his wife a favour. If client not happy, maybe he go home and take out his... annoyance on wife, or beat children. And it's your fault. You've made him angry.' The Ukrainian's phone rang. 'You,' he pointed at the Scandinavian girl who had tried to cover her legs with the short dress, 'lift your dress higher. Show your legs.' He looked at the phone, grunted, said: 'be ready when doorbell rings.' He looked at each of the girls. 'Smile,' he said. More, baby bear. Chin up. Up. Up, like a model. Parallel to a mantelpiece.'

Rebecca raised her head.

Satisfied, the Ukrainian lifted the phone to his ear and walked out. The bodyguards followed.

The new woman raised a middle finger to the departing men's backs, dug into a clutch bag, produced an electronic cigarette, and jetted a cloud of vapour into the air.

'I'm Zita,' she said.

'Hi.' One of the girls extended her arm to shake hands. Zita shook her head. 'In this business, we never shake hands. We bump shoulders or elbows. I don't know where your hand was five minutes ago.'

'Oh.'

Zita grinned, made her voice low and husky and mimicked the Ukrainian. 'You must make them feel like they're giving you the best time ever. Hah! What happens when they're too drunk to get it up and act like it's your fault, and then demand their money back? What happens then, huh?' She pointed out the kitchen window. 'I moan so loud you can hear me across at those apartments, and it does no good.' She exhaled another cloud of vapour.

'Has anyone got nail scissors?' the blonde with the bruised lip asked.

Zita dug into her clutch bag again and found some. She left down her e-cigarette and said to the girls: 'Let me show you what I do.' She looked around to see where the old Asian woman was, then sat on the sofa and displayed her hands, palms down, to the girls. Eight nails trimmed neatly, with the two forefinger nails, each a jagged quarter-inch long. 'That's deliberate,' Zita whispered. 'Somebody that's nice to me, I'm nice back. But,' she raised her hands and turned them into claws, 'anyone try to hurt me, I rip his eyes out.' She demonstrated by swiping the air with her fingers. 'Here, let me.' Zita trimmed the girl's nails, but left the forefingers alone. She sucked on the vape pen again. 'What's your name?' she asked Rebecca. 'I'm sure it's not baby bear.'

'Rebecca.'

'That's a nice name,' Zita said. 'You Irish, yes?'

'Yeah.' Rebecca shifted. The cheap flimsy nylon material made her skin itch. She wondered if she was missed yet. Was anyone searching for her?

'I'm Polish,' Zita said. 'I'm from a small town called Człuchów. It's four hundred kilometres from Warsaw.' She twisted her hair and used a hairpin to fix it into an artistic disarray. She stretched her thin, hard as a steel rod body, crossed her long, muscular dancer's legs and patted the seats around her. 'Come, sit. Keep warm.'

The girls huddled together. Zita pulled the blanket from the back of the sofa, and they held it in front of themselves.

'What day is it?' a girl asked.

'Wednesday,' Zita said. 'I know by the number of johns. Monday and Tuesday, light. Wednesday and Thursday, busy. Friday and

Saturday, crazy. Sundays? Very quiet. Every john is at home with his wife and family.'

'But yesterday was—'

'An exception. Because you're new. Everyone wants to be first with the new girls. When they arrive, it's…' she clicked her fingers, 'bang, bang, bang. Literally.'

'We have to get out of here,' Rebecca whispered. 'Otherwise, he'll kill us all. We saw him kill a young girl, didn't we?' She looked around for confirmation.

The girls nodded.

'Where am I?' the girl with the bruised lip asked. 'I was in Berlin. In a car park. A woman asked for me for directions. Next I woke up in a room… Are we still in Germany?'

'No, Ireland, someplace,' Rebecca said.

'I was living in Sligo,' one of the Scandinavian's said. 'I called a taxi. That's the last I remember of my other life. I think that was two weeks ago. I haven't smiled since.'

'I was in my apartment,' Rebecca said. 'I was kidnapped…' she swallowed the lump in her throat.

Zita patted her arm. 'My sister got caught up in drugs and owed people money,' she said. 'She killed herself, but the debt remains. I'm paying off that debt. I've been sold twice.'

'How long have you been—?'

Zita shrugged. 'Eight, nine months. Something like that. I'm not sure.'

'Why me?' Rebecca whispered.

'You must owe him something.'

'No, I don't.'

'Drugs?'

'No. No way. I never touch them.'

'Then maybe your boyfriend did.'

Rebecca stared at the woman. 'I don't have one. My ex wasn't into drugs. Didn't deal drugs—'

Zita shrugged. 'Maybe he did. Maybe he didn't.'

'He didn't. I'd have known.'

'I thought I knew my boyfriend,' another girl said. 'Hi. I'm Nicole. He took me on holiday to Spain. I remember going out for a meal with him and then I woke up in the back of a van with three other girls. I was sold a lie from a person I loved. He must have known these people.'

'We *have* to escape,' Rebecca's whisper was urgent.

'Impossible,' Zita mouthed back. 'I've tried, failed, and got the scars to prove it. I don't remember how many times they've put a dog collar on me, tied me to a radiator and whipped me with a car aerial. See?' Zita lifted the kimono and showed the girls her back, interlaced with white scars. I risked my life to get out. It didn't work. The scars excite some johns. Sometimes they try to do the same. I met other girls who wanted to escape too. They've always been found. And killed. We're disposable. A commodity. Like vegetables. No matter what rock you crawl under, they'll find you, and then they'll kill your family. Slowly. Shhh.' Zita's eyes flicked to the door.

The old Asian woman came in carrying a tray of polystyrene cups. She handed one to each of the girls. 'You drink,' she said. 'Protection.'

Rebecca looked at the container, half-filled with a liquid that had the consistency of gooey jelly. 'What's this? Protection from what?'

Zita gulped hers down, took out the vape pen again, inhaled, and waved her hand through the exhaled vapour. 'It'll stop you getting pregnant.'

Rebecca hadn't thought of that. She looked at the liquid again and took a sip. 'Ugh. Why can't we take a tablet?'

The other girls tasted the syrup and made faces.

'Tablets expensive,' the old Asian woman said.

'It's a concoction she makes.' Zita looked at the old Asian woman. 'It works. Better than having a baby. I find the easiest way is to, you know, down the hatch.'

Rebecca closed her eyes and sipped. The syrupy concoction coated her tongue and throat like thick grease, but thoughts of the alternative made her finish the viscous syrup.

The doorbell rang. The girls drank their brews and scrambled for combs and makeup. The Ukrainian appeared and clapped his hands. 'Client passing through. He's got fifteen minutes.'

'Wow,' Zita said. 'Big spender.'

They smelled him before he appeared; a sickly, pungent odour of rotten vegetables and pig manure.

'Shit, I know that smell,' Zita murmured to Rebecca. 'I've seen this john before. He'll want to do something gross. Don't back away or scream. If you do, he'll pick you. Stare him down.'

A small fat man, ugly as an ogre, waddled in. He smiled at the girls, showing gaps where the central and lateral incisors top and bottom should be. The few teeth that remained were stained dark brown, and his wellingtons were caked with foul-smelling sludge. His grey, dishevelled hair reminded Rebecca of Albert Einstein's.

Nicole gagged.

The man unzipped his trousers, releasing a body odour of stale yeast and cheese. He pulled out an erection, the length and girth of a baby's arm, and waved it over and back like a diviner using a hazel stick to source water. He took a step closer, looking for a reaction.

Rebecca felt her flesh pucker as he edged nearer, but stood stiff and prayed he wouldn't pick her. She stared at a soot stain that seeped through the ceiling and trickled its way down to a shelf, where it pooled in a black circle. In her mind, she recited Sharona's mobile number over and over.

Zita snorted.

Nicole shrank back and screamed.

The man pulled her out of the line and dragged her into the corridor.

Zita held her nose. 'Jezus, how do you stay upwind from that?'

The old Asian woman fanned the air with a dishcloth and liberally sprayed the room with deodoriser.

'Thank you,' Rebecca said to Zita.

Zita smiled. 'He can smell fear. That's what turns him on.' She pulled Rebecca closer. 'From now on, we stick together. We look out for each other, okay? Trust no one. Sometimes they send in one of their own people to see how you perform. If you don't pass, you'll be beaten or starved or drugged and forced to star in videos.'

Rebecca shuddered. 'Okay,' she said.

5:45 P.M.

HUGH EXITED THE port tunnel, drove along Promenade Road, swung left onto Bond Drive Extension Road, and slowed. He was unfamiliar with Dublin docklands. A fog rolled in from Dublin Bay, and through the murky mist, he peered left and right at warehouses, rows of artic trucks and stacked forty-foot containers. The red pin that indicated where Ferdia's phone had been earlier, was off to his right. He looked for a turn, but there was none, until Bond Drive Extension Road veered ninety degrees right. There was nothing here except thousands of snow-covered wooden pallets and a large petrol station on the right. Maybe that's where...? No. The red pin was now on his left, slightly further on. He passed an unlit derelict site and kept driving until a single streetlight lit up a concrete wall that loomed in front of the car's headlights. End of the line. He brakes, stopped, studied the map, and glanced left at a parking lot that appeared to be a graveyard for old trucks, rusted containers and piles of broken pallets. This was where the red dot pointed. An abandoned galvanised shed towered over snow-laden trees that lined the perimeter. Nothing moved. There's nobody there, Hugh thought. Even if Ferdia had been there earlier, he isn't there now. And I'm not going in; could get eaten alive by rats. He reversed, drove back the way he'd come, then swung into the petrol station to get coffee for the journey home.

'LADIES AND GENTLEMEN, we're down to the last five entrants.'

The poker players straightened.

'Texas Hold 'em. No Limit Tournament Style. No more buy-ins. Standard rules apply. Play continues until one player remains standing. Winner takes all. Any questions?'

Malcolm McGuire rubbed his eyes.

Thoughts of the forty thousand euro prize money had kept him focused all day, but he could feel his attention waning. Energy drinks and strong coffee could only do so much.

The cards were dealt. Someone bet. Another raised. Malcolm folded. Same with the second hand. He won the third; a small pot, but it woke him up. He played the next few hands aggressively and bullied his competitors. In the space of two coffees, he'd hoovered up an extra eleven thousand in chips.

Easy money.

A break was called. Malcolm stood, stretched, went for a walk, and thought about his rivals.

The player on his left shouldn't have got through to the final. His features signalled every hand he was dealt, and he tried to mask his true reaction by doing the opposite of what he thought betrayed his hand. Poor cards resulted in false expressions of delight, as he bluffed his way through, forcing the betting up in the hope that everyone else would fold.

Nobody was fooled.

The player on Malcolm's right was better, but too eager. He squandered good hands, increased bets too fast, and blew the other players out, instead of reeling them in.

The two men across the table were cool professionals: their facial expressions never varied. This is what they did for a living. They followed no pattern, sometimes folded with reasonable cards, sometimes played with rubbish, going with their hunches. But they weren't getting a run of luck. I'm the one on a winning streak, Malcolm thought. He splashed water on his face. After a month of bad beats at the race track and casino, his luck had turned. He just needed to hold it together. The money and title were his. For a second, he thought about the promise he'd made Ciara, and was sorry he'd broken his vow. But he couldn't stop now. She'd understand.

He walked back to the poker room, and his hand brushed against the plastic bag in his pocket. He needed something to help stay alert. He removed two tablets, shoved them into his mouth, resumed his seat, took a swig of Red Bull and swallowed the pills.

One pot bled into another.

Rainbows of coloured chips changed hands and were won back. Malcolm got caught in a lousy bluff with one of the professionals and lost five thousand. Next hand, he was dealt pocket kings, and raised all the way to the river, when his opponent flopped an ace to go with his pocket ace. Another three thousand down. Malcolm rubbed his neck, frustrated. He could feel nerves build. Usually cool as ice, his heart rate increased, and the room was getting warmer.

'Bet.'

Malcolm refocused. New hand. His insides dissolved into a pleasant wave. Tense muscles relaxed. The dealer spoke, the words jumbled up and disintegrated, but Malcolm smiled and nodded. One of the professionals pushed three thousand into the centre of the table. He glanced at his hole cards. Ace and King of diamonds. The flop had the Queen and seven of spades, and ten of diamonds. Loads of potential. Confidence radiated from every brain cell.

'Raise.' Malcolm doubled the kitty.

Two players folded.

The professional checked his pocket cards. 'Call.'

The turn brought the ace of spades.

Malcolm bet again. The professional raised. Malcolm scratched his neck. A creepy crawly was running down his back. He shook his shoulders to ease the tickle. His pair of aces looked good—unless his opponent had two pocket spades to fill a flush.

Malcolm peeked at his hole cards again. The King of diamonds moved and spoke to him. 'He's bluffing.'

'Call.' Malcolm added chips to the pile, and the dealer added the river card. Three of clubs.

'Ow.' Malcolm jerked. The King of diamonds had pierced his finger with his sword. 'What did you do that for?' He rubbed his sore finger and looked at the river again. The Queen of spades winked at him and nodded. 'Now's your time, Malcolm.'

'All in.' Malcolm pushed his piles of chips into the centre of the table. They fell, cascading like dominos. The rush was like flooring the accelerator of a high-powered car. The other player pushed his stack forward too. A charge of electricity surged around the room. Beads of sweat popped on Malcolm's forehead. Whatever was biting him had moved into his scalp, flooding his brain with poison. He slapped at his head and tried to dislodge it. The soles of his feet were burning. Had to get out. Run. He looked behind and raced ahead at the same time. He'd collect his prize money later. First, he'd get rid of… Malcolm ploughed headfirst into a concrete pillar, bounced, careened into the poker table, unconscious before he hit the floor.

6.30 P.M.

'S'UP, BUD,' Decaf grinned at Ferdia.

'Man, I'm buzzin' like a box a bees. Needed tha' blast before the fun starts. It'll keep me goin' 'til Dessie gets here. Me an' Dessie? We're solid. Rock solid. Dessie knows I'm not here for the bullshit; I'm only here for the good shit. He's a class act. Know wha'?'

'Wha'?' Ferdia asked.

'It's gonna be… I'm not tryin' ta frighten ya or anythin' bud, but I'm predictin' bleedin' carnage. In a few hours, there'll be more devils here than in hell. Jus' sayin'. I'd beat the lard outta ya meself, no problem, 'cept I've a bad back.' Decaf went to a corner of the warehouse, urinated against the galvanised skeleton, and spoke over his shoulder. 'But the lads need their fun.' He wiped the fingerless gloves on the seat of his tracksuit and took a crumpled cigarette pack from a pocket. 'Killin' for a livin'. That's wha' the lads do.' He lit the last cigarette and threw the empty box at Ferdia. It hit him on the chest and fell at his feet. 'An' lemme tell ya, they're bleedin' good at it. You'll die screamin', an' when they're finished, they'll toss ya out that winda.' Decaf pointed the cigarette at the window frame. 'You'll spin like a flywheel and then… splash. It's bleedin' skull crack city 'round 'ere lately. I betcha…' Decaf stopped and cocked his head, when he heard boots on the metal staircase. 'There's the lads now. I've news for ya, bud. Your bad day jus' got worse.' He sucked in a final drag of nicotine, flicked the cigarette butt out the window, and waited at the top of the stairwell. Four men shouldered past him and stood in front of Ferdia.

'Where's Dessie?' Decaf looked around, confused as a gun dog that had lost the scent.

'Away,' one man said. 'Negotiating business.' He produced a knuckleduster, slid it over his fingers and flexed his hand until it fitted snug.

'Negotiate?' Decaf said. 'He couldn't negotiate a fookin' roundabout. Away where? Where's me gear?'

The blank stare he got spoke its own language. The man shrugged and eyed Ferdia.

'Where's yer man from Ukrainia?' Decaf asked.

'It's the Ukraine.'

'Wha'?'

'It's not Ukrania, you dumb shit. It's… forget it.'

'Whatever. Where's he?'

'Down the country, minding a few flesh houses.'

Decaf nodded. 'All the new honeypots down there too?'

'Most of them. Why?'

'Jus' wondered.'

One man said something in a foreign language and they all laughed. Decaf pinched the boil on the side of his nose, looked at the men, and laughed too. 'Come on, lads,' he said. 'Stop messin'. Where's me gear? I was promised gear.'

'We don't have gear.' The man pointed at Decaf and then at Ferdia. 'Untie him.'

'Why? Jus' kill him.'

'New instructions,' the man said. 'He must stay alive until Dessie comes back Saturday. You've to babysit him until then.'

'Saturday? Defuk youse on abou'? I'm not stayin' here 'til Saturday.' Decaf shivered. 'Dis place gives me the heebie-jeebies. Too many dead souls floatin' 'round here at nigh'.'

'Whoooo,' the man said. 'Don't worry, he won't cause trouble. It'll be like minding a sleeping baby when we're finished with him.' He pointed again. 'Untie.'

Decaf muttered, went behind the pile of rubble and dragged out a stepladder. 'Dessie, the little bollix. Twisty as a garden hose, he is. Off wit' one of his fancy women, I 'xpect.' He dragged the stepladder behind Ferdia and tried to yank it open. 'Been in more beds than a garden rake, an' as usual, leaves me to clean up his crap. Not long ago he didn't have a pot to piss in. Now he's drivin' a big rig an' livin' in a fancy-schmancy gaff in Fox fookin' rock. Few years back he useta get lost goin' to the dole office. He wouldn't've been able to *find* Foxrock. Now it's shiny suits an' dickie bows and two-tone bleedin' shoes. No homeless shelter round there, I betcha, or walk-in drug rehabs.' Decaf climbed up the stepladder. 'If the beautiful people of Fox fookin' rock knew half of what was goin' on, man, house prices would fall, bleedin' rapid.' He climbed another step and started to undo the rope knots. The four men formed a semicircle around Ferdia.

HUGH SIPPED COFFEE and walked back towards the vacant lot for a final look.

Two cars were now silhouetted in the street light, parked beside the shed. Hugh moved towards them, feet crunching through snow and ice. Taxis. Their engines pinged as hot metal cooled. They've only arrived, he thought. Is Ferdia here now? Hugh edged past the cars. Hair bristled on the back of his neck. He searched for an entrance and remembered a similar experience the previous week; after following Adam Styne, he'd ended up in a fight-to-the-death.

If there'd been moonlight, Hugh wouldn't have seen the soft glow shine from a window high up, but the dark surroundings made the weak glimmer shine like a beacon. He left down the coffee cup, stepped nearer the building, made out the shape of a doorway and walked through. It was dark as pitch inside. Hugh swiped his phone, touched the torch app, and its white light revealed the skeletal steel structure of a small area that must have been a foyer one time. A stairwell to his right, ran up into more darkness. He ascended the first few steps, stopped, listened, and climbed a few more. First floor. He flashed the torch around. Two steps on the flat and then the metal stairs turned forty-five degrees to the next floor. Hugh put the phone in his pocket and continued, then stopped. There was muffled noise coming from… in the cavernous building, it was difficult to pinpoint, but it seemed to be all around him. Then, a thud from above. Second floor. Two more steps on the flat and the stairs turned forty-five degrees again. Same for the third floor. The sounds were louder. Hugh strained to hear Ferdia. Nothing. Now, a noise below him. He tiptoed towards the fourth floor. From here, he could see a yellow light beam and hear sounds like someone hitting a punchbag, but there were no voices. Another two steps. Now he could see the light bulb overhead. The grunts and groans were audible. Someone was getting hammered. The landing opened directly into the room. Hugh crouched and craned his neck to peer over the remaining steps.

TROUBLE CAN ONLY come from six places: front, back, left, right, above or below.

Tied up for nearly seventeen hours, Ferdia's body had locked. His arms felt like lead and he could barely stand. Even though his body was broken, his head was clear, and he knew he had no chance against these killers. He flexed his fists. Nerves tingled and he tried to get circulation going. He knew the type he was dealing with; he'd seen dozens of them over the years. Musclebound bullies who'd smash you into pieces, but if you could keep your distance and weather that initial storm, you'd win the fight because they couldn't sustain the attack. There was still no way he could win and escape, but the fact they had orders not to kill him yet, was a small bonus.

Decaf pushed the stepladder aside and stood to Ferdia's right, legs twitching, eyes darting over and back. The muscle men watched like cats with a cornered mouse. Veins stood out on their necks. Muscles, taut from pumping iron, bench presses and steroid injections, twitched in anticipation. If they come one at a time, I'm dead, Ferdia thought and made his move. He feinted left, and the four muscle men charged. It gave Ferdia a second to move a step to the right and grab Decaf. He held him tight in a full-length lover's embrace and forced himself to crash backwards, with Decaf on top. Ferdia recoiled in pain, but clamped his legs around the small man, pinning him in place, and then used one hand to scrabble around and find the empty cigarette pack Decaf had discarded. His fingers found it, crumpled it up, and forced it into his own mouth and bit down, using it as a crude gum shield. Then he tucked his head into Decaf's chest.

In a rush to get in the first blow, the muscle men had got tangled up. They pushed each other out of the way, kicking the bundle on the ground. Ferdia didn't escape punishment; his arms and legs took a battering, but Decaf took the brunt of the heavy blows. Ferdia cringed as boots thudded into Decaf's body. His moans drove the muscle men to even greater extremes of violent frenzy. They can't keep this up much longer, Ferdia thought. What then? What the feck am I gonna do then?

THREE STEPS. TWO. ONE.

Hugh stood on the landing, peered in the doorway, and tried to make sense of the scene. From his pocket, the mobile phone chirped like a cricket. Muffled and low, it seemed loud as a siren in the sudden stillness.

Hugh fumbled for the phone. Two men broke free from the bunch and ran towards him.

Fight or flight. It's a biological reaction. Nothing to be ashamed of.

Hugh did neither. Like a rabbit caught in headlights, he froze. One of the men punched him on the jaw, grabbed him, twisted him around, tugged his head back, and Hugh felt an arm encircle his throat. His strangled scream was choked off, the tight arm, unrelenting. He couldn't breathe. He felt his eyes pop, and for the second time in a week, everything faded to black.

Ferdia pushed Decaf off him. The muscle men milled around, their blood lust momentarily sated. More used to obeying orders than making decisions, Hugh's appearance had knocked them off-kilter, and they weren't sure how to react. Afraid of the wrath a wrong decision would bring, they did nothing.

Decaf groaned and tried to stand. His leg buckled and he fell. 'Me leg. Ye broke me bleedin' leg.' He saw Ferdia and rolled away.

The man with the knuckleduster dug out a mobile, pressed a number and walked to the window. He kept his back to the others, talked a little, and listened a lot. He disconnected and turned. 'Put him back,' he pointed at Ferdia. 'Tie him up,' he nodded towards Hugh, crumpled on the ground. 'You,' he looked down at Decaf, 'you babysit. Mind them.'

Decaf stared at him 'How defuk can I mind 'em? Me head's spinnin' an' me bleedin' leg's broken. I'm—'

'If your leg is broke, rip it off and hit them with it.' The man watched his comrades tie Ferdia back onto the cantilevered beam. Then they pinned Hugh's arms behind his back, trussed him up with more rope, and left him lying face up.

'Don't leave. I come back later with food for you,' the man said to Decaf. 'Now, we've business to run.'

The men moved to the stairwell. Decaf rolled to his feet and hobbled after them, holding his side. 'Me head's meltin',' he shouted. 'I need some gear.'

The footsteps faded, and Decaf limped back. 'Run a business? Between then, they couldn't run a fookin' bath.' He kicked Ferdia's leg. 'You bit me. That's for bitin' me, ya bleedin' vampire. This's all Dessie's fault, the disloyal little bollix. It boils me blood, bud. I do all de heavy liftin', and here I am livin' the dream on bleedin' minimum wages.' He kicked Hugh in the ribs. 'I work, an' he goes swannin' off. Low life meetin' high life. Him slingin' white with the bow-tie set in Fox fookin' rock, wearin' bleedin' sunglasses in the middle of winter. An' now, de lads tell me he's added a fookin' fada to his name.' Decaf kicked Hugh again. 'Where defuk did you come from?'

Hugh was still out cold.

'We know nuthin' 'bout runnin' skin. Those European lads are the experts there. But Dessie? He wants to be stuck in every bleedin' thing like a fly 'round a picnic table. Wasn't happy makin' nice money in nightclubs and headshops. Oh, no. Hadda get in wit' the big boys.' Agitated, Decaf scratched his arms, coming down off his heroin kick. 'Hasta be the big fella, throwin' coin around Fox fookin' rock like it's goin' outta fashion. Don't get me started, bud.' Decaf sniffed mucus and swallowed. 'I don't get it. Fairview, Foxrock, they're all the same to me. Designer clothes. Designer Watches. Designer stubbles. Designer drugs. Doesn't matter what part of this city you live in, every day's a race to night time.' Decaf rubbed his leg. 'Bleedin' funny, how Dessie still comes back to Sheriff Street nearly every night, even though he's got his big pad in Foxrock. Misery mansion, I call it. Never been invited in, mind.' Decaf roamed, scratched, twitched and searched his pockets for something that wasn't there. 'I need gear, bud. I gotta get a fix.' His eyes narrowed, thinking. He bent over Hugh, searched his pockets, and held his discovery up: two twenty euro notes and a single five. 'Don't go away,' Decaf said. He limped towards the stairwell. 'Remember yer man in tha' film. Big fella. What's his name? He useta say, "I'll be back." Decaf giggled like a schoolgirl.

Ferdia waited a minute, then shifted forward and tried to nudge Hugh with his foot. Hugh? Hugh? Wake up for feck's sake…'

9 P.M.

'WHERE'S YOUR HAPPY face, baby bear?' the Ukrainian asked Rebecca. 'Smile.'

Rebecca's smile was thin as a knife blade.

The Ukrainian walked out. Zita stuck her tongue out at the doorway and raised her middle finger. 'You set my heart a-flutter with your silver tongue,' she said, and tucked a blanket around Nicole who was sunk into the settee, bunched into a ball, legs drawn up to her chin, hands clasped behind her knees. The room was warm, but her body shook in a constant shiver.

The door slammed, a departing john, and the Scandinavian with the bruised lip stumbled into the room. The cut had been reopened. Blood welled and flowed from the split. It dribbled down her chin and turned the white blouse into a red bib. The old Asian woman appeared. Rebecca didn't think she noticed anything that was going on, but grasped now that she saw, and probably heard everything. The Tasze chant was all a front. The old woman pressed a warm washcloth against the cut for twenty seconds, followed up with an ice cube for fifteen seconds and then dabbed on lip balm. She had a new top slung across her shoulder, and she motioned at the Scandinavian girl to take off the bloodied blouse. She exchanged it for the new one and then walked away without a word. All done in under a minute.

'I bet in a previous life, she was a cut man in a boxer's corner,' Zita whispered to Rebecca.

Despite her nightmare, Rebecca smiled. 'Yeah, it's just—'

'Bizzness,' Zita finished.

'I hate when they slobber all over me like a St. Bernard dog,' Nicole said. 'Having to pretend they're the best lovers ever, to make them finish quick. Then a quick wipe down, comb my hair and go again. Yuk.'

'Or when they massage your knee and the inside of your thigh,' Zita took the vape pen from her clutch bag. 'In ten seconds you *know* they're gonna pinch you and there's nothing you can do about it.'

The girls nodded, all in this together, making the best of a bad situation.

'Never let them know you don't want to,' Zita added. 'That turns them on. Gives them more power over you.'

'I hate when they come in and stare at us,' the Scandinavian said. 'Comparing our body sizes. Once, just once, I wish we could line them up and strip them, and then we could point and giggle like they do.'

'I try to talk to them,' Zita said. 'Married men are suckers for women who take them seriously. Ask questions. They love when you seem interested. Wife is never interested in what he has to say, so this is something he's not getting at home. Let them talk. Most just want someone who'll listen to them, make them feel like they're the most important thing in the world. Tell them how good they are.'

'Doesn't stop them raping us,' Rebecca said. 'How can anyone think that we'd enjoy being—'

'It's simple,' Zita said. 'You trade sex for survival.'

The doorbell rang. Rebecca's stomach churned. The girls dived for makeup. In the thirty seconds it took the punter to pay, they'd applied lip gloss, ran combs through their hair and were standing in line, smiling. The Ukrainian came in, followed by a man dressed in a business suit, shirt and tie, and talking into a mobile. Average height, he looked mid-thirties with short, light brown gelled hair. Podgy, but not overweight. Not particularly attractive nor ugly. Ordinary.

'Huh-uh. Huh-uh,' he said into the phone, eyed the line-up, and pointed at Rebecca.

At least he looks clean, she thought, walking ahead of him to her room.

'Huh-uh. Huh-uh,' the man said.

A bodyguard closed the door behind them and Rebecca heard the bolt lock. She handed a condom to the man, waited and wondered what this one would be like. She'd told every john that she didn't want to do this, but so far, her pleas went unheard. Would this one be different? She hoped so.

The man jammed the phone between his shoulder and jaw and pulled Rebecca closer. Rough fingers unhooked, unzipped and tore garments when he got impatient.

'Listen,' Rebecca whispered. 'I—'

'Huh-uh,' the man said, and pushed her face down on the bed. A belt slithered over her skin like a snake. Across her back, down her legs. She closed her eyes and winced in advance, knowing the pain was coming a second before the sharp smack bit into her skin. She hissed to prevent a cry of pain.

Three hundred and twelve. Three hundred and thirteen. Three hundred and fourteen...

'Huh-uh. Huh-uh,' the man said.

'Oh that's marvellous,' Rebecca said.

'Hold on a second, Jack,' the man said. 'What'd you say?' he asked Rebecca.

'I said, that's—'

'Well, shut up and don't say it again. Jack? Are you there? Huh-uh. Huh-uh.'

Three hundred and seventy-one. Three hundred and seventy-two. Three hundred and seventy-three... God. Not even halfway there yet.

Rebecca could feel more spite in the belt lashes, and then they stopped. A hand slithered over her body. She could feel him position himself, and she clamped down on her lips as he drove into her body like a pile driver, deliberately trying to hurt her. He succeeded. Rebecca closed her eyes and counted.

'Huh-uh.' The man said, and then stopped. 'Jack? Hold on a second. Sorry about this.' The man slapped Rebecca's head. 'What are you doing?'

'I'm... I'm not doing anything.'

'I don't like it when women make noise in bed.'

'Oh? Did I make a noise? I didn't think I was.' Rebecca expected another slap. 'I thought—'

'Shut up. Your moans are taking me out of my moment. Sorry, Jack, what were you saying? Huh-uh.'

Rebecca closed her eyes and suffered the pain. He was rougher now, determined to prove by sheer strength that he was the superior being here. A thump on the door, followed by a 'two minute' call out from a bodyguard made Rebecca sigh in relief.

'I'll ring you back,' the man said. He pulled away savagely and Rebecca felt she'd been torn inside out. 'You've ruined me for any other man,' she said. 'I'll never be the same again. Never.'

'I don't care whether you liked it or not,' the man said. 'I'm not paying for *your* enjoyment. If it's good for you, consider it a bonus.'

He tossed his mobile beside his trousers at the bottom of the bed, went to the en suite, then stuck his head back into the bedroom. 'Clap your hands,' he said.

'What?'

'Clap your hands and keep clapping while I tidy up. That way, I know you're not riffling my wallet.'

Rebecca sat up and clapped. She listened to the shower gurgle and eyed the phone. The screen was still lit, which meant it hadn't locked yet. Could she dare? What would the consequences be if...? It was now or never. It would have to be a text. If he heard her voice... The mobile would self-lock in seconds. She bounced to the bottom of the bed, grabbed the mobile with her right hand, and smacked a thigh with her left. She pushed the phone symbol, pressed 'contacts,' then pressed the plus sign, added a fictitious name and Sharona's number, hit 'save' and typed her message:

its Rebecca. Help. Kidnap. Barrack st bishop st castle st cecil st conven

The shower turned off.

Rebecca tapped 'send,' slapped her thigh harder, deleted the contact, dropped the phone face down beside the trousers, and sprang back to her previous position. She hoped the phone would power off before the john picked it up. Otherwise, the screen light would be a dead giveaway. She had to distract him somehow. Still clapping, Rebecca walked to the en suite. 'May I dry the back of the world's greatest lover?' she purred, and took the towel from the man before he could refuse. 'What broad shoulders you've got,' she whispered. 'And those muscles... hmm.'

Three sharp knocks on the door. 'Time's up.'

'Give me that.' The man grabbed the towel from Rebecca, rushed into the bedroom, scrambled into his trousers and refastened his belt. 'I'm not paying for another fifteen minutes.' He fixed his tie and jacket, picked up the phone, stepped over the used condom he'd left on the floor and rapped on the door. Before the bodyguard opened it, he'd dialled a number. Rebecca heard him say 'huh-uh, huh-uh,' as he walked up the corridor.

9.30 P.M.

THREE THINGS CAUSED Hugh to regain consciousness.

Arctic sea air forced its way through clothes and pain. Like a wraith, it seeped into muscle and bone and demanded a reaction. A drip plopping on his face also helped. He swallowed rusty water coming from the galvanised roof, and gagged. The third was Ferdia's voice. 'Hugh. Hugh? Wake up for feck's sake. They'll be back any time.'

Hugh groaned, stirred and tried to move his hands. He shook his head to clear the haze. 'What happened?'

'I'll tell you later. Now, listen to me.'

'What are you doing here, Ferdia?' Hugh tried to sit up. It took him precious seconds to figure out he was tied up. 'Why am I—?'

'Now's not the time, Hugh. Listen to me. You've gotta focus.'

'I'm focused. I'm focused. What… how—?'

'You need to roll to your left,' Ferdia said. 'Towards that pile of rubble. Again.'

Hugh strained to comply with his hands tied behind him.

'Two more and then stop.'

Hugh stopped and panted with exhaustion. 'Lemme sleep for a bit—'

'Hugh? Focus. Or we're both dead.'

'Huh?'

'Twist your body ninety degrees.'

'What's ninety degrees?'

'Just feckin' twist, yeah like that. Good. Now, push back with your legs. And again. Stop. Right behind your hands, you should be able to feel my wallet.'

'I don't feel anything,' Hugh said.

'Search around. Move a tad to your left. Anything there?'

'Yeah. Something. It's a wallet.'

'There's an embossed design on the front. Feel for that and get it in your left hand.'

Hugh closed his eyes and concentrated. 'I feel it.'

'Great. Open the wallet, and in the top left, you'll feel a credit card.'

'Top left?' Hugh said.

'Yep. Top left. Got it?'

'I think so.'

'Good. Take it out slowly. It's not really a credit card. There's a knife—'

'Yeah. I've seen you use it. I've no idea how it works.'

'It's simple. Press the card edge and the blade springs out,' Ferdia said. 'Be careful. It's sharp. Tell me when you've managed to do that.'

'I'm pressing, but there's nothing... oh, right. Got it.'

'Good man. When you're comfortable with the grip, find a spot between your wrists, and saw through the rope. Don't feckin' cut an artery, or—'

'Thanks.'

'Any joy?' Ferdia asked.

'Will you give me a minute?' Hugh stretched his shoulder muscles and tried again.

'Take your time, but hurry up,' Ferdia said. 'I know it's hard from that position. Don't break the blade, whatever you do.' He listened for footsteps on the stairwell.

'I won't. It's working,' Hugh sliced. He could feel the threads shift and split. 'Couple more should do it... There.'

Cutting through the binds around his legs took seconds.

'There's a stepladder somewhere behind me,' Ferdia said. 'Steady, steady.'

Hugh staggered to his feet, waited for the dizzy spell to pass, then dragged the ladder over. He balanced himself on the third rung and cut through Ferdia's bonds.

'Phew,' Ferdia said. He took the credit card knife from Hugh. 'Let's get the feck outta here. Be quiet though. There's a fella coming back to babysit us shortly. I'd prefer to be gone when he gets here.'

'Okay,' Hugh said. 'Did you see where my phone went? And car keys?'

'Phone's over there,' Ferdia pointed. 'Your car keys—?'

'Still in my pocket.' Hugh patted his jacket and stooped to pick up his phone.

Ferdia replaced the credit card knife in his wallet. 'Can you shine your phone light over here? My mobile's here someplace. It's smashed, but the SIM card's all I need. Got it, let's go.' He pushed Hugh towards the stairwell. 'On tiptoe,' he whispered. 'Every few steps, stop and listen. Easy now...'

'Seems a lifetime ago since I came in here,' Hugh said when they were out in the open air.

'Less than two hours,' Ferdia clasped his hands around his stomach. 'And you slept through most of it. What day's today?'

'Wednesday. Why?'

'That's okay. Niamh's funeral is tomorrow. Didn't know if I'd missed it.' Ferdia looked around. 'Where's your motor?'

'Across the road.' Hugh pointed and blenched with pain. 'I think I've a broken rib.' He stopped walking.

Ferdia used one hand to drag Hugh along. 'If you'd a broken rib, you wouldn't be walking. You've no idea what the pain of a broken rib is like. One man choked you out. No big deal. Another fella smacked your jaw and kicked you. Might be a bruised rib. Walk it off, you'll be grand.'

'He really belted me.' Hugh rubbed his jaw.

'Yeah, you moved your body back outta range, your feet were out in front of your chin, so you weren't connected to the ground when the punch landed. That's why your brain took the full—'

'Aww, shut up, Ferdia.'

'I'm only saying. That's why you got flat-lined.'

'And what flat-lined you?' Hugh could see his mother's car in the distance. 'You went after Dessie Dolan, didn't you?'

'Yeah. Met his hatchet men and I got overpowered. We both made rookie mistakes, but sure, that's how you learn.'

'Where's my car, by the way?'

'Don't worry, it's safe,' Ferdia said. 'I'll pick it up tomorrow. Do you have anything to drink?'

'There's water in the car.'

'That'll do till we hit Ganestown.' Ferdia squeezed into the passenger seat. 'The way we look, if we go in anywhere, they'll call the cops.'

'Ganestown? Jesus. I've gotta ring Emily. I told her I'd be home by eight.'

'When you're on the phone can you give the Presbytery a bell too? Tell Jim Kelly I'm grand.'

'Father Kelly? How's he involved in—?'

'Long story. Gimme that water…'

SHARONA WATERS REREAD the text message and showed it to Ronan.

its Rebecca. Help. Kidnap. Barrack st bishop st castle st cecil st conven

Ronan frowned. 'Who'd you tell about meeting Rebecca? Is someone acting the—'

'Only you and Hugh. Look,' she pointed at the screen. 'See the way it's typed?'

'Yeah.' Ronan tapped on his own mobile. 'Those names? They're streets in Limerick city.'

'I *knew* it,' Sharona said. 'I *knew*... What'll we do? Look at the way the last word's not finished, it's—'

'Convent Street,' Ronan said.

'—like someone was gonna take the phone away if they caught her texting?' Sharona ploughed on. 'We *have* to do something. This is definitely—'

'What can we do? Limerick's two hours away. If we *do* go there now, what'll—?'

'I don't know. We've gotta do *some*—'

'And there's no address,' Ronan reasoned. 'Cecil Street. Castle Street... Where do you start looking for someone within that radius?'

Sharona chewed her bottom lip. 'There *must* be something we... Can you do your geek thing and see if the phone's located somewhere on those streets?'

Ronan sighed. 'I suppose I won't get any peace until—'

'You won't.' Sharona waited for Ronan's verdict.

'Sorry,' Ronan said. 'Location settings aren't switched on. I can't track the phone.'

'Shit.' Sharona pounded a cushion. 'Shit. Shit. Sh—'

'You have the number, though, so I could do a reverse phone lookup,' Ronan said.

Sharona's fist stopped in mid-air. 'Which means what, exactly?'

'It's an app.' Ronan swiped through icons and pressed one. 'If you get a call from a number you don't know, you can do a reverse phone lookup that'll give you the details. It's handy if you're making a list of potential scam calls, or if you wanna know the name and address of the person who called. It'll give you...'

'Do it,' Sharona said.

'Cool. What's the number?'

Sharona read it out. Ronan inputted and waited for the app to do its thing.

'Well?' Sharona leaned into Ronan.

'Huh,' Ronan said. 'Belongs to Adrian Fitzgerald-Gilligan. Lives in Castletroy, outside Limerick city. Monaleen Heights, Castletroy. That's, lemme see... seven kilometres from Castle Street. Nearly eight from Cecil Street.'

They stared at the phone screen.

'You gonna phone him?' Ronan asked.

Sharona thought, then shook her head. 'That text,' she said, 'isn't a fake. It's a genuine cry for help. We'll go to Limerick tomorrow.' Her voice didn't brook debate. 'I wanna eyeball this guy when we ask him how he knows Rebecca.'

10:30 P.M.

FERDIA PASSED OUT from the pain.

Hugh thought he was asleep, but when they reached Ganestown and Ferdia still didn't respond, he drove to the hospital. Two ambulances were lined up at the emergency department. One of the crew got a wheelchair and helped Hugh bundle Ferdia into it. Ferdia regained consciousness as he got wheeled through the pungent odour of alcohol swabs, pre-injection wipes and soiled bandages. For once, he didn't resist.

Inside, the intense, chaotic, organised rollercoaster was packed solid. A combination of the bad weather and seasonal flu had led to a deluge of patients over Christmas and New Year. The human torrent continued into January, and there was still no end in sight. Staff, hallow-eyed from exhaustive work shifts, moved between making patients comfortable and filling out paperwork. Most of the elderly had oxygen masks or used hand-held inhalers to help relieve asthma and breathlessness. A teenage girl got a drip attached to her arm. Next to her, a toddler was throwing up violently. Over in a corner, a drunk sang 'The Fields of Athenry,' and waved his hands around, making it nigh impossible for the irritated nurse to take blood. She clamped his arm between her arm and body and tried again to find a vein. It looked like she was digging for worms.

Hugh watched Ruth talk and reassure a frail old lady on a trolley. She folded a sheet around the woman's neck, smiled, patted her arm, straightened, and stared across the waiting area. Their eyes locked. She walked over and folded her arms.

Hugh grinned. 'Cometh the hour, cometh the—'

'Warriors,' Ferdia said.

'I was thinking assholes,' Ruth said. She smelled of methylated spirits. 'Just when I thought we'd got a lid on the mayhem, you pair come along. I presume this is Ferdia. And where's my pizza?'

'I can explain,' Hugh's grin turned sheepish. 'Umm, yeah, this is Ferdia. Ferdia Hardiman, Ruth Lamero.'

'Hugh's been talking about you non-stop,' Ferdia said.

'Really?' Ruth raised an eyebrow.

'The thing is,' Hugh rushed to explain, 'Ferdia got into... a fight with some guys. He wasn't answering his phone and I figured out where he was and I had to rescue him. I didn't have a choice.'

Ruth stared at him.

'Well? Say something,' Hugh said. 'You agree with me?'

'Silence doesn't mean I agree with you, Hugh,' Ruth said. 'In this case, silence means your level of stupidity has rendered me speechless.'

'Listen,' Ferdia said, 'I'll be perfectly honest with you. It—'

'Whoa,' Ruth held up her hand, 'whenever anyone says "I'll be perfectly honest with you," I always go hide my purse.'

'No, seriously, believe me—'

'Uh-oh. I'm definitely gonna hide my purse.'

Ferdia tried again. 'Gimme a few plasters and some painkillers, an' I'll get outta your way. I'll be grand.'

'Did you see your face?'

'Argh, it's only a bone bruise.'

'It's shredded,' Ruth said. 'And that haematoma over your eye looks nasty. She peered at the swelling. 'Looks like you've been kicked and punched.'

'He has,' Hugh said. 'That's why—'

'It's nothing,' Ferdia said. 'You wouldn't have any vinegar lying around, would you?'

'No, I wouldn't. Let's see.' Ruth bent and lifted Ferdia's shirt. 'Broken rib, I'd say. Torn and lacerated skin. Arm joints strained and hyperextended. Muscles cramped and pulled. Tendons stretched, torn ligaments... you're not going anywhere. Hmm, and you'll need an anti-tetanus jab. Let me see if I can find someone to give you a big fat injection. Oh dear, there's no doctor free. I'll have to do it myself. Lucky, lucky me.'

Ruth elbowed Hugh out of her way and wheeled Ferdia over to a porter, gave him instructions, and busied herself with paperwork. She seemed to have forgotten Hugh.

Hugh limped over and rubbed her arm. Ruth turned and peeled his hand away.

'Err, what about me?' Hugh asked. 'Should I, you know, hang around, or…?'

Ruth gave him a dismissive glance. 'You're fine. Go home, take two Panadol and lie down.'

'Oh. Okay. Is Ferdia—?'

'He's gone for a CT scan. He'll be here for a few days.' Ruth turned back to her paperwork.

'I'll go, so,' Hugh said.

'This isn't an airport, Hugh. You don't have to announce your departure.'

'Aww, Ruth I can't leave like this. You're upset, and—'

'I'm fine, Hugh. Why would I be upset? I've been on my feet for fifteen hours. In that time, I've had one ten-minute break and eaten half an apple. I'm looking after twenty-three patients, and four will die before morning. That's a real number. Right now, I'm about five seconds away from either taking a break or doing something that'll send me to prison for life.'

'Ruth, he needed help. He'd have been killed if—'

Ruth turned on Hugh. 'How can you listen to someone who's so obviously wrong in their judgement and whose actions are probably illegal? You don't even agree with him, and yet you continue to… Why?'

'Because he's a friend. He's helped me in the past and now he needs me to return the favour. That's what friends do.'

Ruth pointed at the door. 'Out there, do what you like. In here, I drive the bus. Stay out of my lane. Go home, Hugh.'

'We'll talk tomorrow,' Hugh said.

Ruth's folded arms accentuated the distance between them. 'No, we won't. Tomorrow I sleep.'

Hugh tried again. 'Next day then?'

'Next day I'm back at work.' Ruth picked up a kidney-shaped bowl. 'Look around you, Hugh. Everyone here wants to relieve pain and stay alive. You're dead set on ending yours and hell-bent on causing mayhem before you do. I'm…' Ruth shook her head. 'I'm going for a break. I need to recharge my patient care curve.'

6

THURSDAY 24 JANUARY. MORNING.

'WE'RE A DAY late with your evaluation tests,' O'Brien said, 'thanks to the mini riot. I assume George played a major role.'

'I'd nothing to do with it,' Styne avoided the question. The whine of electric drills and hammers was present since early morning, as workmen bolted and welded furniture back in place. The canteen had been reopened for breakfast, but half the space had been corralled off with yellow crime scene tape. Additional security still didn't stop George from singling Styne out.

'Hear you're havin' a meet with the suits today.' George leaned closer and muttered. 'Not a word 'bout yesterday. Not. A. Fuckin'. Word. I'll hear if you do.' He slapped Styne's back and disappeared amid the flow of moving bodies.

'I'm supposed to be seen professionally within twenty-four hours,' Styne told O'Brien. 'I want you to issue a formal complaint. Before we discuss these tests, what's happening with my business?'

'Hattinger's locked up, Adam. No sign of life, and no, I haven't made any enquiries about its future and my colleague hasn't come back with any updates. Count yourself lucky you're away from all that stress and strain. Now, let me address your formal complaint. The system is overloaded, and people are often stuck for weeks before they're assessed. This place is full at the moment. In fact, jailed prisoners with severe conditions have to wait four months on average for a transfer. *Four months*, Adam.'

'Am I supposed to thank you for getting me here within days?'

'Don't need your thanks, Adam. Also, the fracas at breakfast yesterday didn't help.'

'When I've been assessed, what then?'

'There'll be several assessments, Adam. Any case that has the potential to end up in court will be gone over with a fine-tooth comb. If psychiatrists are satisfied you suffer from a mental disorder, they'll make an involuntary admission order, under the Mental Health Act's relevant section. You'll be given a general description of the proposed treatment and if we feel it's beneficial, we can have the admission order reviewed by a Mental Health Commission review tribunal. If that goes against us, we're entitled to appeal to the Circuit Court against the decision.'

'And when I'm found sane?'

'If the psychiatrists are satisfied you don't suffer from a mental disorder, you must be released immediately, back into the arms of the Gardaí.'

'To jail?'

'We'll see,' O'Brien said. 'It's a blight on our society, Adam, that psychiatric disorders are the only illnesses that we, as a nation, regularly respond to with handcuffs and incarceration. It's deluded and archaic. And as more humane and cost-effective ways of treating mental illness have been cut back, we increasingly resort to the tried and trusted law-enforcement method: prison. Oh, don't get me started about this antiquated system. I wonder what the next generation of psychiatrists and psychologists will say about how we handled our most vulnerable. The growth in the number of mentally ill prisoners over the last five decades can be traced directly to poverty, transient lifestyles, and the closing or downsizing of state hospitals. The... the *chronic* underfunding of public services, restrictive insurance policies, a lack of an adequate range of community support programs, and the likelihood of adults with serious mental illness who have a substance-abuse disorder, is a disgrace.' O'Brien took a breath. 'The result? More than *twenty-five* per cent of prison inmates have a mental condition or have been hospitalised in a mental facility. Most mental-health professionals say the figure is substantially higher.'

'Thanks for the information download,' Styne said, 'but it's not pertinent to me. I'm not mentally ill. But if I stay here much longer, I—'

'Don't worry,' Adam. 'If you're deemed fit to leave, you'll be whisked away before you can say cheerio. It's a matter of economics. It costs around three hundred euro per day to keep a prisoner in jail, not including educational expenditure. And that figure has reduced because extra prison capacity and less staff equals lower costs. In here, you cost the taxpayer almost eight hundred euro per day, so they'll want you out. Pronto. You're right, in some respects, it is just like a jail, except for one bonus feature you won't find in a real lock-up: you're pumped full of drugs in order to bring your brain back to as close to normal as possible. Out there,' O'Brien waved at the wall, 'in prison, there's a good chance someone will beat those brains out and leave you a vegetable.'

Styne scowled. 'I'd take my chances. At least in jail, if you're found guilty, you're given a release date. Here, guilt equals a life sentence. Literally.'

'Not necessarily.' O'Brien flicked a speck of dirt from his dark navy Crombie overcoat. 'New antipsychotic drugs are manufactured all the time. Plus, changing social policy has led to the de-institutionalisation of psychiatric patients throughout the country, which has shifted the burden of their care from the shoulders of the state to the backs of our communities. So, at some stage in the future, even dare I say, George could be deemed psychologically safe to be allowed back into the general populace. Those houses would be a safety net for patients that need a sanctuary as a defence against themselves.'

'Crazy system,' Styne said.

O'Brien smiled. 'Be thankful that crazy is notoriously tricky to assess, Adam. Release patients too early and results can be disastrous. Keep them confined, and they may rot. We're systematically shutting down all the mental health facilities, so the mentally ill have nowhere else to go. Prisons are the new mental health hospitals, and they are bulging with people who shouldn't be there. So, in some ways, it's far easier to get away with a crime when you've been labelled mentally ill. Yes, I know some mentally ill people commit serious crimes, but the vast majority are brought in for offences that *flow* from mental illness. Everything can be overcome, well, almost everything. Murder is the one thing that's still virtually impossible to get away with, thanks to DNA. Today, when a barrister waves DNA at the jury, they convict. End of story.' O'Brien nodded at Styne. 'You mightn't like it here, but trust me, it gives us options we can use to our advantage.'

'What if I'm found sane, but with some... traits?' Styne asked. 'How can you meet the threshold needed to prove someone is legally insane at the time of the alleged offence? Is that what you're planning?'

'Adam, just because you may have some psychopathic tendencies, doesn't make you a mass murderer. We spoke about this last time.'

'This place is driving me nuts.'

O'Brien bounced his eyebrows. 'A locked psychiatric ward is no place for the sane. Nights can be filled with screams unless you've been prescribed a sedative. Have you been given any—?'

'I don't want them. I want to be declared sane and get out of here.'

'Nobody's perfect, Adam. In fact, the list of borderline personalities is endless. Well, not entirely endless; there are almost four-hundred different diagnoses. Lots for us to work through. Now, let's start where we left off last time. Sharona Waters.'

MIDDAY

HUGH GAVE EMILY the day off.

Stiff and sore, he wanted to sleep, but for once, his mother got up early. After a one-sided conversation, Kathleen dozed in her sitting room chair, and Hugh tiptoed to the kitchen and dialled a Zoom call with his four deputies. The suggestion box was half-full. Staff were taking videos of product displays and footage would be uploaded to social media later. Everyone was smiling a little more. They discussed window displays and shelving rearrangements to create hotspots, and agreed a "special offer" area where products would change weekly. He told them about Ronan and the website and asked about Malcolm. No one had seen him.

Managing people was something Hugh liked and was good at. It also gave him a sense of control over other areas of his daily existence. That was one of the best antidotes to relieve stress in caregivers, where life can often end up revolving around the person being cared for. He knew he was lucky to have work as a release. A lot of full time carers had no set routine as every day brought different demands. There was no off switch. He wanted to text Ruth, but knew she'd be asleep. He wanted to phone the hospital, but knew he'd get no information about Ferdia. After the Zoom call, he rang Ronan Lambe.

'Who's the greatest web designer on the planet?' Ronan asked.

'Bill Gates?' Hugh said.

'No, dude, it's me. I've been working most of the night on McGuire's website. Looks good. I'd have my part done today, but I've to go to Limerick.'

'Oh, okay.'

'Yeah. Sharona got a fix on that girl, Rebecca Greenfield, so we're going to check it out.'

'How'd she do that?'

'We did a reverse phone check.'

'Is that a thing?'

'It's a thing, dude.'

Hugh told him about rescuing Ferdia. After, he rang Charlie. 'Website needs updating,' he said. 'I've got a guy who'll do it. It won't cost much, and the sales uptake will more than pay for it.'

'I've been leaving that project on the long finger,' Charlie said. 'I'd hoped Malcolm would get stuck into it. Wishful thinking, I suppose. He hasn't been in touch, has he?'

'No. I—'

'One gambler can make beggars of a whole family,' Charlie muttered.

'Sorry, Charlie? I missed that.'

'Nothing. I'm... I heard you and Ferdia went on an adventure last night.'

'God, news travels fast.'

Charlie laughed, the first time Hugh has heard him chuckle in weeks. 'Phoned me earlier. He bribed some nurse to loan him her mobile.'

'Should we organise a collection for him?' Hugh asked. 'Everything he has was destroyed in the fire.'

'God, no,' Charlie said. 'That would mortify Ferdia. Anyway, he doesn't need money. Ferdia is very wealthy. He bought a lot of buy-to-rent properties in Dublin and Galway throughout the late eighties and early nineties. Did you know that?'

'No.' Hugh shivered. There was a breeze coming from someplace.

'Well, that's Ferdia. He doesn't need to work; only does it because he loves it. All those properties are mortgage free now, so I guess the money he banks every month makes him one of the richest people in the Midlands. Don't just judge the exterior, Hugh. Underneath that gruff demeanour, Ferdia is a shrewd operator. Having said that, he should have more cop on than to tangle with... Still, I understand why he did it. I'm finding it hard to forgive, too. Easy to say, but in practice, forgiveness is hard.' Charlie sighed. 'Our business has picked up.'

'Slow and steady.' Hugh straightened his back and flinched in pain. 'Attitudes are improving. New layouts will make a difference. Many goods can be bought online, but we're also social animals and like human contact. People want to see and feel a product before buying. McGuire's gives them the shopping experience. We'll push social media hard; staff are doing it already. Their attitude is the main reason for the swing.'

'Hmmm,' Charlie said.

'You okay, Charlie?'

'Lost my train of thought for a second, Hugh. I'm a long way from where I want to be, but I'm much better than I was. I'd be happier if Malcolm would...' Charlie's voice filled with regret. 'If only Ciara was still around. She'd make him see sense. God, wish I could unwind all the errors I've made. But you're right; we need to do something different. Trimming fat has run its course. It's great to see new ideas gain momentum. Work away on the website. Let me know if you need anything else.'

'I will,' Hugh said.

He disconnected and went to check on his mother. The sitting room was empty. 'Mum?' The downstairs bathroom was empty, too. 'Mum?' Hugh tore upstairs and looked into each room. Couldn't believe his mother wasn't in her bedroom, and double-checked everyplace.

Nothing.

Panting now, Hugh pounded downstairs and tried the sitting room again, even though he knew she wasn't there. Outside, he thought. Did she go outside? Heart thumping, he raced to the hall door, and stopped when he saw it ajar.

'Phone. Phone. Where's my phone?' Hugh ran into the kitchen, grabbed his car keys and mobile from the table, and punched in Emily's number on his way out to the car. When she answered, he gasped, 'Mum's missing.'

THE DRUGS HAD taken a heavy toll on Malcolm McGuire.

The last thing he remembered was the card table. He'd no idea how he got back to his apartment. Again. The past few hours had been horrendous: nausea, incontinence, coughing up blood, cramps, chilling fantasies and skeleton apparitions. His heart thundered against his ribs. Now, half-conscious, he made a decision.

'I'll kill myself.'

Malcolm tried to consider suicide rationally.

Drowning? Too slow.

Jump off a building? But what if I don't die? Run in front of a bus? Maybe the driver would brake or swerve. Close my eyes and drive into an oncoming truck? No. A train. Jump in front of a train. It wouldn't be able to stop. Couldn't avoid a collision. That's it. One step off the platform.

His jaws ached. He was lying on the sitting room floor, surrounded by smashed crockery. Plants had been taken from their pots and trails of compost were visible on every surface. How did that happen? He saw the head of a china figurine that Ciara had bought him, and that made him crawl to the bathroom and vomit again. From somewhere, his phone rang, but he was too weak to look for it. 'Water,' he whispered. 'I need water.' His movements were spasmodic, like a broken windup toy, and his face and body were sticky with sweat. 'Sweating like a racehorse,' he mumbled. 'That racehorse in Cheltenham. Ten to one.' He tried to think of its name, struggled to turn around, but couldn't figure out how. He flushed the toilet, scooped up water in his hand and lapped it like a dog. He heard himself babbling, but couldn't fathom the words. He closed his eyes and concentrated on what he was saying: 'Never again, never again, never again…'

RONAN LET THE Sat Nav direct him to Castletroy and then onto Monaleen Heights.

They passed a large playground that was closed. 'We're here,' he said, and parked outside a two-storey detached red-bricked house overlooking a large front garden. There was no car in the driveway, but tracks in the slush indicated that one or more had driven out earlier.

'Nice,' Sharona said. 'Very nice.'

'No one home.' Ronan gnawed a fingernail. 'Now what?'

Sharona stared at the house. 'What do we know and what do we need to find out?'

'We know Rebecca texted you from a phone owned by a guy who lives here,' Ronan said. 'We need to find out how that happened.'

'Without tipping him off,' Sharona added.

'Agreed.' Ronan thought about that. 'As long as it doesn't mean, like, a physical confrontation. I've already used up my lifetime ration of courage.'

'Hmm. Maybe we're reading this all wrong,' Sharona said.

'You think?'

'No, I think we've got it right. But, you know...'

'Yeah.'

They fell silent.

'So, how do you want to work this?' Ronan massaged the steering wheel.

'The thing is,' Ruth said, 'maybe he gave her the phone and let her send the text—'

'You think?'

'No, but still.'

Silence again.

'Know what I think?' Sharona said.

'What?'

'I think we should check out those streets. You know, have a look around. Scout the lay of the land. Have some lunch. We'll swing back here later and see if anyone's home.'

'I LOCKED THE door and left the key in it. I shouldn't have. I never thought she'd—'

'Whoa, Hugh. When? How long's she been gone?' Emily asked.

Hugh started the car and tried to think how long he was on the Zoom call, plus talking to Charlie and Ronan. 'Maybe up to forty minutes,' he exited the driveway and headed towards Ganestown.

'Say that again? I lost you,' Emily said.

'Forty minutes,' Hugh repeated.

'Oh.'

Hugh could hear the blame in Emily's voice. 'I'm driving into Ganestown,' he said. 'I'll—'

'You take the ring road, and I'll check the old way,' Emily interrupted. 'You don't know if she put on a coat, do you? This weather...'

Hugh tried to recall what coats were on the hall stand. 'I think the red coat's missing,' he said, taking a right turn for the bypass.

'Okay, I'll meet you at Ganestown hotel in a few minutes...'

HUGH SWUNG ONTO the ring-road that looped Ganestown. Could she have wandered from the main thoroughfare and got lost, he wondered, eyes scanning the road ahead. That's impossible. How could she? She's lived here all her life. I should have stayed with her. He visualised Kathleen alone and confused. Wandering in circles, frightened, expecting him to collect her. The road ahead was clear, but snowdrifts were still piled up on both sides. Hugh found himself plunged back into the panic he'd felt three weeks earlier when his mother had been diagnosed with Alzheimer's. Ahead, a man out walking his dog. Hugh pulled over and let the passenger window down. 'Have you met or passed a woman? Sixtyish?'

The man stooped, glanced in the window and shook his head. 'Sorry.' The dog strained at the leash.

'Thanks anyway.'

Hugh drove on.

A black cat streaked across in front of him.

The ring-road ended at a roundabout, and he turned towards the town centre. Ahead, a woman out for an afternoon jog. He pulled alongside.

The woman pulled an earbud free.

'Sorry. Have you seen anybody on your run? Sixtyish—'

'I passed a man with a dog.' The woman edged away from the car, suspicion showing in her dark eyes while she jogged on the spot. She pointed backwards.

'No, it's my mother I'm looking for. Thanks.'

Hugh drove around Ganestown Square, trying to pick out a lone figure, possibly wearing a red coat. He shivered, panic solidifying. The quick solution options were disappearing. Fast. Where could she have gone? He should have bought a wristband with his address and mobile phone number on it, or a tracking device, and make her wear it… A car swung into the square. Emily. He checked the passenger seat. Empty. His heart stopped. Through the windscreen, Hugh could see the panic in Emily's stare, head swivelling as she checked doorways and alleys. They drove into the hotel car park.

'She has to be around.' Emily tried to keep up with Hugh's long strides as they ran towards reception. 'She couldn't just disappear.'

'She's probably come back here, looking to dance more.' Hugh barged into the foyer. The receptionist smiled. 'Hi, Hugh. You've—'

'

'Have you seen Mum? Was she here in the past hour?'

'I saw her last Saturday night—'

The one spark of hope got quenched like a candle flame being snuffed out. Hugh turned away. 'Dammit, she has to be close. The hospital. I'll try the hospital. I bet someone brought her there, and she can't remember her name or address—'

'I'll phone, the receptionist said, and made a call. Hugh rang Meadow's supermarket. 'Kathleen isn't here,' a manager told him.

'No one with Kathleen's description has shown up at the hospital,' the receptionist said.

The trio looked at each other for inspiration.

'How could I have been so thoughtless?' Hugh ran a hand through his hair.

'It's not your fault,' Emily said. 'It wouldn't matter how many of us were there. If Kathleen wants to sneak out, she'll find a way. It's not unusual. We'll just have to hide the keys from now on...' She snapped her fingers. 'Taxi rank. Someone might have picked her up. I'll go.'

Hugh tried to think rationally. 'The only other place I can think of is the hostel. But that's a two-mile walk. Surely she'd... I'll run over. If she's not there, we'll go to the Garda station and report her missing. At least they know her since the last episode.'

'Call everyone in your phone contacts,' Emily called over her shoulder. 'To help search.'

They sprinted out, spreading in different directions. Hugh stabbed at his phone key pad and sent a mass text to his contacts while he ran. What if she'd got a bus? She could be halfway to Dublin or Galway by now, he thought. How would they find her? He didn't even have a photo on his phone to show the Guards. But they knew her. Last week, she'd parked and locked her car in the middle of Main Street, causing a minor tailback. Beads of cold sweat dampened his brow. The homeless shelter loomed ahead. You don't have to have Alzheimer's for it to destroy your life, he thought. Just being in contact with it is enough. He took a shortcut through Bread Lane and careened up Main Street, dodging a delivery man pushing a trolley. Outside the homeless shelter, half a dozen men congregated, cigarette smoke hanging like a pall over their huddle.

His phone rang. Emily. 'A taxi driver saw Kathleen going into the hostel with a man five minutes ago,' she said. 'She's wearing the red coat.'

'I'm there now,' Hugh panted. 'Hang on. Please let her be here. Please let her be here.' He burst through the door into the hallway. He stopped, breathless and in a lather of sweat. Over the hum of voices coming from the dining area, he could hear his mother laughing.

'Is she there? Is she okay?'

'Haven't seen her, Emily, but I can hear her. I'll meet you back at the hotel in a few minutes.'

Lunch in the hostel had finished. Most of the men sat alone, contemplating another day. Kathleen was sitting across from a medium-sized, heavily muscled man with a full beard and curly brown hair that fell below his shoulders. Hugh hadn't seen him before. He had a ruddy weathered complexion, a hawkish nose and hooded eyes. He watched Hugh approaching, projecting an air of alertness and quiet strength. Hugh put his hand on his mother's shoulder. She looked up and smiled. 'There you are. I knew you'd be here. I was telling Bill about you. Bill, this is... go on, tell Bill your name.'

'Hugh. Hugh Fallon. Kathleen's my mother.'

'Bill Timothy.'

They shook hands. A bowl of soup and a book rested at Bill's right elbow: the biography of Nicolaus Copernicus.

'Tell him where you work, Hugh.'

'I manage a local hardware shop.'

'Omnium rerum principia parva sunt. Everything has a small beginning,' Bill said. 'Small opportunities are often the start of great enterprises.'

'You're not from around here, Hugh said.

'No. Passing through. Manchester, originally, but I've travelled a lot. Picked up bits of dialects along the way.'

'Including Latin,' Hugh said.

Bill said: 'Your mother's very kind. I met her on the street and she insisted I come in here for something to eat. She's made sure I'm fed for the day. And organised dry clothes.'

'Great. Well, nice to meet you, Bill.' Hugh wanted to get his mother home safe. 'We'll let you finish your lunch in peace.'

Kathleen picked up her handbag and allowed herself to be led away. She linked Hugh as they walked out. 'That's a nice man. He promised to paint my house when the weather gets fine. Where are we going?'

'Across to the hotel, Mum. I parked there.'

'I'll stay in the hotel. I want to dance. My son will come to collect me.'

'It's okay, Mum. I'm your son.'

'Indeed you're not. My son is…' she groped for an elusive word. 'Do you dance?'

'Badly, Mum. Very badly.'

'I'll teach you. What do you do for a living? I used to be a nurse. I have a son, you know. He looks like you.'

'I know.'

Kathleen stopped. 'Do you know him?'

'Yes. We're very close.' Hugh sent another mass text to his contacts, calling off the search.'

'Oh. That's nice.'

Hugh hugged his mother. 'Let's have coffee before we go home.'

AFTERNOON

ADAM STYNE WAS wheeled into the bare-walled office where the initial assessment would take place.

Styne settled into the wheelchair and thought about what Allister O'Brien had told him.

A doctor will give you a physical examination that'll include blood pressure and blood and urine samples.

Why?

They need to understand your general medical condition to properly assess your psychiatric symptoms and their potential causes. They'll also check any requirements for medical care, and choose the best psychiatric treatment.

For what purpose?

Lots of reasons. It establishes a baseline measurement before treatment begins. It also includes or excludes a diagnosis and aids in the choice of treatment. Likewise, it detects or rules out disorders or conditions that have treatment consequences. For example, urine screens for substance use disorders, neuropsychological tests to verify the presence of a learning disability, and brain imaging tests to attest the presence of a structural neurological abnormality. Oh, that last one won't be done because of time constraints, lack of funds and staffing issues.

What staffing issues? Does that mean I could be here indefinitely?

Funds are low. Staff turnover is high. But tests of haematological, thyroid, renal, and cardiac function will be conducted. In a patient with bipolar disorder, it may help the clinician choose—

I'm not bipolar. This is—

You asked a question. I'm answering it, Adam. Learn to play the game.

Can blood tests detect... abnormalities in the brain?

No, but they will examine your blood and compare it to individuals from a population of similar patients, in a similar age group, gender. The laws of probability, you know...

I don't want my blood samples to be compared with George or Ronnie. Why would you allow—?

This probability is also referred to as the prevalence of the condition in that population. Relax, Adam. There is a thing called false negatives and false positives. Have you heard of them?

No.

The key point to remember in clinical practice, is that false negative and false positive test results do occur. You don't need to concern yourself about it. Roll up your sleeves. Let them take samples. Afterwards, you'll have a face-to-face interview and you'll be given the first of your written tests. It's quite long. Don't rush it. It should take you an hour and a half. True or false questions. Don't overthink the answers. Just remember, sympathy, empathy, compassion.

How will I know which is the right answer?

There are no right or wrong answers. A hundred people can do the test and come up with a hundred different results. It's called the MMPI-2 test and it measures personality traits such as paranoia, hypomania, social introversion and psychopathology. It connects individual's responses to dozens of questions scattered throughout the test that are positively or negatively correlated with a particular personality trait. Because these questions aren't obviously related to the trait to which they are associated, it's difficult to fake. Remember, sympathy, empathy, compassion...

A small, smiling Filipino doctor performed the medical and filled three test tubes with blood samples. He examined Adam's mouth, took swabs and made notes. He left, and the shrink arrived.

'Good afternoon. It's Alan, isn't it?'

'Adam.'

'Oh?' The psychiatrist amended the name on his iPad. Middle-aged, grey hair, he wore glasses and a sports jacket. 'Were you involved in the fracas yesterday?' He stared at Styne.

'No.' Styne stared back.

The doctor's mobile rang. He looked at the screen before accepting the call. 'Tina?'

From the conversation, Styne assumed the caller was a patient. He listened to the psychiatrist ask questions and discuss details. He seemed to be researching new material, and the specific questions were designed to reduce his patient to the sum of her symptoms. There was a lot of head nodding. The psychiatrist nudged the caller like a lab rat being prodded through a maze. A frown suggested that the answers were contradicting his pet theories; they weren't conforming to whatever label he wanted to stamp on her.

The doctor tried another battery of questions, but his scowl remained. This test case wasn't working, his theories weren't being supported. In the end, he gave up. 'Alright. I'll write you a prescription for a new antipsychotic drug. We'll try that for a few weeks and see if there's any change.' He disconnected without saying goodbye.

There was no apology. 'Where was I... Alan?'

'Adam.'

'Yes. Adam. Adam Styne.' He stabbed at his iPad. 'Yesterday. What started it?'

Styne shrugged. 'What starts any row?'

'I suppose you saw nothing.'

Styne thought about his barrister's words.

Sympathy, empathy, compassion.

He wondered if this was some sort of test. Better assume it is, he thought. He remembered George's fake frown of concern, and replicated it, glanced squarely for a few moments at the psychiatrist's face, he maintained eye contact. 'I wish I did, doctor. But there was a huge scrabble and I was too far away. I can't believe that something like that could happen, so quickly. In truth, doctor, I can't stop thinking about it. It scared the life out of me. It could have...' Adam stopped. He didn't want to overdo it. 'I'll have nightmares forever.'

'Hmm.' The psychiatrist tapped his iPad and flicked to another screen. 'I'm obliged to explain why we're here today.' He settled into the chair. 'The purpose of a psychiatric evaluation depends on who requests it...'

Styne half-listened and wondered how Ronnie had digested this verbal overload. He tuned back in when he saw the psychiatrist adjust his body language, indicating he was near the end of the statement.

'In other words,' the psychiatrist continued, 'your safety, and the identification of signs, symptoms, or disorders that require urgent treatment will take precedence. In such instances, emphasis may be placed on obtaining information needed for immediate clinical recommendations and decisions. Do you understand?'

'Yes.'

'Good. The first part of the assessment is a face-to-face client interview.'

Allister O'Brien had talked him through this process.

Evaluations based solely on record review and interviews of persons close to the patient are inherently limited by a lack of the patient's perspective.

For what purpose?

This face-to-face interview provides the psychiatrist with a sample of the patient's interpersonal behaviour and emotional processes. It can either support or qualify diagnostic inferences and aid in prognosis and treatment planning.

I don't need treatment.

Adam, the psychiatrist can glean important information by observing the patient's general style of relating, how they minimise or exaggerate certain aspects of their history, and whether particular questions appear to evoke hesitation or signs of discomfort. Additional observations concern the patient's ability to communicate about emotional issues, the defence mechanisms the patient uses when discussing emotional topics, and the responses and reactions to the psychiatrist's comments.

'Okay,' Styne said.

'Any questions? Any concerns?' the psychiatrist asked.

'No. I'm delighted to be allowed an opportunity to give my account of events leading up to this point.' Adam maintained eye contact.

'You can begin by telling me about yourself,' the psychiatrist said. 'There's no rush. If you need toilet breaks, that's fine.'

They'll ask if you've any concerns. This is a way of making the patient feel at ease. Then they'll tell you the purpose of the interview and make sure you understand the process. After that, they'll start back at your childhood, what you did, what your parents were like, etcetera. You'll be asked lots of open questions designed to make you talk and expand your replies.

What has my growing up got to do with anything?

Because structured, systematic questioning is useful if you want to elicit information about substance use and traumatic life events. It also helps to ascertain the presence or absence of specific symptoms and signs of particular mental disorders. That's why they'll go back to the beginning.

There's nothing to tell.

You're in their territory now, Adam. Play the game according to their rules.

Will I be told how I've scored on these tests?

Not on tests. I'll get them. But during the interview, yes. Patient satisfaction is best when the psychiatrist provides feedback during the interview.

What sort of questions will I be asked?

They aren't trying to trick you, Adam. There's no hidden agenda. They're compiling important information. Obviously, you won't say anything stupid like "As a youngster I loved dissecting frogs or killing puppies," but useful clinical information is obtained by asking questions concerning your early development, culture, health, literacy, schooling, disabilities, sexual orientation, religious and spiritual beliefs, social class, and physical and social environment. All these have an influence on the client's symptoms and behaviour. Just answer what you're asked. Don't volunteer additional information. And remember, eye contact, but don't overdo it. Also, sympathy, empathy, compassion.

'Who is your family doctor?'

'I've never had one.'

'Where are your records? Your medical history?'

Adam shrugged. 'Don't have any I'm aware of.'

'Who was your parent's doctor?'

Adam didn't know, but was certain the psychiatrist wanted for a name. He searched his brain and recalled a headed sheet when he was burning his mother's belongings. 'Doctor Higgins. Tullamore.'

The psychiatrist made a note. 'And your wife. Madeline, isn't it?'

Adam paused again. The psychiatrist waited.

'Yes. But she's away. Abroad.'

'I understand. We'll catch up with her at some stage.'

'May I ask why?'

'You may. Medical records, family members, work colleagues and other important people in your life are useful sources of information. Family members, in-laws, work colleagues… these are the people who know you best and may provide important information about your personality before… well, before all this happened. It's all confidential.'

Adam knew what Madeline would say about him. What the rest of the Hattinger's and their friends revealed was a different matter.

O'Brien had told him not to worry, but this was an area of concern. Dorothy Ridgeway, for example.

That bitch could ruin me. I wonder what ideas she's whispering to Madeline. What are they concocting behind my back? How can…?

Adam mentally refocused but seethed inside. He smiled at the psychiatrist. 'Thank you for that.'

The questions continued.

'I'm not one of those doctors who believe pills solve every problem,' the psychiatrist said, 'but I know your leg is causing pain. I can prescribe some pain killers.'

'That would be great. Thanks.'

'Also, perhaps some sleeping pills? Are you having trouble sleeping?'

'Yes. Yes, I am. Thank you.'

'And maybe something to calm you down, after what you witnessed yesterday?'

'Thank you again, doctor. What do you suggest?'

Some amphetamine and dextroamphetamine salts for hyperactivity disorder, and perhaps...' the psychiatrist thought for a moment, finger poised over the iPad. 'Perhaps we'll start you on some Olanzapine as well.'

'Okay. Thank you, doctor,' Styne said. Drug pusher, he thought.

'Thank *you*. I'll check the tests tonight and write a report over the next few days. Would you like a break before the written test?'

'Can we keep going if that's okay with you,' Styne said.

The psychiatrist handed Adam a bunch of A4 sheets. Adam scanned the questions on page one, as the doctor explained the test.

True or false: I need to take risks to feel alive.

True or false: In important ways, I am superior to most people.

True or false: I rarely feel guilty.

True or false: I rarely connect emotionally with others.

True or false: I have difficulty staying committed to long-term goals.

True or false: I am a truthful person.

True or false: I like to take chances.

True or false: I care about the welfare of others.

The list went on. Thirty-five questions per sheet. Fifteen sheets. Five hundred and twenty five boxes to be ticked in an hour and a half. Ten point three seconds each, Styne calculated. He quickly spotted the ones that acted as a double check to see if he'd lied previously. The doctor tapped on his iPad and ignored Styne.

Sympathy, empathy, compassion.

Bend the truth, Styne thought and ticked another box. Create a new reality. Present a story they'll buy into and understand. What proof of a crime is there against me?

EVENING

SHARONA AND RONAN peered at the two cars sitting side by side in Adrian Fitzgerald-Gilligan's driveway.

Lights blazed from the house.

'So...' Ronan prompted.

'What do you think?' Sharona asked. 'What's the logical thing for us to do?'

'Hey, don't ask me. I usually make decisions by the eenie, meenie, miny, moe method. If I'm the voice of reason here, we're in a bad situation.'

'We could go to the cops, I suppose,' Sharona said.

'O...kay,' Ronan sounded dubious. 'And tell them what, exactly? The only thing we have is this guy's phone number, and if there's an innocent explanation, we don't want squad cars with sirens and lights coming into this small estate. Maybe he's Rebecca's uncle, and something like that could butcher his reputation, if, you know—'

'Yeah. No.'

'This could go sideways real quick,' Ronan said.

'Hmm, I know. We *could* knock on the door and ask some questions,' Sharona added. I mean, what's the harm in asking questions, right?'

'Right. You're a reporter.'

Sharona nodded. 'I am. And we *did* get a text from Rebecca asking for help.'

'Who do we work for?' Ronan asked.

'Err, The Limerick... Leader?'

'Sounds good,' Ronan said.

'Okay, then. Let's do it.' Sharona took a notebook and pen from her bag, got out, marched to the front door and rang the bell. Someone switched on a hall light, opened the door and stood silhouetted in the doorway. 'Yes?'

'Adrian Fitzgerald-Gilligan?' Sharona asked.

'Yes?'

'We'd like to ask you some questions with regards your activities around Limerick city last night, at approximately nine, nine-thirty p.m.'

Adrian Fitzgerald-Gilligan froze. 'Who—?'

'Limerick Leader,' Sharona said.

'We're working on a special investigation,' Ronan added, matching Sharona's sharp tone.

'Who are you?' Fitzgerald-Gilligan asked.

'He's my photographer,' Sharona said.

On cue, Ronan used his mobile to snap a photo of Adrian Fitzgerald-Gilligan.

'This is an official investigation,' Sharona opened her notebook. 'What exactly *was* your business—?'

'Who's that, darling?' A female voice floated through the hallway.

Adrian Fitzgerald-Gilligan shrunk. 'I've no idea what you're talking about. Now, if you'd please leave—'

'Last night?' Sharona raised her voice. 'Nine? Nine-thirty?'

'Shhh,' Fitzgerald-Gilligan said. 'Listen…' he glanced backwards, then turned to Sharona and Ronan.

'Darling? Close the door. It's freezing.' The voice was closer now, in the hall.

Adrian Fitzgerald-Gilligan's face paled in the hall light glow. He put a finger to his lips. 'I'll tell you if—'

'Oh, hello.' A woman joined Adrian Fitzgerald-Gilligan. A head taller than the man, she wore a loose-fitting dress that bulged over her pregnant belly. She smiled at the visitors.

'People from the council,' Adrian Fitzgerald-Gilligan looked at Sharona and Ronan. 'About the, um—'

'Playground.' Sharona's eyes burned into Fitzgerald-Gilligan's face.

The man pointed out at the estate. 'Yeah. The playground.'

'Now?' The woman seemed surprised. 'With a foot of snow on the ground?'

'Well, funds have to be allocated in advance, or else…' Sharona gave a what-can-you-do shrug. 'Even when research is complete, it'll still take six months for new equipment to be installed. When are you due?' Sharona asked the woman, but kept her eyes on Adrian Fitzgerald-Gilligan's face.

'Six weeks. Can't wait, can we, darling?'

'You go in and stay warm, dear,' Adrian Fitzgerald-Gilligan said. 'I won't be long.' He stepped out, closed the door behind him. 'What do you want?'

'The address you visited last night,' Sharona said, 'and what can you tell us about Rebecca Greenfield, the woman who was with you.'

'I've no idea what her name was. Listen, it's not what you think. I—'

'I don't think anything, sir. Your private life is not my concern. For now. The address please.'

Adrian Fitzgerald-Gilligan slumped against a wall and told them. Sharona wrote it down.

'Describe the girls,' Sharona said.

The man struggled to remember any physical details.

When Sharona had mined all the information she could think of, she closed the notebook. 'If we require further information, we'll be in touch,' she said. 'I'd advise you not to phone or enter that premises again. It's under observation and Gardaí could charge you with obstructing an ongoing criminal investigation. Understood?'

'Yes. Yes.' Adrian Fitzgerald-Gilligan clasped his hands in prayer and beseeched Sharona and Ronan. 'Please, don't contact me here. My wife… she, she's—'

Sharona nodded. 'Pregnant. I know.'

'Yes, but,' Fitzgerald-Gilligan lowered his voice, 'she wouldn't understand. I've had the worst week of my life, and last night was… a release. I've never, I mean, I'm not the usual type who goes out looking for—'

'What type do you mean?' Sharona asked. 'Do you have a perception that all johns are—'

'I hate that word johns,' Fitzgerald-Gilligan said.

'Do you have a perception that all *johns* are dirty old men in raincoats?' Sharona asked. 'They aren't. They're from all walks of life: black, white, thin, fat, young, old… Maybe they're all having a crap week, or involved in a bad relationship, or going through a rough patch in their marriage. Or maybe they just want the thrill of been able to do whatever they want with anonymous women because it gives them power?'

'That's not true,' Adrian Fitzgerald-Gilligan said. 'Well, maybe in some cases, but not in mine.' He checked the front door was closed and came forward a step. 'Last night was positive for my marriage.'

'Really?' Sharona couldn't let that go. 'So, paying for another woman is acceptable, while your wife is ready to go into labour? Hmm. Interesting.' She stared the man down and he looked away.

'You've no idea,' Fitzgerald-Gilligan make a track in the slush with his shoe. 'She… she makes me feel like a pervert for asking. I'm not hurting anyone. If I have sex with another bird, so what? That's it. It's over. Never to be thought of again. But she,' he pointed towards the house, 'doesn't believe a man can have sex and walk away. Actually, we can. Which would *you* prefer, huh? Your boyfriend going off with a girl who's doing it for nothing because she likes him, or he goes to a prostitute, pays for it, no emotions, and he never sees her again? Huh?' He looked to Ronan for support. 'You're playing with fire if you fall for another woman. It's something I've never done. The secret is never to go back to the same woman twice. That way, everybody wins.'

'Sir, I don't need your justification, but if you think prostitution is a victimless crime and that every woman enters the profession willingly, you need a history lesson.' Stony-faced, Sharona put the notebook into a pocket. 'We'll do our best to be discreet, but I can't guarantee anything.' She wasn't in the mood for clemency. 'We'll check your statement against other accounts. If we find you've lied, all bets are off. Good evening. Oh, congratulations on the imminent birth of your child.'

'WHAT A PRICK,' Sharona said when they were driving away from Monaleen Heights. 'Suburbia holds some dirty secrets. Criminalise johns, I say. That'll put a stop to guys preying on women for sex.'

'Or drive it further underground,' Ronan said. 'Good job he was so rattled he didn't ask to see ID. Photographer, eh?'

'Something else to add to your long list of talents, Ron. You were great. Convinced me.'

'Thanks. You were great too. Glad we didn't have to ask about the text message. He thinks we're watching the premises. Getting the information this way was best.'

'Hmm. Now what?' Sharona looked at Ronan. 'Any ideas?'

Ronan shrugged. 'We must have enough to tell real cops what we've found, and—'

'And how long will it take them to act?' Sharona asked. 'Paperwork, get a team organised, questions. Rebecca needs to know we're on the case, *now*.'

'We could call 999 and say there's a fire on the premises,' Ronan suggested. 'The firemen would have to clear the place and—'

'Sounds good in theory,' Sharona said, 'but the bodyguards Gilligan spoke about? There's no way they'll let the girls mingle and answer questions. They've been *trafficked*.'

'Hmm.' Ronan steered around a bend and approached the roundabout that led back to the main road.

Sharona flicked a glance at Ronan. 'I suppose we could... no, that'll never work. *How* can we let Rebecca know that we're working on getting her free? I wonder if...' A large sign loomed in the headlights. Motorway and Dublin to the left. Limerick city to the right. Sharona looked at Ronan, waiting, but Ronan wasn't taking the bait. Sharona plunged ahead. 'You'll have to go into that house and talk to her. Give her a phone so she can keep in contact with us, and—'

'What? Who? Me?'

'Well, *I* can't go in,' Sharona reasoned.

'Aww, Jeez.' They stopped at a traffic light and Ronan knuckled his eyes. 'Don't go down that road with me, or we'll be enemies for life, Sharona.'

'Just pretend you're a john, I mean, customer,' Sharona patted Ronan's leg. 'That way, you'll have an opportunity to talk to her. Alone. Imagine how she's feeling? Imagine if it was me or your sister in there, and—'

'Aww, Jeez,' Ronan said again. The lights changed.

Left for Dublin. Right for Limerick City.

The driver in the car behind blew the horn. Ronan swung right and took the exit for Limerick.

Sharona smiled and relaxed.

'This was always the plan, wasn't it,' Ronan said.

'Maybe. But that's all part of my charm. Don't you agree?' Sharona arched an eyebrow.'

'I agree, but if there's ever gonna be a replay of this, delete my number now.'

'This is a one and done.' Sharona pinched Ronan's earlobe. 'Imagine all the brownie points you've collected today.'

'Huh. We need to find a phone shop.'

'I'll Google it.' Sharona reached for her mobile.

'You'd better describe her, so I'll know who to look for,' Ronan said

'No problem,' Sharona said, scrolling.

Another thought struck Ronan. 'Um, how much will I have to, you know, *pay*, to, like, *see* Rebecca?'

Sharona looked at him. 'God, I've no idea. I'll Google that too…'

7 P.M.

'THAT'S A NICE LADY.' Kathleen Fallon looked at her face in the mirror. 'What's her name?'

'Kathleen,' Hugh said.

'That's my name too.'

'It is, Mum.' He'd always assumed his mother retirement would involve community and charitable work, coupled with going to cities she wanted to explore. This slide into a disease devouring her brain, cell by cell, was difficult to accept.

Kathleen walked over to Hugh and stretched out her hand. Hugh shook it. 'So good of you to call,' she said. 'Nice to see you again. You should be getting home now.'

'I am at home, Mum. We're here together.'

Having missed several hours work earlier, Hugh wanted time to explore ideas he had for McGuire's, but with Kathleen, that was impossible. Hourly, he was finding out things about himself that he didn't like. He'd thought the love he had for his mother was infinite, but Alzheimer's was making it millimetres thick. Add resentment, helplessness, guilt and irritability to the mix, and he was forgetting the person his mother was before this disease took over. To watch an adult become a child, was unnatural and unnerving. Alzheimer's contaminated everything in its path.

When he took on this caregiver role, he'd no idea what was in store. It was borne out of obligation, love, duty, and doing the best he could for his mother. He'd read up on the disease, knew about the behaviours associated with it; the hostility, anger and violence, but he assumed a lot of that was due to external factors; people weren't given the care they needed. By home caring Kathleen, exposed to a familiar environment, he assumed he'd be able to supply quality time and cushion his mother's descent. This was misguided, and after today, he knew something had to change. That something was him. *I have to change,* Hugh thought.

Kathleen sat beside him and silence settled around them for the first time in two hours. She made a bandage out of a newspaper and wrapped it around a doll's leg. Hugh sent Ruth another text. She hadn't replied to any all day.

'I want to go home,' Kathleen said.

'Okay, Mum. When would you like to go?'

'Now.'

'It's too late now. Everyone's asleep. We'll go tomorrow. After breakfast.'

'Okay. Do you dance?'

'Badly,' Hugh said.

The doorbell rang. Hugh answered it and stared at Ferdia, framed in the doorway. 'What the—?'

'Not staying,' Ferdia stepped inside and closed the door. 'I've a friend bringing me to Dublin. Howaya, Kathleen.'

'Ferdia! How wonderful of you to call.' Kathleen trotted down the hallway towards the big man, arms outstretched.

'Jesus, she sees me every day and doesn't know me,' Hugh groused. 'You call once in a blue moon and—'

'You look younger every time I see you, Kathleen,' Ferdia said.

'Oh, stop, Ferdia.' Kathleen patted her hair. 'I look terrible.'

'Nonsense. I've been hanging around boxing rings for thirty years.' Ferdia enveloped Kathleen in a hug. 'I know a knockout when I see one.'

'You look lovely, Ferdia.'

'Clean living, Kathleen. It's all down to clean living.'

'Will *you* dance with me?'

'Pleasure.' Ferdia slow-waltzed with Kathleen.

'You're crazy,' Hugh said. 'Why aren't you in hospital?'

'Had to go to Niamh's funeral,' Ferdia said. 'They bandaged up my ribs. I'm grand. Might as well hang around Dublin as sit in a hospital.'

'Except you'll go after Dolan again, and this time I won't be there to rescue you.'

Ferdia twirled Kathleen. 'Even if I wanted to, there's nothing I can do about Dolan. He's away until the weekend. I might plan a welcome home committee for him, though. Besides, I need to collect your car.' Ferdia eased Kathleen onto the settee. 'I've got a new phone. Same number, so keep in touch. Let me know what's happening.' Ferdia tossed Hugh's house keys at him. 'Thanks for that.'

'Anytime,' Hugh said. 'Where are you staying?'

'Don't know yet. Any word on Malcolm?'

'No.'

'How are things at McGuire's?'

Could do with spending more time there.' Hugh pointed his eyes at his mother.

'Delegate,' Ferdia said.

'I'm doing that. I—'

'See? You've learned from the best. Delegation doesn't mean abdication, Hugh. You don't *hafta* be there when you've got a good team. They'll keep an eye on the overall show. Slán.'

'Make sure the location thingy is turned on,' Hugh said.

Ferdia kissed Kathleen's cheek and promised he'd see her soon.

Hugh gave Kathleen her tablets and got her ready for bed. Later, he texted Ruth again, wished her goodnight and that he'd try calling her tomorrow.

His mobile jangled Ruth's reply.

k. thx. bi.

8 P.M.

THERE WAS NO neon sign or flashing light to indicate a brothel was in operation.

Sharona squeezed Ronan's arm. 'Good luck, babe. Thanks for doing this. You know it's important.'

Ronan rang the bell, and the door opened a fraction. One eye peered out.

'Erm,' Ronan said.

'Been here before,' a voice asked.

'Um, no. No.'

'We're fully booked,' the man said.

'I'm passing through,' Ronan explained. 'You were recommended, for, um, you know…'

'Who recommended us?'

'Erm, John,' Ronan said.

The eye appraised him for twenty seconds, then undid the chain and opened the door. 'Sixty-five. Cash. Fifteen minutes. Pay upfront.'

'Sixty-fi—?'

The man shrugged. 'Don't like to pay? Is no problem. Not negotiable. Goodbye.'

'No. I'll pay, dude.' Ronan handed the man three twenties and a ten.

'No change,' the man said. 'You want tablet?'

'Huh?'

'Tablet. Make you big and strong. Help satisfy the lady.'

'Argh, no. I'm good.'

'Okay. Only the best and cleanest girls here.' The man pocketed the money. 'Follow me.' He walked down the hallway, stood in a doorway, folded his arms and gestured for Ronan to go in.

Four girls were crowded into a small room, standing beside a dingy sofa. Ronan spotted Rebecca and wondered if he should pick her straight away, or pretend to be undecided. What did punters normally do? 'Um,' he said, rubbed his chin and studied the panoply of flesh. One woman chewed gum and watched him, a faint smile playing on her lips. The other three smiled too, but he knew from the downward glances that these were people who didn't want to be here.

The man shifted in the doorway.

Ronan took a stick of chewing gum from a packet and folded it into his mouth. 'Her.' He pointed to Rebecca.

Rebecca peeled away from the line-up and walked down the corridor to her room. Ronan tried to hide his face when he saw the red light blinking from a monitor attached to the ceiling, but knew his image had been captured. The bodyguard's footsteps were right behind them.

Rebecca walked into a bedroom. Ronan followed.

'Fifteen minutes,' the man said, and bolted the door.

Rebecca stood in the middle of the bedroom, waiting for instructions.

'Rebecca? Sharona sent me,' Ronan whispered. Apart from the bed, the room was bare, and cold as a decompression chamber.

It took a second to register, and Rebecca's face transformed from despair to hope. 'Sharona? She got the text?'

'Yeah. Hi. I'm Ronan. She wants you to know we're gonna get you outta here.'

'This is a set-up. I know this is a set-up to see how I'll react.' Rebecca's eyes narrowed with suspicion.

'No, no. Listen. I remember you. I was in Whispers the night Sharona gave you her number,' Ronan said. 'We can ring her now, if you want. I read your text message. You didn't get a chance to finish the—'

'Okay.' Rebecca grabbed his arm. 'When? I can't take any more—'

'A day, two days, tops,' Ronan whispered. 'Here. I got you a phone. My number and Sharona's is programmed in. We'll text you—'

Rebecca shook her head. 'No way. There's no way. I'll get caught. Everything is watched. Everything is searched twice, three times a day. It's impossible to hide—'

'It's tiny,' Ronan showed her. 'Look. It'll fit into the toe of your shoe—'

'Not a chance,' Rebecca said. 'You've no idea—'

'Shit,' Ronan looked around, frustrated. 'Can you tell me how the gang operates?'

Rebecca shrugged. 'Leader's Ukrainian. Bodyguards all seem to be Eastern European. I've no names. They don't allow us to get close to them. Never talk business in front of us. And if they *do* talk, it's in their language. They control us like sheep in a pen. We're money machines for them. On-call, twenty-four seven. No breaks. No choices. Refuse to work, you're beaten. A young girl got shot dead right in front of me. If I don't do what they say, they'll get my sister and—'

'That's not gonna happen,' Ronan said.

'How do, how can…? You've…' Rebecca lowered her voice. 'You've no *idea* what these people are capable of. Even when I'm not… working, it's impossible to rest. I'm afraid to sleep. I wonder what tomorrow will bring, or the day after. Is the next guy gonna kill me?'

'Um,' Ronan swallowed, unable to think of a reply. 'I promise you'll be out soon. Everything will look brighter once you're—'

'Anyone that pays for us, only wants to hurt, humiliate and degrade,' Rebecca whispered, eyes wide with fear. 'Every hour of every day is an endless… sameness. I'm ruined. Physically and mentally. Even if you smuggled me out now, I don't see anything different to look forward to. Tomorrow, Next week. Next month… it's all the same big black blob. I'm existing. That's all I'll ever be able to do. This constant pain… My head hurts. My heart aches. My body, my brain… The agony can't be separated. It's so unfair. I was going about my life. Making plans, hurting no one, and this happens. Girls come and go. I've no idea where they disappear to.'

'The gang will soon be behind bars,' Ronan muttered. 'Then you'll be able—'

'Some prisons don't have bars.' Tears streamed down Rebecca's cheeks. 'I wouldn't have thought it possible, but it's scary how quick I've adapted to what's considered normal in here. I still can't say the word brothel.' She shook her head. 'Sometimes I think in here is protecting me from having to deal with everything out there. At least, the abuse we know is better than the future we don't know.'

A knock on the door. 'Two minutes.'

Rebecca slid out of her thin as tissue dress. She ruffled Ronan's hair, undid two buttons and pulled his shirt loose from his waistband. 'Have to make it look like, you know.' Rebecca crumbled up the bedsheet and lay on it.

'Yeah. Listen.' Ronan's voice was low and urgent. 'Expect us anytime. Keep the faith. Stay strong for a few more days.' He dug into a pocket, pulled out a small object, no bigger than a hearing aid battery and showed it to Rebecca.

'Time's up,' a voice said from the corridor.

Ronan took the chewing gum from his mouth, wadded it into a ball, stuck the battery into it, grabbed one of Rebecca's shoes and pushed it into the point between the heel and the outer sole. 'It's a transmitter,' he whispered. 'Even if they move you, I can keep track of—'

Another knock. Louder this time.

'Go, go,' Rebecca said.

'See you soon,' Ronan dropped the shoe. Before he'd taken a step, he heard the bolt slide back. The door opened and the bodyguard stared at him. Ronan waited in the doorway as a girl stumbled past in the corridor, followed by another minder. Rebecca frowned. She'd seen that girl before… someplace.

'Thanks,' Ronan said and followed the pair up the corridor.

The bodyguard looked at Rebecca. 'Wash. Get ready and come to living room. A special client wants you. Wear something nice.'

JAW SET, RONAN navigated turns and roundabouts and followed signs for the motorway.

In the yellow street lights, Sharona saw a gel of tears trickle down his cheek. When they got on the motorway, Ronan took a deep breath. 'Well, that was a fun thing I won't be doing again.'

'How's Rebecca? What happened?' Sharona caught Ronan's hand and held it.

'She's getting raped. Repeatedly,' Ronan said, staring at the road. 'I think she's already experiencing some form of Stockholm syndrome. Not surprised with the abuse, which is being enforced by a culture of fear and brutal violence. A girl was killed in front of her. It'll take years of therapy to... *Years*. How the *fuck* can this happen? Huh? In this day and age? God*dammit*.' Ronan pounded the steering wheel. 'How can this be allowed to happen?'

8.30 P.M.

NIGHTMARES CHASED Malcolm McGuire all day.

The headache felt like a woodpecker was drilling through his skull. The drugs had dissolved but his brain was fuzzy from the chemical haze. He could sense clouds gathering again, just over the horizon of his consciousness.

What day is it, he wondered. Dad'll disown me. The jangle of his mobile stopped the reverie and brought him crashing back to reality.

'The boys'll be around to collect the money in an hour,' Dessie Dolan said.

'There's a money issue,' Malcolm staggered to the window. A rigid-body truck drove past displaying the logo of a national bookie along with betting odds on tonight's greyhound races.

'What issue?'

Malcolm turned back into the room. 'I don't have it.'

'Oh? Thought you were gonna do the devil an' all in Jurys Inn, Mal. A man told me he spotted you splittin' tens at some stage. Ya must've heard the sayin' "never split ten's".'

'I ran into a straight, Dessie.'

'You ran into a fookin' wall,' Dolan said.

'It... I got crippled by two big pots.'

'Mal, Mal. How come it's always someone else's fault? Why don't you blame technology, huh? Any gobdaw with a phone can download an app an' throw a few euro on a horse or a fiver on the first goal scorer in a soccer match. Sure it's all a bit of craic isn't it? 'Til it isn't.'

'I'm not blaming—'

'Or why don't ya blame the bookies for your bad luck, huh? It's their fault that they send out texts an' shit, pushing deals. Hey, yesterday this horse was twelve to eleven, but just for the next six hours, he's, wait, a bleedin' bargain at three to one. It's all their fault, isn't it, Mal?'

'I'm not saying—'

'Gone are the days, Mal, when a man useta call into a bookies once a year an' have a bet on the Grand National. Now, he decides to try his luck on a phone, loses, and starts chasing losses. But it's the bookies fault. Amirigh' or wha?'

'Yeah, Dessie. It's just that—'

'You've seen the ads, Mal: When the fun stops, stop. But not you. Oh no. You won't admit you've a problem, so what can anyone do to help ya. Huh? Poor Mal's drained his bank account again 'cos he's chasin' cash. Way too easy to bet now, and adverts are designed to push punters into things they shouldn't do. Next, you'll sue *me* for givin' ya money, an' I amn't even in the country. You lost, an' I'm the bollix, wha?'

'I'd never do that, Dessie. And I *will* deal with it,' Malcolm said. 'Tomorrow. No, not tomorrow. In a few days. When things get back on an even keel.'

'I'm not waitin' 'til next week, Mal. We had a deal. Cough up.'

'Dessie.' Malcolm was desperate. 'Just give me a few days. A week, max.'

Dolan snorted. 'You're havin' a laugh, Mal.'

'Just this once, Dessie. Please.'

'Mal,' Dolan sighed, 'I'm in business to make money, not throw it down the drain. I'd be ran outta town if people heard I've given you more leeway.'

'This is the only way you'll get paid, Dessie. I've... I'm out of friends.'

'You've got twelve hours, Mal. Sell the beemer, or I'll sell it for ya.'

'I can't. How'll I get around—?'

'Use the bleedin' bus. Twelve hours.'

'There must be another way, Dessie.' Malcolm voice shook. 'I've always paid you back.'

'Not the last time you didn't.'

'I will. I swear, I will. I need a break. Dessie? Hello? Dessie?'

'I'm thinkin'.'

Malcolm waited.

'Tell you wha', Mal. You can do me a favour.'

'Oh? What's the favour?'

'That doesn't sound too eager, Mal, for someone with a big debt. Fergeddit.'

'No, no, it's… this signal. Tell me the favour. I'll deliver.'

'There's a package I need to collect in Berlin airport tomorrow. Fly over, pick it up an' fly back. All expenses paid. I'll write off the debt an' give you two grand for your troubles.'

'What's the package? Who's it for?'

'See? There ya go again, Mal. Look, if ya wanna keep bitin' the hand that feeds ya—'

'No, I'm not. Honest. Gimme the details. I'll do it.'

'Good. I'll get one of the taxis to call for ya tomorrow 'round half-twelve. The driver'll give ya two boardin' passes. You hop on the plane. My solicitor will meet ya in the departure lounge, hand you a briefcase, an' you turn around an' fly home. The taxi man'll pick you up, give you two grand for your troubles an' bring you back to your pad. You'll be home in time for the nine o'clock news.'

'How big is the briefcase?' Malcolm asked.

'Small. Important papers I need.'

'Okay.' Malcolm was already thinking of ways to spend the two thousand.

'This gives you breathin' space, Mal,' Dolan said. 'Don't mess up. Be ready at half-twelve tomorrow. Don't forget your passport.'

DOLAN DISCONNECTED AND dialled another number from memory. 'Whassup? Huh? Wha? How dafu—' Dolan paced the hotel bedroom. 'Whaddaya mean he got away? He can't have… An' where's Decaf now? God almighty. Bleedin' Decaf. He'd one bleedin' job… When word gets out, we'll be laughed outta the city. Yeah, yeah, I know you did, but we go way back. We grew up together, an' all.'

Dolan listened for a minute. Then: 'You're righ'. We need to make an example outta 'im. Causin' too much grief, but fuck it, he's... Yeah, I know he'll prob'ly kill himself soon, anyway, but... We're doin' him a favour, righ'?' Dolan listened some more. 'Huh. Make it quick, though; a double dose of full fat Mexican black tar. Have it done before I get home. I don't want people thinkin' I'd anythin' to do wit' it. In other news, I've cut ties wit' the golden goose. Before we finish up, though, he's doin' me a favour tomorrow. Guess wha'? Yeah, Berlin.' Dolan gave a short bark. 'Can ya sort the details, an'...? Huh. Righ'. I'll see you Saturday.'

Dolan disconnected, pulled the back cover from the phone and inserted a new SIM card. He flicked through TV channels, thinking things through, and then went clubbing.

9 P.M.

EYE DROPS MADE Rebecca's eyes sparkle.

She used a finger pad to apply a dot of concealer underneath them to hide the tiredness, then added mousse to her hair, smudged on some mascara and dusted powder on her cheeks. A sweep of lipstick each side of her cupids bow and another stroke for her lower lip. A week ago, that would have taken me an hour, Rebecca thought. She shoved everything back into her clutch bag, and on her way to the door, sprayed a mist of cheap perfume, and stepped through it. She could tolerate whatever was next, knowing help was on the way.

In the living room, Rebecca and the new girl stared at each other. 'I've seen you before,' Rebecca said, 'but I don't know where.'

'I kinda recognise you too.' The girl moved and the flimsy negligee flashed open to expose a crystal tattoo on her midriff.

Rebecca snapped her fingers. 'Whispers. You were picked...' she pointed at the tattoo. 'I remember—'

'Yeah, I remember now,' the girl said. 'I thought it was gonna be the start of something, and next night I got kidnapped. Seems like a lifetime ago.'

'No way.' Rebecca stepped closer. 'That's what happened me. Some drug debt my ex-boyfriend—'

The girl stared at her. 'That's what I was told too...'

'Whispers,' they said, simultaneously.

'The modelling gig,' the girl said. 'A scam to—'

The front door slammed and Rebecca moved away.

Zita and the bodyguard came in. Zita was angry and punctuated her petulance by kicking the couch. 'That was a waste of makeup,' she said.

'What happened?' Rebecca asked.

Zita kicked off her shoes, threw her purse on the couch, went to the kitchenette, washed her hands and filled a glass of water. 'Nothing. I caught a newbie. Five minute hook-up. He wouldn't come in here in case someone saw him. He exploded the minute I touched him. Big, awkward guy. Built like a ship, but with a small rudder. Shortest booking in history.'

The new girl, pale now, asked to go to the bathroom. The minder grunted and followed her down the corridor.

'Long as you're okay.' Rebecca checked they were alone and edged closer to Zita.

'Pfft. Impossible to understand men.' Zita sipped water. 'Men without rings, needy. Men with rings, horny. Tell some of them that you're being forced to do this, it gets them excited. Tell others you're afraid, and that turns *them* on. If we come across as weak, they don't like it. Come across as bolshie and they see it as their right to try and tame us.' Zita shrugged. 'Hunters and their trophies.'

'And like all hunters, deep down they want to kill us,' Rebecca said. 'They would if they knew they'd get away with it.'

'Least I've someplace warm to come back to.' Zita took her vape pen from a pocket. 'Better than getting out of a car and being stuck on the stroll, half-frozen, waiting for the next one. Bad hook-ups on the street are an easy way to get killed.' Zita exhaled and studied Rebecca through the vapour. 'Yours was a newbie too, wasn't he?'

'That last guy? Yeah. Listen,' Rebecca glanced around again and murmured, 'he's going to rescue me.'

Zita laughed. 'If I had a euro every time I heard that, I'd be living the life of—'

'It's not like that.' Rebecca rushed her words. 'I used a john's phone to call a friend for help.'

Zita stared. 'What friend?'

'That's beside the point,' Rebecca said. 'All that matters is, a plan's in place to get me out of here. I don't know when exactly, but be ready. You're coming with me. We *have* to get out of here before he kills us.'

'Okay.' Zita whispered back. 'Keep this between ourselves. If we tell everyone else, they'll be, how you say, they'll act different.

Nervous, excited. Bodyguards will pick up the vibes. Once we're free, the first thing we do is give police directions so they can rescue the other girls.'

Footsteps sounded in the hallway.

Zita caressed Rebecca's arm. 'Thank you for telling me.' She moved away as the bodyguard came in. 'I gotta pee, too,' Zita said.

Rebecca sat on the sofa. The new girl joined her. Rebecca could see a dozen questions on her face, but she shook her head. The bodyguard ignored them. Rebecca thought about Whispers. The modelling gig. A scam to recruit new sex workers. She wondered how many young missing people ended up like her. Every week people disappeared. Was this part of the reason why? Zita returned with the old Asian woman. She bypassed the sofa, sat on one of the chairs, used a toe to push a small circular table away and crossed her long legs. For once she'd nothing to say. The old Asian woman pottered about in the kitchen. The only sound was the rumble of the tumble dryer. The front door opened. Maybe this is the special client, Rebecca thought.

The Ukrainian stood in the doorway. His glance fell on everyone before it landed on Zita. 'What's so urgent?' he asked her.

'Baby bear is working with a john to escape.' Zita pointed at Rebecca. 'Police could be here anytime.'

Rebecca could feel the Ukrainian's eyes bore into her skull. She stared at Zita. Zita adjusted her position, re-crossed her legs and smiled at Rebecca. The Ukrainian rubbed a three-day growth of black beard, pushed away from the door and pointed at the new girl. 'Go to your room and pack.' He turned to the old Asian woman. 'We move out in twenty minutes.' He nodded to the bodyguard. 'You and Rusty. Dismantle security and sweep this place clean.' The Ukrainian walked into the room and stood behind Rebecca. Inside she cringed, but she sat straight and stared at Zita, numbed by the woman's treachery.

'You think you're different, baby bear,' the Ukrainian said. Rebecca heard the lighter flick a second before the whiff of tobacco smoke. 'You think any man would be lucky to have you because you're different, huh? The truth is, you're the same as everyone else here. Clients say you're ordinary. They say you cold as fish in frozen river. They say you have attitude. No smile. No eye contact. No spirit. Clients come here for a treat. You cheat them after they pay for service. I have to give refunds. You get paid to do what client wants, not what you want. They pay, you play. But since you came here, nobody said to me, "I want to be with that woman again. I can't live without her." Nobody.'

'I *knew* she was trouble the minute I saw her,' Zita said. 'I *told* you. Jezus, it's either screaming self-pity or sulky silence. Sell her to the Russians. They'll teach her how to be a whore.' Zita used her finger to comb her tangled hair. 'Remember that last girl? The Russians cut her gums with a dirty blade. The infections... every tooth is like a sore tooth. It's what they do. No cuts or bruises to turn off clients. Yes, sell her to the Russians. They love dealing in pain.'

'You'll never work out,' the Ukrainian told Rebecca. 'Because you don't stand out. She is a goddess. Look at Zita. Clients pay double to be with her.'

Zita grinned.

'Men will play you like a toy for a while,' the Ukrainian said. 'And then they'll dump you. Why? Because you're a bore, baby bear. A filler, until another comes along. At Christmas, you're a turkey. At Easter, you're a lamb. That's your role. Pump and dump. A back-up plan. Now, what am I going to do with you? Huh?'

'Sell her to—'

'Shut up, Zita.' The Ukrainian leaned his elbows across the back of the settee and shared his phone screen with Rebecca. The moving images caught her attention, and she turned away from Zita. Her sister, videoed as she got off the school bus and walked to her parents' bar. Rebecca bit her lip.

'For your punishment, Rusty will pick up your sister tomorrow, baby bear,' the Ukrainian said. 'Clients like girls in school uniforms. After that? Who knows? If she's good, I'll keep her for a while. But, I've got a frien' in Abu Dhabi. Verrie rich man.' The Ukrainian tapped the phone screen. 'He likes young girls. I know he'll pay me, hmmm, a hundred thousand, plus flights. He'll keep her for a week, maybe two, depends how much he likes her. Then he'll sell her to one of his sheikh buddies for a hundred gran'. See? It's cost him nothing. But, then, the fun's over, and your sister's work begins. She'll end up someplace outside Islamabad, servicing tribesman for six months, before getting sold to a pimp in India for one hundred and fifty gran'. Now, this Indian has a choice. He can force your sister to spend the next three years looking after twenty men a day, seven days a week, until she's so diseased even clients that roam the back alleys of Bangalore won't touch her. Or, he can sell her straight away for organ donation. Her liver, kidneys, lungs and heart will be, how you say, removed and sold.' The Ukrainian lit another cigarette. 'He will decide which is the most profitable. Everyone must make money along the line, baby bear. Oh, sometimes, girl gets lucky. My frien', Mr Sheik, might keep your sister for his harem, and she'll end up in a tent in the desert, surrounded by a thousand miles of camel shit. Or, maybe she's like you and thinks she can escape. But, where will she go? No money. No passport. Can't speak the language. No way back. No way out. And your family can't collect her, because they won't know *where the fuck* she is. And it's all your fault.' The Ukrainian grabbed Rebecca's shoulders and shook her. 'You're lucky I've promised you to a special client tonight. Otherwise, I'd cut your throat.'

Two bodyguards appeared and the Ukrainian spoke to them. He leaned down again to Rebecca. 'We'll talk later. For the next few hours, all you have to do is shut up and look stupid.'

'She's good at that,' Zita said.

The Ukrainian clapped his hands. 'Go.'

Rebecca stood. 'The stories you told me,' she said to Zita. 'Your sister? All lies?'

Zita smiled. 'I'm a good actress, yes?'

'I *trusted* you,' Rebecca said. 'How could you?'

'I'm good at being bad. First day we met, I told you there are no friends in here. It's everyone for themselves.'

'Yeah. I never thought about betrayal,' Rebecca said.

The Ukrainian grabbed a clutch bag, tossed it at Rebecca, and pushed her towards the door.

'Yes, yes.' Zita laughed and clung onto the Ukrainian's arm. 'Eventually, we're all betrayed by those we trust. Except me. *This* is my boyfrien'. Any man that messes with me, he'll cut his throat.' Zita kissed the Ukrainian's cheek. 'See? I'm his eyes and ears when he's not here. He needs me as manager. He knows that only a woman can deal with a roomful of women. Every whorehouse needs a strong madam to keep everyone in place.'

'If he needs you that much, why'd he rape me?' Rebecca asked. 'Maybe you're not a goddess after all.'

Zita's grin faded. Her eyes flashed, and she hissed at the Ukrainian. He answered, shrugged and shook his head.

'You lie,' Zita spat at Rebecca. 'Lies, li—'

'Shove it up your ass, Zita,' Rebecca said and walked out, sandwiched between the two bodyguards. Shoulders back, head high, the dark night swallowed any last remnant of hope

10 P.M.

FERDIA SPENT THE day driving around Dublin, alternating between the docks and Stephen's Green.

Decaf was easy to find: he never ventured further than a few blocks from the shed in Dublin docklands. Most of the time he loitered around the petrol station, either begging or looking to score drugs. Ferdia wanted another way in through Dolan's armour, but Decaf wasn't high enough up the chain. He'd hoped Tiny would supply the key. That didn't look to be the case, as Tiny was a no show. Going back to Whispers was out of the question. He'd keep looking for an opportunity.

Ferdia swung left at the dental hospital. Two girls, still in school uniforms exited a casino near Tara Street station. He drove across the Liffey and turned right for 3Arena and the docks. Much as he wanted intelligence on Dessie Dolan, he didn't want to beat it out of a drug addict, but with no Tiny, Decaf was his only chance.

Ferdia turned into the petrol station area and saw Decaf wander between rows of big rigs just off the ferry, begging the drivers for a handout. He looked like he hadn't eaten for days. A security guard moved him away from hassling people at the petrol pumps, so he went back to the trucks. The truckers ignored him.

A taxi drove in. The driver guided the car around the parking area perimeter and repeated the process twice. When Tiny shuffled into view, headlights flashed, and the taxi slotted into a free space. Ferdia peered at the two men who got out. He recognised Fu Manchu from Whispers. They're gonna kill Decaf for letting me go, Ferdia thought, and eased out of the car. He crouched and hobbled between vehicles. He wouldn't be able to fight, but he'd raise a commotion, and the truckers would respond. He edged around a rigid body lorry, took out his phone, ready to press 999, and then slipped it back into his pocket.

The two men were chatting with Decaf like old friends. They smoked cigarettes and clapped Decaf on the back. Then, cigarette butts got flicked away. They skidded and sparked along the icy ground as Fu Manchu pulled a bundle from his pocket, peeled off some notes, handed them to Decaf, and got back into the taxi. He was still holding his ribs, Ferdia noticed. The second man said something and laughed. Decaf laughed with him; two friends having a chat. The man gave Decaf's back a final slap, and Ferdia almost missed the small packet handover. Decaf palmed it and walked away, tracksuit bottoms dragging in slush. The bouncer got into the taxi, and it drove out. Ferdia watched Decaf walk towards the shed.

Ferdia returned to his car, started the engine and turned up the heat. That scene makes no sense, he thought. After the grief he caused the gang, why treat Decaf like he's the prodigal son? I'm missing something here. And why give him money *and* drugs? Why not give him the money to buy his own gear? *Has* to be a reason. His mobile rang. Ferdia looked at the caller name and pressed the accept button. 'Howaya, Father,' he said. 'Still spreading love the Ganestown way?'

'Still trying, Ferdia. Haven't seen you around for a few days.'

'No. I'm sorting out a few things.'

'You've not gone to live in the shadows, have you, Ferdia?'

'Not at all, Father,' Ferdia lied. He watched Decaf disappear. 'I've things to do before I get back to ordinary living.'

'So... that catastrophe we spoke about has been diverted, Ferdia?'

'Postponed, Father.'

'You're dealing with dangerous people, Ferdia. It's easy to get submerged into their mentality.'

'Argh, it's nothing like that, Father. I've got a handle—'

'How long will it take, Ferdia?'

'Not long. A few days. Maybe a week at most. You'll hear reports.'

'Keep me informed, Ferdia. Ring me every night. None of this "I'm grand" text nonsense. I want to hear your voice. Every night. Okay?'

Ferdia sighed. 'Sure, Father.' He disconnected, turned off the car engine, got out and followed Decaf.

The deep, bass, mournful sound of a foghorn echoed from the port. There was no taxi, no sign of life at the shed. Ferdia climbed the metal stairs, stopped every few seconds to listen. Nothing stirred. He could see the dim filament lightbulb cast its weak glow and a bubbling groan made him climb the last few steps fast. He peered through the doorway, stepped through, ducked under the girder and walked across to Decaf who was lying beside the pile of junk. Ferdia pressed the torch app on his phone and let the light play around.

Rodent eyes glittered a few meters away, and Ferdia threw a piece of rubble at it. Decaf's drug paraphernalia, spoon, lighter and water bottle lay strewn around him. A clear plastic bag was empty at his foot. The thick elastic band he'd used as a tourniquet to make the vein pop, was tight on his arm. The needle, still stuck in a vein, the syringe empty. Ferdia knelt and studied Decaf's face. His eyes were closed, his nose bleeding, and there was foam on his lips. His breathing was shallow, and his fingers had a blue-black tint. He patted Decaf's cheek. 'Decaf? You gotta wake up.'

No response.

Ferdia dialled 999 and went over to the window for a better signal. He looked across at Clontarf's lights while the operator patched him through to the ambulance service. He answered the quick-fire questions, gave the exact location and tried to rouse Decaf again.

Decaf's eyes opened. The corner of his mouth lifted, and he attempted to smile. 'Willya lookit tha'?' He slurred and coughed up a bubble of blood. 'The fookin' vampire's back.' He swallowed, started to choke. Ferdia rolled him onto his side and removed the needle.

'Backstabbin' bastard,' Decaf said. His previous dilated eyes were now pinpricks. 'Should've known when they said t'was a gift from Dessie to keep me going. Knew the second I plugged into the needle that it wasn't right.' He coughed again. 'Am I gonna die, bud? Am I running outta road?'

'Doesn't look good, Decaf,' Ferdia said. 'This isn't Lourdes. There'll be no miracles here.'

'Bleedin' Dessie. Jus' as I was gettin' straight. The amount of shit, I've shovelled for that fella, an' he gives bleedin' clampers more respect than he gives me. He's forgot that he comes from the shallows like me. No place for us in the heights. Got more money than a bank, an' he still can't buy class. I'm gonna die, aren't I?'

'Doesn't look good, Decaf,' Ferdia said again. 'Where does he hang out in Foxrock?'

Decaf grinned, his few remaining teeth coated in blood. 'I'm sayin' nuthin', bud. Snitches get stitches 'round here. Anyways, t'wouldn't do ya any good. You rarely see him. He's in an' out like a sniper.'

'Okay.' Ferdia straightened and heard rats scrabble away. 'See you on the other side, Decaf.'

'Listen,' Decaf tugged Ferdia's trouser leg and coughed, his breathing weaker now. 'Will ya tell me Ma, that I'm dead?'

'I'll try,' Ferdia said. 'What's your name?'

'Coffey,' Decaf said. 'Me auld fella calls me Paddy. Me Ma calls me Patrick. Everyone else calls me Decaf.' A cramp twisted Decaf's abdomen, and he curled up, groaning in pain.

'Does Dessie owe you money?' Ferdia asked. He could hear an ambulance wail in the distance. 'If he does, I'll get it for your mother.'

'Fergeddit, bud. He keeps money like a bleedin' prisoner. More chance of gettin' shite from a rockin' horse.' Decaf looked at Ferdia. 'He's sneaky as a snake, but he's got friends in high places, bud.' He coughed up more blood. 'That makes him bulletproof, 'til he's no longer needed. I keep tellin' him, but he won't listen. Went from small-time to movin' serious weight too quick, an' it's still not enough for him. Then he got involved with those European fellas. Them lads can chew six-inch nails an' spit out thumbtacks. It's them that uses the nightclub as a hunting ground for fresh meat.'

Ferdia knelt down. 'Whispers?'

Decaf was fading fast. 'Yeah. An' now lookit me? Dyin' in the dirt.'

The ambulance siren scream got closer. Seconds away. 'Has your Ma enough money to give you a decent burial?' Ferdia asked. 'The least you deserve.'

Flashing lights cast a blue halo on the shed. 'Nah,' Decaf said. 'Me auld fella takes whatever she gets an' drinks it.'

'Tell me where Dessie keeps the money, and I'll guarantee you Mrs Coffey will give her son the best burial ever.'

Decaf spat blood. 'That'd have the neighbours talkin,' bud.'

'Let them,' Ferdia said. The ambulance crew were on the stairs. 'You deserve it.'

'There's money in my pocket. Give her that, an'…' Decaf tried to swallow and gagged. 'Yeah, fookit, Dessie owes me. Big time.'

Ferdia found the money and Decaf's ramble got more incoherent. In the time it took the ambulance crew to navigate equipment and stretcher up four flights, Ferdia learned a lot. Not everything, but enough.

The paramedics got to work. One picked up the syringe, sniffed the plastic bag and murmured to his colleague. The second man administered an antidote used to reverse the effects of opioid drugs. After a discussion, they placed an oxygen mask on Decaf's face and decided not to put up a drip until they got to the ambulance. They strapped him onto the gurney and began the tricky process of moving downstairs. Ferdia carried some of their equipment and walked ahead, his phone torch app lighting the steps.

'Will he survive?' Ferdia asked when the ambulance doors closed.

'He injected uncut high-grade heroin,' a paramedic said. 'If we took it, we'd be dead. He's built up an immunity. Could survive, but who knows?'

'Where're you taking him?'

'James's.'

'I've a car across the way,' Ferdia pointed. 'I'll follow you.'

Ferdia turned the heater on, searched his pockets for cigarettes, forgetting he'd given them up a week earlier. His fingers found Decaf's money; a hundred euro in tens. He tried to fold the notes and couldn't because they kept sticking to his fingers. He turned on the interior light, looked closer, and got the whiff of peanut butter. 'Feck,' he muttered. 'Feckin' peanut butter. Rats crave peanut butter. Bastards wanted to make sure.'

10:30 P.M.

THE TWO MINDERS didn't speak.

From the back seat, Rebecca watched the M7 motorway signs. Ballinahinch, Southill, Carrigatogher. She tried to stay alert, but a combination of the blanket of snow that made everything look similar, and the hypnotic effect of kilometres of identical motorway, made her drowsy. They drove past the Nenagh exit. Rebecca closed her eyes and wondered again who this special client was. In one way she was thankful because, without this diversion, unpleasant as it may be, she would surely be dead. Zita's betrayal meant her time was limited. But she had to find a way to warn her sister.

A sign for the Barack Obama Plaza loomed out of the dark. The taxi slowed, and the driver took the ramp, turned left at a roundabout, and the next right. In the pitch-black night, surrounded by white, Rebecca lost her sense of direction. Another right turn. This bumpy road cut through woodland, and then they were back in the open again. A left turn. Through the rear window, Rebecca could see the lights of the Barack Obama Plaza. We haven't travelled far from the motorway, she thought. Maybe a few kilometres. The taxi was crawling now. The driver's companion pointed at a high, cut stone wall on the left. The car stopped, reversed, and went through the gateway. Alert now, Rebecca watched. There were fields on either side.

A few hundred meters on, they drove under an enormous bridge, an underpass built on the motorway. The lane got steeper, the driver changed gear and gunned the engine to keep traction. At the top of the hill, the laneway ended at the edge of a two-story house. A car was parked at the front. The taxi driver drove into the yard, around the back of the house and stopped when the car's nose was within a metre of the back door. No automatic sensors flared, but an outside light over the door got switched on. The back door opened a fraction, but no one appeared. The driver turned off the engine, opened his seatbelt, reclined his seat, settled back and closed his eyes. The other man got out, went to the door and stuck his head inside.

11:15 Rebecca read on the car dashboard. The bodyguard stepped away from the house, counted a wad of notes he placed in his pocket, then opened the taxi door and gestured for Rebecca to get out. Gripping her clutch bag, she stepped out and could hear motorway traffic trundle over the bridge. The minder pushed Rebecca inside the house, followed, and closed the door. Rebecca looked around. They were standing in a beautiful, modern kitchen. The bodyguard took a magazine from an inside jacket pocket and pointed it at a doorway.

'Upstairs,' he said. 'Three hours.' He sat into an armchair and thumbed through the magazine.

Three hours?

Rebecca went through the doorway and walked up a double-width, mahogany stairs. Half-a-dozen black and white framed paintings of people from a bygone era hung from a wall. At the top of the stairs, there were several doors off the landing, all closed, except one with a light shining into the hallway. Rebecca tapped on that door. 'Hello?' she said.

'Come in,' a high-pitched male voice answered.

Rebecca went in. The room was enormous. A free-standing wardrobe and a fireplace with a real fire. It glowed and sparked and threw out a heat haze. A drinks cabinet showed an array of bottles. Two full-length mirrors on adjoining walls gave occupants a simultaneous back and front view of themselves. High ceiling, elaborate cornices, a large antique dressing table and chaise longue, two armchairs and a king-sized bed. And there was still lots of space.

'What's your name,' the man asked.

'Rebecca.'

'That's a nice name.' The man was tall, thin, white-haired and beyond middle-age. He wore a striped shirt, umber coloured trousers and burgundy shoes. His walk was effeminate, dainty and precise. If Rebecca met him on the street, she'd have assumed he was gay. He stretched out a small hand and she shook it. He pulled away quickly.

'Drink?' he asked. He closed the door, turned a key in the lock, and walked back across the room.

'Err, okay,' Rebecca said. This is weird, she thought. She followed him to the drinks cabinet, and the man opened the glass door with a flourish. 'You choose,' he said.

Rebecca pointed to a large bottle of white wine.

The man looked at the label. 'Good choice. Why don't you tidy up after your journey, and I'll pour.' He pointed to a door that Rebecca hadn't noticed.

'Oh, thanks.'

Rebecca locked the en suite door and sat on the toilet. It's a trick, she thought, looking around. No window, but it was the size of an average bedroom. Floor to ceiling dark brown polished marble. Each tile had a seashell embedded in it. Double shower, double wash hand basins, and heated towel rails. She wondered how long she could stay there to use up some of the three hours. After handing over a fortune in euros, he wouldn't leave her many minutes. How many seconds in three hours? Nine hundred by twelve. She couldn't do the math. And anyway, what's the rush? I'll be dead tomorrow. How much time has passed? Rebecca walked over to the wash hand basins, looked at herself in the mirror and rummaged through her clutch bag. Stopped. Removed items. This wasn't hers. Similar, but not hers. The usual accessories were there; lipstick, a small compact mirror, comb, rouge, eye shadow and a half-empty bottle of Visine eye drops. Rebecca pulled out a small aerosol can and read the label: Mace. Self-defence spray. This is Zita's, Rebecca thought. The Ukrainian threw me the wrong purse. Her mind churned, and she upended the rest of the contents into the sink. A few condoms, an unopened packet of chewing gum, and a small plastic bag with white powder.

Rebecca got to work. Thirty seconds to apply thick black liner and a stroke of mascara on her lashes to emphasise her eyes. A pencil rub on her brows and a dab of red lipstick enlarged her mouth. She crammed everything back into the purse, leaving the Mace last. It made her feel empowered and more in control as she walked back into the bedroom. The man was using a poker to prod the fire. He added more timber, straightened, handed Rebecca her wine glass and topped up his own. The bottle was already three-quarters empty. Rebecca wondered where to sit, or if she should wait. Emboldened with the Mace, she sat in one of the armchairs, kept a firm grip of the purse, sipped her wine and looked at the man over the glass rim. The white hair was a bit mussed, and his eyes glittered. He was getting pissed. He took another gulp of wine. 'Are you ready to be saved, Rebecca?'

'Pardon?'

'Are you ready to be saved? If you open your heart to the Lord, there's nothing He won't do for you.' The man thumbed a sign of the cross on his forehead, his lips and his heart. Then he kissed the thumb. 'Do you realise God is watching you?' He poured the remainder of the wine into his glass. 'The Bible says in Hebrews 9:27 that "it's appointed for every man once to die, and then judgment." That means everyone dies and is judged before Almighty God. So, as you stand before God on Judgment Day, will he send you to heaven or hell? Have you been a good person, Rebecca? Huh? Have you? There is only one principle by which we can all be judged, and that's God's Law, also known as the Ten Commandments.

Is this what the Ukrainian meant when he said, "shut up and look stupid?" Rebecca wondered. Well, if he wants to rant for three hours, that's fine. Better than being groped.

The man opened another bottle of wine and filled his glass. 'Once, I was a sinner like you,' he said. 'I used to visit service providers and am familiar with the emotional pain that some of you are in and are trying to fill with sex.'

Rebecca blinked but said nothing.

'I'm also aware,' the man continued, 'of your financial reasons for doing this, and I'm conscious of the dangers that you put yourself into every time you see someone. I want to save you, Rebecca. Jesus Christ rescued me from a life of sin and depravity and I want to share the Gospel with you. Our God is a God of love and forgiveness. He'd never send anyone to Hell…'

Rebecca nodded, sipped wine and tuned out. The heat from the fire was making her drowsy again. She hoped she wouldn't fall asleep. That could freak him out. How many seconds are gone, she wondered. If she blasted Mace at him now, how would she get by the bodyguards? Maybe an opportunity would come, but the time wasn't right. Yet.

'… And you're right. No one can live up to the standards set by the Ten Commandments. Man isn't perfect. We were born into sin. Have a sinful nature. God is so holy and so flawless that his standard is unattainable to mortal men.' The man took another gulp of wine, left the glass on the mantelpiece and staggered to the en-suite.

Rebecca rooted through the purse once the door closed. She'd heard that the ingestion of eye drops caused cramps and diarrhoea. Maybe it wasn't true, but… She bounded across to the fireplace and added half the remaining contents of Zita's Visine eye drops to the wine glass. Rebecca put the eye drop bottle back into the purse, and her fingers touched the plastic bag. She took it out and looked at the white powder. Had no idea what it was. A toilet flushed. Should she? Could she? What if? She ripped open the packet and tipped the contents into the wine. It fizzed like an effervescent tablet and Rebecca added more alcohol. She heard a tap run, then it turned off, and she was back in her chair when the man reappeared. He made a beeline for his drink and continued from where he'd left off. 'What does God need from us?' he asked Rebecca.

'Repent,' Rebecca said.

The man drank. Rebecca kept one hand in her purse, ready. 'Yes, exactly,' he said. 'Repent and trust in the Lord with all our hearts. That's from Romans 10:9. When we do that, Jesus washes away our sins, and we can stand before God, blemish free on Judgment Day.' Another gulp of wine. 'He doesn't want to send you to Hell. He loves you. You've heard John 3:16 "God so loved the world, he gave his only begotten Son, that whosoever believes in Him, will not perish but have eternal life."

'Amen,' Rebecca said.

'Prostitution is a terrible chasm you've fallen into, Rebecca. Jesus has no mercy for women who make a living from pleasure.' The man topped up his glass again, face flushed. His movements got jerky and agitated. ' "The harlot's pathways leads straight to hell. Down to the chambers of death." That's Proverbs 7. And Revelations tell us "all fornicators shall have their part in the lake of fire." Repent or go to hell, Rebecca.'

Rebecca nodded.

'Stop that,' the man's shout took Rebecca by surprise. 'You're a whore, and you're a bad woman for tempting me.' He jumped onto Rebecca's lap and sucked her ear like a limpet. Caught underneath him, trapped in the chair, Rebecca couldn't move, but it felt like she was being attacked by a ravenous beast. She hoped whatever drugs she gave him brought on a heart attack. He puffed, panted and grunted, sweating with exertion and started to tear her clothes. Rebecca got hold of the Mace and squirted it straight into his face. The man screamed in agony. Blinded, he leapt up, tripped over a rug, and bounced his head off the fireplace. The scream turned to a moan and the air turned fetid as he soiled himself. The Visine's working, Rebecca thought. She listened for footsteps on the stairs. Nothing. The bodyguard probably thinks it's all part of the fun, she reasoned. Adrenaline pumping now, brain working overtime, she pulled the man onto the bed and started a search. A jacket in the wardrobe produced the phone.

'Great.' Rebecca glanced at the bed. Stomach cramps had forced the man to curl into a ball. She swiped the screen and it looked for a passcode.

'Shit.'

Rebecca put the phone back, hunted again and found a wallet fat with money. 'Keys. There's a car outside. His keys must be here.'

They were. In an overcoat pocket.

She took the coat from its hanger, pushed the wallet into the pocket beside the keys, draped it over one of the armchairs, and left her purse and Mace on top.

One chance, Rebecca thought. Please, God, give me one chance. She picked up the poker, slashed it through the air and lost her grip. The poker bounced off a wall and landed on the carpet with a dull whump. She tried again, wondered how hard she'd have to hit the minder to knock him out. Gripping the poker tight, she bashed a cushion. Whacked it again. Harder this time. And again. Satisfied, she looked at the man on the bed, moaning in agony.

Now or never.

Rebecca slipped the right dress shoulder strap down her arm and pulled the flimsy garment down to expose her breast. She ran to the door, pounded on it. 'Help, help.' Then she twisted the key, opened the door and shouted again. 'Help, help.'

The minder ran upstairs, two steps at a time.

'I think he's having a heart attack,' Rebecca gulped and pointed into the room. 'We were on the bed and he started… moaning and panting.'

The minder charged past, into the bedroom.

Rebecca slipped the dress strap back on her shoulder and followed.

'Is… is he going to die?' she asked.

'Resuscitation,' the minder said. He bent over the preacher man, started to turn him onto his back, and with the back of his head exposed, Rebecca blasted him with the poker. Technically illegal, but by more good luck than good management, the blow landed behind the bodyguard's ear, one of the most effective targets in a street fight. The strike disrupted the cochlea and vestibular system, wrecked the minder's balance and equilibrium. The brain shut down, defending itself from the attack, and rendered the man unconscious before he slumped across the preacher on the bed. Rebecca swung again, this time striking the bodyguard's neck, and damaged the vagus nerve. In a fight, either blow would deliver a knockout. Coming together, they guaranteed the minder would sleep for hours.

The stench was overpowering. The preacher had soiled himself again. For good measure, Rebecca sprayed both their faces with Mace, shrugged into the overcoat, which was way too big, grabbed her clutch bag and stuffed it into a coat pocket. She held onto the Mace can, ran from the room, locked the door behind her and stuffed the key deep into a large flower pot filled with compost. 'I can act too, Zita,' Rebecca muttered and tiptoed downstairs.

In the hallway, she peered into the kitchen. The magazine was on the chair where the bodyguard had left it. She walked along the hall, around a right-hand curve to the front door.

Five minutes, Lord. Just give me five more minutes.

She took out the car keys, opened the hall door, slipped out and closed it quietly behind her. She let her eyes adjust and looked down the hill to the vehicles trundle over the bridge. The preacher's car was three metres in front of her. Scuttling clouds caused sporadic patches of moonlight to shine on the car. Its frame glistened with frost. Like most men, he'd performed a three-point-turn, so the car was ready to go.

Rebecca pressed the fob and ducked behind the car when the alarm chirruped. Hazard lights flashed twice. She watched the house corner, waiting for the second minder to appear.

Nothing.

She looked down the hill again. If I can move the car twenty metres, she thought, gravity will take over and it'll freewheel at least down to the bridge. At *least*. Maybe even further. Every metre was a bonus.

Rebecca opened the car door and tensed with the interior light came on.

Jesus, why are you doing this to me?

She got in and closed the car door. Trapped and vulnerable if someone came, she kept her thumb on the press-down Mace can button, squinted through the windscreen and said, 'aww, *shit*.' The windscreen was covered in a glaze of frost and ice. 'Shit. It'll take the heater at least five minutes to thaw that out.' Rebecca considered her options and looked at the control panel. She didn't own a car but was used to driving tractors on the farm at home, and her father's Toyota. This car was bigger. Way bigger. With more dials. She peered closer. The starter was a button. Okay. Lights. Wiper. Heater. She turned them on and off. Checked the gearstick. Manual. Good. She pulled the seat forward and touched the pedals. Everything was ready, except she couldn't see out.

I'll run, she thought. Take my chances in the open space. But how far will I get in high heels and a bulky overcoat? 'Think, Rebecca,' she said. 'Think. Is there another way? There *is* no other way. Do it. Just do it. Do it. Do it.'

She pushed the start button, pressed the switch on the door that opened the drivers' electric window, eased the car into gear, and stuck her head out the window. Then, aiming for the lights on the overpass, Rebecca released the clutch.

Twenty metres. Give me twenty metres, Lord, without being seen or heard.

The tyres, crunching over fresh snow and ice, sounded like a hail of gunfire, but she was moving. An alarm dinged, and a seat belt sign flashed. Rebecca ignored it. After twenty metres she put the gearstick in neutral and let the car freewheel. Her eyes stung from the cold and the car was going faster now. Too fast. She touched the brake to slow down and measured the distance to the bridge. A kilometre, maybe less. She had to get that far. Then she'd have a view back up the hill to see if the taxi followed her. She had a head start.

'A head start and Mace. That's all I need.'

The bridge loomed ahead. The car passed under it and then slowed, slowed, slowed.

Rebecca braked and turned on the windscreen heater full blast. A digital clock lit up from the console. 00:35

No way, she thought. All that inside an hour and a half.

She got out, shivered in the cold, walked back to the underpass and looked up the hill. No lights. No car chased her. Traffic rumbling overhead was a comfort; it meant other humans were nearby, going about their lives. Soon, she'd be in the Barack Obama Plaza. Dublin was an hour away. Elated, Rebecca went back to the car. The frost and ice on the windscreen had turned to mush. The wipers cleared it off, and she fastened the seat belt. In minutes she was driving back through the forest, the plaza lights ahead. She came to a T-junction. Was it right or left? She thought it was left.

'Stop second guessing yourself, Rebecca,' she muttered. 'Just do it.' She swung left.

There was another turn near here... wasn't there? I'm sure we... Yes. Left again.

The Plaza lights were within touching distance. Coffee, Rebecca thought. Decent coffee and food. Anything except pizza. I'll never eat pizza again. The thought of coffee made her mouth water. She speeded up. The exit ramp was just ahead. 'Doughnuts,' she murmured. 'My kingdom for three chocolate doughnuts.'

A fox streaked across the road. Rebecca jammed the brakes and skidded. She tried to control the skid, tore at the steering wheel too hard, and spun. The airbags deployed, setting off a chemical charge that produced an explosion of nitrogen gas, a microsecond before she got showered with talcum powder. The car mounted an earth embankment, slithered along the surface, and then toppled nose-first into a fast-flowing water table, swollen from weeks of runoff from ice and snow. Rebecca's temple cracked against the side panel and she blacked out.

7

FRIDAY 25TH JANUARY. 1.15 A.M.

'MUM? MUM! What are you doing up again?'

'Get away from me.' Kathleen shook Hugh's hand off her shoulder. 'I don't want you here. I can take care of myself.'

This was something new, getting up in the middle of the night and putting on a fire. Tired and irritable, Hugh wanted to yank her away from the hearth that she'd piled fuel on and set ablaze. If one of those logs fell out... He pressed his cheek to hers. 'I'm here,' he said, 'and we're going to take care of each other.' Hugh led Kathleen over to the couch. They sat in silence and watched the flames dance. He closed his eyes. Even when she's supposed to be asleep, I can't rest, Hugh thought. This caring sucks the oxygen from any optimism. I'll have to think about locking her bedroom door.

'Who's your mother?'

'Huh?'

'Who's your mother?' Kathleen asked again.

'You are, Mum.'

'No, I'm not. I never had a boy.'

'Okay, Mum.' Hugh swore silently. I've no idea what I'm doing, he thought. My old fashioned notion of obligation and love and duty isn't working.

'Can I eat this?'

Hugh opened his eyes and took the flower stem from Kathleen. 'Not that, Mum. It might make you sick. Would you like a snack?'

'I'd love one,' Kathleen said.

'I'll find you something nice.' Hugh dragged himself from the couch. 'Memory loss isn't the worst thing about Alzheimer's,' he muttered, opening presses in the kitchen. 'The worst is losing learned skills, ability to walk, talk, to go to the shop. It's about not putting an electric kettle on an electric cooker ring. It's about—'

'Hugh?' Kathleen had followed him into the kitchen.

'Yes, Mum?'

'You know I love you, don't you?'

'I know, Mum. I love you too.'

These moments of lucidity are seductive, Hugh thought, because they make me believe Alzheimer's is a phase, and we'll get through it. Nothing is further from the truth.

2.10 A.M.

THE SHRILL GRANDE Valse Nokia ringtone pulled Sharona Waters from a deep sleep.

Eyes closed, she stretched out an arm, groped around the bedside locker, found the phone and hit the connect button. 'If this is you, Ronan, you're dead.'

'Sharona? It's Rebecca.'

Sharona bolted from the bed and switched on a bedside lamp.

'Where are you?' She squashed the mobile between her shoulder and jaw and started dressing. Rebecca's voice gabbled in her ear, hyperventilating. 'I'm in the Barak Obama Plaza, near Nenagh. I escaped, but I crashed a car. One of the workers here gave me her phone to make a call. You're the first one I thought of.'

'I'm an hour away.' Sharona grabbed a coat and ran downstairs. 'I'm leaving now.' She snatched her keys from the hall table. A staccato of illegible words, laced with hysteria, rattled from the phone speaker like bursts from a Gatling gun.

'Say that again, Rebecca? I lost you.'

'I'm gonna lock myself in the toilets.'

Sharona nosed her car out of Mountain View estate. 'Stay on the phone. I'm—'

'I have to give it back to the girl—'

'Okay.' Sharona steered off Ganestown loop road, veered left onto the N62, and pressed the accelerator. 'Don't move. I'm an hour away.'

'I'll be in the toilets,' Rebecca said.

'I'll find you. Stay put...'

JUST BEFORE 3 A.M. Sharona rolled her car into a space in the Obama car park and ran through the entrance door of the Plaza, glanced around for the toilet directions and headed down a long corridor. She pushed open the toilet door and called, 'Rebecca? Rebecca? It's me, Sharona. Are you here? Rebecca?'

A bolt clicked on a cubicle door and Rebecca peeped out. 'Oh, Jesus,' she said, opened the door wider and stepped towards Sharona. 'It's so good to see you. Thanks for—'

Sharona enveloped Rebecca in a tight embrace. 'God, girl. Ronan told me about that... prison in Limerick. You're one amazing lady to find a way out of that.'

'When it's life or death...' Rebecca said. 'And it literally was. Besides, I had this.' She lifted an arm and showed Sharona the Mace can welded to her hand. 'A girl's best friend in a bad situation.'

'I hope you used it and blinded them for life,' Sharona said. 'That coat is wringing wet. Here, let me swap you.' She peeled off her coat, gave it to Rebecca, and linked her arm. 'Let's get outta here.'

In the car, Rebecca told Sharona about braking to avoid a fox and skidding into a water table. 'The crash stunned me, but the water lapping at my knees woke me up,' she said. 'I managed to loosen the safety belt and, lucky enough, I'd the presence of mind to grab the purse, climb into the back seat and get out that way. It wasn't far to the plaza, but, God, it took me ages in these heels. There was no traffic on that back road, but as I got nearer the plaza, I had to hide every time I saw headlights. Any car could have been them searching for me.' Rebecca shivered and Sharona turned the heat up to maximum.' You're safe now,' she said. Thank God you remembered my number.'

'I've recited it so often, I'll remember it forever,' Rebecca said.

'What do you want to do now?' Sharona asked. 'Go to the Gardaí?'

'Not yet,' Rebecca said. 'I've been thinking about it, but I'm not ready to... I can't let them get away, but I need time to think. That modelling competition? In Whispers? It's a scam. I only figured it out a few hours ago when I met saw another girl who won the competition same night as me. First thing cops will think is: what was she doing alone in Whispers? Thinking she won a bloody high paying modelling competition?'

'No, they won't—'

'Yes, they will. I'm a reasonably intelligent woman who does stupid things on a semi-regular basis. They mightn't say it, but they'll think it. Same as they do with every girl who goes into a bar alone, dressed in a tight mini, or has a few drinks to many and walks home alone… I've watched enough soaps and TV courtroom dramas to know that behaviour is seen as compliant.'

'I think—'

'And the waiting room, the forms, the endless questions. Swabs, tests, exams… Ugh. Not tonight, Sharona. I couldn't handle all that now.'

'Okay. Whatever you decide, I'm here for you,' Sharona said.

'Thanks. And thanks for coming out in the middle of the night. I'd no one else to turn to. I couldn't phone Dad. Wouldn't know what to say to him. My mind…'

'I understand.' Sharona saw a motorway sign for Tullamore. 'Do you think we should go into Tullamore hospital just to get you checked out? Physically? Make sure you've got no, err… STD? You might need antibiotics.'

Rebecca thought about that and nodded. 'Yeah. I could say I'd a one-night stand and—'

'Yeah.' Sharona took the Tullamore exit.

'Least I'm not pregnant,' Rebecca said. 'An old housekeeper gave us some contraceptive concoction she made up herself. Tasted like something she dragged from the bottom of a dirty river.'

'What?' Sharona looked across at Rebecca. Rebecca thought about what she'd said and started to giggle. Sharona joined in. In seconds, the two women were in peals of laughter.

'Seemed like a good idea at the time,' Rebecca said, and they both cracked up again.

'Shit, I needed that.' Rebecca used the coat sleeve to wipe tears from her eyes. 'All I've seen for the last five days are leery, creepy, needy, hostile, angry men, looking for any excuse to get violent. They're the masters, in control, and they'll make the woman pay for whatever perceived snub their wives or girlfriends or bosses or co-workers has dealt them. While they're here, by God, they'll conquer, even if it means taking something that hadn't been consented. See, that's the thing about rape,' Rebecca said. 'It's about power. Power and control. They know I can't refuse. I learned within six hours not to show any emotion, cos any response just gives them a bigger rush. I told every single john… See? I speak the lingo already. I told every single john I'd been kidnapped, that I didn't want to do this. No one, *not one*, listened or cared. Every hour I made it through alive was a bonus.'

Sharona stopped at traffic lights beside Tullamore hospital. 'You ready?'

Rebecca nodded. 'Yeah. I need to get checked out. After, will you help me come up with a story to tell my parents and sister?'

'Sure.'

'And I'll need to use your phone.'

'No problem.' Sharona pulled into the hospital car park. 'Come on. Let's do this.'

9 A.M.

HUGH WAVED HIS four managers into McGuire's conference room.

They pulled out chairs and Hugh stopped them. 'Let's stand,' he said. 'This won't take long. No point getting comfortable.'

They looked at each other.

'But things have improved,' Maeve said. 'We're all—'

Hugh nodded at the woman who'd questioned him at the meeting. 'So I see,' he said. She still showed leadership qualities.

'We've got great ideas from the suggestion box. And Liam,' Maeve nodded at her colleague, 'had the thought to ask customers to add their ideas as well. There's been an amazing response to—'

'And the video ideas are being uploaded onto Facebook,' Liz added.

Liz was the other female he'd picked.

Hugh looked at Liam. 'Well done for thinking about asking for customer opinion. Should've thought of that myself. Everything we're doing is right, but what is the main thing this business needs right now?'

'More customers,' Maeve said.

Hugh snapped his fingers. 'Exactly. Anything else?'

They studied him, looking for clues.

Hugh put them out of their misery. 'Focus,' he said. 'It's not the customer's job to remember to do business with us. It's our task to remind them. We need one-hundred per cent focus on netting shoppers. Each of you will have to change your work structures. Trying to do what you've always done, plus the extra work I'm giving you, can't keep you efficient, so, delegate most of your regular daily work. For the next sixty days, farm out everything that doesn't directly involve your focus to get and keep customers. I spotted some of the videos on Facebook,' Hugh said. 'They're great. Who's co-ordinated them?'

'I did,' Maeve said.

'I did,' Liam said.

'I did,' Liz said.

'I—' Tim started.

Hugh laughed when he saw the collective muse hit. 'One person, one focus,' he said. 'It's not always about being busy, is about being effective. Decide among yourselves who manages the video demonstrations, the newsletter content creator, and the suggestion box. I also think a podcast could be an interesting idea to explore. Ask some of our suppliers to talk and demonstrate products here in the shop. Three-minute how-to videos. Any of you good at that?'

'I deejay at weekends,' Tim said. 'I have equipment—'

'Okay,' Hugh said. 'Try it, upload them onto social media. Let's see what happens. How to… prepare a wall before painting. How to, I don't know, reseal a shower tray. How to re-grout tiles. How to remove moss from lawns. There must be a thousand everyday practical demonstrations we can do to help customers and sell them a product for the job.'

'Leaky taps,' Liz said.

'Putting up wallpaper,' Liam added. 'Nightmare if you don't know the tricks.'

'How to remove oil from tarmac,' Tim chipped in.

'See?' Hugh said. 'How to… cut a curve in a tile without smashing it. Write down ideas, but funnel them to Tim. Tim is the how-to guy. This is different to the demonstration videos that are being uploaded at present. Can you arrange between you who does that?'

Everyone nodded.

'We'll be called on to make difficult decisions,' Hugh said, 'but if we work together as a team to find creative solutions, we've got a chance to turn this business around. Now, unless anyone has anything to add or ask, the meeting's over.'

When the managers left, Hugh checked his phone. No text from Ruth. He debated sending her another message and decided it would be over the top.

The mobile buzzed in his hand. Ronan.

'Dude, have you seen Sharona? Has she phoned you?'

'No. Why?'

'Aww, man. I bet she's gone back to Limerick—'

'Whoa, Ronan. What happened in Limerick?'

Ronan explained. Then, 'I worked on your website most of the night and we'd arranged to meet at her place for breakfast. I'm here. She's gone. Her car's gone—'

'She's driven into town to get food,' Hugh said. 'Chill. She'll be back in—'

'Fridge was full last night, dude. I *know* she's gone.'

'Nonsense,' Hugh said. 'She'd have phoned you if… And if she *did* go back to Limerick, what'll she do? But the fact that she's not there is a bit strange—'

'She's concerned about Rebecca.'

'I'm in McGuire's,' Hugh said. 'I'll be there in five minutes.'

Hugh left immediately. Sharona was his best friend's sister. James Waters and himself has hung around together throughout their teenage years, and used to let James's young sister, Sharona, tag along to some concerts with them. Hugh saw her and treated her as the sister he never had.

RONAN MET HIM at Sharona's house.

His facial expression answered Hugh's unspoken question. 'We gotta go to Limerick, dude.'

'Did she leave a note?'

'Why would she leave a note? She could pick up the phone and call me, but she knew I'd talk her out of it, so she's gone on her own.'

'But what'll she do when she gets there? Did you phone her?' Hugh speed dialled her number.

'Yeah. It's switched off, dude.'

'Still off. Got a key?'

'No.'

'I know where she keeps a spare,' Hugh ran around the back. He found the key, opened the hall door, pushed into the hallway, and looked around. 'Sharona?' He opened the sitting room and kitchen doors and looked inside. 'Let's check upstairs,' he said. 'What about her other phone? The new one with—'

'Jesus, dude. I'd forgotten that.' Ronan stabbed a button on his mobile. 'It's ringing,' he said. Together, they stood on the landing and waited for Sharona to answer. 'Come on,' Ronan muttered.

Hugh frowned, walked across the landing and put his ear to a bedroom door and opened the door. They peered into the bedroom,

Ronan still holding the mobile to his ear, stared at the bedside locker and watched Sharona's new phone vibrate and shimmy across the wooden surface.

'Shit,' Ronan disconnected. 'Dude, we've gotta do something, like, proactive.'

'Okay.' Hugh was focused now. 'Do you have the address in Limerick? Can you—?'

The front door slammed.

'Hugh?' Sharona called. 'Ron?'

Hugh and Ronan almost got entangled on the stairs.

'Jesus, Shar…' Ronan stopped. 'Rebecca?'

'You've met Ron,' Sharona linked Rebecca's arm. 'Say hi to Hugh Fallon. He's, like, my big brother.'

'Hi.'

'Now that's out of the way. Let's have breakfast,' Sharona said.

'WHAT'S OLANZAPINE?'

Allister O'Brien peered over his glasses rim at Adam Styne. 'Medication used for psychotic patients. Why?'

'It's been prescribed to me along with amphetamine and dextroamphetamine salts.'

'Have you taken them?'

'No.'

'Good. Flush them down a toilet. Unfortunately, some hospitals can become a pill-mill, Adam. Many patients are given drugs to keep them passive. It makes an easier life for staff. Because of last Wednesday, you're going to have two tests today. First one shortly, the second one after lunch. I don't want them to flow into next week. By the way, I've made contact with Madeline.'

'Oh?'

'She's fine.'

'What's happening to my business?'

O'Brien ignored the question. 'She refuses to visit you. Pity. It would've been good to show that the wife supports her husband, but it's not the end of the world. The good news is she told me that you never lifted a hand to her in anger.

'I wouldn't—'

'But what she *did* say, was that you're a genius at using your brain like a truncheon to slap people around with words that club, condemn and censure. She said that hurt more than physical blows, and if I could see inside her psyche, it would be black and blue. Oh. She's applied for a divorce.'

'Make sure she doesn't get her hands on my personal bank accounts,' Styne said. 'And answer my question. What's happening to my business?'

'Nothing, Adam. All closed up.'

Styne stared at the barrister, his eyes narrow slits. 'Keep me posted,' he said.

'Certainly, Adam. But your priority is to get out of here a free man. The bank accounts issue, by the way, is being handled. I've asked Madeline to write down her thoughts about what life was like with you.'

'Why don't you ask her to explain why she thinks she can run my company? She already wrote to me, remember?'

'That's different, Adam. That was a letter from a wife to a husband, telling him how pissed off she is. This will be an official document. Yes, it's a slight gamble, but I feel it's worth the risk. If a document is on file, it'll stop the state from going after her to dig up additional information. And no matter how bad things are in a family, nobody ever writes down every single detail. Things become starker when they're written in real time. Rather than deal with remembering the pain, a lot gets omitted.'

'It won't be good,' Styne said.

'I hope not.' O'Brien chuckled. 'Otherwise, who'll believe it? We're all agathokakological to various degrees. If she writes something... unsavoury, I'll find three psychiatrists to refute and contradict. It's for the best. Trust me.'

'Huh.'

'I hear you did well on your Minnesota Multiphasic Personality Inventory test. It didn't show up any emotional disorders.'

'Why would it?' Adam asked.

'Ooh, you're a little erinaceous today, Adam.'

'And you're full of big words.'

'Thank you. Now, tone down the attitude a fraction, but not too much. We don't want you to appear too confrontational. Just a few things to remember when you're having today's discussions.' O'Brien consulted his notes. 'Don't overdo the niceness. You're a hard-headed businessman. Act like one. You're indignant at being locked up, oh, and hold the eye contact for a few seconds more. And *even* if your childhood was exemplary, scatter a few grains of untruths here and there, just to keep them interested. Otherwise… well, no life is perfect.'

'What's this psychiatrist like?' Styne asked.

O'Brien consulted his notes again. 'Like everything in life, Adam, there are shrinks for the rich and shrinks for the poor. You'll be fine.'

'I won't plead insanity,' Styne said.

'It's not my intention to let you,' O'Brien answered.

'But, I thought… all this…?'

'I *hate* insanity pleas,' O'Brien said. 'With an insanity plea, you're at the mercy of psychiatrists, and you never want to be in that situation. It like relying on a Doberman; you never know when it's going to rip you apart. In the past, I've represented real dangerous people, and every time I've sent one to see a psychiatrist, the shrink turned out to be crazier than my client on his worst day. Luckily, the legal insanity business is in recession, at least in this country. Bottom line, Adam, psychiatrists know they're often not even *remotely* aware of some of their patients… um, quirks. So, regardless of tests, and without failsafe proof, they can't guarantee whether a patient committed a crime or not. However, as I've said before, one scintilla of DNA and—'

'There won't be.'

'Good. We'll work on uncontrollable impulses and temporary insanity. That equals diminished capacity with no intent to harm the victim. We can work wonders around that with a jury when the time comes, with, of course, the use of a few selective facts.'

'I see. I still can't understand how anyone could compare George to me. I mean—'

'Comparisons are odious and appearances are deceptive, Adam.' O'Brien stood and buttoned his coat. 'I recall a case where an ordinary suit and tie bank teller cut up two sixteen-year-olds with a meat cleaver. Don't try to justify anything. Don't twist words to suit your narrative. These people are professionals. Everything you say, every *twitch* gets recorded. So, more eye contact. You're a hard-headed businessman…'

'COFFEE?'

Sated, Hugh covered the mug with his hand. 'I'd better get back to work.' He looked across the table at Rebecca, still unable to comprehend what she'd physically witnessed and mentally gone through over the past week. 'What now?'

'Now, we get a few hours' rest,' Sharona answered. 'I'll phone the Gardaí and get them to take Rebecca's statement here. Then we shop. Rebecca will stay with me for a few days.'

'Should've phoned me,' Ronan shook his head.

'Why?' Sharona arched an eyebrow at him. 'It was the middle of the night. You needed sleep. And I'm not some helpless old lady. If I've to call you every time I go for an hour's drive…'

'But still,' Ronan said.

'I thought it was you phoning, and I wasn't gonna answer it.' Sharona tussled Ronan's hair. 'When I heard your voice, Rebecca, I just… took off. Sorry for not phoning you, but it took the hospital staff ages to read the X-Rays and tell us the physically Rebecca was fine, and that the bang on my head wasn't serious. Then talked to her parents and sister until the battery gave up.'

'Feel okay now?' Hugh asked.

'Sore, but I'll get over it,' Rebecca said. 'The bruises will heal, but—'

'You're alive,' Hugh said.

'Surviving.' Rebecca slipped off a high-heeled shoe and massaged her foot. 'Time will heal the wounds, but the scars will stay forever. You know the saying, "what doesn't kill you makes you stronger?" That's crap. What doesn't kill you leaves you scarred and beaten and… feeling helpless from the shame, the self-blame, the pain, the humiliation I've experienced—'

'It's not your shame,' Hugh said.

'Then why do I feel guilty? I'll *never* be the way I was. How can I face any boyfriend again? How can I tell him? We'll have a row. He'll disappear.' Rebecca blinked away tears. 'We take everything for granted until it's gone.'

Sharona patted her arm. 'Anything we can do to help you get through what you're—'

'I want the one thing I can't have; my old life back. I don't want to spend every day hiding behind layers of makeup and sunglasses.' Rebecca wiped her eyes. 'It's hopeless. Actually, hopeless is such a weak word. It feels ten times worse than that. After the last week, life seems irrelevant, unimportant. I'm a loser. I put myself into this situation. Nobody wants a loser.'

'Bullshit,' Sharona said. You got out. You're free. You've taken back ownership of your life.'

'Have I? I've been thinking about that. I don't want my family or friends, people who really know me, to find out the real truth about what I've gone through. It would destroy my dad, and he'd want to kill someone. Mam would be heartbroken, guilty and embarrassed. My friends wouldn't know what to say, and they'd be angry with themselves that they couldn't think of something that would wash the hurt and pain away, so the awkwardness would show, and they'd start putting distance between us.'

Sharona noticed Rebecca massaging her foot. 'You don't have to make any life decisions now. Go have a shower and rest. Later we'll shop for clothes and shoes.'

'CAN I BORROW your phone?'

John looked at the fifty euro note in Adam Styne's hand, handed the mobile over, sat on the bed and waited.

Styne scrolled through business news feeds:

A new board of directors will be appointed at Hattinger's next week.

Styne nearly jumped from the wheelchair. 'They can't. Stop them. This is a travesty. It's impossible,' he muttered.

John stood and came forward.

'It's okay.' Styne handed him the money and waved him away. 'Just saw some bad news about my business.' He kept scanning and talking to himself. 'Board members should be chosen by merit or representation or... or a combination of both. Consideration must be given to the level of business knowledge and the amount of time running the office. How can a board be appointed? Is the ballot open or secret? How and by whom are any evaluations carried out?' Another article caught his eye:

Madeline Hattinger and unnamed investors purchase Hattinger's for an undisclosed sum. Madeline has assumed responsibilities of the day-to-day running of Hattinger's Fine Art and Antiques. "This is a transition phase in our family business," she told us during our interview. "A new direction, if you will."

'What?' Styne blinked and tried to focus on the words. His face went from ashen grey to blood red.

"Ms Hattinger blames recent troubles and the current drop in earnings on poor strategic decisions taken over the previous eighteen months, and "a new board of management will be announced next week." She added: "We are confident this downward trend can be reversed in the second quarter."

Styne scrolled further.

"We're currently in the process of rewriting the family creed, which will include a total transparency in all transactions. My years of working both inside and outside the family business will ensure added value to the Hattinger brand. I want to assure all our customers, that my skill set and management style differs completely from those of former executives, and I've dozens of new ideas ready to showcase. The new board of directors and I can't wait to get started."

Styne's face turned back to puce. 'This is an... *outrage.*' Spittle flew from his mouth. 'I'll—'

'We gotta go,' John said. 'You'll be late for your assessment, and I'll get blamed.' He snatched the mobile from Styne and wheeled him into the corridor.

THE PSYCHIATRIST'S NAME badge said Gloria.

'This is called the Thematic Apperception Test,' Gloria said. 'It won't take long, I promise. Did your barrister tell you we'll conduct another one after lunch?'

'Yes.' Styne was still fuming.

O'Brien lied about my business. What else is he lying about? Whose side is he on?

He tried to remember what O'Brien has said about this test.

TAT test consists of pictures showing fairly ambiguous scenes. You've to make up stories about what you see. One for example, is of a woman holding her face in her hands. Maybe she's crying. Maybe she'd received bad news. You'll be asked: what's the lead-up to this event and what's happening at the moment. What are the characters feeling or thinking, and what do you think is the outcome of the story? One card is completely blank, and you'll have to create your own story. Just say what you see.

What's the point?

People express their inner motives through the stories they frame, Adam. TAT is used as a tool for research around areas such as dreams, fantasies, mate selection and what motivates people to choose their occupation. It's used to assess disordered thinking, and in forensic examinations to evaluate crime suspects, or to screen candidates for high-stress careers. It reveals repressed aspects of our personalities. Just let your inner actor loose, Adam. You'll walk through this. Remember the three magic words: Sympathy, empathy, compassion...

'If you're ready, we'll begin.' Gloria held up a card. 'Look at the picture and tell me what you think has led to the event shown.'

Her words barely registered as Styne struggled to concentrate.

Sympathy, empathy, compassion.

12.30 P.M.

THE TAXI DRIVER grunted at Malcolm. 'Passport?'

'Yeah.'

From the back seat, Malcolm alternated between scrolling through Twitter feeds and staring out the side window as the taxi sped past big-box storage units and distribution centres along the M50. At the airport, the driver halted in the set down area. He reached into the glove compartment, pulled out an A4 sized envelope and gave it to Malcolm. 'Two boarding passes,' he said. 'All ready to rock 'n' roll. You know the drill. When you get to Berlin, there's a Starbucks beside the information desk. Buy a coffee and hang around. Someone will contact you.'

'How will——?'

'Don't worry 'bout it,' the driver winked. 'All organised. When you get the briefcase, don't let go of it 'til you see me. I'll be in the arrivals hall with your dosh.'

The double doors whooshed as Malcolm walked into the departure hall. On the escalator he opened the envelope and took out the outbound boarding pass, plus five twenty euro notes. A scanner accepted the boarding pass barcode, the turnstile's padded arms opened, and Malcolm joined the queue for security check. The human chain snaked forward, slow as molasses. He watched passengers haul strollers and carry-on luggage onto the conveyor belt, remove coats and shoes and place all other personal items into trays, ready for the x-ray scanner. Security personnel shouted instructions about shampoo bottle sizes. Malcolm placed all personal items in a tray, pushed it towards the x-ray machine, and waited in line for the body scanner, walked through, and he was in the duty-free area. Checked the departures computer screen: the flight to Berlin was on time. He headed to the boarding gate.

'GANESTOWN'S CHANGING.' Charlie stared out of Hugh's office window.

'Not enough, you mean,' Hugh said. He remembered this time last week he was at Ciara McGuire's funeral.

Charlie turned and smiled. The corners of his eyes creased, but the eyes remained clouded with pain. He looked like a hollowed-out version of his former self. 'Maybe,' he said. 'Well done at the meeting. Good job on getting people on your side. Already moral is changing and there's a little more cash in the tills.'

'Thanks, Charlie. We benefit more from cooperation than conflict. When staff come up with their own ideas, they'll try harder to implement them. I think it's a myth that morale improves once sales figures increase. It increases when employees believe business *will* improve. It's up to management to present a clear vision of the future and lay out practical, achievable steps. That's all I'm doing. Basic psychology 101.'

'Hmmm. Pity Malcolm isn't around to see this, Hugh. Kids no longer follow parental footsteps. We've lost that continuity.'

'Maybe it means a better educated workforce,' Hugh said.

'Perhaps,' Charlie said, and changed the subject. 'The death of a child is like no other.'

Hugh knew this was the real reason Charlie had come into the office: Malcolm wasn't around and he needed to talk with someone. 'Life's different. We're different. Parents say that when their child dies, a part of them passes too. Ciara was a symbol of the future and losing her is a loss of hopes and dreams.' Charlie rubbed his eyes. 'Pain and loss are universal, but the grief process is still an individual, personal experience. Especially for fathers. Men aren't supposed to cry. We're meant to support, be strong and attend to practical matters like funeral arrangements and such. Most of us are determined not to grieve, which can lead to all kinds of emotional distress and depression later.'

'Don't go there, Charlie,' Hugh said, and wondered was he talking about himself or Charlie. Or a mixture of both.

'Grief's a killer,' Charlie sighed and walked towards the door. 'It makes you feel abandoned, isolated, overwhelmed. I thought I could cope, but I'm going to have to get support from family, friends and...' he looked at Hugh, 'co-workers.'

'I mightn't have the words to console,' Hugh said, 'but I'll listen anytime, if that's any help.'

'Most times, that's all we need.' Charlie stood in the doorway and pinched the bridge of his nose. 'Thanks for listening. I'm going to visit Ciara's grave and then I'd better get back to Mullingar. No matter what my personal situation is, Hugh, it's still up to me to decide when the fight's over with regard this business. Not the banks. Not the government. Not Philip. Me. And I'm not giving in yet.'

'Good. I'll send you a report—'

Charlie waved the offer away. 'I want to see results, Hugh, not progress reports.'

AFTERNOON

DETECTIVE MARCUS MULRYAN stood and stretched.

'Shouldn't be too difficult to track down a two-story farmhouse accessed by its own motorway underpass a few miles from Obama Plaza,' he said. 'Can't be too many of them.'

His two female colleagues remained seated either side of Rebecca. The tape recorder was still running, and they'd also taken notes. Ronan had given the brothel's exact location. The detectives pushed hard for the name and address of the man in Castletroy, but Sharona refused to budge. She'd give up the guy in a heartbeat—had zero sympathy for him—but his pregnant wife didn't need the additional stress.

Ronan described the brothel's interior and a sparse description of the man he'd seen. Rebecca filled in more pieces of the jigsaw. She told them about the young woman with the crystal tattoo, the murder of the young girl and Whispers role in the trafficking recruitment scam. She broke down several times.

'There's a guy they call Rusty,' she told the detectives. 'Rusty and Zita are the only names I heard. The main man was never named. All I know is that he's from Odessa, Ukraine.'

'Your bravery is astounding,' one of the female detectives said. 'We know this is going on, but these details are brilliant. When we arrest these people, we'll need you to confirm their identity from a line-up. It'll count as evidence at trial.'

'Will they see me?'

'No. It's done through one-way glass.'

'I'm not giving evidence in court,' Rebecca said. 'I don't want to relive and answer the same questions over and over. It won't help me and at best, they'll serve a few years. Victims serve a life sentence.'

Detective Mulryan grunted, turned away and tapped a text on his mobile. Then he punched in a number, held the phone between his shoulder and ear and ambled outside. The people inside watched him walk to and fro along the short driveway.

'I understand how you feel,' the second female detective placed her hand on Rebecca's arm. 'But right now, you are speaking for every woman who has suffered at the hands of pimps and traffickers. Every woman who walks home with her house keys wedged between her fingers to use as a weapon. Every woman who crosses a street or switches train carriages because some guy won't break eye contact. *You* are their saviour. This is literally hashtag MeToo. If one person speaks out, others will join in and say: "I've gone through that, too. Those people did the same to me." They build a business on broken bodies, false promises and shattered dreams. We'll need your evidence to break this gang up.'

'I don't know.' Rebecca bit her lip. 'I want to forget. How can I forget if I know there's a court case pending in, what, a year? Two years? How can I erase what happened if I've to remember every detail? Those nightmares bring up the fear and terror of being bought and sold like a cow at a mart. I was too happy. I should have known something would...' Rebecca choked, her voice faded like a whisper in the wind.

'How could you know? It—'

'It's impossible to move forward. All my thoughts are different from what I envisioned a few weeks ago. My life got robbed by people who...' Rebecca shook her head and stared at the floor.

The detectives communicated through eye contact. 'We'll leave it there for now,' one said and gathered up the papers and notebooks. The second unplugged the recorder, placed it in a briefcase, and looked at Rebecca. 'The little that's been done in Ireland about trafficking is window dressing,' she said. 'Political rhetoric. Long as it's brushed under the carpet and not spoken about directly, any public outrage will be muted, because they don't know the truth about what happens in the house or apartment next door. If we *ever* stand a chance of winning this trafficking scourge, it'll be won by women like you.'

Rebecca used her fingers to untangle a snarl from her hair, sniffed quietly, and stared out at detective Mulryan, still on his mobile.

'Yeah,' the second detective said. 'The public attitude is: so long as it doesn't happen to me, let's pretend it doesn't exist, so we don't feel uncomfortable in our daily lives. I know that abusers violently attack victims, but so long as it's away from *my* neighbourhood, I can ignore it. *I* teach *my* kids how to engage in healthy relationships. If others teach theirs that frustration and anger is best vented by beating the shit out of someone vulnerable, that's not my problem. Oh, and if others gaslight victims of abuse, so they won't whistleblow in order to try and save others from violence, that's okay, as long as I don't know about it. Tell you what, why don't we all look the other way and stay quiet and make it easy for traffickers and abusers and predators to get away with it. That's why the bastards win, Rebecca. Don't let them win. They *depend* on our silence. Please think about letting your story become someone else's survival guide.'

'They've taken my soul,' Rebecca said. 'I've nothing left to give.'

'Whatever you decide, no one will judge you.' The detectives handed Rebecca business cards, stood, buttoned their coats and nodded at Sharona and Ronan. 'Phone us any time,' one said. 'We'll be in touch.'

'Phew,' Sharona said after the detectives left. 'I'm glad that's over.' She clapped her hands. 'Let's go into Ganestown, Rebecca, and kit you out. Wanna join us, Ron?'

'Ahh, no. I'd better finish McGuire's website. Will I see you later?'

'Yeah, come over for dinner at six,' Sharona kissed Ronan. 'We won't be more than a few hours. Ready, Rebecca?'

Rebecca nodded, listless. Relaying her ordeal to the detectives had worn her out. She stirred and dragged herself off the couch.

'We can wait if you're too tired,' Sharona said.

'No, it's fine.' Rebecca pointed at her shoes. 'I can't walk around in these high heels much longer.'

'See you both later,' Ronan said. 'Enjoy shopping.'

GLORIA HAD PLANNED to wrap up this second test quickly.

She selected eight cards from the set of thirty-two and watched Adam Styne's grip tighten on their corners, as he tried to interpret the pictures without revealing his true impressions of personal relationships with family, peers, parents, figures in authority, and subordinates. In addition to assessing the content of the stories that Adam was telling, Gloria also evaluated his manner, vocal tone, posture, hesitations, and other signs of an emotional response to particular pictures.

Styne's reactions concerned her.

He was showing stark contrasts to results in the previous assessments. She wondered why he struggled with these pictures. And why so nervous? He's hiding in plain sight, she thought, and that makes *me* nervous. His empathy was leading to sarcasm and her additional questions led to evasion tactics or silence.

Gloria decided to take Adam through the whole set in order to get a complete picture of his needs for achievement, fears of failure, hostility, aggression, and the way he internalised relationships with others. In particular, the extent to which he was emotionally involved in relationships with others, and his ability to understand the complexities of human relationships. Styne's inability to distinguish between viewpoints and the perspectives of others, was a red flag. Gloria watched his demeanour change. The small room crackled with tension as Styne stammered, evaded, fidgeted and for the first time, found it difficult to make or maintain eye contact. Gloria watched his cobalt blue eyes turn ice cold when she asked him what he felt the stories' outcome were. This is a devious, dangerous man, she thought, and wondered if he imagined killing her. Styne's index finger and thumb were white from the death grip he had on the card, and Gloria sneaked a hand into her pocket and gripped the mobile alarm.

4.25 P.M.
A TALL, BLONDE female stood beside Malcolm McGuire.

'For you.' She dropped a briefcase beside his chair outside the coffee shop.

'I thought you weren't coming,' Malcolm checked his watch.

The woman shrugged. 'Very busy. Safe journey.' She turned on her heel and walked away.

Malcolm picked up the briefcase and shook it. Small and light. The brass Franzen three dial combination locks were set at 000. He tried to open them, but the case was locked. He finished his coffee, left half a sandwich behind, and moved towards the Berlin Schoenefeld Ryanair departure lounge. His thoughts turned to the best possible financial return on investment he'd make from the cash he'd have in a few hours. He'd run out of friends he could borrow from and this could be the last opportunity to get his head back above water.

Thirty metres behind, the blonde tailed him to the departure gates. Through a glass wall, she studied Malcolm as he stood in line for security check, and saw the briefcase go through the CT scanner. Her eyes flicked back to Malcolm as a security man motioned him forward through the metal detector. He passed through, picked up the briefcase, checked the departure screen for his gate number, and disappeared into the crowd.

She dialled a number from her mobile. 'He's through,' she said, disconnected, walked towards the car park and paid the parking fee. In her car, she phoned another number. When it answered, she spoke slowly and distinctly: 'I have information. A twenty-three-year-old man boarded a Ryanair flight from Berlin Schoenefeld, and he'll be landing in Dublin, local time 19:10. He has no luggage except a small burgundy briefcase, and there is a quantity of drugs hidden inside. The man is wearing…'

4.40 P.M.

AN ANONYMOUS GREY Seat Alhambra with a green and blue taxi sticker on the front doors, and tinted windows all around, turned right on Ganestown square.

The car in front, a Renault Clio, parked on the street, and the taxi driver's head swivelled as he passed by. His eyes darted to the rear-view mirror, tried to keep the Renault in view, but sleety rain and the sodium street lights made it difficult to distinguish one car from another.

'Turn,' a voice ordered from the back seat.

The driver gunned the engine, sped toward a roundabout, spun around the large snow-covered flowerbed, and drove back the way he'd come.

'Slow down,' the voice said. 'Stop.'

The taxi halted. The indicator flashed as if the driver was dropping off a fare. The three men in the Alhambra eyed two women get out of the Clio.

'Rusty, get behind them,' the voice said. The driver pressed a button and the electric sliding door opened. Rusty hopped out. The driver and the man in the back seat watched him walk along the footpath and then step between cars, closing in on the women from behind.

One of the women opened the Clio boot and took out an umbrella.

'Drive,' the voice said. He reached up and turned off the interior light. 'Ask if they need a taxi.'

The taxi driver shifted the car forward and stopped beside the Clio. He buzzed down the window and stuck out his head. 'Was it ye that ordered a taxi?'

Attacking from behind, Rusty violently pushed the two women to the open slide door. The man in the back seat dragged them in, and Rusty clambered up after them. The driver pressed a button, and the sliding door closed. The taxi drove away.

'Hello, baby bear,' the Ukrainian said. He pinned Rebecca's arms. She screamed with terror and tried to kick out, futile in the cramped space. 'You didn't think I'd let you go that easy, did you? We have unfinished bizzness. And you've brought a friend to meet me. That's nice.'

Sharona, trapped against a sweaty armpit, and unable to assimilate what had happened, went rigid with fear.

Rusty laughed.

The abduction had taken six seconds.

Shocked, disorientated and now book-cased between the two men, the women were helpless. Rebecca squirmed to escape.

'Relax,' the Ukrainian said. He turned on the interior light and stared from Sharona to Rebecca. 'Hush now. We go for a drive. Save your energy for later, baby bear. You'll have lots of time to tell me about your adventure. No money for you for a verrie long time.' He wagged a finger in Rebecca's face. 'I pay back client you didn't make happy. And his eyes… big issue. Double clients for you tomorrow. But no problem, baby bear. Work, work, work.' Flesh struck flesh with the sound of a whip crack. And another, harder, the slap full of evil intent. Rebecca moaned in pain. 'And we'll have time to get your frien' ready for Valentine's night. Verrie busy…'

6.30 P.M.

'SHARONA'S MISSING, DUDE. She and Rebecca haven't come back from shopping and they should be back now 'cos she said to call over for dinner at six an' I'm here an' the house is locked, an'—'

'Aww c'mon, Ronan,' Hugh said. 'Not this again. You're turning into an old fuddy-duddy.' He pulled the car onto the road verge. 'When girls shop they forget time. Jeez, give them a bit of slack, man.'

'Sharona told me to call over for dinner at six, dude. They should be back by now. She's deadly about time. Her phone's off. It's going into voicemail.'

'Probably forgot it again. Bet it's on the kitchen table.' Hugh could hear Ronan breathe into the phone.

'Okay,' Ronan said. 'You're probably right. It's just that—'

'I know. You're concerned.'

'Yeah. I'll hang around. See what happens.'

'Okay. Let me know when they turn up.' Hugh disconnected. He pulled into his mother's driveway and the mobile rang again. Ronan.

'That was quick,' Hugh said. 'See? I told you they'd—'

'Trouble,' Ronan panted. 'They're not home. They're on the way to Dublin.'

'Oh? Sharona rang you?'

'No. When I met Rebecca in Limerick, I stuck a tracker in her shoe. I checked it now, and she's on the motorway, heading to Dublin.'

'What?' Hugh tried to make sense of this.

'Dude, something happened, and they're on the move. What'll I do? Will I phone the cops? Will they laugh at me? I've no evidence of a crime. They'll say I'm bonkers, but I *know* something's up.' Ronan's voice quivered. 'No way would Sharona do this without… she knows how pissed off I was this morning when—'

'You're right, she wouldn't.' Hugh switched the phone to his other ear, thinking. 'We assume they're still together?'

'Right. Sharona wouldn't leave Rebecca.'

'Where are they now?'

'I can't talk to you and track them at the same time,' Ronan said. 'I'll—'

'Keep tracking. Meet me at Griffin's petrol station in five minutes.' Hugh tossed the phone on the car seat and barged into the house.

'Emily? I've an emergency. Can you hold the fort for a few hours? I've gotta go to Dublin.'

'Oh. It's just that—'

'I wouldn't ask if it wasn't... this could literally be life and death.'

'Okay.' Emily took off her coat. 'I'll change my plans.'

'You're a star, Emily.'

'Hugh. You've *got* to start thinking about... long term.' Emily gestured towards the sitting room. Hugh could hear his mother talking to the television.

'I know, I know. And I will. I'll look at all options this weekend. I promise. Hafta go. Sorry.' Hugh ran back to the car.

RONAN WAS WAITING at the petrol station.

He jumped in and Hugh had the car rolling again before the door slammed. 'What's happening?' Hugh asked.

Ronan pointed at his phone. 'They're between Kilcock and Lucan at the moment. What'll we do, dude? This is—'

'Have you tried Sharona's phone again?'

'Yeah. Still voicemail.' Ronan kept his eyes on the phone screen.

Hugh indicated left and thundered onto the motorway. Traffic was light, so he took liberties with the speed limit.

Ronan gnawed a fingernail. 'Still moving. Nearly at Liffey Valley.'

Hugh pulled out his mobile and speed-dialled Ferdia. As usual, Ferdia didn't answer. He went through the voice mail routine and left a message: 'Call me. It's urgent.' A car, driven by someone in an even bigger hurry, zoomed past. Hugh waited until the taillights were pinpoints in the distance and then speeded up, keeping the lights at the outer edge of his vision.

'Turning onto the M50,' Ronan said.

Hugh concentrated on the road. 'How accurate is that thing?'

'Within a metre.' Ronan hunched over his phone, eyes glued to the screen.

Hugh said: 'We still don't know if we're—'

'We are, dude. We are. Sharona would've made contact by now. Somehow. Something's going down. I can feel it.'

They barrelled past a sign for Mullingar and Tullamore. Hugh's mobile rang. 'What's so urgent?' Ferdia asked.

'Are you still in Dublin?' Hugh pressed the speaker button so Ronan could hear.

'Yeah. In St. James. Why?'

'You okay?'

'Yeah, yeah. Visiting a guy. Sorting out a few things. What's up?' Hugh told him.

'I know Sharona,' Ferdia said. 'She wouldn't let her friend head off on her own. Ronan's right. Something's up. Where are they now?'

'Still on M50, near Ballymount,' Ronan said.

'And where are ye?'

Hugh glanced at a motorway sign. 'Coming up to Kinnegad.'

'Grand,' Ferdia said. Hugh could hear traffic through the phone speaker. Ferdia was on the move. 'Listen, I'm with a few people here. I'm gonna hang up. Gotta make a few calls. You keep tracking. I'll ring back in a few minutes.'

'What are you—?' Hugh started, but Ferdia had disconnected. The lead car took the Kinnegad exit, and Hugh shot past.

'They've turned off the M50,' Ronan said. 'Looks like they've stopped.'

'Heavy traffic, maybe.' Hugh's eyes read the sign:

Toll. Five kilometres ahead

He dug coins from a pocket.

Ronan watched the phone screen, silent.

Hugh steered around a sweeping curve and lights from the toll plaza loomed in the distance. He threw the exact change into the basket and gunned the engine as soon as the barrier lifted.

'They're moving again, dude,'

'We're only twenty minutes behind. What direction are—?'

Hugh's mobile rang. Ferdia.

'I've set the wheels in motion,' Ferdia said. 'Actually, they were already in motion; we've moved the timeline forward a tad. Gimme an update?'

'They've turned off the M50 at junction 11 and now going down the R137 towards Bushy Park,' Ronan said. 'They've stopped again.'

Hugh passed the Maynooth exit, stayed on the outside lane, and whizzed by half a dozen cars. The traffic was heavier now. He could hear Ferdia murmuring.

'Is there someone with you, Ferdia?'

'Yeah. I'll tell you more when we meet up. What's happening now?'

'Heading towards Bushy Park,' Ronan said.

'Grand. Look…' Ferdia began. 'I don't wanna say too much over the phone, but don't worry. All you lads have to do is tell me where that feckin' tracker is going, okay?'

'Okay,' Ronan said. 'Sorry for—'

'Nothing to be sorry about,' Ferdia said. 'In fact, you might have supplied the missing piece of a puzzle. Where are ye?'

'Passing the Spa Hotel,' Hugh said. 'We'll be on the M50 in a minute.' He hunched over the wheel and searched for any traffic breaks that would gain precious seconds.

'Tracker's past Bushy Park, heading towards Terenure,' Ronan said.

'Hasn't left the R137?' Ferdia asked.

'No.'

'Grand. Let me know if that changes.'

Hugh followed the M50 signs and looped south onto the motorway, got on the outside lane and speeded up. He half-listened to Ronan's commentary. 'It looks like… yeah, it's moved onto the R114.' Agitated, Ronan rocked forward and backwards in the seat.

'Tell me if it stops for more than two minutes,' Ferdia said.

'It's moving… slow, dude. Coming into Rathgar.'

Hugh swung into the left lane, ready to take junction 11 exit.

'Now passing the Rathgar Avenue, Orwell Road junction,' Ronan said. 'Staying on the R114.'

'Huh. It's a straight run from there into Rathmines,' Ferdia said. 'I wonder if that's where they're going. That's a serious bit of kit you've got, Ronan.'

'It's just a standard—'

'Hey, no one's bothered what the hell it is, so long as the feckin' thing works,' Ferdia said.

'It works.'

'Grand.'

Hugh drove by Bushy Park.

'There's a fair amount of housing estates between Rathgar and Rathmines,' Ferdia said. 'If they turn off—'

'Still on R114,' Ronan replied. 'Passing Winton Avenue now.'

'We're fifteen minutes behind,' Hugh said.

Whoever was with Ferdia murmured, and Ferdia grunted in reply. 'Can you give me another exact location?' he asked.

'Um, coming up to Auburn Villas... now.'

'Deadly,' Ferdia said.

'They've turned left onto Charleville Road.' Ronan's high-pitched tone rose another notch. 'Now turned right onto... hold on, Wynnefield Road. Oh, they've turned into an apartment block.'

'I don't suppose that yoke can give you the number?'

'It can, once they go inside, dude.'

They all waited in silence until Ronan called out the apartment number.

'Magic,' Ferdia said. 'Feck sake. Only a stone's throw from Rathmines Garda Station. I'm hanging up now. Ring me when ye get here...'

7.55 P.M.

THE PASSENGERS FROM Berlin made their way through the corridors of Dublin Airport.

Malcolm McGuire sauntered along, swinging the briefcase. On the flight home, he'd mapped out a sure-fire route to riches. Down the escalator, into the baggage claim area, his pace quickened, and he made a beeline for the exit. Couldn't wait to get his hands on the cash. He entered the green channel, dodged around a person whose baggage was being searched. The exit door was straight ahead.

'Excuse me, sir?' A uniformed figure materialised by Malcolm's side.

'Yes?'

'Can you come this way, please?' The customs man pointed to a free table.

'Nothing to declare,' Malcolm held up the briefcase.

'I understand, sir. Purely routine. Step this way. Place the briefcase on the bench, please. Where are you coming from today?'

'Berlin.'

'When did you travel to Germany?'

'Earlier today.'

'I see. And what was the nature of your visit to Berlin?'

'Business.'

'Is the briefcase yours?'

'Yes,' Malcolm answered.

'And has it been out of your sight at all today, sir?'

'No.'

'May I see your passport please?'

Malcolm dug it out. 'Look, I've a taxi waiting—'

'This should only take a minute, sir.' The customs man examined the passport. 'Can you open the briefcase for me please?'

'Erm, I can't. I've um, forgot the code.'

The man looked up from the passport. 'Oh? What's in the briefcase, sir?'

'Just papers.'

The officer smiled. 'Well, that's alright then. No problem. We'll put it through the X-ray machine.' He held up the passport. 'I'll hold on to this for the moment. Follow me, sir.' The official walked over to a baggage scanner.

Only now, Malcolm realised that two other custom officers flanked him. His heart rate doubled as he watched the customs man place Dessie Dolan's briefcase on the conveyor belt. Something bumped into him. 'Excuse me,' an eastern European passenger said. His trolley had five king-size suitcases, and he was having trouble steering straight while talking on a mobile. 'Sorry,' he smiled at Malcolm, readjusted his grip on the trolley and manoeuvred it towards the exit. He piloted it through the doorway and disappeared into the arrivals hall.

'Sir?'

Malcolm turned back to the baggage scanner and the customs officer. 'Yes?'

'Can you remember the lock combination for your briefcase?'

'No.'

'Then, I'm afraid we'll have to detain you a little longer while we check the contents.' The man picked up the briefcase. 'Need to take a closer look. We'll leave this area and go to another zone—'

'It's not my briefcase,' Malcolm was desperate. 'I'm carrying it for… a friend. It only contains papers. He told me—'

'A few minutes ago you told me it was yours,' the customs man reminded Malcolm and steered him through an employee-only doorway and down a metal stairway. The two other officials followed.

'Yes, but... I... it's not mine. I don't know what's in it,' Malcolm's body shook. 'I'll make a phone call and sort it out.'

'Let's see what's in it first, shall we?' the customs man said. Their footsteps echoed in the empty corridor. 'You can make a phone call later.' He stopped, opened a door, and gestured Malcolm inside. The room was of average size. Several people milled around. Others watched monitors or used handheld equipment to examine luggage.

'If you can't remember the combination, we'll have to cut open the briefcase,' the customs man said.

'I wasn't given the combination.' Malcolm began to cry.

The official shrugged and passed the briefcase to a colleague who worked a small angle grinder around the hasps until they fell off. He opened the case, removed sheets of blank paper, then used a knife to slice around the briefcase's interior and expose a false bottom. Glancing at Malcolm, the man removed four plastic bags, filled with a white substance. He used a spoon to remove a sample, added it to a test tube and showed the results to the official.

The men nodded. 'Okay, sir,' the customs officer spoke to Malcolm. 'You've brought an illegal drug, cocaine, into the country. Want to tell me what the story is?'

Malcolm stared at the briefcase.

'We're going to take you to a custody cell,' the officer said. 'You're not obliged to say anything unless you wish to do so, but anything you *do* say may be used in evidence...'

AT THE BUS stop across from the arrivals hall in Terminal 1, the eastern European with the five suitcases lit a cigarette and blew smoke at a no smoking sign.

A taxi sped up, stopped beside him, and the driver who'd dropped Malcolm off earlier, hopped out. He helped transfer the luggage into the boot and back seat.

Leaving the trolley on the footpath, the men got into the taxi and drove away.

8.10 P.M.

UNLIKE THE SPECTACLE in TV docu-drama police raids, the Irish Drugs and Organised Crime Bureau entered the Wynnefield Road apartment by ringing the bell.

When the old Asian woman opened the door and peered out, six armed officers pushed their way past. Her warning scream, though, caused a flurry of activity. Bedroom doors opened, and half-dressed johns peeked around door jambs to see what the commotion was. Officers pushed them back into bedrooms and stood guard until they'd secured the apartment.

Rusty was in the living room when three detectives swarmed in. As the first line of defence, he barged forward and head-butted one Garda. The other pair tackled him. Furniture got smashed and overturned in the confined space. The Ukrainian, standing in the kitchen area, grabbed a large monkey wrench and swung it at a kitchen sink tap. They broke off and a jet of water shot through the outlet hole, drenching himself in the process. 'Plumber,' the Ukrainian shouted, as another detective came through the doorway. 'I no speak Eeenglish.' He came forward, hands raised. 'Need to get tools from van.' A fire alarm sliced the silence. The detective looked at the water pool on the kitchen floor and seep into the living area, and that split second hesitation was enough. The Ukrainian stepped forward, poleaxed him with a blow, and walked into the hallway. 'Plumber,' he edged past Gardaí. At the outside door, he shouldered past a policewoman who'd handcuffed the old Asian woman, and walked down the steps.

Across the street, a shadow extracted itself from the gloam. Ferdia crossed the road, held up a hand like a traffic cop to slow an oncoming car, and saluted the driver when he was three-quarter ways across. He met the Ukrainian in the gateway. 'Where are you going?'

'Plumber,' the Ukrainian said. 'Burst pipe. Need tools from van.'

'What van?'

The Ukrainian raised a hand to point, then swung at Ferdia with an overhand right. Ferdia ducked and countered with a blow to the Ukrainian's stomach. Hitting the man was like punching a tractor tyre. His fist bounced off the Ukrainian's hard muscles. A right uppercut jerked Ferdia's head back, and a kick planted to his ribs sank him to his knees. Another kick stretched him out. When Ferdia staggered to his feet, the Ukrainian was gone.

THE FIRE ALARM had stopped wailing when Hugh and Ronan arrived.

Ferdia was slouched on the apartment steps, holding his side. He waved a paramedic away.

Ronan brushed past. 'They're fine,' Ferdia called after him. He tried to stand, winced, and sat down.

'Another fight?' Hugh asked.

'Yeah. It's feckin' concussion central here.'

'What's happened?' Hugh asked. 'Are Sharona and Rebecca—?'

'In shock, but not harmed. Physically, anyway. They got bundled into a taxi in the middle of Ganestown. Fair play to Ronan all the same. Only for that gadget—'

'Yeah. Who was that in the car with you?'

'Long story,' Ferdia said. 'Remember Decaf?'

'The guy that tried to kill us in the warehouse?'

'Argh, he's dead sound. We're getting on grand. He's given me lots of info on Dolan and his gang. The bould Dessie's mixed up with some shady people. Into bigger crimes than loan sharking. This,' Ferdia jerked a thumb at the apartment, 'is part of a bigger picture. He's due back into the country tomorrow, an' he's heading for Ganestown. I've got a surprise lined up for him.'

'Ganestown? What's in Ganestown?'

Ferdia lowered his voice. 'It's a perfect location for drug transfers. Sleepy village in the middle of Ireland with plenty of escape routes if needs be. And it's on the motorway.' He stretched and changed position. 'Your car's at St. James's. Can you give me a lift to Ganestown tonight? I want to be there to meet Dolan tomorrow.'

'Sure.'

'Grand, so.'

'Let me check on Sharona and Rebecca.' Hugh walked inside the apartment and was stopped by a Garda.

'Tell them you're with Pete,' Ferdia shouted.

'I'm with Pete,' Hugh said.

A man appeared from the living room. He had grey-brown hair and the solid build of a wrestler. What made him stand out was his posture; it commanded authority, and his eyes, accustomed to decades dealing with criminals, missed nothing. 'Someone mention my name?'

'I'm Hugh,' Hugh said. 'I drove Ronan—'

Pete beckoned him forward. 'Watch your step. Place is a mess. Ronan and the girls are down here. Quick chat, then I'll have to get you out.'

Hugh followed Pete into a bedroom. Sharona, Rebecca, another blonde-haired girl, and Ronan were with detectives. Sharona waved Hugh over, stood, and hugged him. 'You've come to my rescue again.'

'This is all the Ronan show,' Hugh said. 'I'm just the driver. You okay?'

'We're fine. It'll take me a while to process the… It was kinda dark, but still, to get kidnapped in the middle of Ganestown on a Friday evening. It happened so fast, I mean, seriously, I didn't even realise… those guys are on another level.'

'Sharona, you're gonna have to steer clear of—'

Sharona looked hurt. 'We were in the wrong place at the wrong time. And I'm *glad* I was with Rebecca. Least she wasn't alone.'

'Yeah, but it—'

'We didn't *ask* to be kidnapped, Hugh.' Sharona lowered her voice. 'You heard Rebecca earlier. She's a victim of circumstances beyond her control.'

'Dude,' Ronan slapped Hugh's back. 'Awesome driving. Gardaí want to get more details from Sharona, so we'll stay tonight.' He pointed at Rebecca, in deep conversation with a female detective. 'Her dad's on the way. She's going home to rest up. That other girl sitting beside Rebecca? They were, err, working together in Limerick.'

Rebecca caught Hugh's eye, and she waved, half-smiled in recognition.

Hugh waved back. 'We'll catch up again soon.'

Rebecca nodded.

'Can you move my car from Ganestown Square?' Sharona handed Hugh a car key. 'Park it at my house. Or yours. I'll pick it up over the weekend.'

'Thanks again, dude,' Ronan said. 'Monday, I'm back in action. I've finished McGuire's website. I think you'll like it.'

'Great. See you then.' Hugh looked for Pete, but couldn't find him. At the front door, Ferdia was on his mobile. 'Huh,' he said, and when he saw Hugh, he raised his eyes to heaven and followed him to the car and settled into the seat. 'Leave him. Let him stew for a few days. It'll do him good.'

They were back on the M50 before Ferdia disconnected. 'Feckin' Malcolm's got himself in deep shit this time.'

'What now?'

'He's a drug smuggler.'

Hugh nearly crashed. 'What?'

'Yeah, well, he's a feckin' drug mule. Flew out to Berlin today. Picked up a briefcase for Dessie Dolan and brought it back through customs, the feckin' eejit. Had a kilo of cocaine in it.'

'Jesus,' Hugh said.

'Customs got informed before he arrived.' Ferdia twisted in the seat to make himself more comfortable. 'The guy I talked to said that the only people who could've known that level of information about the suspect were the people who gave him the stuff. Dolan, the bastard, set him up. Probably needed a decoy to let a bigger consignment slip through. You can't feckin' fix stupid.'

'Man, that sounds serious,' Hugh said. 'What are the penalties for—?'

'Six to nine months' jail before a trial. Then it depends on the judge. Could get anything from a suspended sentence to six years.'

'Aww, Jesus,' Hugh said. 'Can he plead, I don't know, ignorance, maybe? Or duress?'

Ferdia rubbed his stomach and hissed through clenched teeth. 'Good luck with that. That defence hasn't got a hope in hell, because anyone could raise it.'

'So? What are you going to do?'

'Me?' Ferdia looked across at Hugh. 'Not a feckin' thing. A taste of prison life will do him good.'

'I've no sympathy for Malcolm,' Hugh said. 'It's Charlie I feel sorry for. First Ciara and now this. I haven't seen Malcolm in McGuire's all week. He must be still gambling and this is a way to get a stake. He's not a hardened drug smuggler, but it shows how detached he is from reality, if he'll—'

'Yeah. That's—' Ferdia groaned and clutched his side.

Hugh slowed and turned on the interior light. 'Ferdia's eyes were closed. Sweat trickled down his face. 'What the hell, Ferdia?'

Ferdia gasped. 'A fella kicked me…'

Hugh lifted the edge of Ferdia's shirt and saw the blood-soaked bandages underneath. 'Hospital,' he said.

'No way. I'm grand.' Ferdia gritted his teeth. 'I'm not missing tomorrow—'

'Stop, Ferdia. Just stop.'

'Get me a few painkillers, an'—'

'Shut up, Ferdia…'

HUGH PROPPED FERDIA up and staggered into Ganestown emergency department.

The wall clock read 22:35 and there was no change in the chaos since the last visit. Staff were still under severe and sustained pressure. Hugh left Ferdia slumped against a wall, queued at reception, and watched frazzled nurses calmly administer care. With no facial indication of the stress they must feel, working in what seemed like third-world conditions, Hugh wondered how their worth was calculated. Per hour or by how much pressure they can take? Whatever wages they received, it wasn't enough.

Two Gardaí escorted a man in. He was handcuffed, bleeding from a knife wound that ran from ear to lip. The man screamed profanities and kicked out. Patients scrambled out of harm's way and the handcuffed man resorted to shoulder-butting the guards.

A receptionist handed Hugh a form and pen and told him to fill out the details. Someone would be with him shortly.

'What's your date of birth?' Hugh asked Ferdia.

'January twenty-fifth, nineteen seventy-one.'

'Today's January twenty-fifth. Happy birthday.'

'Is it?' Ferdia was hunched over in pain. 'Niamh, Lord have mercy on her, had booked this weekend away for us. She never got a chance to tell me where we were going.' Hugh saw the flash of pain in Ferdia's eyes.

'I'm sorry,' Hugh said.

'Yeah. A week ago I didn't think I'd end up… uh-oh.'

'What?'

'Don't look to your left.' Ferdia spoke out of the corner of his mouth. 'Man, does that woman ever go home? Dammit. She's spotted us. Looks like she could chew bark off a tree. Stoop down and keep schtum.'

Hugh looked across at Ruth Lamero. She bent to reassure a frail old lady in a wheelchair, folded a blanket around the woman's neck. She straightened and stared across the waiting room. Hugh waved half-heartedly. Ruth made her way towards them, stopped to chat with a man wearing an oxygen mask. He took off the mask and Ruth smiled and patted his shoulder. 'I know. Oh, and if you *still* insist on smoking, take vitamin C, vitamin E and beta carotene. They'll help counteract the damage you're doing.' She replaced the mask and weaved through the patients until she stood in front of Hugh and Ferdia.

'We're back,' Ferdia said.

'Yay,' Ruth said.

'Ferdia was erm...' Hugh began. 'He's bleeding. Needs help. He... he got into a fight. I think his ribs, or something, got busted again, and—'

'Nothing serious,' Ferdia said. Minor bumps and bruises. I need a few bandages, is all. I won't be staying.'

The men looked at Ruth.

'Well,' Hugh said, 'say something.'

'I don't know what to say.' Ruth's glare burned like a laser beam. She lifted Ferdia's shirt, looked at the bloody bandages and pursed her lips. 'I've seen worse who lived.'

'That's good,' Hugh said.

'And I've seen better who died.'

'Oh.'

'I'll be grand.' Ferdia tried to straighten. 'Throw a bandage on it—'

Ruth's look stopped Ferdia. 'Someday,' she said, 'you'll wow me with an intelligent comment, but not today, though.' She snatched a wheelchair one of the porter's was returning. 'Sit,' she pointed to Ferdia, 'before you fall.' She asked him questions, and he lied through his teeth, thinking it would stop him spending the night in hospital. Ruth swiped the admittance sheet from Hugh's hand and wheeled Ferdia away. 'We need to get you X-rayed and—'

'Hey,' Hugh called, angry at Ruth's snub. He hurried after them and handed Ferdia a key. 'That's for Sharona's car. It's parked on Ganestown Square someplace. It'll keep you mobile for a day or so.'

Ruth frowned. 'Why's Sharona's car on Ganestown Square? Why can't she—?'

'Long story,' Ferdia said. 'She got kidnapped a few hours ago. Only for Hugh and Ronan... You wouldn't have any vinegar, would you?'

Hugh walked out.

8

SATURDAY 26 JANUARY. 8 A.M.

HUGH FIELDED SEVERAL "Did you?" "Have you?" and "When will we?" questions from his mother, and tried to remain calm.

He wanted to say, "I've told you that six times already today," but there was no benefit in antagonising his mother. It was easier to accept rather than fight, but he found himself wanting to react. He twisted his neck and shoulders to relieve some tension. I don't have the skill set to be a caregiver, he thought, and looked at the assortment of items Kathleen insisted she needed at the breakfast table. Her handbag. Two books. A glass of water and a glass of milk. A doll and hairbrush. Like the Jenga board game, he knew it would end in disaster, but the aftermath was easier to deal with than the cause. Appeasement instead of confrontation.

'I'm freezing. Is the heat on?'

'It is, Mum. I'll get you a blanket.'

'I don't want a blanket. Can you check the pipes in the attic and make sure they haven't frozen?'

'I'll do that, Mum, once we've finished breakfast and taken tablets.'

'When are we going shopping?'

'Soon, Mum. The shops aren't open yet.' Hugh examined Kathleen's features. Seeing her meticulous appearance gradually fade was heart-breaking. 'I need to make an appointment to get your hair done,' he said.

Kathleen patted her head. 'We can do that after shopping.'

'Okay, Mum.' Hugh opened a cupboard and looked at the myriad of tablet containers. 'It's like living in a stash house,' he muttered.

'What?'

'Nothing, Mum.' Is a care home the right option? he wondered. Or is it a cop-out on my part? Once Mum's in there, I'm off the hook. If I go down that road, it's a long-term commitment; there's no turning back. He counted out pills and left them on Kathleen's plate. Her elbow caught the milk glass, and it fell. Glass got strewn across the floor. Her other hand grazed the handbag and it toppled, spilling its contents into the milk. 'Don't stir 'til I clean up,' Hugh said. 'I don't want you to stand on glass.'

The doorbell rang.

Hugh raced to open the door. Ruth was outside. 'I'm heading home from night duty,' she said. 'I shouldn't have judged you last night. I'm sorry.'

'Erm, can you come in? As usual, I'm in the middle of a minor crisis.'

Ruth followed Hugh inside. He gestured at the whitewashed floor. 'Watch where you walk. Make yourself a coffee while I clean up.'

'Who's that?' Kathleen stage whispered.

'You remember Ruth?' Hugh used a brush and dustpan to sweep up the glass. 'She looked after you in hospital.'

'Morning, Kathleen.' Ruth's voice floated from the kitchen.

'I've never been in hospital,' Kathleen said.

'Ferdia told me what happened yesterday,' Ruth shouted over the boiling kettle.

'Where's Ferdia?' Kathleen smiled. 'Is he taking me shopping?'

'No, Mum. I'll take you. So ye're talking?' Hugh asked Ruth.

Ruth appeared with two coffee mugs. 'One-sided conversation. He talked. I listened.'

'Did you see him before you left? How is he?'

'No idea. He signed himself out sometime in the middle of the night.'

'Oh? You don't like him.' Hugh finished mopping up.

Ruth handed Hugh his coffee, sipped her own and made a moue with her lips. 'I'm not a Ferdia fan. In every imaginable, measurable way possible.'

'Can we intellectually discuss, or maybe even debate our differences?' Hugh asked.

'I don't understand how you can listen to someone who's so obviously wrong, Hugh. His actions are reckless at best, probably illegal or criminal at worst. You don't even agree with him, and yet you continue to… to be at his beck and call. Why?'

'Because he's a friend. He's helped me out in the past. If he needs a favour returned, I will. That's what friends—'

'He thinks there's no situation he can't either punch or smart-ass his way out of. Bulldozes his way through life and if someone gets hurt, well, tough. Most people would go into mourning after the horrific death of their girlfriend, but Ferdia—'

'That's not accurate. You don't know him.'

'You're right. And I don't want to.'

'You're passing judgement on someone you don't know,' Hugh said.

'Oh, horse manure. I'm no angel, but Ferdia makes me look like one. He may have got you a job once, but you *have* to cop on. I care about you, Hugh, and I see the trouble he gets you in. You've *got* to see that Ferdia isn't relevant anymore.'

Kathleen frowned.

Ruth patted Kathleen's arm to reassure her and lowered her tone. 'He has the ability to irritate and annoy me,' she added.

'Why?'

'Because...' Ruth shook her head. 'There are no words.'

'His big heart drives him,' Hugh said.

'Thirst for revenge drives him,' Ruth answered.

'No. Desire for justice drives him.'

'No. He—'

'I like Ferdia,' Kathleen said.

'He lost Ciara, his niece,' Hugh said. 'Then his girlfriend, Niamh, got killed. Murdered. He wants to bring those killers to justice. And his nephew, Malcolm? He doesn't want to lose him, too. It's natural to grab on and try to protect those closest to us when we realise they could be gone forever. Yes, sometimes his impulsive nature leads to flawed thinking, but everything Ferdia does, *everything*, is sewn together with good intentions.'

Ruth sighed and sipped coffee. 'We won't agree on this.'

'That's okay. We can't agree on everything. Can we move on from here?'

Ruth left down her mug on the table and fastened her coat. 'I'm wrecked. I need forty-eight hours sleep. Without that I can't make any rational decisions. Maybe, *maybe* someday I'll find out my prejudices are unfounded.'

'Or maybe your judgement is right,' Hugh said, 'and I'll be proved wrong. Either way, it shouldn't stop us moving on with our lives.'

'Hmm. We'll see. Goodbye, Kathleen.'

Hugh's mobile rang and he reached into his pocket for it.

'I bet that's fucking Ferdia,' Ruth said.

Hugh looked at the screen and showed her the caller ID. It was fucking Ferdia.

Ruth's smile was thin. 'Don't do anything stupid, Hugh. Chat soon.'

The hall door closed and Hugh answered Ferdia's call. 'Where are you?' He noticed Kathleen hadn't taken her tablets, so he handed her one and gave her the glass of water.

'Not far away. Listen—'

'You signed yourself out? Why?'

'I'm grand. A leaky kidney. Nothing serious. Listen—'

'Jesus, Ferdia. When will you—?'

'Will ya listen up, man? Bad news.'

'What? Malcolm?'

'Nah. Haven't even thought about him. It's Rebecca.'

'What about Rebecca?'

'She took an overdose last night.'

'Aww no. Is she okay?'

'She's dead.'

'What?' Hugh's legs buckled and he slid to the kitchen floor.

'Yeah. Shocking. Her father took her home and a while ago Rebecca's mother brought her in a cup of tea and found the poor girl dead.'

'No.' Hugh rubbed his eyes and groaned.

'Must've gone home to die,' Ferdia added. 'Poor lass.'

'How'd you hear—?'

'I phoned Sharona to tell her I'd her car. Mrs Greenfield had called her a few minutes before that. Rebecca left a sealed envelope addressed to Sharona. Everyone's in bits.'

Hugh was finding it difficult to breathe. 'It can't be. I spoke to her last night. It's—'

'I don't know the ins 'n' outs,' Ferdia said. 'But she must've decided she couldn't cope, and wanted to die at home with her family around her. But what the feck do I know?'

'I saw her talk to detectives last night.' Hugh was breathless now. 'Where's the help? Where's the professional support? What provision does the Department of Justice provide for—?'

'You're asking the wrong man, Hugh.'

'It's not right,' Hugh said. 'That's so unfair. A young girl... Those people that abducted her *have* to pay. End of story. Were they all rounded up last night?'

'Most were. A few weren't there. An' the main fella got away. For now.'

'God. So it's not over?'

'No, not yet,' Ferdia said. 'But nearly. The next few hours should round up more of 'em.'

'What are you doing about Malcolm?' Hugh staggered to his feet and gave Kathleen the rest of her tablets.

'I told you. Nothing. I'd a chat with Charlie last night. We'll let him spend a few days reflecting on his... life choices. Tough love, I know, but he can't wriggle out of this one so easy. There's a slim chance he'll get a light sentence, but Malcolm's gotta think the minimum he's looking at is six years. There's a solicitor gonna see him later this morning. I hope that conversation softens his cough. Anyway, I knew you'd want to know 'bout Rebecca. Lord have mercy on her. Sharona's gonna meet the parents today. I've sorted out a hire car in Dublin for her and Ronan. When they get back to Ganestown, I'll pick it up from her and bring it back to Dublin and collect your car. That okay?'

'Fine.'

'Wanna see our loan shark friend get handcuffed later?'

'No, thanks. Far as I'm concerned, Ferdia, that ship has sailed. This whole thing, Ciara, Niamh, bloody Malcolm and now Rebecca's death, sickens me. I want nothing more to do with any of it. I'm out.' Hugh tossed the phone aside and stared at the wall. It was only when he felt the tears running down his face, he realised he was crying.

9.30 A.M.

'WHASSUP?' DESSIE DOLAN spoke into the mobile. 'Any hitches?'

He stared out the taxi window and watched a Lufthansa plane skim warehouse rooftops as it descended. 'Huh-uh. An' the golden goose?' Dolan laughed at the reply. 'Good enough for the little bollix. An' Decaf?'

The taxi changed lanes and headed for the airport exit.

'Huh?' Dolan frowned. 'Did the lads give him the...? Then he couldn't have gone far. Ye searched the alleyways?' He listened to the explanation. 'I hear ya, but strange all the same that there's no trace. Should be 'round there, somewhere. Maybe he staggered into the sea. Good job I hadn't sent his auld fella a mass card, innit?'

The voice at the other end said something, and Dolan thought about it. 'Yeah, that's possible. All set for today? Everything locked 'n' loaded?'

The taxi driver got in lane for the Ryanair departure hall.

'Wha'? An' you're only tellin' me this now? When did that happen? An' more important, *how* defuk did it happen? Who knew about the apartment? Huh? How many—?'

Dolan saw the taxi driver eye him in the rear-view mirror. 'I'll phone ya back in five minutes,' he said. 'I'm not happy 'bout this. Not bleedin' happy at all.'

The taxi stopped. Dolan threw the driver some euros, grabbed his overnight bag, went into the airport and rang his contact back. 'Gimme the details.'

Cagey as a cornered rat, Dolan could smell danger. He wandered up and down the cavernous hall and assessed the facts. 'Someone grassed,' he said. 'Someone who wasn't there, fuc—'

He listened some more. 'Who's replacing Rusty today? Where's...? The lookouts are needed. We need all the manpower...' Dolan's voice shrilled. 'I'm tellin' you now, don't skimp on the setup. If I lose this shipment, I'm... Wha'? How can I relax, when you're...?' Dolan swapped the overnight bag strap to his other shoulder. 'Wha? Yeah, I'm *supposed* to be on a plane in less than an hour, but I think I'll sit this one out. You're gonna be there to oversee, aren't you? Yeah, I know, but you've *gotta* be on the ground for... This deal's too big to fail. I'm tellin' ya now, if it goes pear-shaped, I'll take you down—'

The caller's attempts to appease Dolan were unsuccessful. 'Don't bleedin' mess up,' Dolan warned. 'I'll phone you tonight.'

Dolan disconnected and brooded. Too many slip-ups. Too many things out of his control. Too much money at stake in one shipment. The raid on the Rathmines apartment worried him. *Had* to be an inside job, he reasoned. How else could they have found it so fast? In his head he ticked off names of potential whistleblowers and this thought process fed into his paranoia. What else could they do to him? What other information could the bastards give the cops to save their own skins? The house in Foxrock didn't concern him; the property wasn't in his name. The cannabis plants he was growing there needed to be checked, but the four million euro in cash he'd stashed in the house—that was his biggest worry. What if... It was well hidden, but still... With all that was going on, could he risk going back for it? Should he? Was it worth it? He checked the departure and arrival times on the big screen, added in the driving times, reckoned it was doable, and allowed avarice to trump his personal safety. He punched a number into his mobile, and when it answered, he said: 'It's me. That large consignment you mentioned last Tuesday? Has it arrived? Huh. Good. I'll call around seven tonight. Whatever you've got, I'll take it. Wha'? Yeah, cash. Four large. *Very* large. Righ'. Have 'em ready, I won't have time to hang 'round.'

Dolan disconnected, tore up his boarding pass, prised the SIM card from the phone and dropped it into a bin. He checked his passport, placed it into the overnight bag, and swapped it for a different one. Then he walked to the Ryanair customer service area. 'Wanna buy a ticket to Dublin,' he told the girl behind the desk. 'For the flight that's leaving at...' he looked at the monitor, 'ten past two, an' another for the one that's comin' back at nine-twenty.'

'Certainly sir. Can I have your name, please?'

'Newman.' Dolan handed over the passport. 'Paul Newman.'

12 P.M.

A CONVOY OF cars and jeeps left Dublin docks at one-minute intervals.

In the lead, a reconnaissance van ran surveillance. Behind it, a twenty-year-old Toyota Corolla with bald tyres and a broken taillight trundled along. If they came across a Garda checkpoint, this decoy would get pulled in and the driver questioned, allowing the rest of the cavalcade to pass. Next, a 4x4 with a reinforced bull bar drove out, in case something needed to get rammed out of their way. The driver and passenger were armed and dangerous. The fourth vehicle, a taxi, transported the cocaine shipment, and it was followed by another 4x4, for security. The last car was a nondescript black Passat. The lone driver was the person in charge.

The convoy passed the M50 toll bridge and exited onto the N4. They stayed within the speed limit, and maintained that one minute distance. The lone driver speed-dialled the driver in the observation car. 'Anything?'

'All clear.'

The man disconnected, continued past Lucan and Leixlip, and speeded up when he got onto the M4 motorway.

'IRISH LAW,' Malcolm McGuire's solicitor said, 'states that if you commit a crime where your will is overborne by *imminent* threat to your life, then that works as a full defence. It means you could be acquitted of the crime.'

'So, that means if we can prove I was forced—?'

'No.' The solicitor's sharp reply shut off Malcolm's glimmer of hope. 'Drug mules pleading duress won't cut it. The keyword is "imminent." While a person can *say* they are under threat, how can you prove it's *imminent,* especially if you walk through an airport where you have oodles of opportunities to seek help? How do you show the threat to your life is *imminent* if you've done nothing to seek protection? Our courts are reluctant to allow this rule to be procured legally, because they know, especially in the drugs game, it's a defence anybody can raise.'

After the night in a holding cell at Dublin airport Garda Station, Malcolm looked wretched. Pale, unshaven and scruffy, he toyed with a paper cup of water. 'How long am I gonna be here?'

'You'll be brought to Cloverhill prison sometime today and held on remand while the Gardaí prepare their book of evidence.'

'How long will that take?'

The solicitor shrugged. 'The packages you were carrying has to be sent to FSI, Forensic Science Ireland, to get analysed. That could take a week, ten days. Then, someone has to issue a cert, and that timeline depends on the backlog or if people are on holidays. It's usually two weeks, but the judge can hold you on further remand if all the evidence in the case isn't ready. They could, for example, be waiting on phone record analysis or other pieces of evidence.'

'Will I get bail?'

'That's... rare,' the solicitor said. 'Flight risk.'

'I'm not a flight risk. I've—'

'Maybe not,' the solicitor cut in. 'You *could* get bail, but as I said, it's rare. Gardaí would definitely invoke Section 2 bail application.'

'What's that?'

The solicitor puffed out his cheeks and recited: 'Under Section 2 of the 1997 Bail Act... basically, Gardaí would object because cocaine is a Class A drug. It's a serious crime.'

Malcolm groaned. 'What prison sentence can I expect?' Three months? Six months?'

'Unlawful importation of coke can incur custodial sentences from four to eleven years,' the solicitor said. 'It depends on quantity. The kilo you carried in? I'd say… eight years.'

'What? But I… Does Dad know what's happening? Or my uncle, Ferdia. Ferdia Hardiman? They'll vouch for me. I—'

The solicitor ignored the question. 'There are some circumstances that can help lessen jail time,' he said. 'Plead guilty. Co-operate with Gardaí. Give them information about your supplier. Conviction of dealers higher up the chain would be beneficial to your—'

'I don't have a dealer,' Malcolm said. 'I was set up. Forced under duress to—'

'Then maybe you can convince the trial judge, and he or she will take pity on you.' The solicitor held up his hands. 'Look, I'm only telling you the facts. It's no skin off my nose. I won't be pleading your case when it comes to trial.'

'When will that be?'

'Eighteen to twenty-four months—'

'Eighteen to…? But I *told* you—'

'That's a standard time,' the solicitor shrugged. 'On the positive side, if you take a plea, then whatever sentence is passed, your time on remand will count as time done. Understand?'

'I think so.'

'Also,' the solicitor smiled, 'lots of people who serve jail sentences report that being caught had helped them to refocus their lives. Some gain qualifications whilst in prison. You'll have opportunities to complete courses, pass exams…' He stopped when he noticed his words were having an adverse effect on Malcolm's delicate disposition. He coughed and tapped his pen on the table. 'Any questions?'

Too numbed to think, Malcolm shook his head.

'Right, so.' The solicitor pushed back his chair. 'If you think of something, ask to speak to me, and I'll see what I can do.'

The interview room door clanged shut. Malcolm put his face into his hands and sobbed. He'd never felt more alone.

THE OLD COROLLA peeled off the exit before Ganestown. It stopped on the bridge, and had a clear view of the motorway, from both directions, but the driver watched the westbound traffic flow. The 4x4 with the bull bar, speeded up, overtook the observation car, continued another two kilometres to the exit after Ganestown, and the men repeated what their comrade in the Corolla had done. The jeep stopped on the bridge overlooking the motorway. The men got out, strolled over to the barrier wall, leaned against the guard rail, lit cigarettes and watched the traffic head east. One man pulled out his mobile and dialled a number. 'In place,' he said. 'All clear.' He grunted and disconnected, eyes never leaving the motorway.

Bunched together now, the taxi, the second jeep and the black Passat all indicated for Ganestown.

FERDIA PARKED SHARONA'S Clio at Green's westbound petrol station.

He heaved his large frame from the confined seat and went into the coffee shop. Green's had a petrol station on either side of the motorway. Connected by a tunnel that ran underneath, this was a perfect pick-up or drop-off point for a drug courier. Whichever side a squad car appeared, it was simple to drive through the tunnel, exit out the opposite side of the motorway, and escape on the maze of backroads throughout the Irish Midlands.

Ferdia bought coffee and scanned the area as he ambled back to the car. Nothing out of place. Cars queued for the car wash. Drivers pumped fuel, bought newspapers, milk and treats to chew on their journey. If detectives were in the courtyard, Ferdia couldn't see them. He thought for a moment about checking the petrol station on the opposite side of the motorway, but figured this one, on the westbound side, would be Dolan's choice, as it was directly off the motorway. The drug bust didn't interest him; he wanted to witness the arrest of Dessie Dolan, the man who'd destroyed countless lives, was responsible for Niamh's death, almost killed Decaf, and played a big part in ruining Malcolm. Ferdia wanted to look into Dolan's eyes and let him know who was responsible for his downfall. He moved the car over to the side, where artic trucks parked, sipped coffee, and waited.

A taxi pulled into the service station. A 4x4 followed and parked beside it. Nobody got out. A black Passat drove in and disappeared into the tunnel. Ferdia lost sight of it, but moments later, it re-emerged from the tunnel and parked alongside the jeep.

Two more minutes passed. Still no movement from inside the three vehicles.

Ferdia toyed with his mobile and yawned.

Fifty metres away, three burly men in black overcoats got out of a Mercedes and walked towards the taxi. When they reached the car, the taxi driver opened the door, stood, stretched and fist bumped the men.

Ferdia left down the coffee and straightened in the seat.

The taxi man opened the boot and the trio stooped and peered inside. Huddled together, they appeared to confer, then, satisfied, they straightened and nodded. Watery sunlight glinted on metal as the taxi driver handed over the car key. The days of transferring drugs from one vehicle to another were gone. Now, dealers swap cars, and money gets transferred electronically. More fist bumps. One of the trio passed a key fob to the taxi driver, and he tossed it in the air, caught it on its descent and stepped towards the Mercedes. The person in the Passat never appeared. The three burly men got into the taxi and drove slowly towards the exit. The 4x4 tucked in behind it, riding shotgun.

TROUBLE CAN ONLY come from six places: front, back, left, right, above or below.

This time it came from left, right and above.

Three cars, lined up for a car wash, peeled away. It took three seconds for two of them to block the entrance and exit. The third slid lengthways into the tunnel opening. Drug unit detectives used the cars for cover and pointed automatic weapons at the gang. More plain clothes Gardaí materialised from parked cars and herded customers away from the petrol pumps and into the coffee shop.

Ferdia stayed put and watched.

The gang was ready and willing to shoot it out, but the suddenness of the bust, plus the cacophony of sounds and shouts helped disorientate the dealers. The arrival of two helicopters, the chuff-chuff of their whirring rotor blades, a man with a bullhorn shouting "put your hands up," distracted them further. Ropes got tossed out of the helicopters and half-a-dozen gunmen used a doubled rope coiled around their bodies to rappel within a few meters of the gang.

The three burly men were pulled from the car and handcuffed. The taxi driver lay on the ground, hands behind his neck; a detective's knee planted on his shoulder blades. With guns trained on the 4x4, the two occupants stepped out, and the driver in the Passat took off. Tyres squealing, car aimed at the tunnel, the driver was intent on ploughing through the blockage. A detective fired a short burst, hitting the number plate and the two back tyres. The driver lost control and skidded into a stationary car. Steam rose from the Passat's bonnet. The driver's door opened, a man got out and ran. Two detectives chased after him.

Ferdia frowned at the man running towards him. It wasn't Dessie Dolan. This person was bigger. The man got nearer and Ferdia thought he recognised him. He eased open the car door and swung his legs out. As the man ran past, Ferdia timed his charge, powered forward, and rugby tackled him from the side, driving the man's body into the side of a lorry. His head dented a hubcap and he lay on his side, stunned. Ferdia knelt over him and waited for the detectives to catch up. Pete was first.

'Good job I was on hand to help ye out,' Ferdia said.

'I'll send you a medal.' Pete watched his colleague drag the man away. 'Good result,' he said. 'We caught them all. Decaf's information about the lookouts was spot on.'

'Good man, Decaf.' Ferdia watched the gang get separated and bundled into cars. The drug unit officers started to pack away their gear. 'Where the feck's Dolan?'

'Still abroad,' Pete said. 'He didn't make the flight he was booked on. Could be any number of reasons. We'll watch the airports.'

'Huh. When he finds out his haul got seized, he'll never come back,' Ferdia said. 'Whoever supplied the drugs will want their money. If he doesn't have it, it's lights out.'

'It is what it is.' Pete slapped Ferdia's shoulder. 'Call me next time you get a tip.'

'Yeah. That guy from the Passat? I know the face, but I can't put a name on him.'

Pete smiled. 'I've watched him for two years, Ferdia. Marcus Mulryan. One of our own. He's up to his neck with Dolan. In fact, he's the main reason Dolan and his friends were able to slip under our radar for so long. Nothing worse than a bent cop.'

Holding his ribs, Ferdia limped to Sharona's Clio, sat into the car, sipped dregs of cold coffee and watched detectives on sentry at the shop door allow customers to go about their business again. Everything had returned to normal. His mobile rang. He looked at the caller ID and sighed, 'howaya, Father.'

'Is it over, Ferdia?'

'Almost, Father. Still one skittle left standing.'

'The one you wanted?'

'Yeah.'

'Pity,' Father Kelly said. 'I heard you were involved in rescuing Sharona Waters and her friend yesterday.'

'News travels fast, Father.' A car transporter pulled in and start to load the gangs' vehicles. 'Aye, I was there but wasn't involved. Sharona's boyfriend, Ronan Lambe, used some kinda phone app to track their movements, and I passed the word to a few cop friends. No big deal.'

'I see. This vendetta needs to end, Ferdia. Too many people have got hurt or killed. Do you know where... the skittle is?'

'Europe, somewhere.'

'He'll come back,' the priest said.

'You can't predict the unpredictable, Father.'

'He'll be back,' Father Kelly said again. 'If he's left anything here, he's got to. A thief's hell is the fear of thieves, Ferdia. They can't trust anyone, not even their own kind. It's—'

'What'd you say, Father?'

'They can't trust anyone, not even their own—'

'No, before that.'

'A thief's hell is the fear of thieves.'

Ferdia clicked the seatbelt into place and started the car. 'Father, I've gotta go. You've given me an idea.'

'Ferdia? Ferdia?'

'I'll phone ya in a few hours, Father.' Ferdia turned off the phone. Cursing the cramped space, he drove out and pointed the car towards Dublin.

2.40 P.M.

ADAM STYNE TWISTED in the wheelchair.

'It must be serious if you're here on Saturday,' he said.

256

'I didn't want you spend the weekend fretting.' Alistair O'Brian took off his hat, unwound his long scarf and removed a file from an inside coat pocket. 'Yesterday afternoon's session didn't go well. But all's not lost.'

Styne hadn't needed to read Gloria's body language to know the session had been bad. He hadn't concentrated on the task in hand, his mind stuck on the Hattinger business. He'd tried to engage with her at the end, but Gloria remained tight-lipped as she gathered up the cards and left.

Another bitch to add to my shit list.

For the first time since his schooldays, Styne found himself not in control. Anxiety twisted and churned him up leaving him on tenterhooks. All night, he'd limped around the cell-sized room, hyper, yet exhausted. Rest was impossible. Now, he was too tired to focus but wanted to discuss his next move. Although he didn't trust O'Brien.

If he'd told me about Madeline and the business…

Just for a second, he wondered if he swallowed the tablets he'd squirrelled away, would it be enough to end it all? He felt for the knife lodged into the plaster of Paris, and touched it for reassurance.

Anything is better than this hell hole. There has to be a way out.

O'Brien clicked his fingers and brought Styne back to the present. 'Are you with me, Adam?'

'Yes, yes. What do I need to do to get released?'

'I said, on Monday you'll be taken back to the hospital for a check-up. That'll give the psychiatrists here an opportunity to discuss your case.'

'What does that mean?'

'Exactly what I said. They'll read each other's notes, have a discussion, and make a decision about your… um, condition.'

'I don't have any condition. What've you heard?'

'Nothing.' O'Brien scratched his head. 'But there's a strong possibility that they're going to bring in another psychiatrist—'

'What for?' Styne gripped the arms of the wheelchair to stop himself springing forward and throttling the barrister. 'I've answered everything they asked. What else could they—?'

'Hmm.' O'Brien shrugged. 'It's not usual, but sometimes they look for another opinion.'

'You're useless,' Styne snapped. 'I've done everything you asked, against my better judgement, and now you're telling me… what? It's all for nothing?' His grip tightened on the wheelchair arm. 'That these so-called professionals are so stupid they can't agree on facts, so they have to bring in some other quack? For what? So that they can dream up with another scenario to keep me here? You're fired. I demand—'

'Calm down, Adam.'

'I *won't* calm down. I want a new barrister that'll get me out of here and into a regular prison.'

'O'Brien shook his head. 'You don't want that, Adam. Trust me.'

'Trust you? What has trusting you got me? Your job was to get me out, not keep me locked up at the mercy of those... fraudsters who think they know what's going on in my brain. Pffft. You know, and *they* know there's nothing wrong with me. Now, recommend me a new barrister. One that isn't as inept as you.'

O'Brien looked over his glasses rim at Styne. 'If that's your wish, Adam, then I'll make the necessary arrangements. However—'

'It is,' Styne said.

O'Brien nodded. 'Okay, then. I'll set the wheels in motion.' He buttoned his coat, picked up his hat from the bed, tucked the file under his arm and walked away and spoke over his shoulder. 'I wish you all the best with your defence. He opened the door.

'Wait,' Styne said.

O'Brien turned and raised his eyebrows.

'What exactly is the purpose of another... evaluation?' Styne asked.

O'Brien stepped back into the room. 'I've only had brief conversations. I don't have the final reports yet, but two psychiatrists are of the mind that you're using a farrago of facts and fiction to convince them you're sane.'

'I am sane.'

'Regardless of what you think, Adam, these people aren't stupid. They've spent years studying human behaviour and aren't that easy to sway or influence. But they're professionals and won't make any rash decisions, hence the reason to call in another colleague for his opinion. As I said, it's not usual, but it's not unheard of either.'

'What's their issue?' Styne asked. 'Is it possible to—?'

O'Brien held up a hand. 'Adam, they're uncomfortable in your presence. They feel you're playing games, assessing them, turning the tables, and then tailoring your remarks to give the best impression that'll help your cause. Like people do at job interviews.'

'That's—'

'One told me,' O'Brien interrupted, 'that you are unable to admit you're wrong, or have ever done wrong. You blame stress, work, tablets, the weather... whatever. Nobody's an angel, Adam. We hurt people emotionally and physically, yet *you* manage to project blame on everyone else. Apparently, you're always looking for an angle. Always reframing reality to fit your narcissistic delusions.'

Styne stared at his barrister.

'Basically,' O'Brien said, 'on the one hand, you're trying too hard. A second shrink told me he found no signs or symptoms of psychosis. Nothing that would indicate incompetency or arouse suspicion. You don't hear voices. There's no valid depression or elevation of moods. Your outer perceptual reality is accurately recognised; social values accredited. You have excellent logical reasoning, which I would expect from a man in your position, and you can foresee the consequences of injudicious or antisocial acts. However, you seem... unable to respond with adequate feelings when discussing your wife or deceased parents. You've an inability to criticise your own mistakes, Adam, and while it's not end game, it's a big warning sign when a patient can't acknowledge former mistakes.'

'Is that it?' Styne asked. 'My freedom is in the hands of—'

O'Brien looked over his glasses at Styne. 'One of the psychiatrists is an ex-colleague of mine,' he said. 'We had a phone conversation just before I came to see you. I was told that you don't suffer from any mental disease or defect. You were never a victim of physical, sexual or psychological abuse. This colleague is convinced you murdered those women. With premeditation and deliberation. That you're uninhibited by any moral concerns or considerations. You kill because you want to kill, a psychopath, incapable of empathy. No one else matters unless they serve a purpose. You've no problem hurting others, physically or emotionally. No guilt. No shame. No remorse.'

Then I'll never get out of here. If one of them argues against me, they'll all agree. Should I overcome O'Brien now? There's very little staff on for the weekend. Or do I wait for a better opportunity at the hospital on Monday?

Styne's hand edged around the back of his knee and eased the knife free.

'You're a deceptive, clever liar,' O'Brien continued, 'who has learned to live in the conventional, social realm with everyone else, and also in your private world. You're extremely skilful in separating these two worlds, Adam. People with this ability can commit the most horrific crime and then come home and have dinner with their family,' O'Brien clicked his fingers, 'like nothing happened. They can switch roles as easy as changing socks. This colleague called you a chameleon, and that's why they need another opinion.'

'Was it Gloria?' Styne asked.

'Doesn't matter,' O'Brien said.

'Will this new person be someone you know?'

O'Brien shrugged. 'It's possible, but I won't be told. I've done all I can for now, plus I've manipulated the system to get you in here where you have a certain amount of freedom, as opposed to the prison system, where you'd be chewed up and spat out. But,' O'Brien slapped the file against his thigh, 'it's your decision, and if you feel your best option is in prison, then so be it.' He turned to leave.

'Maybe I was too hasty,' Styne said. 'You're still my best hope.'

O'Brien gave a crooked grin. 'Apology accepted. There's nothing we can do now. Let's see who the new psychiatrist is, and then we can discuss tactics, eh?' He turned towards the door.

'What's happening with my business?' Styne called after him.

If he tells me a lie, I'll kill him. If they think I'm mad, I'll show them mad.

O'Brien leaned a shoulder against the door and sighed. 'Nothing, Adam. There's nothing happening and there's nothing you can do at present, except stay in control. You're going to the hospital Monday, and I'll see you when you get back. Now, try and get some rest.'

'You dropped something,' Styne pointed to the side of the wheelchair.

'Did I?'

'Yes, just here.'

O'Brien came back and hunkered down beside the wheelchair. 'I don't see—'

Styne drove the knife into O'Brien's throat. Blood trickled out and O'Brien chocked and tried to pull the knife free, his fingers slipping on the bloodied plastic handle. Styne stood, pushed O'Brien onto his back, pulled off his shoes and trousers and ignored the man's gurgles and gasps for breath. He dressed himself in O'Brien's clothes—the trousers were tight over the plaster—then grimaced in distaste when he saw the blood on O'Brien's scarf and coat.

At least the coat is dark, so it won't be noticed.

Styne whipped off O'Brien's scarf. The coat was more problematic, as O'Brien wouldn't let go of the knife, but Styne prised the barrister's fingers away long enough to free the coat sleeves. The coat was also tight, but he buttoned it, then wound the scarf around his neck and lower face. He searched through pockets, found the phone, a wallet and car keys. Placing the file under his arm like O'Brien did, Styne stepped over the groaning man, walked into the corridor and closed the door behind him. He held the phone to his ear and talked into in as he walked towards the exit. A security man nodded at him from the glass hut, and followed him along the corridor, a set of keys jingling in his hand. At the first locked door, Styne turned away and kept talking into the phone, as the security man unlocked it, then brushed past, ignoring the pain in his knee. Through the next doorway, and Styne could see the front door ahead. He took out the car key and was pressing the fob before the security guard has the front door opened. A car alarm to his left chirruped and without acknowledgement or hesitation, Styne walked to the car, scarf tails flying behind him. He heard the door slam behind him as he got into O'Brien's car and drove out. He didn't look back.

I need to get to the farm. Then I can start to take my revenge.

3.10 P.M.
'WELL, IF IT isn't the bleedin' vampire back for more blood.'

Washed, shaved and off drugs for a few days, already Decaf looked a different person. His skin was pale, but he appeared years younger. Ensconced in a private room, away from the main St. James's hospital artery, he had round-the-clock protection, courtesy of Pete.

'Story, bud?'

'It went down like you said, Decaf. Everyone's busted. But Dessie didn't show. He's still abroad.'

Decaf shook his head. 'Sumptin's wrong. He never misses a handover. Hasta make sure it goes off clean. Too much at stake. This deal was huge, so he'd defin'ly be sniffin' round like an ex-wife. Unless… he somehow got wind. Dessie's cagey. He's like a bleedin' virus that thrives on penicillin. Still, he's gonna throw a bleedin' wobbler when he finds out his gear's gone. You gotta find him, bud. We're not safe while he's out there.'

'You're safe,' Ferdia said. 'You won't get abandoned. I think he'll wait for a phone call to tell him everything's cool, and when he doesn't get it, he'll panic. If he has anything stashed in Ireland, he'll come back for it. Then he'll scamper to Europe and stay low 'til the heat dies down.'

'He'd better stay very bleedin' low, 'cos them fellas that gave 'im the gear will be gunnin' for 'im. They'll want their money, an' they won't ask nicely.'

'Exactly. That's why he needs cash. Where would he keep a stash for emergencies?'

Decaf giggled. 'Bud, he wouldn't trust his own mother, so t'would hafta be someplace that no one knew. His auld fella would find it at home. Too many people around Whispers an' his place on Thomas Street. I'd say the gaff in Foxrock. He bought it last year an' no one's allowed in. I was there once, a few months back, in the middle of the night, an' he made me wait in the car. An' me dyin' for a piss. Anyway, when he went in, I pissed on his big gate.'

'Where in Foxrock?'

'Aww, man.' Decaf closed his eyes. 'I was fried that nigh'. Haven't a foo—'

'Think,' Ferdia urged. 'Gimme something.'

Decaf thought. 'I remember Cornelscourt shopping centre on my righ'. An' after that we turned left.'

'Good,' Ferdia said. 'And then?'

Decaf scrunched up his face. 'Bud, I... there was a roundabou' an' we turned righ', or was it left? Yeah, defin'ly left. The house is on a corner, an' there's a high wall around it, an' there's a line of trees growin' inside the wall. The electric gate's massive. When I was pissin', I remember thinkin' "that gate's massive".'

'That's great, Decaf. Keep going.'

'That's it, bud. There's nuthin' more. We were only there to drop off or pick up sumptin'.'

'Can you remember how long it took to get from Cornelscourt to the house?'

'Minutes, bud. It's not far.'

Ferdia moved towards the door. 'Grand. I'll have a look around, see if I can spot anything. I'll get back to you. Stay loose, Decaf.'

'You too, vampire. Oh, wait.'

'Yeah?'

'That night in the car, Dessie said if the neighbours knew wha' he was doing in the house, they'd have a fookin' fit. He laughed at the good of it, like 'twas a game to him.'

'Huh,' Ferdia said. 'See ya.'

'Hey,' Decaf called. 'Make sure that cop fella stays on his side of the door. I don't want his kind stinkin' up my air.'

'Yeah, yeah…'

FERDIA PASSED CORNELSCOURT shopping centre.

Decaf's directions weren't bad. Because of his years driving getaway cars across the city, he'd an inbuilt instinct for remembering routes. But the affluent suburb of Foxrock was a warren of roads, roundabouts and electric-gated houses built on corners. Ferdia also couldn't afford to hang around. Residents were apt to call Gardaí if they spotted a loiterer.

He made several passes, widening his search area. Decaf's words about Dolan being up to something, replayed on his mind. He wondered what that meant. He doubled back to Cornelscourt centre and began again. It would soon be dusk. Have to make a decision, he thought, and circled by the half-dozen potential houses. As his focus narrowed, his considerations became clearer. Stupid me, he thought. Dolan's away all week, so there'll be no car going in or out. His driveway will have a fresh bed of snow.

That idea eliminated four homes.

Something stirred in his brain as he checked the other two houses. He couldn't grasp the thought, so he drove around again, in the hope his eyes would latch onto whatever niggled him. On the third circuit, the solution popped, and Ferdia smiled. He stopped and stared at the house.

'Would you believe it?' he muttered. 'In the middle of feckin' Foxrock.'

He drove around again, convinced himself he was right, parked fifty metres away, where he had a partial view of the gateway, and tried to judge the situation from Dolan's perspective. I'd grab cash and run, he thought. Cash is king when you want to stay under the radar. With no idea if Dolan would appear in an hour, or a day, or at all, Ferdia reckoned that if he did, it would be sooner rather than later. He squeezed some feeling into his cramped legs and settled in to wait.

5.25 PM

THE INBOUND RYANAIR flight was twenty minutes late landing.

Dessie Dolan pushed through passengers standing in the aisle until he was almost at the front. Then he hopped from foot to foot and willed the door to open. Seconds were precious. That twenty-minute delay could be a disaster. He wanted to be in and out, pronto.

The customs man gave the passport a cursory look. Dolan walked into the baggage area, through the arrivals hall, and out to the short-term car park. He cursed the parking fees, fed the required notes into the machine and snatched the ticket it spat out. Thirty-five minutes later, he was at Cornelscourt. He calculated how long it would take to complete his work, and relaxed. Maybe he'd even have time to park in the long-term park going back, and save himself some money. Robbin' bastards, he thought. He'd have to book online, but he could do that in the house. He swung left at the roundabout, happy that he'd a workable plan. The gate fob was in the cup holder and Dolan pressed it before getting to the corner. He swung into the entrance and waited for the gate to open, his eyes taking in the pristine snow-covered driveway. He tapped the steering wheel, impatient, steered up to the house, leapt from the car and unlocked the front door. Dolan was inside the house when a figure slipped through the electric gates seconds before they clicked shut.

STAYING IN THE tracks the car had made, Ferdia walked to the house. He debated whether to smash his way in, or wait and see what Dolan did. His mind gave off a series of bad ideas. He reached across the car bonnet, snapped off both wiper blades and put them into his pocket. That'll slow you down, he thought and wondered if Dolan had left the keys in the ignition. He chanced opening the driver's door. The keys weren't there, but the gate fob was on the dashboard. Ferdia grabbed it. Noises inside the house made him step back around the side of the house. The decision to move in or wait was taken out of his hands when Dolan reappeared, lugging a large suitcase. He angled it into the car boot, pushed it in, ran back into the house and dragged out another case. Ferdia was close enough to hear Dolan grunting with exertion. He watched the man slam the boot shut and return to the house, leaving the front door ajar. A chink of light escaped but apart from that, the place was dark.

After five minutes, Ferdia pushed away from the wall and approached the car. Whatever's in those suitcases, must be important, he reckoned. He checked the front door. All clear. He opened the car boot and pulled the cases out. They weren't heavy, maybe twenty-five kilos each, but with his busted ribs, it felt like they weighed a tonne. Ferdia closed the boot, picked the cases up by their handles and half ran down the driveway. At a large tree near the electric gate, he dropped them and walked back towards to the house, panting. Half way up the drive, his mobile rang, and he swore under his breath. He pulled out the phone, glanced at the caller ID. Ronan Lambe. Ferdia disconnected, turned off the mobile and waited to see if Dolan would appear. Nothing. He staggered to the house, sagged against the wall, and bent over, breath hissing through gritted teeth. He'd have no trouble taking on a scrawny individual like Dolan, but knew he didn't have the energy to chase around the house after him. Better let Dolan come to him.

The clack of shoe leather on a tiled hallway made Ferdia straighten. The footsteps came towards the front door. Ferdia eased onto the small portico and stood directly in front of the door. When Dolan opened the door, Ferdia said 'knock, knock,' and drove his left fist into the middle of Dolan's face. Ferdia knew from experience how disorientating that punch was. It only takes a few pounds of pressure to break a person's nose, but the pain is excruciating. The nose is also connected to eyes via tear ducts, and a direct blow usually results in a temporary loss of vision. Dolan flew backwards and slid along the marble floor. He came to a halt when his head hit the stairs. Ferdia followed, crouched over Dolan, and knocked him out with a crack to the jaw. He turned Dolan onto his side, straightened, shook the pain from his wrist, and had a quick scout around. Standard hall and stairway. Doors to the left and right. Locked. A third door at the end of the hall was unlocked. Ferdia put his shoulder to it and forced it open.

Light and heat blasted him in the face, and the smell, a combination of pine needles and pig slurry, was stifling. Ferdia ventured into what was once a kitchen. The kitchen units, studded walls, partitions and doorways had been ripped out, leaving a new ground floor plan shaped like an inverted U. Every centimetre of wall, window and ceiling had foil insulation tacked to it. Dozens of

Infrared lamps shone directly on knee-high crates containing cannabis plants, turning the place into a hothouse. Ferdia wandered along a narrow path that allowed the grower ease of access and looked at the crates on either side. 'Huh. A grow house in Foxrock.' He knew nothing about cannabis growing, but this looked like a sophisticated set-up. Back in the hallway, he checked on Dolan, then went upstairs. This was a replica of the ground floor. He spotted half-a-dozen carbon filters, and some of the Infrared lamps were switched off. Probably on timers, Ferdia decided as he plodded back downstairs. He nudged the unconscious man with his shoe. 'You must have some electricity bill,' he said, and waited for him to wake up.

A siren wailed in the distance.

Now that he had netted Dolan, Ferdia didn't know what to do with him. He'd focused so much on the capture, he hadn't given much thought to the next stage.

The yowl of a squad car siren grew louder.

Yes, he wanted revenge, but...

It wasn't one siren. There were several.

Ferdia frowned, moved to the hall door and looked out. He couldn't see beyond the high wall and trees, but the reflections of flashing red and blue lights were clear in the dark. Close now, and they were coming this way.

Dolan groaned.

Ferdia hopped back into the hall and delivered another short, sharp punch to Dolan's jaw, knocking him out again. Then he walked down the driveway. The sirens were almost at the other side of the wall. He crouched beside the suitcases, concealing his big frame in the shadows of the large tree. A siren yipped and swung into Dolan's gateway. From this angle, Ferdia couldn't see, but he could hear a lot of chatter. How'd the cops find out Dolan was back so quick, he wondered. Well, they're here now. Might as well let them in. He pressed the fob and heard the gates clank open.

Engines revved.

The first squad car raced up the driveway. And another. And another. Car doors opened and Ferdia heard footsteps crunch through snow and ice. He lifted his head and counted eight officers surround the open front door. He inhaled a deep breath, caught the suitcase handles, and stumbled through the electric gates as they closed. The Renault Clio was fifty metres away. He glanced around at the other secluded residences. Nobody was out on the roadway, but that didn't mean people weren't watching from inside. Ferdia zigzagged to the car, fumbled for keys, opened the boot, threw the suitcases inside and sped away.

Back at Cornelscourt, he turned into the shopping centre car park and shut off the engine. He got out, exhaled, and let the night air soak up the sweat plastered on his face. He unbuttoned his shirt and looked at blood spots that had seeped through the bandages again. Then he opened the car boot, looked at the suitcases, unzipped one, opened it, and blinked. Bundles of hundred, fifty and twenty euro notes filled the interior, and he stared at the windfall for a long time. He'd never seen so much money. What now, Ferdia thought. He walked over to a bin and pushed Dolan's car wipers into it. What the feck am I gonna do now?

9

SUNDAY 27 JANUARY. 9.30 A.M.

'WHAT'S THE STORY, vampire?'

'It's all good, Decaf.' Ferdia threw a Sunday newspaper on the bed. Decaf peered at the writing.

'What's it say?'

Ferdia read out the bold print:

"Following a phone call reporting a domestic disturbance, Gardaí discovered a sophisticated grow house in Foxrock, south Dublin. During the search, they found the entire house had been converted into a factory, and fitted with extractor fans, timers for lighting and heaters and an irrigation system.

A large number of plants in various stages of growth were seized, and a man was arrested at the scene. The drugs will be sent to Forensic Science Ireland for analysis. A Garda spokesperson said the seizure was worth an estimated €1.5 million euro…"

'Dafuk?' Decaf laughed. 'Neighbours won't be impressed, wha?'

Ferdia said: 'That cocaine bust yesterday? That's serious jail time. The grow house will add a couple more years to his sentence.'

Decaf shook his head. 'You don't know Dessie, bud. He's a bleedin' gouger. He'll squeal on anyone to get a lighter sentence.'

'Then he's safer inside,' Ferdia said. 'Drug lords will take him out if he rats. Anyway, just wanted to let you know it's over, Decaf. I'm moving you to a private hospital tomorrow where you'll heal up for a month or so.'

'Then wha?'

'Then I'll get you a proper job.' Ferdia stretched. 'I know a garage man who's looking for a mechanic.'

Decaf grinned. 'I fookin' love cars, me.' 'His eyes narrowed and he looked at Ferdia, suspicious. 'Why're doing this, bud? What's your angle?'

'No angle,' Ferdia said. 'I'm gonna go see your mother now. I've got some stuff for her.' He winked. 'See you tomorrow.'

'Diya know howta find her?'

'Yeah, yeah. I'll get her.'

'Thanks, bud,' Decaf said. 'Tell her I said hello.'

'Will do.' Ferdia opened the door.

'Hey,' Decaf called. 'How'd you find the house yesterday? Didya fly all over Foxrock with other vampires?'

Ferdia grinned. 'The directions were good, Decaf. You gave me a general location and house description. The gates were important. Then I looked for houses with no car tracks going in or out, 'cos Dessie was away, right? I'd an idea that if he wouldn't let you into the house, he must've a reason. It took me a while to figure out what was different from Dessie's place to any other in the area. One house had no snow or ice on the roof, which meant there was serious heat being generated from inside.' Ferdia shrugged. 'That got me thinking, and I'd figured it out before Dessie arrived.'

'Sweet,' Decaf said. 'An' then you called the cops?'

'No, that wasn't me. Some of the neighbours must have seen me snoop around. It happens. Oh, do you remember a guy who worked for Dolan that wore a cowboy hat?'

'Yeah. Tommy Mellon. Why?'

'He's dead, isn't he?'

'Yeah.'

'Do you know where the body is?'

'Maybe.' Decaf squinted at Ferdia.

'I want the cops to find it. His parents need closure.'

'I was there, bud,' Decaf said. 'I know exactly where he is…'

FERDIA DROVE ALONG the quays, towards Dublin's north inner city.

Sheriff Street was empty except for three hardy smokers loitering at a corner. They stared hard as Ferdia passed. He swung into Castleforbes road, parked, grabbed a bulky Dunnes Stores bag from under the passenger seat, and walked to Decaf's house.

'Howya, missus,' he said to the suspicious woman who opened the door a crack. 'I'm a friend of Decaf's. He asked me to call.'

'Patrick?' I haven't seen him in—'

'Yeah. He's grand. Told me to say hello. He's getting cleaned up. Here,' Ferdia thrust the plastic bag at her. 'Asked me to give you this.'

Eyes full of doubt, Mrs Coffey opened the door a fraction, took the bag and peered into it. The door opened wider, and Ferdia got a partial look at Decaf's mother. A dressing gown was wrapped around her small-boned frame, and permanent worry-lines creased her face.

'He also said not to give any to his auld fella.'

Mrs Coffee looked at Ferdia and back at the bag. 'Is this…?'

''Tis, missus.' Ferdia looked around. The smokers were walking towards him. 'Listen, I'll be off now. Take care.'

'Who are you?' Mrs Coffey called after him.

'Friend of Decaf's,' Ferdia said. 'Keeping a promise I made him.'

GRIEF CAN DISSOLVE a person.

Sharona Waters looked washed out as she stumbled into Kathleen Fallon's hallway. Ronan Lambe followed, red-eyed from lack of sleep. He was ashen as a corpse.

'We spoke to Rebecca a few hours before she died,' Sharona sniffed and wiped her nose with the back of her hand. 'I keep asking Ronan, did I say something wrong? Should I have tried harder to… I don't know, make her stay with me? I wanted her to talk about her ordeal. I hoped she'd share some of the painful experiences. It would relieve a bit of the agony. Maybe I pushed her too hard and something I said triggered a reaction.'

'I doubt that,' Hugh said.

Ronan rubbed Sharona's back and said nothing.

Sharona handed Hugh an envelope. 'She left this for me.'

Hugh unfolded the single sheet of paper:

> *Sharona,*
> *We can put up with pain once we know there's a cure, but when hope dies and all that's left is constant agony, with no way out… what's the point? You've been an amazing support, but what's the point living, if I can't even control my thoughts? I want to get back to where I was before, but I*

know I never will. Seeing how easy it was for those men to pick us up off the street confirmed that. Now, every minute, I face the unbearable terror of the unknown, and that fear will never end.

I feel ashamed, and I don't know why. The only reason I can write this is because you know the truth. I can't tell my parents everything that happened. They'd feel they were somehow to blame. Relieving my burden and putting it onto them isn't an option. And if there's ever a court case and trial, just the thought of that media circus makes me physically sick. It would be like getting violated all over again.

People scare me.

Being alone scares me.

If I see an open window, I'm afraid someone will break in. If I close it, I get claustrophobic. This fear will never go away, and that's my biggest fear. I know my family will support me, but I feel so alone, hopeless, and desperate, even surrounded by people who love me.

I'll never be able to get emotionally involved in a relationship. How can I attain any level of intimacy after what those bastards put me through? I'll always be vulnerable, suspicious, afraid to let go, never be able to relax enough to form a connection. I'd be scared he'd find out, afraid he'd ask me something I'd have to lie about. I'm a shit liar and someone always finds out. How'll my parents and sister cope then? How will I cope? I can't process all this. My brain's on fire. Death will be a relief compared to a life sentence for something that wasn't my fault.

Don't hate me, Sharona. I know you see me as a heroine and a survivor, but I see myself as a victim. I'll always be a victim. I know you want me to focus on the future, but there's no future. This is for the best. Thank Ronan and Hugh for everything. Please remember me. Goodbye.

Rebecca. Xx

Hugh rubbed his eyes and looked at his mother, who sat quiet in her armchair, sensing the sombre atmosphere. Sharona slumped on the settee, staring at the fire. Ronan, beside her, chewed his bottom lip. Hugh handed the letter back to Sharona.

The back door opened and Ferdia tramped into the living room. 'Was passing and saw the hire car. Thought it was you.' he tossed the Clio car key to Sharona. 'We can swap.'

'Ferdia!' Kathleen stretched out her arms like a child wanting to get lifted up.

Ferdia leaned over and hugged her. 'You look younger every time I see you, Kathleen.' His gaze skimmed the faces of the glum trio. He straightened, put his back to the fire, and rocked back on his heels. 'I hope Rebecca's at peace,' he said. 'If it's any consolation, most of the trafficking gang have been rounded up. Ye missed it yesterday. Gunfight in Ganestown.'

No one responded or asked a follow-up question.

Ferdia tried again. 'Guess what? Marcus Mulryan, the detective, was part of the gang. He worked hand-in-hand with Dessie Dolan *and* the traffickers. He was the main reason they got away for so long.' Ferdia looked at Sharona. 'Probably him who tipped the kidnappers off 'bout your and Rebecca's whereabouts.'

Sharona nodded.

'Oh,' Ferdia clapped his hands. 'Dessie Dolan was nabbed last night. He'd a grow house in Foxrock. Imagine? Cops found him face down in the hall. Must've tripped over his shoelaces when he was trying to get away.'

Silence.

'Did ye hear that Adam Styne escaped? He's on the loose.'

That got a reaction.

In unison, three people said, 'What?'

'Do none of ye buy a newspaper or listen to the news?' Ferdia asked. 'Yeah, he stabbed his barrister yesterday afternoon, took his clothes to disguise himself, walked out and drove away. There's a warrant out for his arrest. The barrister's alive. "Stable" the newsman said.'

Hugh and Sharona looked at each other. 'He knows where you live,' Hugh said. 'You're not going back to Mountain View until he's caught.'

'It'll be grand,' Ferdia said. 'I've asked Pete to get police protection for ye. It'll be only for a day or so, before they'll find 'em. There's a squad car outside here already. I expect there's one at 29 Mountain View as well.'

Hugh groaned. 'What am I gonna tell Ruth?'

Ferdia stepped towards the door. 'Huh. Aye. Well, I'll leave that to you. Anyway, I've to see Father Kelly about something before I pick up Master David.'

'Did he get you yesterday evening?' Ronan asked.

'Who?'

'Father Kelly.'

'No. Why?'

'He rang me. Wanted to know how I tracked Rebecca to Rathmines. Asked if I could trace your phone, an' see where you were.'

'He did, did he?'

'I rang to tell you—'

'Yeah, I saw the missed call,' Ferdia said. 'Did you...?'

'Yeah. Easy peasy. He said it was urgent.'

'Feck sake,' Ferdia grumbled. 'I can't go for a... Next phone I get, it'll have no feckin' gizmos. Man's got a right to his privacy. Right. I'm off.'

Sharona heaved herself from the settee. 'We'd better go too.'

Hugh linked Kathleen outside to wave goodbye and looked at the squad car parked at the gateway. Sharona handed Ferdia the hire car fob, and he used his hip to nudge her away from Ronan and Hugh. 'Whatcha gonna do?' he asked.

'About what? Styne?'

'No. Rebecca. She has to be remembered. You should set up some kind of hostel for trafficked women.'

'What?'

'A secure place to help those people,' Ferdia scratched his jaw, 'in Rebecca's memory, like.'

'Christ, Ferdia. I wouldn't even know where to begin,' Sharona said. 'It's not as simple as getting premises. It would have to be secure, and you'd need experienced staff: doctors, nurses, psychologists, a chef, housekeepers, individual and group therapy, personal defence lessons—'

'If change ever comes for these people, it'll hafta come from a woman, Sharona. If you don't champion the cause, who will?'

'Hmm. A detective said something similar to Rebecca the other evening,' Sharona said. 'It would cost a fortune,' she added.

'I'll fund it,' Ferdia said. 'There'll be grants you can apply for once you're up an' running. It wouldn't be a sprint. More a marathon.'

'There'd be uproar in Ganestown,' Sharona said.

Ferdia shrugged. 'Feck the begrudgers. Trafficked people don't get enough government support, and the general public don't wanna know.'

'You can't fight the system,' Sharona said.

Ferdia looked at her. 'Well, if you can't fight it, change it.'

Sharona stared back. 'You've thought about this, haven't you?'

'A bit,' Ferdia said. 'Look, think about it, is all I'm asking. You'd be great, fighting for those with no voice of their own.'

'I'll consider it,' Sharona said. 'I got a call from my solicitor last Friday. I've to appear in Ganestown court next Wednesday to give evidence against Milo Barnes and this stalking case. I could do without that right now.'

'Huh, snap. I've a court date tomorrow,' Ferdia said, 'to try and convince a judge that Malcolm isn't the feckin' eejit everyone thinks he is.'

'That'll be hard. What'd he do this time?'

'Long story, but he's an international drug smuggler now. Anything for a gambling stake.'

'Sweet baby Jesus,' Sharona said. 'What a… Charlie spoilt him.'

'Yeah. Easy got, easy squandered.' Ferdia saluted Hugh and Ronan. 'I'll have your jalopy back tomorrow, Hugh,' he said, and moved towards the cars.

'That hostel funding?' Sharona called after him.

'What about it?'

'Where's it coming from?'

'What's that got to do with anything?'

'I know you were in Foxrock last night, Ferdia. We were driving to Westport when Father Kelly rang Ronan. It *is* Dessie Dolan's money that'd be financing it? Isn't it?'

Ferdia opened the Clio boot, removed two suitcases, tossed them into the hire car, and winked at Sharona. 'So what if it is? Wouldn't that be karma? Sometimes karma's a bitch. Slán.'

11.45 A.M.

FERDIA WAITED UNTIL the congregation had dispersed after 11 a.m. mass.

It gave him time to figure out what lie to tell the priest. He walked to the side entrance, a bulky Dunnes Stores bag under his arm, and entered the sacristy. Father Kelly had removed his vestments and was back in civilian gear.

'Ferdia, I'm so glad you're safe. I prayed for you, but I knew the Lord would protect you. God works in mysterious ways.'

'He does indeed, Father.' Ferdia looked around. Portraits of dead priests hung on a wall, alongside a picture of Pope Francis beaming from a lob-sided picture frame. The place hadn't changed since he'd served mass forty years ago. 'If 'twas him who phoned the cops and told them to call around to Dolan's gaff, then that's way too mysterious for me, Father.'

Father Kelly wrung his hands and looked contrite. 'When I thought about what I said to make you cut off the call so fast, I'd an idea what you were up to. I didn't want you to do something you'd regret, Ferdia. Had to phone the Gardaí a few times before I convinced them there might be an issue. I played the priest card.' He cracked a smile. 'Is it over?'

'It's over, Father,' Ferdia lied.

'Then, I'm glad I did it.' The priest removed an overcoat from a hook behind the door.

'So, what've you done about the roof, Father, apart from praying for fine weather?'

'I've spoken from the pulpit. The congregants know I'm hoping their generous nature will—'

'This might help.' Ferdia handed over the bag of money. 'Dessie Dolan specifically asked me to make sure you get it.'

The priest looked into the bag and then at Ferdia.

'Restitution for ahh, past sins,' Ferdia said. 'God. Mysterious ways, an' all that.'

'This's a lot of money, Ferdia.'

'It'll help you keep the lights on, Father. Sure, if there's any left over, you'll find a way to put it to good use.'

The priest looked at the money again. 'You didn't have to do this, Ferdia. You could've kept it and—'

'Not my style, Father.' Ferdia opened the sacristy door and stepped out.

'Will I see you at Mass, Ferdia? You're welcome… to see how the roof repairs turn out.'

Ferdia smiled. 'We'll see, Father. We'll see. Don't look now, but the window blinds in the house across the road are moving.'

'Ahh, the curtain twitcher. What's next for you, Ferdia?'

Ferdia scratched his head. 'The insurance company have agreed to pay out. Builders will start to demolish the shell of my old house soon.'

'That's great, Ferdia. We'll never forget the dead, but the living have got to live.'

'Huh. The money will buy a soft bed, Father, but I'm not sure it'll help me sleep. Slán.'

'Stay safe, Ferdia,' the priest said.

'You too, Father.' Ferdia walked away.

'Ferdia?' the curtain twitcher called.

Ferdia shaded his eyes against the dirty, copper-coloured winter sun and crunched across the icy road. 'Howaya, missus.'

'Ferdia. How can you walk around without a coat? It's freezing.'

'Argh, I think warm thoughts, missus.'

'I never got a chance to sympathise with you after Ciara's death,' the curtain twitcher said. 'God love her. Must've broken your heart. And she'd such a big funeral.'

'Thanks, missus. Aye, she had. That's Ireland for ya. People will walk twenty miles to your funeral, but won't cross the road to congratulate you.'

'I haven't seen you around the church much, Ferdia. Do you mind me asking what you and Father Kelly were—?'

'Don't mind at all, missus.' Ferdia turned back towards the car. His mobile buzzed and he read Sharona's text message:

Bring it on. I'm ready.

Ferdia grinned.

On a grass verge, a single daffodil bulb had pushed through a speckled carpet of half-thawed snow. Spring was on the way.

ACKNOWLEDGEMENTS

When I had this novel half-written, a brief overheard exchange forced me to rethink, start from scratch again, and dig deep into areas I knew little about.

That led to many conversations with detectives working the greater Dublin area, and I want to thank them for their time, patience and advice in helping me figure out various strands that were important to the story.

Also essential were the discussions I had with past and present staff from Dundrum Mental Hospital. Insider knowledge is crucial in sprinkling real facts into a fictional narrative, and these chats were vital in keeping that balance.

Once I'd assembled the manuscript, I handed it over to my trusted beta readers, who collectively (and not too nicely) told me what worked and what didn't. A massive shout out to Sinéad Ní Ciardubháin, Simon Armstrong, Jane Badrock, Peter McCauley, Jack Keaton, Emily Rainsford and Jonathan Black. As in my previous book, crime writer Martin Keating came up with more brilliant suggestions. I'm privileged to have him in my corner.

The Tullamore Book Club trundles on every month, taking pandemics, lockdowns and Covid in its stride by switching to Zoom. These amazing readers and writers keep me grounded and make me read "stuff" I normally wouldn't touch. Sincere thanks to Lisa-Marie McKeown, Maura Flynn and Loraine Walsh. Your critiques and recommendations were invaluable in tightening up plotlines.

As I write this acknowledgement—early December 2021—and still several months before you, dear reader, will have an opportunity to get your hands on the novel, a number of online book clubs have already volunteered their support. It's difficult to describe how important these groups are to writers. With over 5,000 books published worldwide *every day*, it's impossible for new writers to get noticed without the assistance of people who spend their free time reviewing novels. The Fiction Café Book Club is one example. Ran by powerhouse literary lovers Wendy Clarke, Emma Louise Bunting, Melanie Thomas, Pam Devine, Ellie Bell, Katy Baldwin, Michaela Balfour, Lauren Roberts, Emma-Louise Smith and Sarah Price, these committed individuals are a lifesaver to authors. Huge, huge thanks to them for their help and support.

Tracy Fenton, the driving force behind The Book Club, is another incredible inspiration, as is reviewer Dee Groocock, and live interviewer/podcaster, Donna Morfett. Fellow crime writer Noelle Holten also blogs and reviews crime novels at CrimeBookJunkie Book Reviews.

In Ireland, we have the Rick O'Shea Book Club, and bookblogger Mairéad Hearne. Both go out of their way to ensure the Irish literary scene is front and centre for readers. My deepest gratitude to all of you, and every online book club, for the work and commitment you put in, day after day, for little or no recompense.

Special thanks to Sean Coleman and his team at Red Dog Press for pulling my manuscript from the submission file, and deciding it had potential. His phone call validated all the solitary hours spend hunched over a laptop. Also, the welcome I received from other Red Dog authors, was humbling.

Finally, to you, the reader. None of this would make any sense if you didn't continue to read, share, comment and review. You are the heartbeat that drives me, and every writer, to create better work.

ABOUT THE AUTHOR

A native of Co. Roscommon, Ireland, Eoghan wrote his first story aged nine. At college, he studied Computer Programming, works in Sales Management & Marketing, but his passion for reading and writing remain.

Eoghan's stories were shortlisted for the 2018 Bridport Short Story Prize, and Listowel's 2019 Bryan McMahon Short Story Award Competition. Others have been published in various anthologies. He has also completed two crime fiction novels in a planned trilogy set in the Irish Midlands, and has started work on the third.

A graduate of Maynooth University's Creative Writing Curriculum and Curtis Brown's Edit & Pitch Your Novel Course, Eoghan divides his time between Roscommon and Dublin.

Eoghan constantly explores ways to increase his knowledge in the art of writing. He enjoys attending literary festivals and is excited about the prospect of getting back to face-to-face discussions with readers and writers. He's also a heavy metal fan, and, post Covid, can't wait to headbang at a rock gig.

Find him on Twitter @eoghanegan